DEATH
COMES FOR CHRISTMAS

A Camelia Belmont Mystery

PJ Donison

Death Comes for Christmas
A Camelia Belmont Mystery

www.pjdonison.com

ISBN: 978-1-7780387-1-6
First Edition, February 2022
Cover Design: https://100covers.com/

Thank you for purchasing my book!

Get updates and information on

new releases, deals, discounts, and more

when you join my mailing list.

https://pjdonison.com/

Already a subscriber? Thanks so much!

pjdonison

26 Letters, Rearranged

DEATH COMES FOR CHRISTMAS

Book 1

Camelia Belmont Mystery Series

Always tell the truth.
There's a lot less paperwork.
Claude E. Ducloux, Esq.

The world is full of obvious things which nobody by any chance ever observes.
Sherlock Holmes
Hound of the Baskervilles

1

The End

December 24-25

The dark stain of night spread over the city as lights winked on. Any lingering twilight was snuffed out by an Alberta Clipper, a rolling wave of cloud and snow pushed along at 50 miles an hour ahead of the jet stream. The barometer dropped. Windows whistled and moaned. Doors whined and thumped. Animals burrowed and huddled. The flatlands from eastern Alberta to Manitoba were in thrall to the storm, a tsunami of ice crystals blasting everything in its path.

This was no winter wonderland.

Freda Swenson had lived through eighty-five Saskatchewan winters. Some small part of her could tell by the keening wind it was going to be a wicked blizzard, but she had more serious worries. Death was coming, riding hard on a frost-rimed steed, setting a course for Freda, hungry for what was left of her life.

Through a foggy shimmer of consciousness, Freda looked up into a face so like her own.

Mama?

She felt a warm breath against her cheek as a voice softly murmured, "I'm here, just like I promised. Are you ready to go home?"

Freda realized she *was* ready. Despite Arthur, *because* of Arthur. She couldn't put him through this. She blinked slowly, twice, tears blurring her vision.

Death's cool fingers had been grasping at her ankles for years, or so she imagined, but tonight his chill crept into her bed. His cold breath wrapped around her, growing inside her like frost covering a window. Death lay next to her in the dark, a palpable entity, whispering a sweet invitation.

This time, Freda didn't pull away.

There came a cold grip on her yet-beating heart.

Then, a little gasp of surprise and a deep sigh of instant knowing as Freda's last breath rushed out, chasing her spirit into the night.

As the bitterly cold, gray dawn of Christmas approached, Freda lay lifeless, her wavy hair radiating on the pillow like a frosty silver halo. Her skin was a macabre hue of purplish-blue—her lips and fingernails an even deeper shade—making her appear frozen.

Dr. James Frederick Fitzgerald shook his head and clicked his pen open and closed, repeatedly, for what seemed like an eternity. Strains of Tchaikovsky's Nutcracker Suite filtered in from the hallway.

She looks like the queen of the sugar plum fairies.

He made a simple entry on the death certificate in his best scrawl.

Natural Causes.

What else could he do? It was Freda Swenson for god's sake.

2

Wish List

December 18

It was another painfully bright winter morning in Phoenix and the intense sunshine bouncing off the desk only made Camelia Belmont's hangover dig in its heels. She flinched against the light ricocheting off the high-rises and got up to lower the blinds. The vista to the east—dusty pink Camelback Mountain against a flawless turquoise sky—was breathtaking. Wasn't this what she had worked so hard to get? And yet, she wasn't content.

Despite the envious view, Camelia was relieved it was her last day in the office for two whole glorious weeks. She craved a change of scenery, a white Christmas back in Canada, away from Arizona's relentlessly cheerful weather, and far away from her demanding, irate clients. Her mind slipped into the daydream, stepping off the plane into a Narnia-like wonderland, crunching around Wascana Lake in her new boots, hugging a mug of cocoa at Willow Bistro, watching the sun set across the frozen lake.

Crisp, cozy, idyllic.

Surely, reconnecting with her roots would help put her work woes in perspective.

Camelia paused to remind herself that while her clients might nip at her like hungry coyotes most days, they weren't *all* bad. But even on a good day—and those were increasingly rare—the divorce work didn't satisfy her inner justice warrior. If she could just convince Byron to promote her … but advancing to partner was only the first step. And it wasn't nearly enough if she was just going to be heading up the firm's family law department. Laughable, really, since the so-called department was just her, a paralegal, and a shared junior associate with an attitude problem.

No, Camelia wanted more.

Like her name on the law firm letterhead and a lot more money.

You listening, Santa?

The firm's monthly billing requirements were a painful reminder of her status as a senior associate. No power, no control, no clout. And yet, she was subsidizing her mother's independent living rental, funding her husband's new startup, and paying cash for therapy. On top of that, she was spending precious billable time on pro bono refugee cases. The work was urgent and compelling, so it was easy to rationalize, but it was killing her bottom line. She had to make partner—and a bigger paycheck—or give up on someone, but who? Her mother? Her husband? Herself? Desperate Central American refugees?

Camelia shook her head to dislodge the fog of alcohol clawing its way out of her system and swallowed another ibuprofen. These workday hangovers were torture and coming too often, lately. Her eyes burned, her insides were shaky and uncontained, and the misty bits of the evening she couldn't quite remember made her feel vaguely ashamed. She tinkered with the thought of just a nip of vodka, some hair of the dog. Instead, she emptied the carafe of coffee into her cup and reviewed the list her paralegal, Cate Sanchez, had prepared.

I'll be working overtime. Again.

Not that there was any such thing as overtime pay in a law practice. She didn't dare do the math on hours versus income because she was pretty sure she was earning about the same as Cate when it came right down to it, and for what? There was no justice or moral high ground in divorce work. She couldn't stomach the greed, the sense of entitlement, outright lies, rage attacks, and petty retributions that landed on her desk daily. It was exhausting to referee round after round of petty bickering between adults acting like toddlers. Most days, she was just aiding and abetting rich people in extracting their pound of flesh. And *all* her clients were rich, because ordinary people couldn't afford the fees.

Hell, I can't even afford me.

Camelia didn't want to think about all these … *issues*, especially through the haze of a hangover. Besides, the pile of pleadings Cate had stacked neatly in order of priority wasn't going away. As soon as she finished up—it wouldn't take that long—Camelia could slip out for a little lunch. And a big glass of wine. A reward for diligence. A prize for not running into the street screaming.

She grabbed the first sheaf of pleadings and began to read, pen in hand.

3

FRAMILY

DECEMBER 18

Camelia had barely begun working when her mobile phone buzzed: Rita Becker. Despite the weight of work, her face broke into a smile for her second cousin and lifelong friend.

"Rita! How's my favorite cuz?"

"Hey Cam, is now a good time?"

Camelia assessed the stack of work in front of her.

"Absolutely." She wished it were true. "Now is perfect. Way better than this stack of pleadings."

"Sorry, you're at work? I thought you'd be home packing. Don't you guys leave tomorrow?" Rita asked.

"No, Sunday."

"Okay, well, I'm just calling to nail down some time together before the entire holiday gets sucked into the Swenson vortex …" Rita said.

"And the Belmont vortex, too. Leon's mother is over-scheduling, as usual."

"Okay, let's be real. I just want to make as many plans as possible so I can avoid being one-on-one with Mum and Kenna for more than an hour at a time," Rita giggled.

"I do love my feisty Freda, but then she's not my mother," Camelia said. "As for your baby sister? Yeah, count me out. I can't take the drama."

"Speaking of drama, have you talked to Mum? She called this morning, going on about what to wear, and the Boxing Day menu. Again."

"No, I haven't talked to her. And if I'm gonna get out of here any time soon, I need to get my butt in gear," Camelia said. "I'm way behind thanks to a huge shit show I had to deal with on Monday," Camelia said.

"Ooooh. Details, please!"

"Okay, the short version. I represented the wife at a hearing, kind of a high profile case. Lawyer husband is a big swinging dick in litigator circles, represented by Spencer Ashcroft the third, and you know how I feel about Numeral Men," Camelia said.

"Oh yeah, I remember a certain Jeremy the Fourth," Rita said, laughing.

"Ashcroft is no better. Anyway, Wife is a scorned socialite. But, to be fair, I like her. She's not your typical sucked and tucked Scottsdale bobble head. So, the case is barely a minute old, and I stepped in for a routine scheduling hearing," Camelia said, relishing the retelling. "Just before the hearing kicks off, Ashcroft pulls me into the hall to make some bullshit settlement offer. And before I can even respond, here comes the wife, freaking out, saying the husband is having a heart attack," Camelia said.

"Whaaaat?"

"Right? Then here come the deputies and the medics, clearing the area. Meanwhile, husband is down for the count …"

"Wait, he died right there?" Rita said.

"No, he lived, but he collapsed in the courtroom. And get this," Camelia took a sip of coffee. "When the medics wheeled him out, I saw a Narcan box on the gurney, and he was purple. Looked like they just pulled him out of a snowbank …"

"Cyanosis …" Rita said.

"You'd know better than me. But, *Narcan.* He obviously OD'ed on something. And the wife is a nurse, or she used to be, so I expected her to be doing CPR or something instead of freaking out. It was a mess."

"Jeez. Sounds like it. Did she slip him a little something to speed up the divorce?" Rita laughed. "Even compared to hospice—I mean, people die at my work every day—this sounds pretty crazy."

"Well yeah, people go to your office to die, not mine! And these two are high rollers, at least by Phoenix standards. By the time I got back to the office, the media were all over us, so on top of having my hearing blow up, dealing with the cops, and managing my client, I gave my first press conference. All this on a Monday, for god's sake," Camelia said.

"Wow, look at you! Where can I watch it?" Rita asked.

"I'll text you the link," Camelia said. "Anyway, the husband lived and they're saying it was a heart attack, but that open Narcan box makes me wonder."

"Hmmm," Rita paused. "My first guess would be cardiac arrest secondary to opioid overdose."

She delivered the information so nonchalantly, Camelia thought she was kidding.

"Oh yeah, right. Mr. Litigator snorting oxy before a hearing? I kinda doubt it," Camelia said, laughing.

"Or fentanyl. If he was purple, had a heart attack, and there was a Narcan box on the gurney …" Rita said.

"Really? I mean, he's super successful, so why would he risk it all for something like that?" Camelia said.

"Did you just say that out loud?" Rita laughed. "Ever hear of addiction? Opioid crisis ring a bell? You'd be surprised who's using. It's *everywhere*."

Camelia scribbled on a fresh legal pad: *Anders / Fentanyl / opioid overdose?*

It seemed so unlikely, so farfetched. But if Aaron Anders was using opioids, she could credibly argue he wasn't competent to be running a law firm with access to millions of dollars of client money. With the new state rules about law firm ownership, Suzanne could end up running the firm.

"Yeah, I suppose, huh?" Camelia made a note to subpoena Anders' medical records. "Anyway, enough about me, what's going on with you?"

"Oh, you know, I see dead people," Rita laughed. "It's a one-eighty from working in Emerg, where you're fighting tooth and nail to save everyone who walks in the door. Now I'm not saving … anyone."

"It sounds like you kinda miss the ER."

"I miss the comradery and the hustle, but I do not miss 12 hour shifts on my feet with no pee breaks and having drunk people vomit on me. Palliative care is just *so* different. I mean, we call it palliative but really I do MAID service." Rita half laughed, but Camelia could hear a pang of sorrow in her friend's voice.

"Huh?"

"It's a joke. M-A-I-D. Medical Assistance in Dying. Maid service, get it? I know, I'm going straight to hell," Rita said.

Camelia snorted. "Got it. Very clever. And you're not going to hell, just a mild purgatory. It's where all the best people are," Camelia joked. "I always forget you guys legalized the act of dying. Very civilized."

"That's exactly what Mum says. When I talked to her this morning she told me for the 47th time that we are not to let her linger. Like that would happen," Rita laughed. "Ben would unplug her if she had a hangnail!"

"Yeah, your brother's not exactly the sentimental type. God, I hope she's not sick? She would tell you, wouldn't she?"

"I'm sure she's fine. You know how she is when she gets an idea in her head, and Mum's always been terrified of being bedridden, like her mother was at the end. And even though I do this for a living, it's still weird to discuss end of life arrangements with her," Rita said. "Plus, she doesn't understand how strict and convoluted the rules are, and honestly, I don't think she cares. I mean, it's hard enough explaining it to my patients, never mind getting the point across to my mother. But, it's my job now, right?" Her voice sagged into the phone.

"If it helps, I can talk to her about it. You know, as the lawyer in the family," Camelia said.

"Well, she's always listened to you more than the rest of us."

"Isn't that always the way?" Camelia asked, with a laugh.

"Yeah, pretty much. We can talk about it next week. What time do you guys land in Regina?"

Rita and Camelia compared calendars.

"We're still on for New Year's Eve, right?" Camelia asked.

"Yep. Do you guys want to go out, or stay in?"

"We're gonna do a little of both." Camelia paused. "Okay, I can't keep this secret another minute. We have a little surprise Christmas gift for you and Dave."

"Oh? I thought we weren't doing that …"

"I know. No gifts. But this is different. We got tickets to the Colin James New Year's concert at the old Trianon Ballroom. Can you believe it?" Camelia said.

Rita squealed. "Oh my god. Are you kidding? Dave will be over the moon! But how on earth did you get tickets? I thought they sold out ages ago!"

"They did, and I'm as shocked as you that I managed to get such great seats. So, Merry Christmas!" Camelia said.

"That's a helluva Christmas present! I can't wait to tell Dave," Rita said. "Can we get together on the 27th, too? Just the four of us? We'll come to you for a break from the family. We'll no doubt need it after the Boxing Day party," Rita said, laughing.

"Hey, I'm family too," Camelia laughed.

"No, hon, you're *framily*, and that's completely different," Rita said. "And promise me, next year, we go lay on a beach somewhere, okay? Now, get back to work and I'll see you next week."

Camelia's mood had lightened with something tangible to look forward to: enjoying time with Rita and Dave, people she could relax with, away from the rest of the family. Almost like a real vacation.

But first, this godawful pile of paperwork.

4

THIRSTY

DECEMBER 18

It was barely 11 o'clock but Camelia already needed a drink.

It's coming earlier every day.

She rolled her shoulders to dislodge the thought, took a long drink of water, and bent to the tasks her assistant had organized for her. She was reviewing a financial affidavit when Cate walked in.

"Nina Garry is on line three. She wants to buy you lunch, so she must have another pro bono case," she said. "And here's the asset list on the Forman case. You'll see there are a couple of account numbers missing, but I'm following up on it."

"Forman? That's not our case."

"Hate to break it to you, but it will be. Byron wants to see you as soon as you have a minute," Cate said, peering over her shoulder through the open doorway. She stepped into Camelia's office and pushed the door shut. "Brace yourself. He seems really pissed off."

"About what? Wait, hang on," Camelia said, holding up her index finger.

Camelia really wanted to slip away and meet Nina at the Biltmore, drain a bottle of pinot noir, and call it a day, but an angry Byron coupled with the stack of files on her desk were like ominous clouds, warning her away.

"Hey Nina, can I get a rain check?"

"On lunch, yes. On this emergency hearing? No. Can you take it? The hearing is Tuesday," Nina said.

Camelia paused. "Is it telephonic?"

"It can be, if you think you can cover it. Mom and two kids are about to be deported back to Nicaragua if we don't get an extension," Nina said.

Camelia looked up. Cate was shaking her head, pointing at the stack of files on her desk. She stage whispered, "No way. Don't do it."

"I just ... dammit Nina. I really wish I could, but I'm under the gun. I'm so sorry," she said.

"I get it. You weren't my first call and you won't be my last and hey, have a good Christmas. Let's catch up after the holidays," Nina said.

Camelia hung up the phone and turned back to Cate. "I hate telling her no. Anyway, what's up with Byron?"

"Remember the Hallman case? We're being sued for malpractice," Cate said.

"Are you kidding me? When were we served? And what did we do to inspire Joan Hallman's wrath? I thought she loved us," Camelia said.

Camelia ran hot anyway, but Cate's announcement had her heart rate ticking up. Anxiety was a warming spice, creating a low flame in her solar plexus, radiating heat throughout her body. She could hear her blood flowing in her ears.

"We were served a couple of days ago, but the new docketing clerk is way behind so I just got it this morning. I haven't read it all the way through, but it seems like a slam dunk for us. Joan didn't get her way and her life is a big mess, so she shouldn't have to pay our fees. And she claims you smelled of alcohol at a meeting," Cate said, cautiously. "I'm sure it won't hold up, but Byron is upset because the response is due while he's in Utah for his ski trip," Cate said, rolling her eyes. "And his new client, this

Forman guy, needs a quickie divorce to get assets out of his name. Gonna be a busy end of the year."

Camelia took a deep breath.

"Jesus. I'll have to report the malpractice …"

"Done," Cate said. "I sent a copy to Byron's assistant and scheduled a call with the liability carrier. And I drafted a letter to Hallman's attorney regarding the arbitration clause in the fee agreement. It's in your stack." She nodded at the pile of files on Camelia's desk.

"I knew I liked you for a reason," Camelia quipped. "About Forman. Do we even have room for another case? How many are on our docket as of today?"

"We're right at the firm limit. The Forman case will make 41. Should be easy, though, since he's giving the wife everything. Obviously, she's not arguing about it. I've already drafted the Petition and it's here," Cate held up a thin sheaf of papers, "for you to approve. As soon as you're done with Byron."

"Okay, I'll be back in a minute." Camelia headed for the hallway, coffee mug in hand, heart in throat. Her phone buzzed in her pocket. Auntie Freda.

Shit.

She stopped, took a deep breath, and returned to her office, pulling the door closed behind her.

"Good morning! How's my favorite auntie today?"

"Good morning, dear. I hope I'm not calling at a bad time?" Freda said.

"Not at all. Things are winding down for the holidays, so I'm just catching up on some paperwork," Camelia said.

If only it were true.

"I'm terribly excited to see you all, and I just want to double-check the dates and times. You're arriving on the 21st, is that right?"

Camelia recited travel dates for Freda, who reciprocated with her own list of events.

"I hope I've caught you before you finish packing? I don't want to spill the beans just yet, but please bring something dressy for New Year's Day," Freda said.

"Oh? And what's that about?" Camelia responded.

"It's a secret for now, so don't be a buttinsky!" Freda said, laughing.

"Well, okay Mystery Woman. But define 'dressy'. Like formal wear?"

"No, more garden party cocktail," Freda said.

"Does Leon need a suit, or is a sport coat okay?"

"It never hurts to see a man in a suit, but I suppose a sport coat will do," Freda said.

"That's probably the best we can hope for, Auntie. You know how these computer geeks are—they live in their jeans!"

"Yes, well, the working man's uniform has certainly changed. I remember when men wore three-piece suits and a fedora to work every day, but I guess that time has passed, hasn't it?"

"Not even trial attorneys wear three-piece suits anymore. I'll make sure we look presentable for your mysterious event, but don't count on Leon wearing a suit," Camelia said.

"That's all I can ask, dear. And please let Sophie and Steve know, too. It's a very special surprise, and I wouldn't want any of you to feel out of place by being under-dressed," Freda said.

Ouch.

"Thanks for the heads up! We're looking forward to our visit, Auntie. I better get going. Duty calls." Camelia said, smiling through Freda's little passive-aggressive dig.

She tried to shush her irritation, but this request prickled, reminding Camelia how demanding Auntie Freda could be. As if the piles of winter clothes weren't enough, now she had to pack yet another outfit for some secret event.

What next?

It was still early in the day, but Camelia desperately wanted a drink. Since she wouldn't have a chance to go out for lunch … she slipped her desk drawer open and ran her hand over the cool copper flask. It didn't take long to convince herself to unscrew the cap and pour a couple of glugs of vodka into her coffee mug. Just for now, just to get through this last day in the office.

January 1st, I'm done for good.

She gulped half the mug.

Crap. Byron was still waiting.

5

Byron's Lump of Coal

December 18

As Camelia made her way to Byron McCaffrey's office, she rifled through her mind, scanning recent events to find the flaws, the horrible oversights, the incredibly stupid mistakes, proof that she was nothing more than a mediocre imposter who should never have been hired in the first place. Had that windbag Spencer Ashcroft called Byron about her panic attack in the bathroom after Anders' heart attack? If so, she'd never make partner. And now, thanks to Auntie Freda, she'd kept Byron waiting.

As founding partner of McCaffrey Rhodes & Rodriguez, Byron was an experienced—and ruthless—criminal defense attorney with the instincts of a great white shark. Byron's office looked like him: serious, successful, masculine, intimidating. He was on the phone when Camelia approached, so she hovered in the open doorway until he waved her in.

"Okay, thanks Rick, I'll let the client know, and we'll get back to you next week," Bryon said, as he hung up the phone. "Shut the door, Cam."

The set of his jaw was a warning. This meeting wasn't going to be pleasant. Camelia pushed the door shut and perched on the edge of one of the leather chairs facing his ornate, antique desk.

"Cate said you wanted to see me? What's …" Camelia began.

Byron slammed his palm on the desk.

"Stop. Talking. Everyone—*everyone*—has heard by now that Camelia Belmont lost it in Court and blacked out in the ladies' room stinking of booze. Let that sink in. I'm not kidding, Cam. If you intend to keep your job, you've gotta lay off the alcohol," Byron said, glaring. "And whatever else you're adding to the mix these days," he added.

So here it was. The talk she'd been dreading since Monday.

Fucking Ashcroft.

She cleared her throat. Her mouth tasted of last night's wine and … well, to be honest, this morning's vodka. She wished she were spending more time defending justice than defending herself, and now that she was facing Byron's accusations, she regretted that little splash in her coffee mug.

Can he smell it?

Camelia let out a mirthless laugh. "I didn't lose it, and we weren't in the middle of a hearing. Who's saying all this crap?" she asked, knowing full well who was responsible.

"I was at Durant's last night for dinner. Spencer Ashcroft couldn't wait to tell anyone who would listen. And *everyone* at the bar was listening." Byron drew a ragged breath as if exhausted by the tawdriness of it all. "I saw your potential six years ago when I hired you and I still do, but your habits are getting ahead of you. Potential requires performance."

"Isn't this a bit of the pot calling the kettle …"

"No, Cam, it *isn't*," Byron interrupted, anger coating his words in contempt. "There's a big difference between having a pint with lunch versus passing out in a Courthouse bathroom at 9 a.m., and I shouldn't even have to say it. And this isn't about *me*, it's about *you* and your future at the firm, so don't quibble. You've got a lot of clean up to do."

He leaned forward on his elbows, clasped his long fingers, and rested his chin there for a moment, staring at the legal pad in front of him.

Typical Byron. Finessing his words to jab just so. Camelia knew she couldn't outmaneuver him, so she waited. When he looked up, his eyes revealed only resolve, no mercy.

"Seriously, Cam, I wanted to discuss this privately, in person, because it has to stop. Your ego is probably writhing in pain right about now, and frankly, it should be. Word of your bathroom scene has traveled like wildfire. On top of that, your former client is suing for malpractice and claims you smelled of alcohol at a meeting. I can't afford to look the other way. Not this time." He smoothed his heavy grey silk tie with his palm and twisted his neck to one side, like a boxer readying for a fight.

"I know how it sounds, but it wasn't … Ashcroft took a lot of creative license," Camelia said.

She'd spent all these years camouflaging her demons in order to impress Byron. She couldn't very well confess now. There was too much on the line.

"Whatever. The *actual* truth doesn't matter. What matters is how it looks, and you know it. Do you think anyone cares about your side of the story? Not that vulture, Ashcroft, that's for sure."

"I get it. But I didn't pass out. I sort of fainted. I think it was low blood sugar," she said, but her words sounded weak even to her. It was no defense against the rabid rumor mill of the Phoenix legal community.

Breathe. Focus. Act contrite.

There was nothing else to say. The humiliating scene replayed in her head like a movie.

Anders had his heart attack. The deputy wanted her statement.

A statement about what? I don't know anything!

She was there, in the Courthouse bathroom, panting, sweating, the grip of a full blown panic attack wrapping around her like a python, squeezing the air out of her. She slid down the wall onto the floor, pulling her knees close. The terrazzo floor smelled of urine and disinfectant. Bile rose in her throat.

Ma'am. are you okay?

I think she might be sick or something, a woman said.

Camelia saw Spencer Ashcroft leering over the cop's shoulder.

A bit too much hair of the dog, Belmont?

"Are you listening?" Byron said.

"Yes, of course," Camelia said, gripping the seams of her trousers with sweaty hands. She tried to calm her hammering heart as it banged away, constructing its own gallows.

"I didn't bring this to *all* the partners out of consideration for your privacy, but I talked to the name partners this morning. Trent and Arturo are with me on this. You've got 'til the end of January—six weeks—to demonstrably clean up your side of the street, or we're gonna have to part ways."

Byron was the kind of person who used words like *demonstrably* in everyday conversation. He tapped his Montblanc pen on the legal pad in front of him, more or less keeping time to the pounding in Camelia's head.

He wouldn't actually fire me, would he?

But she knew he would.

"Just a reminder, I'm going out of town for Christmas. I'm supposed to leave on Sunday. This trip's been booked for months, so I hope that's not a problem now," she said. She could readily imagine the fight with Leon if she had to cancel their trip.

"Not the best timing, Cam, but maybe the break will do you good. Give you some perspective on your behavior and time to think about your future with the firm." The vein running up Byron's left temple was like a barometer indicating the level of his fury; right now it was thumping in bas relief.

"I want to make sure I clearly understand. Can you tell me, in measurable terms, what you require from me in order to make partner?" she asked, attempting to appear professional and cooperative, even though her pulse was racing.

"Jesus, Mary, and Joseph! Are you even listening? First off, we're not even *discussing* partner right now. This is about you keeping your damn job. In *measurable terms*, I want you to get sober. In *measurable terms*, I want you to bill more than 25 or 30 hours a week. In *measurable terms*, I want you to bring home some bacon instead of just eating whatever the firm feeds you. In *measurable terms*, I want you to be partner material and not just another shitty associate who has to be micro-managed. Is that clear enough for you?"

A red-hot slap of shame rushed to her cheeks. Camelia's eyes filled with tears, even though now was most definitely not the time to get *histrionic*. That was how Byron had once described a sobbing secretary. Camelia's tongue was thick and her throat was dry. She carefully sipped her spiked coffee, blinking toward the wall of windows facing Camelback Mountain, trying to compose herself.

Byron's pen tapping was more insistent now. The combined percussion of her headache, heart rate, and his pen was making her sweat and pushing bile up her throat.

Why couldn't he just stop stop stop that incessant tapping?

"Okay, I get it. I just want to make sure I'm coloring inside the lines."

There was an element of challenge in her tone and Byron's temper crackled.

"Do *not* blow me off or you know how this conversation will end. Can you please for just one fucking minute listen to me? I'm trying to help you before you crash and burn. And Cam, you *will* crash and burn, if you keep this up." Byron's eyes darkened and his prominent jaw clenched repeatedly, as if he were chewing the bones of his enemies. He looked every bit the Irish Viking, and his childhood brogue, usually kept under wraps, was flaring out at the edge of his words. "But you're not taking the firm down with you. We have a reputation to protect, and I won't sit by and let you drag us through the mud with your … what should I call it? *Alcoholic bullshit?*"

Camelia flinched. No one had called her an alcoholic before, not seriously. She recognized this tone. It was condescending and biting and there was no percentage in arguing. Byron was an intensely virulent litigator, and he could eviscerate her with her own words. Just like he did with pretty much every witness he cross-examined. He smoothed the paper in front of him and laid his pen aside.

"Go to AA or rehab or whatever you need to do, but get your shit sorted by the end of January. Is that clear enough for you?"

"It's clear. How do you want the results quantified?" she asked, feeling the defiance in her voice.

"Jesus," he said, and shook his head. "I want the results quantified by showing up to work without a hangover and coming back from lunch sober. I was going to leave this at a verbal warning, but it sounds like you need it in writing, so I'll draft a memo to the file, with *measurable goals.* Will that be clear enough for you?"

Camelia fought to swallow the lump in her throat. She couldn't very well recite her entire mental health history or reveal that she was relying on a cocktail of anxiety meds just to make it through the day. Performing in a courtroom week after week was like being held under water: she couldn't breathe, the emotional darkness engulfed her, and she was never more than a few heartbeats away from collapsing. But she couldn't say any of that. Weakness didn't play well in the firm—any firm, really—but particularly a high-profile criminal defense firm. She took a deep breath and blinked back the tears.

"It was just low blood sugar. It won't happen again," she said.

Byron huffed out a bit of scorn and flipped the pages of his desk calendar. "Whatever. This is not a three-strike situation, by the way," he said, and circled January 31 on the page. "First and last chance. Don't fuck this up."

"Got it," she said, and rose to leave.

"Sit your ass back down, we still have actual work to do, in case you've forgotten," Byron snapped. And just like that, he was on to other things, as if he hadn't just gutted her.

Byron and Camelia went through her case list in staccato form, using the shorthand common in the office, straight to the deadlines, eliminating all the unnecessary words that might take another second away from billing.

"Anything else?" she asked, as they reached the last case. Camelia stood to go.

"No. That's it. Think about what I said, Cam. I don't want to replace you," Byron said.

His tone had softened, but Camelia heard the unsaid end to the sentence. Byron *would* replace her if she didn't clean up her act. And soon.

Camelia trudged back to her office with the weight of Bryon's accusations pulling her shoulders into a slump.

Alcoholic. Just like dad.

She locked her office door and collapsed into her chair, contemplating Camelback Mountain through a shimmer of tears. Not that the sandstone hills had any answers, but it was soothing to watch shadows play on the rocks. Clouds were gathering, and it looked like they might get some winter rain.

She'd heard somewhere that water symbolized emotion, so what did the bone dry desert represent? Why did she always feel like she was drowning, gasping for air, struggling to reach the surface? And what of the Canadian prairies, awaiting her return? Were the deep drifts of snow a vast community of frozen feelings just waiting to inundate everyone with all the nasty little things they'd put on ice winter after winter?

Camelia tossed back the last of her coffee and vodka. She knew she was in trouble, and not just with Byron. But was she actually an alcoholic? She could feel the current beneath her quickening, picking up speed, heading for … something out of her control.

But there was still plenty of time to change, to fix it, to start over, stop drinking, get focused, clean up her mess.

Wasn't there?

She drained the copper flask into her coffee mug.

Might as well finish it off.

She turned back to the pile of documents on her desk. Vacation couldn't come soon enough.

6

Kenna Plays Santa

December 18

Kenna grunted as she wriggled her considerable girth into a more comfortable position on the long, sapphire-blue velvet sofa. It was a relic of her childhood, its rich fabric remarkably intact except for a couple of burn marks from parties back in the day, when everyone smoked. She wedged herself in place with pillows and arranged her iPad on her lap, then pulled a fluffy cream-colored throw over her legs.

She was rolling rye and Diet Coke around in her mouth, reveling in the sweetness followed by the burn of the whisky, when her older sister, Rita, texted.

> Everyone confirmed for Boxing Day except Lewis. Cass isn't coming as usual. Any word from Tony?

Kenna gave her a thumbs down emoji and laid her phone aside. Within seconds, her phone dinged again.

Jesus, Rita …

But it was her son, Micky, texting.

Coming over in a few, need anything?

She smiled. He was such a good kid, always looking out for her. She texted him back.

Sure I'll take a lotto and a diet coke

"Mum, Mickey's coming over. Aren't you going out with your friends tonight?" she said.

Freda leaned into the living room, stirring cream into a cup of tea.

"Stop screeching, I'm not deaf. And I'm staying in this evening. The Feast of the Seven Fishes is tomorrow, so the club will be deserted tonight. Plus, I have to finish my cards. Christmas is almost here, and I still have so many to write."

As Freda turned away, Kenna scowled and stuck her tongue out. She wanted Freda to go out so she could relax with Mickey, just the two of them. It could be a lovely mother-son visit, but not with Freda throwing in her two cents, like the Queen of goddamn England. The crotchety old bat sucked the joy out of things. But what could Kenna do? Freda lived here, too. For now, anyway. But she was about to be 85, for chrissake, so how much longer could it be?

"Do you want anything from QuikMart? Mickey's picking up lottos and some DC on his way over," Kenna said, fighting the resentment in her voice.

"I would love one of those pumpkin spice lattes from Timmy's, thanks," Freda said.

Kenna started to respond that Mickey wasn't going to Tim Horton's, and that it wasn't right to ask him, but she reconsidered. Let Mickey see for himself how unreasonable and demanding Freda was, how her relentless air of entitlement was rude and childish.

Kenna sent Mickey the text with an eye-roll emoji and went back to her online poker game. She was up a few hundred but still needed a big win to break even. She fortified herself with another deep gulp of her cocktail and focused on her game.

Mickey showed up a half hour later, stomping off snow and ushering a billow of cold air into the front hall. He kicked off his boots before stepping into the living room holding two coffees aloft, like trophies.

"Ladies! Your champion has arrived!" he said.

"Aren't you just full of the Christmas spirit?" Kenna said, her face lighting up at the sight of her only son. She motioned him in, her arms open for a hug. "Come warm up, it's cold as a well-digger's ass out there tonight!" she laughed.

"That it is, Mum! Like a witch's tit, eh?" Mickey said, laughing as he set the coffees down.

"Language, you two!" Freda chided, but they ignored her.

"Mum, I'll put your diet Coke and two lucky lottos here." Mickey set a plastic bag on the end table, and swung a tote bag full of wrapped presents onto the faded Persian rug. "I came bearing gifts to hide under the tree for Christmas morning. Can you believe it's Sashay's *second* Christmas?"

Kenna fussed over Mickey as Freda settled between the fire and the bay window in her favorite chair, a wide Bergere upholstered in navy and cream toile. Mickey presented Freda with her latte, the aroma of cinnamon, cardamom, and nutmeg filling the room.

"Here you go, Gram! Still piping hot! Smelled so good, I got one too," Mickey said as Freda tilted her cheek for a kiss. "How about a wee shot of brandy to spice it up a bit?"

"That would be lovely dear, thank you. There's a bottle of Hennessy in the kitchen bar," Freda said, smiling up at him.

"Mum, somebody left the cap off and it evaporated. I dumped what was left. How about rum instead?" Kenna said.

"Don't be an idiot, Kenna. How could an entire bottle of brandy evaporate? And what do you mean you dumped it? Down your throat? I guess you owe me a new bottle, now, don't you?" Freda sniffed.

Kenna glared at Freda.

Fine, you old cow, have the last word.

"That's okay, Mick, I'll have rum. But make it a light splash. I have to write Christmas cards this evening," Freda said.

As Mickey placed gifts under the tree, Kenna and Freda settled in; Freda silently sipping her latte while Kenna noisily slurped her rye and DC. After a while, warmed by the booze and blazing fire, their resentments thawed. Freda turned on the stereo to Christmas music, and soon Kenna and Mickey were singing along, with Freda joining in on a chorus now and then. Before long, the three of them were bantering, competing for laughs. It surprised Kenna to realize they were genuinely enjoying each other's company.

With a soft moan, Freda set her cup aside and pressed her fingertips to her temples. "My goodness, that rum has gone straight to my head. Kenna, be a love and bring me an aspirin and a glass of water, will you? I'm feeling a bit wobbly all of a sudden!"

"Don't be so dramatic, Mum. You're fine. Probably too much caffeine this late in the day," Kenna said, hoisting herself up and lumbering to the kitchen.

She returned with a glass of water and handed Freda a tablet. Mickey knelt by Freda, concern scrunching his eyebrows into an inverted v.

"Jesus, Mum, take your sweet frickin' time while Gram chokes off on pumpkin spice!" Mickey said, reaching for the glass of water and glaring at Kenna over Freda's head.

Kenna shrugged. "It's not a big deal, Mick. She gets like this now and then."

Freda dutifully swallowed the tablet. "I do not. And it has nothing to do with caffeine," Freda said, as she stood. "I think I'd best lie down for a bit. Mickey, help me upstairs, dear." She took Mickey's arm, her right hand pressed to her chest.

Freda shuffled along, leaning heavily on Mickey's arm, gripping the thick oak banister as she slowly climbed the stairs.

For a moment, Kenna saw her mother's true age and felt a pang of regret, but it floated away on a wave of rye and resentment. *Of course* Freda would bring their good time to an end. At least she was out of their hair. Kenna was so tired of the lack of privacy under her mother's roof. And she was tired of the way Mickey sucked up to Freda, bowing and scraping for her approval. When he came down the stairs on tiptoes, Kenna quickly rearranged her face, ditching the scowl for a smile.

"Not sure what got into Gram," he said. His own latte and rum, now tepid, was still on the coffee table, and he downed it in one gulp. "She's just too old to be drinking, I guess," he added.

Kenna eyed him suspiciously.

"Mickey, the only thing in Mum's latte was coffee and rum, right?" Kenna asked.

"What the hell, Mum? Jesus. What a thing to say," he sputtered, his indignation shaming Kenna for her accusation.

"Hey, hey, settle down. I just don't want any blowback if she wakes up with a roofie hangover," Kenna said in a stage whisper, smirking into her glass.

"Really? That was like 10 years ago and a totally honest mistake! That roofie was for me, not Gram, and you know it, so don't throw that in my face again. For real. I mean it," Mickey retorted, his face flushing.

"Oh calm down, Mr. Sensitive. Come on over here and sit with your old Mum," she said, patting the sofa with her plump fingers, the glint of jewels reflecting the twinkling lights of the tree.

Kenna had a more-is-better approach to almost everything in life, including jewelry, layering rings on every finger, at least two pair of earrings, multiple pendants, a Rolex watch and a stack of bracelets, all in various concentrations of gold, diamonds, and—tonight—sapphires. Her nails were painted a frosty blue with tiny crystal snowflakes embedded in the polish, matching her sequined Christmas sweatshirt.

Mickey sighed and plopped down, mother and son bookending the elegant sofa.

"So, what's up with my dear old Mum today? How's your pain doing?" he asked. "Do you need me to get you more fen?"

"It wouldn't hurt to have some on hand because it never lets up these days, hon. And thanks for worrying about me," Kenna said, less irritable now that Mickey's attention was laid out before her. "All the meds they have me on, and I still feel like hell. It sucks. And the pin in my shoulder

… I hope you never have to go through anything like that," she said, her eyes misting over with tears as she rubbed her shoulder.

This was more like it.

"I'll bring you a little something to help with the pain," Mickey said, winking. "Hey, have you talked to Dad lately?" He played with the fringe on the blanket tucked around Kenna's legs, his expression distracted, almost pensive.

"No, why would I? He's too busy with his whore to talk to me," Kenna said.

She still referred to her ex-husband's wife as the 'whore' even though Gina and Tony had been married for a decade. It wasn't that she wanted Tony back in her life. It was that his betrayal still stung.

"Auntie Rita invited him for Boxing Day, but I didn't see his response. Did you?" Mickey asked.

"Nope. He was copied on the email invite just like everyone else. You know Rita. *Family is family*," she said, mocking her sister's position on exes. "She texted earlier and she hasn't heard from him. I bet Gina won't let him come. I'll give him a call next week because I'm not petty, like him," Kenna said.

"Riiiight."

"Whatever, maybe he'll no-show again like last year," she said, gulping the remainder of her drink.

"I don't think Dad and Gina are going away for the holidays this year," Mickey said. "Dad says he can't afford a Hawaiian Christmas every year."

"Oh, cry me a river. Mick, be a dear and bring me another, please." Kenna held her glass out, wagging it at him.

While Mickey mixed her drink, Kenna nibbled the edge of an OxyContin tablet and shoved the remainder in her pocket. They weren't as effective as they used to be. And she didn't want to get into this conversation about Tony and the annual Boxing Day dinner. She just wanted some Christmas cheer with her baby boy and was grateful—glad in fact—that Suyin and Sashay were at home. Otherwise, the whole evening would be all diapers and tantrums. Mickey returned with her drink and popped the cap on a beer for himself.

"So, how's work? I bet real estate's slow at Christmas, huh?" Kenna asked.

"Mum, you have no idea how hard it is. I mean, for sure it's hard all the time, but at the holidays, people don't want to move, they don't want to show their house, and the money just stalls out," he said, putting his foot tentatively into the door Kenna had opened. He chugged half the beer in one gulp.

"Yeah, who wants people tramping through the house when you're trying to get ready for the holidays? That doesn't help you make a living, though, does it?" she asked.

"You know I don't like to talk about it with Gram or Suyin around, but Mum, I'm having a hard time. Dad cut me off and won't even give me a loan because, you know, the whore and all," Mickey said.

"What a dick. He's rolling in fucking dough. He should at least take care of his only son," Kenna replied. "Don't worry. Your dear old Mum is here as usual, eh?" She couldn't let Mickey down, not like Tony.

"No, Mum, you can't be giving me money. You need it to live on, and I'll be fine in a few months when spring sales start up again," he said.

"Well, Mick, here's a little secret for you. Don't tell the Chink—sorry, I know, I know—*Chinese wife*," Kenna said, in response to Mickey's sharp exhale.

"Her name is Suyin and that's all you need to call her. This racist bullshit …" Mickey's lips pressed into a thin slash of disapproval.

God, he looks like Tony when he does that. Ungrateful brat.

"Okay, okay. Don't get your knickers in a twist. Anyway, as I was about to say before you got all huffy, I can loan you as much as you need. Keep your mouth shut, but I'm on Mum's bank account, and she'll never know the difference," Kenna said.

"Oh wow, that's good, I guess. I mean, Gram is getting pretty old. And you've always been good with money," he said.

The oxy and rye were tag teaming through her nervous system, and Kenna was enjoying the fuzzy glow of her boozy high.

"Yeah, I have full access to her account, but for god's sake don't tell anyone. I mean it. I don't want it coming back to me from Tony or Suyin or anyone, you got it?"

"Of course, Mum, who are you talking to here? I'm like a fiduciary in my job, right? I'm used to keeping all kinds of financial secrets," he said, grinding Kenna's resistance to dust with his words.

It sounded so noble when he said it like that. Kenna sighed in satisfaction. Now she had his full attention.

"Just grab the checkbook off the kitchen desk," she said.

"Wait, Mum, do you really want to write paper checks on Gram's account? Wouldn't it be better to do a transfer? I don't want her to worry, you know, because this is totally a loan," Mickey said.

"That's my smart boy," Kenna said. It pleased her to be in cahoots with him, happy they were allied against Freda. "Hand me my iPad, and I can take care of it right now. Whoo!" Kenna giggled. "That drink is hitting the spot! How much, Mickey? Whaddya need to get you through?"

"Oh, I don't know Mum, whatever you think is right," Mickey said. "You know how expensive things are with a baby, a house, and a pretty wife who loves to shop." He rolled his eyes.

Kenna giggled. "Oh yeah, the Princess must be kept in designer shoes and bags at all times," she snorted. Suyin was not one to do without.

"Right? It's like you've met her or something!" Mickey laughed along with her, and Kenna wallowed in his approval.

"Okay, I'm sending you an e-transfer for twenty thou, and you keep your trap shut, got it?" she said, her words melting together like slush. She stage-whispered, "Remember, I got the keys to the castle and the password to the treasure chest, and when the old bird croaks, we'll split it all," she said, giggle-snorting.

"Mum, this is why I love you so much! Because you're the best! And speaking of the princess, I have to head out. Suyin's gonna be pissed if I'm not home soon. How about I mix you one for the road, but then I have to go, 'kay?"

Kenna pushed out her lower lip in a fake pout and said, in a childish voice, “No fairsies. She sees you all the time, and I only get one or two visits a week!”

“I know but geez, Mum, she’s my frickin’ wife. I have to go home now and then,” he said, laughing. “Now, let me pour you a little refresher, and I’ll be on my way.”

After Mickey left, Kenna downed her drink. She turned off the lamp and nestled into the sofa, drifting in a haze of oxycodone and alcohol. Warmed by the fire and rye whisky, unwilling to make the long trek upstairs to bed, she pushed her head into the pillows.

Sashay’s brightly wrapped gifts sparkled under the Christmas tree lights. On the mantle, family photos framed in silver reflected the soft red and green glow.

Kenna pressed her body into the sofa, moldering in her resentment, dreaming of life beyond her mother and her childhood home. An idea was forming in the mist of sleep.

7

Favorite Things

December 19

Even as she got ready to go out, Freda was still feeling a bit off from last night's dizzy spell. The Feast of the Seven Fishes and Christmas dance was *the* annual event at the Italian club, and she intended to dazzle Arthur. She hoped the substantial dinner menu would see her through the evening.

Freda lightly applied a bit of blush, making sure she looked naturally sparkling, unlike some of the old dears. Freda had become more austere in her later years, and it pleased her to be one of the most elegant in the room.

She suddenly felt dizzy again.

What the devil is going on?

She'd had just a splash of rum last night, but it left her feeling very strange. She still felt foggy and her heart was racing a bit, but it wasn't enough to keep her away from this romantic night with Arthur. She took a sip of water as her mobile phone chirped. A message from Rita, her eldest.

We're bringing wine for the Boxing Day party. Is one case enough?

Freda counted family members in her head. She'd confirmed everyone except Tony. She doubted Kenna's ex would show up and rather hoped he didn't.

I count 19 so a case should be plenty. thx

As she dabbed Chanel No. 5 on her neck and wrists, Freda wondered if Arthur would propose tonight. He'd been hinting at it for weeks, but she'd studiously pretended not to notice. If he were to ask, Freda would say yes. Emphatically, enthusiastically yes. But was he really looking for love? Or was she nothing more than a dinner companion?

She pulled pantyhose over her bony knees. Yes, she was almost 85, but there was lingering evidence of her former beauty: a full sweep of wavy silver hair framed a strong jaw and high cheekbones, large sapphire eyes were accentuated by expertly tinted brows, and an overbite made her smile expansive. She fastened herself into a long-line bra and stepped into a full slip, then pulled her new holiday dress up over her shoulders: a buoyant sweep of pale chiffon topped by a shimmering rose gold metallic knit that hugged her frame and flattered her pale skin.

Freda took a deep breath and another drink of water to quell the lingering wooziness.

If Arthur did propose, she would likely sell this fussy old house. His penthouse condo overlooked Arboretum Park to the north and the old Hillsdale neighborhood to the south. It was a perfect perch to watch the seasons pass, and a clean break from the hoard of memories tucked into every crack and crevice of the Crescents house.

She'd spent her entire lifetime in this house, years that showed in the curve of her shoulders, the splotches on her hands, and her pure silver hair. At least she was still fully in control of her mind and body.

Thank god I'm not going senile or banging a walker into the walls the way my mother did those last couple of years.

Freda liked her independence, living among her cherished things, but she had been snared by her own clever plan. She'd invited her youngest to move in to recover from her car accident, but it was also a bulwark against the rising tide of Freda's own advancing age. Then came the surgeries—Kenna's shoulder, then her left knee and ankle—all fraught with complications, and now … well, now it seemed that Kenna was never going to get off the couch and get back to living her life. She hated to admit, even to herself, that inviting Kenna to move in had been a mistake. It had seemed like a smart solution to the question of *what next* because Freda had no intention of moving into a senior home, no matter how much her dear friend, Harriet Johnson, cajoled.

Although she would happily accept Arthur's proposal for only one reason—love—joining him in his condo gave Freda a perfect escape from the tiresome drain of her youngest daughter. It irked Freda that Kenna had the gall to play the victim when the accident was completely her own fault, and she was damn lucky she wasn't in prison for drunk driving. It also irritated her that she had become Kenna's caregiver, instead of the other way around, without so much as a word—or dollar—of thanks.

Not that supporting Kenna was a crippling expense. Freda had plenty of money. More than any of them knew. Even Kenna didn't know the extent of it. Freda had added her to one of her bank accounts as a precaution because she knew Kenna wouldn't dare touch a penny without permission. But if she married Arthur, maybe he should be the one named on her bank accounts. After all, that would be proper. Freda considered the ramifications as she spritzed a little hair spray and took one more turn in front of the mirror. She smiled at her own image, then grabbed her evening bag. It was going to be a magical night, she could feel it.

Freda called out to Kenna as she headed downstairs.

"Arthur will be here soon. Can you zip me up, dear? And I'm going to have a glass of wine. Will you join me?" Freda asked, already knowing the answer.

Kenna never turned down a drink. Freda had yet to fully confront her about draining the bottle of Hennessy XO, an indulgence Freda reserved for special occasions. She didn't believe for one minute that Kenna poured it down the sink.

Honestly, the nerve of that child.

"In here, Mum," Kenna called from the kitchen. "I was just mixing a drink. Do you want me to pour your wine?" Kenna said.

"Yes, a glass of the burgundy. There's a bottle open, unless you dumped that out, too," Freda answered, enjoying the little stab.

Kenna didn't respond, but the clinking of bottles carried her tension. Freda didn't care.

Let her stew.

Kenna stepped into the living room, handed Freda her wine glass, and lifted her own highball.

"Cheers!"

"Salute!" Freda said, clinking Kenna's glass.

"Now, turn around and let me get you zipped. Is this new?"

"Yes, I picked it up at that little boutique over by the salon. Isn't it lovely?" Freda said, smoothing the skirt.

"Yes, very pretty. Must have cost a fortune," she said, fingering the fabric. "By the way you're dressed and the way you're acting … do we need to talk about the birds and the bees?" Kenna gave Freda a lascivious grin.

"What … Kenna Anne! Why would you say such a thing? Do you have to be so vulgar?" Freda asked, her cheeks reddening. "And you act like affection between people over 40 is unheard of. For god's sake, Arthur and I've been seeing each other for months. At our age, we don't have time to burn."

Kenna laughed, spewing a fine spray of her drink. She wiped rye and Diet Coke off her chin with the back of her beringed hand. "So, I guess that's a yes?"

"As for your crude suggestion, I think not. But if Arthur were to ask me to marry him, I would accept. Frankly, I would welcome the companionship," Freda retorted sharply.

"Oh, so I'm not your companion now? Remember me? Your daughter and best friend and caregiver?" Kenna said.

Freda raised an eyebrow, but didn't rise to the bait. "You and I are family. Arthur is my beau, and that is completely different. Besides, I'm referring to *romantic* companionship, something that wouldn't hurt you, either." She sipped her wine and sniffed. It tasted strange, with a metallic tang at the finish.

For pity's sake, it's oxidized already?

"Yeah, right. Because men are just lined up at the door. But, really, Mum, marriage? At your age? What's the point? I mean you could live together ... unless he's just after your money," Kenna said.

"I have never lived with any man other than your father, and I don't intend to start being a loose woman now! Arthur and I are adults with reputations to consider. As for my money, that's my concern," Freda said.

This was not going as planned. She assumed Kenna would be happy for her, or at least have the courtesy to act like she was, but Freda should have known better. Kenna was not exactly Miss Manners, despite a lifetime of Freda harping on about social graces.

"I don't think anyone would think twice about you living wherever you want. But since you mention it—do I need to start packing?"

As usual, Kenna's focus was selfish. In that instant, any lingering qualms Freda had about abandoning her old house in favor of Arthur's condo vanished, if for no other reason than to put her grasping, greedy daughter in her place.

"We'll either live here or there," Freda said, gesturing vaguely east. "But you're getting a bit ahead of yourself since the man hasn't proposed. *If* we marry, I think I would prefer to move into his condo—it's perfect for the two of us. But let's not jump to conclusions."

"I'm not jumping anywhere with this knee. It just seems strange that I barely know this guy, and you're gonna up and marry him. And this late in the game?" Kenna said.

Freda's cheeks flushed red with anger. "You barely know him because you haven't tried. You never invite us to join you, not even for lunch. I thought you would be happy for me despite the eleventh hour."

"Of course I'm happy for you. And don't worry, I can always move, or we could all live here together—the house is big enough—or whatever you want," Kenna said, a tone of conciliation softening her voice. "I'll still love you even if you run off with a strange man," she said, winking.

"Well, there's a thought. Arthur and I can elope!" Freda said, laughing, enjoying her wine a bit more now that the initial bitterness was gone. "Now don't go spreading gossip before it's happened. But if he asks, I'm saying yes." Freda said, a satisfied smile lighting up her face.

"As you should, Mum. And don't tell Ben I said so, but we could use a man in the family," Kenna said.

Headlights swept the big picture window and lit up the driveway.

"Oh, that will be Arthur now," Freda said, as she rose to answer the door. She felt a bit unsteady on her feet, almost drunk, and abruptly sat back down. "Can you greet Arthur, dear? I don't want him to think I've been waiting by the window with bated breath."

Freda pressed her fingertips to her temples, trying to orient herself and push away the dizzy spinning in her head. She heard Arthur and Kenna talking in the front hall.

"Come in, Arthur, I'm just finishing up a glass of wine," Freda called out.

Arthur stepped into her line of sight and pointed at his boots. "Shall I come all the way in, or wait here, darling?" he asked, the remnants of his native tongue weaving in and out of his words. Then he stopped, crossed his hands over his chest, and smiled. "My word, Freda, you are an absolute vision of beauty. I'll be the envy of all the men tonight! But we should go soon, if you're ready. You know how crazy the traffic is."

"Of course, of course. Let's get this party started," Freda exclaimed, feeling radiant under Arthur's gaze.

8

FEAST OF THE SEVEN FISHES

DECEMBER 19

The Italian Club's traditional Feast of the Seven Fishes was a lavish holiday tradition for its members, especially those wistful for the old ways. Garlands of fresh pine, twinkling lights, and candles made the ballroom sparkle and the women glow, even the older ones. The room was warm—some said stuffy—but it created a convivial atmosphere and men were soon hanging their jackets on the backs of chairs and rolling up their sleeves.

The evening began with a benediction from Father Francisco, a toast to about a dozen saints, none of whom Freda cared one whit about, she being of the practical Catholic persuasion. *If there's a god, he's damn late to the party*, she would huff whenever the topic of religion arose, then cross herself just in case.

On cue, servers swarmed with trays of antipasti—traditionally meatless—but the Italian Club knew its members. Paper thin slices of salami, spicy capocollo, prosciutto, mortadella, and bresaola were tucked between the cheeses, focaccia, peppers, artichoke hearts, and anchovies. Ice clinked in cocktail glasses, and now and then a peal of laughter rang out over the crowd. Next came chilled plates of bitter greens tossed with grilled squid and aioli as wine flowed between and over top of the courses, from red to white and back again. In light of her earlier dizziness, Freda tried to pace herself, but the wine was so delicious and Arthur was attentive at topping her glass.

The band began to play softly in the background. They laughed and chatted their way through the next courses: broccoli rabe with peppers and shrimp; fluffy gnocchi with lobster; a delicate cioppino; and perfectly balanced linguini with clam sauce. Finally, servers came around with frozen bottles of liqueur and platters of tiramisu and cannoli. Arthur and Freda relaxed, leaning into each other, savoring sips of icy limoncello.

The Morettis were gathering their things, too tired now for dancing, their 67 years of marriage shuffling along behind them like a faithful old dog, herding them homeward, to their shared bed and little night rituals. Josephine Danchuk and Harriet Johnson, Freda's sorority sisters and lifelong friends, had their arms flung around Father Francisco, singing along to show tunes. And Arthur delighted everyone in earshot with tales of Christmas in Sicily. It was a perfect evening and Freda felt the warmth of satisfaction in her bones.

Sure, Kenna was an irritant from time to time, but at least Freda had nights like these, apart from the family, among her own dear friends and, of course, Arthur. He was stroking the back of her hand with his thumb, dashing in his evening attire, complete with a rose gold bow tie matching Freda's dress.

The quintet, well known around town for their interpretation of the Big Band era, were playing everyone's favorites and had just struck the first notes of Glenn Miller's *A String of Pearls*.

"Shall we dance, my beauty?" Arthur asked, grinning like a school boy.

"I thought you'd never ask," Freda replied, giggling, as she took Arthur's hand, following him to the already crowded dance floor.

He was an expert dancer, smooth and decisive, eager to show off. She felt young and giddy and the wine smoothed the way for flirting. But doubts plagued her. Was she good enough for this very good man? Attractive enough? Attentive enough? *Healthy* enough? She pushed aside the thought of her earlier dizziness. As they glided around the dance floor, expertly sliding between the less accomplished dancers, the glitter ball tossed sparkles across Arthur's smiling face. He pulled her close and whispered in her ear.

"Darling, I thought I was full from that outrageous meal, but you're so ravishing I could just eat you up," he said, with a devilish smile.

Freda threw back her head and laughed. "Oh, you naughty boy! How delightful!"

As the song ended to a spattering of applause, Arthur kept his arm firmly around Freda's waist, holding her left hand with his right, creating a circle around her, a shelter from life's diminishing returns, a little island of solace. Awaiting the next tune, Arthur turned to face her and took both Freda's hands in his.

"Freda, dear, you know I adore you, yes?" Arthur asked, his thick silver eyebrows raised in anticipation.

"Of course, darling, and I feel the same," Freda responded, squeezing his bony knuckles.

"We're sensible old ducks, but please, hear me out for a minute," he said. Arthur lowered his head, and when he raised his eyes to Freda's, they were shining with tears. "You see, I never thought this would happen again in my lifetime. Then you came along and it was like springtime again. So, being old-fashioned and a bit of a romantic, I would like to ask you, Freda Agnes Corelli Swenson, if you would share your remaining days with me. Will you marry me, my love?" he said, his cheeks reddening as a tear escaped.

The band had begun playing *Moonlight in Vermont.* To Freda, it was a perfect accompaniment to the moment she had barely dared anticipate. She gasped a little as Arthur swept her into the dance, their eyes locked, and Freda felt a surge of pure love.

"Oh, Arthur. Yes, yes, of course, I will marry you, my darling," she whispered.

When the song ended, Freda's excitement overcame her usual reticence. She clasped Arthur's familiar face between her hands and kissed him full on the mouth, right there in front of everyone. It was daring and romantic and perfect.

"Dear Freda, you've made me the happiest man on earth, so excuse me while I share my joy," Arthur said, bowing.

He trotted onto the stage and gave a little wave. The band leader pushed a microphone into his hand with a flourish.

Aha. So this was all planned.

Freda beamed, hands clasped to her chest, glittering reflections swirling around her. It was all so … happily ever after.

Arthur broke the news to the 350 or so members in the room, and a thunderous cheer went up. The noise of the crowd drifted away as the room began to spin. She felt her knees give way.

Freda looked up to a sea of faces peering down at her. Someone pressed a cool cloth to her forehead.

Sweet Jesus. What happened?

Freda quickly recovered her senses and, just as quickly, covered for her fainting spell.

"It's nothing, really. I think I just had a bit too much wine and excitement," she protested, as George Camponelli, retired surgeon and long-time member, hovered over her.

"I think you've had quite enough fun for one night," George said, as he and Arthur helped Freda to her feet.

"Have a sip of water, Freddie," Harriet said, a glass in hand.

"George is right, love," Arthur said. "Let's get you home."

"I'll fetch your car," George said, holding out his hand. "Give me your valet ticket, Arthur."

After reassuring Josephine and Harriet that he would alert them immediately if Freda took a turn for the worse, Arthur walked Freda to the entrance, where George was holding the door to Arthur's car open.

"Your chariot awaits, Madame. And call Dr. Fitz tomorrow. I'll want a full report," George said, as he closed the car door.

As they drove away, Arthur gripped her gloved hand.

"Are you sure we shouldn't go to the hospital?" he asked.

“I’m fine. You’ve just swept me off my feet is all,” Freda said, although she wasn’t at all sure that was it.

“Please stay with me tonight? I’m worried about you and would rather be close by so I can keep an eye on you, dear,” Arthur said, as they drove through the snow-hushed streets. “Besides, I promised Harrie and Jo-Jo.”

“Oh god, Arthur! The scandal! Can you imagine what people will say?” Freda said, laughing at the thought of it.

Her heart soared and her cheeks warmed in the dim light of the car. She knew her last days would be happy ones, with Arthur at her side.

Family be damned.

9

Wedding Bells & Wills

December 20

Between the gray, plodding afternoons and white-out blizzards of prairie winters, there were days like this, when brilliant shards of sunlight set the snow aglitter and tricked the eye into thinking it must be warm outside. It wasn't.

It was only a ten minute cab ride home but it felt like forever. Freda was still dressed in last night's gown and heels; she had a headache, was feeling a bit woozy, and all she wanted was a hot shower and another cup of coffee. Despite the blasting car heater, she shivered. Pulling her knee-length fur closer, Freda silently rehearsed what she would say to Kenna. Not that Freda owed anyone an explanation, but if she didn't tell the whole story—the proposal, the fainting spell, Arthur's concern—Kenna would make it sordid. Then again, it was early. Kenna was likely still in bed.

As soon as she opened the back door, she knew Kenna wasn't up. The air held the stillness of morning, a quality of quiet slumber, and Freda exhaled in relief when she heard Kenna snoring in the living room. She slipped quietly upstairs.

As she undressed, Freda's cheeks warmed at the memory of Arthur's proposal and their late night, snuggled in his bed, cooing like doves. When she awakened to Arthur whistling in his kitchen, it surprised her to be so completely at ease—a pleasant surprise, much like Arthur, himself.

Suddenly, her old house seemed gauche and outdated. Freda's bathroom was not nearly as stylish as Arthur's expansive ensuite with its heated floors and towel warmers. Letting this place go might be even easier than she thought.

After a steamy shower, Freda tiptoed into the kitchen and pulled the door closed behind her to buffer the sound of the coffee pot. She lit the gas fireplace, eager for its warmth. The sun pouring into the south-facing kitchen was too bright, glancing off every shiny surface, making her squint. Freda filled her cup, lowered the window shade, and pulled a thick knit shawl close around her neck as she curled into the curve of the antique settee tucked under the window. She sighed in pleasure at the first sip of strong coffee. Freda cherished her quiet mornings, today more than usual.

Despite a persistent dull headache, the happy glow of Arthur's proposal had not yet faded. Freda closed her eyes and felt the warm pressure of his palm on her waist as they danced, heard his laughter—still strong despite his age—and saw the sparkle of love and mischief in his dark eyes. The atmosphere of the Italian Club, with its festive decor and twinkling lights, only added to the charm. Yet, despite months of courtship, Freda had not fully woven Arthur into her everyday life because . . .why would she? They had a companionable little romance: evenings at the Italian Club after an art exhibit or symphony, lunches around town, afternoon drives to the lake for a picnic, movie and takeout nights at his place, snuggled on the sofa. Nothing to warrant a fuss. Until now.

When she thought about marrying Arthur Rossi, she couldn't help but smile. He was a long time coming. It had been decades since Freda lost her husband, Geoffrey. She didn't pine for him—that wound healed long ago—but she had often wished for the company of a man, someone who would dote on her, look after her, hold a chair for her. Arthur fulfilled all of that and more. He was widely read, a lively conversationalist, and a generous man with an unfailing love of the finer things. But he also had a sharp wit, didn't suffer fools, and could be ruthlessly sarcastic with his foes. He was every bit her match, and Freda loved him for it.

She flipped open her planner to make notes for their New Year's Day wedding. She knew better than to seek perfection, but she hoped to create a sweet memory. In her experience, two things made a memorable wedding: an emotional ceremony and a raucous reception. Neither of those appealed to her. Freda was not one to put her feelings on display and drunken partying was an affront to the solemn ritual of matrimony, despite there being no wedding mass. Arthur was as eager for a wedding as Freda, and he readily agreed to forego the religious ceremony. Neither of them were active in the parish anyway and, truth be known, Freda secretly opposed the Catholic church these days. Too many disgusting scandals. Besides, she wanted something lovely and light, like a Vivaldi concerto.

Their late-blooming romance was a refreshing second chance in Freda's last chapter of life. Even before the proposal, she'd decided she would move into his light-filled condo if … *when* he asked. But with her promise—was it really just last night?— it was beginning to sink in that her *grand dame* of a house and everything in it, curated over the last century by her family, would have to be sold. There was no way Kenna could keep up with the place. It was a historic home that needed gentle, constant care. And a lot of money.

Freda's eyes misted over as she ran her fingers along the ornate edge of the settee. She'd paid a small fortune to have it shipped home to Regina after discovering it in a Paris street market in the 60s. The only time she hadn't lived in the old Crescents mansion was when she was away at school. The house was built by Freda's paternal grandparents as a wedding gift for her parents. Freda had grown up here and, when she married, her parents gifted the house to her and Geoffrey. They claimed it was a family tradition, but Freda understood. The "tradition" allowed Geoffrey to save face because he would never be able to afford a suitable house on a military salary.

Freda stared absently out the window as she sipped coffee and felt the weight of her memories, piled into every room in the house. A woodpecker dipped his beak in the heated birdbath just beyond the kitchen window and cocked his head at Freda, his feathers puffed against the cold. Beyond him, she noticed a disturbance in the snow beside the garage. Probably the Berenchuk's spaniels sniffing about. And the driveway needed to be shoveled. Again. She turned her focus back to her lists.

The wedding to-do list was easy. Freda had a closet full of barely worn formal wear to choose from and, for that matter, she might just wear her engagement gown. She'd buy whatever flowers were plentiful and could be delivered on time. Freda had planned plenty of celebrations in her day and, for this small affair, it was primarily a matter of itemizing her wishes for the catering manager at the Italian Club.

Freda had anticipated—and wished for—Arthur's proposal. She was relieved to have given in to her intuition, calling everyone in the family in advance, urging them to pack something dressy. If Arthur hadn't proposed, Freda would have thrown together a little New Year's reception. But, as she'd proven once again, a little forward thinking never hurt. Even though she didn't mean to be imposing, it was only fair that she'd given them all advance warning to dress appropriately. What they did after that was up to them.

As the kitchen door opened, Freda's phone dinged with a message from her friend, Josephine, wanting to know how she was feeling.

"Who's texting at this hour?" Kenna asked. Her face was pink and puffy with the morning after effects of alcohol and oxy. "Any coffee left?"

"Good morning to you as well. The answers are JoJo and yes," Freda said, nodding toward the coffee pot.

Kenna poured rye and coffee into a mug. "So? What happened?"

Freda took a deep breath. She wouldn't start the drinking argument today.

"It was lovely … and I'm engaged to be married."

"Holy shit, Mum! Spill it! I want all the deets," Kenna said, as she plopped down on the other end of the settee.

Freda recounted the story of dinner and Arthur's proposal, but didn't mention fainting. Or spending the night with Arthur. Why create a problem where there wasn't any?

"So I know it just happened, but did you talk about a date?" Kenna asked, slurping her spiked coffee.

"Yes, it's all set. We're marrying on New Year's Day so the whole family will be here to celebrate. That's what I'm working on now," Freda said, gesturing at her planner. "I'm meeting Harrie and JoJo for our Christmas tea this afternoon, so I have to finalize my to-do list."

"Wow. That's not even two weeks. Doesn't it seem a bit rushed? I mean, we could plan a nice spring wedding … in Maui!" Kenna said.

Freda flinched at the "we" and could see Kenna was angling for a paid holiday in Hawaii, but that was the furthest thing from her mind.

"When you remarry, Little Missy, I'm happy to go to Maui. For me, it's here and now," Freda said, pressing her lips firmly together.

Kenna rolled her eyes. "I'll leave you to it, then, since my input *obviously* isn't welcome," she said, draining her mug. "I'll just enjoy some Christmas cheer by myself so you can plan your fancy party." She poured more rye and coffee into her mug and closed the kitchen door behind her with too much force.

Freda let out an exasperated sigh. She wished it wasn't always like this with Kenna. Everything—even her own sweet little wedding—was fodder for Kenna's bickering. It hadn't escaped her that Kenna often used these exchanges as an excuse for drinking. There was no way to ease the tension without becoming a doormat or a shrew and Freda was neither.

Her stomach growled, and a thought popped into her mind. No one wanted to sit around with a grumbling tummy as wedding vows droned on, without so much as a glass of wine to slake one's thirst. What if she inverted the usual order of things? The idea delighted Freda as she wrote in her characteristic slanting scrawl.

Coffee, tea, Bloody Caesars, Mimosas at 11:30 a.m.

A plated lunch would be served at noon, something comforting and warm. She was partial to the chef's seafood risotto. Then Father Francisco would perform a short ceremony, followed by champagne and cake. But not a wedding cake.

I'm no blushing bride, after all.

She made a note to order cupcakes from Sweetie Pies. They would come up with something decadent, pretty, and portable, but she would have to call right away.

The legal tasks were more tiresome: updating beneficiary clauses, naming a new executor, and revising her estate plan. Freda flipped through a thick binder and pulled out her will. Her attorney, Bob Barrett, had been pushing her to set up a trust for years, but she hadn't thought it necessary and suspected he was fishing for fees. Yes, the assets totaled up to a substantial estate, but it was comprised of just the house, her cash accounts, antiques and art pieces, and jewelry. In Freda's opinion, not nearly worth the trouble of creating a trust, and now that she had decided to sell the house, there was even less to fret over.

She hadn't done her annual estate review with Bob—that wasn't until February—so her will still listed her cousin, Jonathan, as Personal Representative, even though he'd died last summer. Freda had put it off, but now she *had* to name a new executor. Who could she trust to oversee everything once she was gone?

The obvious choice was Kenna, since she was living under the same roof, but her last-born wasn't reliable. She drank way too much. Totaling her car, a DUI, the staggering fine, and narrowly avoiding prison hadn't taught her anything. On top of the booze, Kenna was taking way too many painkillers. And she could be so petty and childish. Freda couldn't trust her youngest daughter.

Rita, her eldest, would be the traditional choice and had the advantage of being level-headed and practical. But she was also a traitor who ran off to the West Coast just days after graduating from nursing school, never once considering a return to her roots, or her obligation to her mother. Even though she was by far the brightest of the bunch, Rita was far too independent and contrary, and shouldn't be rewarded with the honor of being in charge of the estate.

As for Benjamin … well, he was too much like his father. He liked to be coddled and, lucky for him, he'd married a woman who catered to his whims. He would no doubt hand all the work of overseeing the estate over to his wife, Norah, which would defeat the whole purpose. To complicate matters further, as the middle child and only boy, Ben defied the birth order prediction of mediator and peacekeeper, instead unifying Rita and Kenna in their disdain for him.

Her niece—Camelia, the lawyer in the family—would be a good choice, but she lived too far away. Arthur would be suitable, but she knew resentments would arise among her children, and she didn't want to subject her new husband to their harangues. Her lifelong friends, Harriet and Josephine, would honor her wishes to the letter, but they were her age and who knew if either of them would outlive her? She could have her attorney administer the will, but he would charge an arm and a leg for the service and, besides, Barrett was already past retirement age.

But there was someone. Someone outside the family, close enough to know the dynamics and strong enough to withstand the inevitable bickering. Someone honest to her bones who had no trouble speaking her mind: Jolene Jarvis. Freda smiled at the genius of her choice. None of them would get away with pilfering a dime with Jolene in charge.

Freda was so satisfied with how things were turning out she didn't for a moment imagine anyone would dare question her decision to marry, sell her home, and revise her entire estate plan, all in the span of a few days. Freda also didn't consider how marrying Arthur would upset the precarious equilibrium of the family dynamic. Not that it would have changed anything. She preferred—demanded, if necessary—that others adapt to her needs, not the other way around.

She pulled her will closer, adjusted her reading glasses, and began editing in her slanted cursive, crossing out, adding in, and making notations about specific bequests. Freda refilled her coffee, stirring in a bit of cream as she called Hillview Salon to confirm her standing appointment with her hair stylist and, as of today, her executor.

10

Days of Auld Lang Syne

December 20

Freda tipped the cab driver with a fresh $20 bill as the valet held the door. She swept into the lobby of the Hotel Saskatchewan, one of the original Canadian Pacific Railway hotels, its old world glamour complementing Freda's own faded glory.

On her way to the dining room, Freda did a quick mental calculation to figure out how many years they had been gathering for this ritual, to exchange gifts, compliments, and gossip. Had it really been 69 years? The first time was for Freda's Sweet Sixteen Tea. Back then, there were eight girls in their group of friends, but life had dwindled them down to just these three: Freda, Harriet Johnson, and Josephine Danchuk.

Harriet and Josephine were already ensconced at the coveted fireside table. They exchanged hugs and air kisses and little compliments before relaxing into deep wingback chairs, at ease in the comfortable elegance of the room. The Hotel Sask was familiar, reminiscent of earlier days when they dressed for dinner and romantic evenings, attended weddings, special anniversaries, and milestone birthdays. They almost felt it belonged to them.

It was only four o'clock, but the sun was already low on the horizon, daylight quickly fading. The dim, golden light of the chandeliers and the nearby fire lent a flattering glow to their weathered faces. When Harrie giggled or JoJo leaned forward to deliver a salty comment, Freda saw the girls she had grown up with, not the elderly women the world saw. She wondered, for a moment, where the time had gone. How had they survived the vagaries of life when so many of their contemporaries were gone?

The waiter delivered ornate plates of bite-size delicacies and poured a round of champagne. Freda raised her glass.

"Let's toast our friendship and 69 years of Christmas tea."

"Oh dear lord, has it really been that long?" Harriet said, dabbing her lips.

"Well, let's go for 70! We have nothing to lose but life itself! And here's to your engagement, Freddie! Can we be your maidens of honor?" Josephine added, laughing.

Having been at the Italian Club the night before, Harriet and Josephine already knew of Freda's engagement to Arthur and the silly fainting spell. But now Freda could regale them with all the wonderful details. They clinked their glasses and sipped the champagne, eyes sparkling with tears of laughter, nostalgia, and affection.

"Well now that you mention it," Freda said, eagerly, "I can't wait to fill you in. What a difference a day makes! I have a lot to do, all of a sudden."

"Down to business!" Harriet said.

"As you know, I'm now engaged to the most lovely man, and it's been a long time coming. I've told Kenna, but we're going to formally announce it to the family at the Boxing Day Dinner, while they're all in town for the holidays. So, you two have to keep it hush hush for a few more days, if you can stand it," Freda quipped.

"Zipped!" Harriet said, pantomiming zipping her lips.

"Who on earth can we tell? Everyone we know is either here or dead," Josephine said, rolling her eyes.

"Speak for yourself, JoJo. I have a lot of friends at The Orchards," Harrie said.

"Will your girls be helping you with the wedding plans?" Josephine asked.

Freda shook her head and rolled her eyes. "Rita doesn't arrive for another couple of days and I can't imagine Kenna being much help with anything," she said. "She's been laid up practically the entire time she's been living with me, going on *two years.* Not that I begrudge my own child some comfort, but if I'm honest, she's no help to anyone, including herself," Freda said.

"She's not the healthiest child, is she?" Harriet said, reaching out to pat Freda's arm.

"She's not at all healthy, Harrie, no thanks to her rotten habits. I had hoped the accident would inspire a change. Instead, she eats junk all day, continues to drink like nothing ever happened, pops pills like they're candy, and never leaves the house. If I bring it up, she pouts. I have to practically drag her to her physical therapy appointments. Rita says I'm an enabler, and I'm beginning to see why," Freda said.

"Well, you tried to do the right thing," Josephine murmured in solidarity. "The younger generations just assume us old women have no life of our own. Pretty cheeky when you think about it."

Freda knew neither of them had much affection for Kenna, but Josephine and Harriet weren't about to judge.

"Don't be hard on yourself, Freddie. Ultimately, Kenna is responsible for Kenna. Really, what can you do?" Harriet asked.

"Funny you ask. I've come up with the Kenna Solution. I've decided to move into Arthur's condo— it's perfect for the two of us—and I'm putting the Crescents house up for sale."

The two friends gasped, Harriet's hands flew to her heart, and Josephine set her fork down loudly.

"Well, I'll be damned," Josephine said.

"This seems very sudden, Freddie. Are you sure about all this? I mean, that house …" Harriet said.

"I know it seems sudden, but it had to happen sooner or later, unless I wait for them to carry me out feet first. It's a lovely home, but it was built for a big family, not one old widow! And it needs constant care. I'm paying a housekeeper all year, a gardener from spring to fall, and the handyman at least once a month. And I don't even want to think about the foundation issues," Freda said, willing herself to look at it dispassionately. "It's not practical."

"True, true. An old house takes a lot of work. I just never thought … well, I guess it's time," Harriet said, tucking a tiny crab cake in her mouth.

"It's worth a small fortune. My god, the real estate prices are ridiculous, but they might be on the way down again, or at least that's what Bruce is saying, so best strike while the iron's hot," Josephine said, wagging her champagne flute at a passing waiter.

"Another good point. And selling the house will make my estate plan that much simpler. There'll be nothing to divide but money. No haggling and bickering over the china!" Freda said.

"Speaking of china, what will you do with all your pretty things, Freddie?" Harriet asked.

"Speak up if there's something special you want, but I expect I'll sell off most of it. Our generation appreciates fine antiques and imported china, but my kids? Pfft. They don't give a flip. They want everything new and modern," Freda said.

"Well, you know my feelings about downsizing. I simply love living at The Orchards, even though most everyone there is incredibly old, unlike me!" Harriet said, cupping her round cheeks in an exaggerated pose. "Maybe you and Arthur can get a place there, too."

"Harrie, we are not all going to live at The Orchards with you, no matter how many times you bring it up," Josephine said. "Although, frankly, the idea gets better every time you mention it, given our impending decline, so maybe we will … someday."

"I'm marrying a younger man, remember? Arthur's just turned 80 and he's still healthy—knock wood—and loves his condo, so we'll stay there for now," Freda said, glancing around and leaning in. "I can attest that I found it quite comfortable last night," she said, suppressing a giggle as she blushed.

"What?!" Harriet exclaimed.

Josephine let loose a peal of laughter. "Why, you naughty little tramp. Did you have a go at old Arthur?"

"Shhhh. Stop it," Freda said, grinning. "It was just … well, I fainted, you know, and he was concerned and wanted to keep an eye on me. I mean, god knows Kenna wouldn't wake up in time to help me if it were something serious."

"And did he? Keep an eye on you, I mean?" Harriet said, raising her eyebrows at Josephine.

"Oh, as sure as I'm sitting here, Arthur had more than eyes on you. The two of you are rather scandalous, aren't you?" Josephine added, laughing into her napkin. "Oh this is delicious news! Who else knows?"

"About last night? No one. And you two busybodies best keep it that way!" Freda said, shaking her head, but grinning in spite of herself. "At least until I announce our engagement to the family. Can you imagine how surprised they'll be?"

"Arthur's a catch. I'm sure they'll be happy for you, Freddie. Well, maybe not Kenna. She's gonna be pretty damn cranky when she realizes she has to move out of the manor!" Josephine said.

Freda's brow furrowed as she considered her youngest child. "Yes, I expect she'll have a fit, but what else is new? She was slamming doors this morning because I won't agree to get married in Maui," Freda said.

"Kenna isn't helpless. I'm sure she'll work it out," Josephine said. "Do you have a date in mind for the wedding, dear?"

"Yes, we're too old for long engagements! Arthur cornered the catering manager at the gala last night and told her to set aside the small ballroom for New Year's Day. So get your dancing shoes ready, girls!"

"Holy moly, that's fast. I guess last night must have been pretty special, eh?" Josephine said, making a shocked face at Harriet before they both burst out laughing.

"Sweet Jesus, will you two stop? It wasn't like that! You girls," Freda said, shaking her head and joining their laughter. "We just thought it would be nice to have the ceremony while everyone is in town for the holidays. I'll sort out the house after that," Freda said. She poured a cup of tea and leaned back in her chair.

"So when will it go on the market?" Harriet asked.

"I was thinking around the first of February, but I need to talk to a realtor. I was hoping your Bruce would manage it," Freda said, nodding at Josephine.

"What about Mickey?"

"I can't let my grandson be the agent. He's—well, you know Mickey—he's not very refined. The boy doesn't even know what dentil molding is, for heaven's sake. He's not nearly experienced enough to manage the sale of a major historic home and, even if he did, I won't indulge the favoritism," Freda said.

"Oh, I'm sure Bruce would be over the moon to list the house, but won't that cause a row with Kenna and Mickey?" Josephine said, a wicked gleam in her eye.

"I'm sure it will ruffle Mickey's feathers, but I certainly wouldn't want him lording that fat commission over the other grandchildren ..."

"What do you mean commission? He's your grandson! Surely he wouldn't take money from the sale?" Harriet said.

"Mickey's always bellyaching about money, so I'm sure he would expect a commission. And since I'm going to pay it anyway, I'd rather skip the nepotism and pay someone who understands historic architecture, don't you think?" Freda said.

"I completely agree, Freddie. It's too important and too much money at stake," Josephine said.

"Well, if they're anything like my grandkids, they're just watching the clock, hoping I keel over before I spend their inheritance. What a surprise they'll have when they find out I've left it all to the art museum," Harriet said. She giggled and clapped a gnarled hand over her mouth. "Oops. Well, I guess that cat is out of the bag."

Freda caught a fleeting glimpse of a younger Harriet, with her auburn curls, freckled nose, gold-flecked hazel eyes, and generous curves. She had always been fun-loving and mischievous, quick to laugh; a faith-filled optimist, able to see a future beyond life's fleeting troubles, even when life's inevitable tragedies piled up at her door.

"Are you really leaving *everything* to the MacKenzie?" Josephine said.

"Sorry, I didn't mean to blurt it out like that, but yes. I've been a docent at the gallery since it opened, and it seems a fitting and worthy heir," Harriet said. "You know how I love art."

"I think it's very thoughtful and generous of you, Harrie. We all know the arts don't receive nearly enough support, and the MacKenzie will probably name a gallery after you," Freda said.

She paused, her thoughts running quickly to tend the sprout of an idea.

"And now that you mention it, perhaps I should do something similar because my progeny don't need the money either. They'll just fritter it all away on designer handbags and kitchen remodels and new cars. It's all they talk about." Freda pushed a bite of lemon cake onto her fork and let the tangy sweetness melt on her tongue. "This cake is delicious!"

"Isn't it? Everything is just lovely, as usual," Harriet said, dabbing the corners of her mouth with her napkin.

"Of course they'll fritter anything they get. That's a given," Josephine said.

"As much as I would like to think they'd do something meaningful with an inheritance, I have to be realistic," Freda said, and her face hardened as she sipped a steaming cup of oolong. "Harrie, you've truly inspired me to think beyond the gene pool and consider my civic duty. And I know exactly what to do with my little hoard. It's just come to me, and it's genius if I do say so. What would you think if I were to endow the garden pavilion project at the Italian Club?"

The idea immediately seized Freda's imagination. It was perfect. She would be immortalized in the Freda Corelli Swenson Pavilion, never to be forgotten for her largesse. She would leave a token to her family and friends, but the bulk of her estate would go to the Italian Club. She visualized a glorious Victorian glass and steel conservatory, a hothouse for greenery and flowers, with rustic tables and chairs for parties and events. Freda was so excited about her new plan she couldn't wait to get home and draft it all up for her attorney. She knew Arthur would heartily approve, as well; suddenly, his approval had become very important to her.

As the waiter cleared dishes and settled their bill, Freda became wistful. Perhaps it was the champagne, or the deepening dark against the warm glow of the fire, or the threat of snow in the low clouds. Whatever it was, it caught in her throat, and she felt uncharacteristically emotional.

"Are you all right, dear?" Josephine asked.

"Yes, what is it, Freddie?" Harriet chimed in.

"Well, I suppose I am getting maudlin in my old age. It's just that here we are, a lifetime between us, and we just never know when our time is up. I'm terribly grateful for the two of you old dears. You know that, don't you? I wish we had another 69 years, even if it's foolish thinking. I'm sorry. I've gone weepy. Never mind me. We're here now, and we should make the very most of the time we have. So, let's be off! I have a wedding to plan," Freda said.

As they stepped out of the lobby, a cold blast of Arctic wind hit them in the face and pulled their scarves this way and that. They scurried into overheated, musty cabs and waved through frosty windows, unaware it was their last goodbye.

11

Christmas Cash

December 20

Kenna sunk into the sofa and took a long swallow of her rye and Diet Coke. Freda would be returning from high tea soon, so she didn't have much time to figure out just how much she had borrowed. Because that's what it was. A loan—not theft, not embezzlement, not misappropriation, not taking advantage— just a loan. She logged into the online banking site, smacking her lips as she slurped the sweet cocktail, looking for a summary of transfers.

When had Freda added her to the account? It was in the summer. August? Or was it earlier? It was so hard to keep track of things these days. Kenna entered the date parameters from June to present and clicked on *Transfers Out*. She wiggled the straw in her insulated cup, taking a long gulp, as the report opened in a new browser tab.

She sucked in her breath when she saw the total.

Is that possible?

Nervous sweat burst through her pores, gathering around her hairline, and made her armpits tingle. Kenna fumbled in her pocket for a nibble of oxy and realized she had already taken the whole tablet. She scrolled through the list of transfers. She'd borrowed a lot more than she thought: a couple of thousand dollars here and there added up quickly. If Freda found out, there would be hell to pay. And of course she was going to find out if she married that old coot, because Freda would surely add him to the bank account.

Goddammit.

Somehow, Kenna had to come up with almost $80,000 and it would have to be fast, before Freda discovered the betrayal and removed Kenna from the account. All of Kenna's money was locked up in an investment fund, which would mean penalties to the tune of 35% if she cashed it in early, but she saw no other way.

This is what I get for being a good mother. Too good, in fact.

The most recent transfer was to Mickey. His Christmas cash. The report confirmed he had received the $20,000 transfer. A wave of resentment crashed over Kenna. Mickey was one-quarter responsible for this mess! She rolled rye and Diet Coke around in her mouth and searched the far corners of her pockets for a crumb of oxy, before remembering she had just come up empty a few minutes ago. This searching, grasping need had become an automatic response to anything upsetting, uncomfortable, or just boring. Kenna rolled one hip forward, and then the other, struggling to get up from the sofa, her attention now focused on more oxy.

By the time she was standing, she was out of breath and seething with misplaced anger. Why had she given Mickey *anything*, when here she was, all by herself, with no one to care for her or help her? And why shouldn't she help herself to some of Freda's wealth? And why shouldn't she get some compensation for everything she did around here? It wasn't like Rita or Ben were front and center to take care of the old bag. Surely, she was owed something for her sacrifices! Kenna's face was flushed with alcohol, oxy, and righteous indignation as she stumbled upstairs.

She rattled the pill bottle and peered inside, surprised there were only six or seven tablets left.

Isn't this just the worst fucking day ever?

She nibbled at the oxy and pushed the remainder in her pocket. Kenna would need a new script, and soon. As she splashed cold water on her face and shuffled resentments around in her head, Kenna realized her mother would ruthlessly use this against her. She would *never* hear the end of it.

But Freda doted on Mickey, and would probably let him off with a stern look. No such generosity of spirit would be offered to Kenna. She knew Freda would demand immediate repayment. But what if Freda thought Mickey had been the recipient of *all* the funds, not just the last bit? After all, he just received $20k, so he wasn't exactly innocent, was he?

Suddenly it made sense to her—and she could easily convince herself—that all the money had gone to Mickey. She felt lighter already. And if she could turn this into a secret they had to keep from Suyin, it would all work out, because Freda wasn't all that fond of Suyin either.

Kenna would rat him out—privately, confidentially—and ask Freda to take the $80k from Mickey's inheritance. When Freda died, which she hoped was soon, Kenna could give Mickey an extra $60k from her own inheritance and none the wiser. Problem solved. She laughed out loud. Or maybe she wouldn't give Mickey anything extra. What had he done to deserve it?

As the little bump of oxy hit her system, Kenna felt the satisfaction of having figured this out on her own. Who could she have discussed it with anyway? Kenna didn't know why her circle had narrowed to the point that it was barely an arc, but she blamed Tony.

Maybe it was the divorce, or Mickey graduating high school, moving in with Freda, or even the accident that made her social life freeze over like a pond in November. It certainly couldn't be her justifiable bitterness over life's disappointments that made people—even her own family—avoid her. Kenna couldn't understand how the horrible things that had happened to her alienated those who had once been part of her life. Isn't that exactly when everyone was supposed to rally to her defense?

Kenna's thought were interrupted when her phone dinged. Again. And again.

When she saw the text messages, she groaned. Of course Camelia would set up a group text to broadcast her every move, and here she was, announcing that her flight from Phoenix was delayed.

Good.

The less interference from her, the better.

Kenna rolled her shoulders and headed back to the living room, taking the stairs carefully, one at a time, the booze and opioids a fuzzy buffer between her and her feet. By the time she got downstairs, Kenna felt like celebrating her creative solution with another cocktail and maybe a big slice of the orange cranberry bread Jan Berenchuk had brought over.

It was going to be a holly jolly Christmas, after all.

12

Christmas Cheer

December 21

Camelia needed a drink. *Badly.*

First, the flight to Regina had been delayed out of Phoenix three times due to a snow storm over the Rockies and, when their connecting flight finally took off from Calgary, the turbulence was so bad the crew canceled beverage service. No booze cart rolling down the aisle to soothe her nerves. And now that they were on the ground—exhausted and impatient—she had to quell her jangled nerves until they got to the rental house.

Camelia took a deep breath and texted Rita.

> We finally made it. Are you here? Heading straight from airport to house. Call me!

She leaned over to let Leon know she was going to the ladies' room.

"Again?" he asked, looking at her a bit too intently.

Why does he have to be so suspicious?

"Yes, again. What are you, the Potty Cop?" she asked, a bit too sharply.

Camelia walked away, not waiting for an answer. Locked in a stall, she ransacked her carry-on one more time for something, anything, to dial down the shaky feeling inside. She found a Xanax in her wallet—*thank all the gods!*—and happily chewed it, eager for the smooth warmth of relief, while watching for a response from Rita. Her phone dinged.

We're here!

It wasn't Rita, but her daughter, Sophie, and son-in-law, Steve, arriving from Toronto. She already felt calmer, knowing they were on the ground and not stranded because of the weather.

Camelia washed her hands and drew damp fingers through her already tousled hair, trying to fluff some gaiety back into her outward appearance. When she exited the washroom, Camelia spotted Sophie and Steve cozied up to Leon at baggage claim and paused to observe them as a stranger would. She saw a happy family reunion, smiling faces, affectionate laughter, and the glow of love around them. Too bad the whole scene was tarnished by her persistent anxiety over every damn thing.

Her phone dinged. It was Rita responding.

We got in this afternoon and headed straight to mum's. I'll call later. Pray for my bitten tongue! Xo

Camelia approached her family, breaking into a smile.

"Mum!" Sophie shouted, throwing her arms around Camelia. They exchanged hugs and dragged their luggage out of the way of other passengers.

"Why don't you guys wait here while I go get the rental car?" Leon said, stacking his backpack on top of their suitcases.

"I'll come along since I'm the second driver," Steve said.

"Make sure you pay our half," Sophie said.

"No, I got it," Leon said.

"No, Dad, you don't. Are we gonna have this argument again?" Sophie said.

"Seriously, do we have to do this every time? How about if we pay for the car and you pay for the gas?" Camelia said. This was a too-familiar conversation, and Camelia wasn't in the mood for haggling.

"Done. Hear that Dad? Do *not* gas up the car!" Sophie said, grinning, wagging her index finger at Leon.

As Leon and Steve walked away, Sophie looped her arm through Camelia's.

"I'm so glad you guys weren't snowed out. The weather is awful," Sophie said.

Camelia shrugged. "It's Saskatchewan in the winter. And it's why we don't live here anymore."

"True. At least we all made it ahead of the blizzard that's on the way. Are we going to pick up booze and food before we go to the house?"

"Yep. We'll stop at the liquor store, pick up some groceries, and go hunker down at the house," Camelia said. "Then who cares if there's a blizzard?"

"Right? A cocktail and a snack would be nice. We're starving," Sophie said. "Those six pretzels they gave us on the plane didn't really fill us up."

"Won't be long. We can all get into our jammies, pour some drinks, and park in front of the fire for the night," Camelia said.

"Perfect. A little Christmas cheer sounds like heaven," Sophie said.

She smiled at her daughter but, for Camelia, Christmas cheer was in short supply. She could already feel the old, familiar ghosts of Christmas past sidling up to her, itching to rob her of any crumbs of joy she might find in the season. She always hoped it would be different, joyful, easy. But memories of home included long shadows cast by her father's drunken rages. Dashed expectations and reminders of her painful childhood lurked around every familiar corner, agitating her demons. If it weren't for Auntie Freda, Camelia wasn't sure she would ever come back to Regina again.

She shook her head to clear the dark thoughts. Despite Byron's dire warning, Camelia was counting on a little vodka to shut those damned demons up. At least for tonight.

13

I'LL BE HOME FOR CHRISTMAS

DECEMBER 21

"Hi Mum, we're almost home. Are you there to let us in?" Rita said, as they neared the Crescents house.

"Yes, of course I'm here, and I have some things to discuss regarding my estate and the Boxing Day dinner," Freda said.

Rita hung up, a ball of worry congealing in her stomach. Whenever her mother wanted to *discuss* something, it was more likely a tirade, or an admonishment or, at the very least, a rant. As Dave navigated the snow-packed streets, Rita freshened her lipstick and smoothed her hair. There was no need to antagonize Freda by showing up looking rumpled and travel-weary, even though that's how she felt after the long, two-day drive from Vancouver.

Rita dreaded the annual Christmas visit but it was mandatory, a duty to be fulfilled, because obeying Freda's edicts was far easier than not. Yet, as they pulled into the driveway, Rita's heart clutched at the sight of her childhood home. It looked like a fairytale castle in the snow, the Christmas tree twinkling in the tall front windows, and a huge wreath on the front door. How could such a beautiful setting be the stage for so many painful memories?

While Dave pulled the car around back, Rita rang the doorbell. She heard footsteps, and Freda swept the door wide, with a scowl.

"My goodness," she said, nodding at the luggage on the steps. "I hope you're not planning to move in, too?"

Rita looked down at their luggage: two suitcases, one toiletry bag, and her medical kit. Her face prickled with the cold and a flush of anger. She quelled the words that rushed to escape and smiled.

"Just enough for the week, Mum. Besides, you've already got a boomerang kid under foot."

"Speaking of Kenna, keep your voice down. Your sister's sleeping."

It didn't surprise Rita that Kenna was in bed because, since the accident, she didn't have anything better to do, other than get drunk and mooch off Freda. Just as well. One less manipulator to deal with.

"Dave's parking the car. He'll be right in," Rita stage whispered.

"Tea's on. Come to the living room when you get yourself sorted," Freda said, leaving Rita in the entry struggling with her boots.

"Great to see you, too, mum," she muttered, as she tucked her medical kit behind her boots, by the door.

Freda was sipping tea by the window, settled into one of two Bergere chairs, a hand-knit throw on her lap. Rita limped into the room, her hips aching from the frigid prairie weather and shifting barometer. That's what 30 years of being on your feet for 12 hour shifts in the ER will do for you—it will break your body and your heart. Taking a job in private hospice care was easier on her back and hips, but it wasn't a cure. Freda seemed not to notice, which was a relief. Rita didn't want to discuss her aching joints or anything else about her life. That was Kenna's specialty, and Rita was determined not to be like her sister.

Dave slipped his boots off and ducked his head into the living room.

"Freda! Great to see you looking chipper as ever! I'm just going to take our bags down to the suite, and I'll be right back," he said, his cheeks and nose red with cold.

"Don't rush. I have some family things to discuss with Rita," Freda said.

A wave of resentment crashed over Rita. They had been in the house less than ten minutes, and Freda was already dismissive of Dave. It was no secret Freda hadn't thought him worthy of her eldest daughter, but you would think, after more than 30 years of marriage, Freda would have come around.

Rita settled into the chair next to Freda's and rubbed her hands as her joints loosened in the over-heated room. She had spent many hours in this room as a child, and it felt reassuringly familiar. The fire blazed next to her, a cozy relief from the bitter cold outside, making Rita instantly drowsy.

"Would you like some tea to warm you up? There's shortbread, too." Freda motioned to the tray on the coffee table, where three empty cups and saucers stood at the ready.

"Not just yet, thanks. So? How're you doing?"

"I'm perfectly fine, thank you. Well, I seem to be a bit dizzy here and there. Maybe I've caught a bug, who knows? I'm sure it's nothing, but I'll see Dr. Fitz after the holidays to make sure all systems are go. And you?"

"We're doing well enough, the new job is interesting, and the kids are doing great, so we have no complaints." Rita filled her mother in on the latest happenings with her children: her youngest, Dana; Darren, his wife, Jessica, and, Clara—Freda's first great-grandchild. When she'd finished recapping their lives, Rita tiptoed into the subject.

"So, is everything okay? You said you wanted to discuss something?" Rita couldn't imagine what was on Freda's mind because her mother looked more radiant and relaxed than Rita remembered. "You look like the cat that ate the canary."

"First, I want to warn you that I'm bringing a guest for Boxing Day, a special guest," Freda said, tilting her chin up as if daring Rita to say no.

"That's fine Mum, we always have room for one more. Who's coming along? Harrie? JoJo?"

It wasn't strange for Freda to invite a friend to the Boxing Day dinner. Harriet, Josephine, and a host of others had joined them over the years.

Freda set her teacup down and cleared her throat. "No dear, it's not the girls. It's Arthur Rossi."

Rita nodded. "Yeah, sure, I remember, your friend from the Italian Club. He's more than welcome. There's always plenty of food," she said.

"That's what I wanted to talk to you about. Arthur is more than a friend. He proposed marriage on Saturday, and I accepted. Arthur is now my fiancé," Freda said, and her face flushed. "I want him to meet everyone and we'll make our formal announcement at the Boxing Day dinner. It will be wonderful to have the whole family with us to celebrate."

Rita was speechless for a moment. She called her mother a couple of times a month, but their conversations were always brief and superficial. Rita didn't have much insight into Freda's daily life, but she could see this was a rare occasion of joy for her mother, so she quickly recovered.

"Wow … Mum, this is very surprising, but in a wonderful way. I'm so happy for you, really, and of course we'll make a place for Arthur. I'm just … well, I had no idea you two were serious," she said, smiling.

"Yes, well, there are a lot of things you don't know about my life because you live so far away," Freda said. "We're delighted to have found each other, even if it is the eleventh hour. He's very decent. I think you'll take to him just as I did," Freda said.

"All that matters is that you're happy. Just like me and Dave. I mean, you didn't think he was a good choice, but here we are, coming up on our 31st wedding anniversary, so it looks like it worked out," Rita said. She couldn't help herself.

"Yes, it seems he was a good enough choice for you," Freda countered, with a sharp glare.

Rita inhaled deeply and willed herself not to respond. She shifted her gaze to the Christmas tree, laden with ornaments from three generations of Swensons. The tree stayed lit from the moment it went up on December 8—the Feast of the Immaculate Conception—until it was taken down again on January 5, the end of the twelve days of Christmas. It was *tradition.* Just like Freda's incessant needling.

"That's quite the news. Who else knows?" Rita said, hoping to move the focus back to Freda.

"Everyone at the Italian Club, because that's where Arthur proposed. Harrie and JoJo were there, of course. I've told Kenna, and now you. I wanted to keep it quiet until we announce to the whole family, but I had to share the happy news with my best friends and dear daughters," Freda said.

"What about Ben? Does he know?"

"No, because your brother isn't here, is he? It's not the sort of thing you send in a text, at least *I* don't. Ben and Norah chose to arrive at the last minute, so they'll find out with everyone else," Freda said.

To outsiders, Freda's words would have seemed innocuous enough, but Rita had a lifetime of experience maneuvering Freda's subtext. Ben was being punished. Rita was angry at him, too, but only because she envied his ability to establish boundaries and stick to them.

"And, of course, with marriage comes change. I've been giving it a lot of thought, and I'll be putting the house on the market after the holidays, so you'll need to remove all your things from the attic," Freda said.

"Whaaaat? You're selling the house?" Rita tried not to strangle on her words. "Wow, Mum, that's even more shocking than getting married! I mean … I just never imagined you without this house, not that you shouldn't sell but it's just … I don't know … such a fixture," Rita said.

She was surprised at her mother's seemingly quick decision to marry, but selling the house? Rita hadn't predicted that. She'd always assumed the house would be passed down, kept in the family, a monument to the family name for coming generations.

Rita's thoughts were ping-ponging around in her head. She suddenly felt attached to the old house, the very house she had run from as soon as she graduated high school. The same house she had vowed never to return to, not as long as her mother lived there. And yet, it wasn't the house, it was the inhabitants that kept her at bay: her overbearing, domineering mother; her odd, prickly brother; and her manipulative, maddening sister.

But there were happy snippets of her father here, too. In that moment, as the sun dazzled on the snow and the warmth of the room swaddled her, Rita became sentimental, possessive even. She couldn't imagine the old house belonging to anyone other than a Swenson.

"It's been my home all my life, but sacrifices must be made, and it makes sense to streamline my estate now, rather than waiting for the inevitable," Freda said, topping up her cup of tea. "Care for some?"

"Yes, thanks, I'll get it." Rita got up and poured herself a cup of tea. "And what about Kenna?"

"What about her?" Freda looked up from her tea. "Oh, you mean where will she live? She'll be fine. God knows she has plenty of money, what with her alimony, and disability pay, and the cash from selling her own house. She can do as she pleases. Besides, there's no way she can keep up with this place, given her health problems. I'm hoping she'll buy one of the new condos down on Broad. It would be good for her to be around people her own age. But who knows, maybe she'll live with Mickey and Suyin," Freda said, shrugging.

"You're right. She needs to meet some new people, get some hobbies or a job or something. It would do her good," Rita said.

And maybe she could quit drinking while she's at it.

"First things, first. I have to declutter, then get rid of all the furniture and housewares so I can list the house," Freda said.

Rita wasn't about to get roped into the decluttering task.

"You should call Gardener's Estates. They did all the work for Margie's folks when they moved to The Orchards. It wasn't very expensive, considering. They took a commission and I wanna say it was 15%," Rita said.

Rita tried to calm her inner panic. If she just went along with it, perhaps Freda would change her mind. She knew better than to give her mother any resistance to push against. Making it seem as if she didn't care might spur Freda to think twice. She knew damn well she would not be able to change her mother's mind, but maybe, just maybe, the enormity of the task would dissuade Freda from making such a rash decision.

"Hunh. Fifteen percent is quite a lot, but of course I'll give them a call. I just thought my own children would be willing to help," she sniffed.

Rita smiled inwardly.

Right on cue.

She hoped Freda would agree to hire out the daunting task of sorting and emptying the enormous house of its treasures. And junk. The attic was full of the detritus of life, left over from three generations. Every room was full of expensive antique furniture. The living areas were crammed with art, mementos from Freda's travels, and bric-a-brac accumulated over the years. The basement storage held all the seasonal ornaments and decorations, and god knows what else.

"Mum, for chrissake, we aren't *children*. That's the problem. We're getting old ourselves and the last thing I need is for Dave to throw his back out again. And my hips …"

"Yes, yes, I know. Everyone has an excuse. It doesn't matter. I'm sure I can hire strangers to sift through your old things. Who knows? Maybe there's a vintage Barbie doll up in the attic worth a few dollars," Freda said.

Rita hated the passive-aggressive shaming Freda was so skilled at, but she refused to cave. The old resentments, however, surged to life in the form of a knot in her stomach.

"Don't worry, Mum. We'll remove all my things before we leave, and I expect Ben and Kenna will do the same. I like Gardener's because you won't have to handle the sales or donations—they do all that. They'll organize an estate auction and everything will go at top dollar. Margie's parents made almost thirty grand on their stuff and they didn't have anything near as nice as all this," she said, waving her hand around the room.

Freda pursed her lips as she quietly poured another cup of tea. She was so proud of her possessions that reducing them to a paltry sum was guaranteed to anger her. And so what? Rita wanted it to sting. If she was going to sell off the entire family collection, why wouldn't Rita be upset? It was her history, too.

"You're right, of course. And since you know so much about it, you can call them and arrange a visit," Freda said.

Touché.

When Rita didn't respond, Freda continued. "One more thing. I'm updating my will. I've named a new executor since Jonathan passed, and a few bequests will be changed, but nothing for you to concern yourself with. Bob Barrett—you remember Bobby, don't you?—will be drafting it all up after the holidays."

Rita didn't flinch at either the news or the name. She'd dated Bobby Barrett a few times when they were both in university. She found him to be a handsy know-it-all, so she wasn't surprised when he went on to law school and became Freda's first choice for the role of son-in-law. And she didn't care to know the details of Freda's will because she had never counted on receiving anything from her mother.

If you were in favor, you were in the will. The next day, if you crossed Freda, you were out of the will. Rita had tired of the game long ago and hated how Freda pitted them against one another. Who needed it? Certainly not Rita. She and Dave had invested their savings well and could live comfortably for the remainder of their lives without a single penny from Freda. Sure, she had assumed her mother would leave them the house, but she had never relied on it. Until now.

"Mum, it's all yours to do with as you please and whatever you decide will be perfect. So, is Kenna your executor?" Rita asked, tentatively.

She had always assumed she would be Freda's executor. It was her right and her role as the eldest, wasn't it? But now she wasn't so sure.

"Never fear, you little coward. I won't put you through the trouble. I've decided to name Jolene as my executor. She can handle the squabbles. And no one else knows, so keep that bit to yourself for now," Freda said.

"Oh my god, Kenna is going to have a fit!" Rita forced a laugh, despite feeling like she might cry. Being Freda's co-conspirator was safer than arguing her position. "But the most important thing is, are your healthcare directives up to date?"

"Yes, but don't be too anxious to pull the plug. I intend to live a good long while, thank you very much. But when it's time, be swift. Be merciful. Don't let them reduce me to some drooling bag of bones. Promise me now," Freda said, her gaze suddenly intense and unblinking.

Here we go again.

Freda always imagined the worst case scenario.

"Well, Mum . . ." Rita began.

"No excuses. You're a palliative care nurse. You know what to do. For god's sake, don't lose your nerve in my hour of need," Freda said.

"We've been over all this. There are forms you'll need to fill out … but yes, I will do what I must," Rita said. She sipped at her tea. "In the meantime, since you're getting married, do you still want to be buried with Dad?"

"I'm crazy about Arthur, but my burial plans remain the same. It's already paid for and arranged, and I promised your father I would be laid to rest with him at the National Cemetery. Arthur will be buried at his family plot in Saskatoon. We're too old to worry about who gets planted where. But I have been thinking about some kind of … I don't know, a *memorial* of some sort that people can visit. Just a little *something*. Ottawa is a world away, and no one there will know me." Freda's mouth turned down as she spoke.

Rita could see the invitation to press for details, but she wasn't biting. No matter what she suggested, Freda would shoot it down, so why bother?

"Mum, if you want to be buried here, that's fine. If you want to be buried with Dad, that's fine too. Or, you can be cremated, and we can send half of you to Ottawa and put half of you at Riverside. Whatever you want is fine with us," Rita said, her voice softening at the thought of sending her mother off into the spirit world with her father.

He was a vague memory now, but a happy one. Rita's childhood was punctuated into two parts: Life With Daddy and Life Without Daddy. Geoffrey had been an affectionate, playful father, full of mischief and secret outings for tiger stripe ice cream at Milky Way, far from Freda's disapproving eyes.

"Really, Rita? As a Catholic I would *never* consider cremation. Besides, I don't like the idea of being reduced to a shoebox full of ashes," Freda said, as she stood and picked up her tea cup. "Now, bring the tea tray with you to the kitchen and we can review the Boxing Day menu. And keep all this to yourself. I want to be the one making the announcement to the family on Boxing Day."

Rita slid the tea service onto the counter and the two women settled at the kitchen island.

"Now, here's what I've planned …" Rita unfolded a sheet of paper and began reviewing the menu with Freda.

"I'm so glad it's your turn. I brought you all up properly, but it only seems to have taken with you. You're a reliable hostess and good enough cook," Freda said. "It will make a good impression on Arthur, even if we're less elegant than we used to be," Freda sniffed. "Remember when we used to hire caterers and a band!"

"Yes, Mum, but that's when you were inviting half the town. Now it's just family, and we can serve ourselves," Rita said. "And Dave will make sure there's a nice playlist of holiday music."

A door slammed upstairs.

"It sounds like sleeping beauty has awakened!"

"Try not to start an argument, dear. Your sister has her burdens," Freda said.

Rita's smirk vanished at the sight of Kenna as she wandered into the kitchen.

"Hey sis, rough night?" Rita asked as she rose to hug Kenna.

"They're all rough when your body is broken in four places," Kenna said. "Not that anyone around here would understand."

"Well, I hope you feel well enough for the Boxing Day Party," Rita said.

"I'm *fine*. How long are you here?" Kenna said, turning on the kettle.

"Dave and I are here tonight, leaving in the morning for his folk's place, and we'll be back early on the 26th with all the food prepped," Rita said.

"I don't know why you insist on traipsing out to the boonies for Christmas. Why don't Dave's parents just come to town?" Freda sniffed.

"Mum, they live on a farm. And it's not exactly the boonies. They're only an hour away," Rita said. "And besides, it's our *tradition*. Christmas with the Beckers, Boxing Day and New Year's with the Swensons. We're not switching it up now!"

"No, of course not. Because you have *rules*, right Rita?" Kenna smirked.

"No, Kenna, I have a *husband*."

Rita smiled at Kenna's shocked expression.
You asked for it.

14

NOT A CREATURE WAS STIRRING

DECEMBER 22

Camelia woke with a start, disoriented and hungover. Again. She rolled over and realized she was home. Sort of. She never felt truly at ease anywhere these days, but at least they were in Regina, a thousand miles from the daily pressures of Phoenix.

She tapped her phone to see the time: 5:47 a.m. The house was dark and quiet, and daylight wasn't yet peeking in the window. Camelia should have been able to relax, sleep in, breathe. But it didn't seem to matter how tired she was, her internal clock didn't care. Leon was sleeping soundly beside her and her daughter and son-in-law were upstairs. She quietly slid out of bed and felt around for her robe.

Camelia tiptoed to the living room and fumbled for the switch. An ultramodern floor lamp lit up a corner of the sofa. The gas fireplace immediately radiated warmth when she turned it on. She sighed with pleasure. The rental was in the Cathedral District, a small neighborhood of heritage homes, trendy cafes, and funky shops along tree-lined streets. It appeared to be just like all the other stodgy century homes—deep sun porches clutched to their stout frames—except for a vibrant magenta front door. That audacious door opened into a completely renovated home with a playful, modern interior. Perfect social media fodder and exactly the kind of place Camelia wanted for a holiday rental.

She pulled the drapes aside and peered outside. It was like a movie set for a festive white Christmas, with pale blue snow banked along the sidewalks and holiday lights twinkling from eaves. So why wasn't she buoyant with elfin spirit? She felt more like a Grinch than Santa's helper. Everything just seemed so … heavy, laden with complexity, bogged down with unmet expectations.

Camelia pulled the drapes closed and settled near the fire with her laptop. She carefully typed in the WiFi password. She regretted it immediately. There were four emails from Byron and two from Cate, both from yesterday.

Camelia pressed her fingertips to her eyes. Would it ever end? She was *supposedly* on vacation, but it was just another work day as far as Byron was concerned. She heaved a sigh and rolled her neck.

Stop the pity party, Cam.

She knew she should be grateful Byron hadn't fired her outright over the Spencer Ashcroft debacle. She should also be grateful for the deluge of work—it was money in the bank—but she was barely keeping her head above water. As for Cate, her assistant was usually respectful of precious vacation time, so Camelia guessed Byron had been riding her as well.

She needed coffee if she was going to work, so she tiptoed around the kitchen, quietly poking around until she found a French press and kettle. While the coffee steeped, she munched on some crackers left from last night's dinner of cocktails and a thrown-together charcuterie board. A half-empty bottle of vodka was on the counter, also from last night. It seemed to be calling her. Like a siren song.

Camelia poured several glugs into her coffee mug and tossed it back. The burn at the back of her throat felt familiar and reassuring.

Just a little kick start to the day can't hurt.

When the coffee was done, she returned to the living room. Camelia opened her billing software and started the timer. She would have at least an hour before Leon woke up.

Might as well do some billable work to pay for this so-called vacation.

15

Crowded House

December 22

Freda awoke to the sound of voices in the kitchen. It took her a moment to recall that Rita and Dave had arrived yesterday. Other than their hushed murmurs, the house was silent. Kenna would still be asleep. It was barely past 7 a.m. after all, far too early for her youngest to be up and around.

It rubbed on her that Kenna was so lazy, and it bothered her even more that Rita was a witness to it. Freda had raised her children to be responsible early risers, hard workers, the type of people to do right by your neighbor and—above all—to be respectable citizens. But here she was, with a layabout under her own roof and nothing she could do about it. Until now.

And then there was Rita. Freda didn't know why Rita irritated her so much when she was in the house, and yet she missed her when she wasn't here. Perhaps it was Rita's blatant nonchalance that prickled. Rita had never seemed to need her mother—unlike Kenna—and she seemed completely unconcerned about any of them, as if nothing bad could ever happen.

Rita, of all people, should know that bad things happen every day.

How had she gone so wrong in raising her children? They weren't criminals or anything like that, but they weren't exactly what she'd hoped for.

Freda dressed quickly and left her room, slamming the door ever so slightly. But as she walked past Kenna's room, Freda could still hear her snoring.

She sleeps like a person with a clear conscience.

Freda shook her head. She had no time for ruminating over the failures of her children. She was meeting her new realtor—Josephine's son, Bruce Danchuk—this morning to discuss listing the house, then she had to mail a copy of her new will to Bob Barrett, then on to Willow Bistro for her grandchildren's annual Cousins Lunch. She had to get a move on.

Freda waved off Dave's offer of breakfast, but poured herself a cup of coffee. She listened to Dave chatter on about the weather forecast as Rita thumbed through the latest issue of *Bon Appetit.* Dave had grown his hair long and was nurturing a beard, which Freda found ridiculous. He was a grandfather, for pity's sake, and yet was reverting to this scraggly old hippie look. Rita wasn't much better, letting her grey hair grow in like some crystal witch. Had they no pride?

Morning was usually Freda's quiet time of the day, and even though she wanted to enjoy their company, she was annoyed. The way Rita pinched the pages of the magazine as she turned them. The way Dave slurped his coffee and kept clearing his throat. It was too much, having them here in the same house, when she barely knew them, yet knew them far too well. The air was heavy with unmet expectations and Freda was growing impatient.

"Did Dana arrive? I didn't hear her come in."

"Yeah, she texted last night. Her flight was late so she headed straight out to the farm. I wish Darren and Jessica were here too, but it's her mom's turn to have them for Christmas. They'll be here on Boxing Day." Rita laid her magazine aside. "Yesterday you said you might be coming down with something. How are you feeling today?"

"Well, I'm no better, but no worse. I just have this nagging headache, but I don't have time to be sick," Freda said, sipping her coffee.

"I have some cold lozenges. I'll leave a few for you," Rita said.

"Are you sure? I mean, isn't sharing a prescription against your oath or something?"

"It's zinc and vitamin C, Mum. Nothing to get excited about," Rita said, with a hard edge in her voice. "I just don't want you to be sick for the holidays, and there's so much going around right now," she said.

"You know how she is, Freda. A walking pharmacy," Dave said, grinning.

"These've got chamomile in them and might make you sleepy, so just use them before bed or when you lay down for a nap," Rita said.

"When have you ever known me to nap? Pffft."

"If you're not feeling well, you're allowed to rest, Mum," Rita said.

"Well, not today, that's for sure. I've got the Cousins Lunch and some last minute shopping to do, but first I'm stopping in at JoJo's to visit with her son, the realtor. You remember Bruce, don't you?"

"Bruce Danchuk? He's a realtor now? Good for him," Dave said, taking another slurp of coffee. "Haven't seen him in ages."

"Aww. I love Bruce. How's he doing these days?" Rita asked.

"Bruce is doing well. He's a successful broker, married to a darling man, and *very* devoted to his mother," Freda sniffed. "Figured I might as well get the ball rolling."

"Rita told me you're selling the house," Dave said.

"Are you sure you want to list it *now*? Houses don't sell that well in the winter. You could wait for spring to get the best price," Rita said.

"I'm not a procrastinator. There's no point in putting off the inevitable." Freda sipped her coffee and fidgeted with a napkin.

"Seems a shame, after almost a century in the family," Dave said, loudly slurping his coffee.

Freda pretended not to notice the slurping, even though it drove her crazy.

"A worse shame would be letting it fall to ruin, which would surely happen if I left it to the lot of you," Freda replied. She laughed at Dave's quick frown. "Oh, don't be so offended. You know it's true. What are you going to do? Leave your precious Vancouver condo to manage this old hulk? I rather doubt it, dear."

Rita yawned and stood up. "Well, Mum, I know you have to be off, and we'll be gone by the time you get back, so give us a hug. I'll leave those lozenges for you," she said.

Freda bristled at being dismissed, but bit her tongue. "Yes, yes, we all have things to do."

She put her cup in the sink and headed for the back door. Freda pulled a heavy vintage fur from the closet and slipped into a pair of short boots.

"I'll see you in a few days. Merry Christmas to all," she said, and pulled the back door closed with a bang.

Freda paused on the landing and took a deep breath. Dave hadn't even offered to warm up her car or pull it around for her. Rita hadn't offered to drive her, even though she knew Freda wasn't feeling well. They were thoughtless and heartless and should just go back to Vancouver where they belonged.

They certainly don't belong here.

16

Cousins Brunch

December 22

Freda's cheeks stung and her eyes watered as she stepped out of the frigid cold into the overly-warm restaurant. As her vision cleared, she saw Sophie waving from across the room.

"Auntie Freda! Over here!"

Freda wasn't Sophie's aunt at all. Freda and Camelia's mother were cousins, and that made Freda an "auntie" to both Camelia and Sophie in the familiar—if not strictly familial—sense. The important part was that they were all family.

"Steve's on his way. Here, let me help you with your coat," Sophie said, as she waved at the waiter to take Freda's fur coat.

Freda settled in to wait for the rest of the Cousins, her children's children, although only half of them would be here. Out of all of them, she was in closest contact with Mickey, but only because he was the last grandchild still living in Regina. Even so, she felt most bonded to Sophie and Ben's son, Andrew, the eldest two of the group. They understood her.

Sophie ordered a bottle of Freda's favorite—Sea Star pinot noir—and they nibbled on chunks of warm, crusty bread as they waited for the others to arrive. Within minutes, Andrew arrived with an androgynous blonde. Rita and Dave's daughter, Dana, was just two steps behind, arm-in-arm with Steve. As the waiter poured the wine, Freda uncharacteristically put her hand over her glass, refusing even a splash.

"Children, I know it may sound strange that I'm not having even one very civilized glass of wine with brunch. I'm driving today and I don't want to ..." Freda began.

"Happy Almost Christmas!" Mickey shouted as he pushed his way through the now-crowded bistro. Suyin was trailing in his wake, her sullen expression all the hint anyone needed as to her mood.

"Mickey! Suyin! We're just getting started. Sophie, pass the wine down the table, will you, dear?" Freda said.

"Gram, you look fabulous! How are you feeling after the other night?" Mickey said.

"What's he talking about?" Sophie said.

"Oh, just a little ... I don't know. Some dizziness. As I was saying when you came in Mick, I haven't been feeling 100 percent lately, but I'm sure it's just a bug, nothing to worry over," Freda said.

But she wasn't sure. She recalled fainting at the Italian Club, and the terror of the darkness as she swam against it, finally regaining consciousness. Freda still had a lingering wooziness and cottony head feeling. And then there were the headaches.

"Hey Gram, try some of this. It's a nose spray I use to keep from getting sick from all the clients I see," Mickey said, passing a little white bottle down the table. "I get it from a Chinese medicine man Suyin's parents use. I have no idea what's in it, some kind of herbal bullshit, but it works!"

Suyin rolled her eyes and drained the wine bottle into her glass.

Sophie put her hand on Freda's arm. "Auntie Freda, don't you think you should know what's in that before you use it?" Sophie asked.

Freda glanced down the table at Mickey. He was glaring at Sophie with such intensity that it startled her for a moment. Then he seemed to catch himself and, like a cloud passing in the sky, he rearranged his face into a smile.

"It's perfectly safe, Gram, just some herbs, that's all,". Mickey said, with a note of contrition in his voice.

"I'm sure it's fine. Thank you, love, hopefully it will ward off the germs," Freda said, and inhaled the mist into each nostril. "Enough of that, let's give our lovely Randy something to do," she said, waving her knobby hand in the waiter's direction.

Freda knew all the waiters by name. Willow was her favorite restaurant and she made a point of being that gracious old woman who was familiar with the staff. She had lived in this small city her entire life and had every intention of leaving it lonely for her someday.

When their food arrived, everyone had to ooh and aah, take photos, and compare notes. Moments later, Willow's chef came out and bowed to Freda.

"I am so happy to see you, Madame! I hope all is to your liking today," Chef Andre said, his chubby face flushed red.

"Oh, Chef, everything looks just perfect, as always. Here's something for you and the kitchen staff. We always enjoy your work so much," Freda said, handing Chef Andre an envelope.

He bowed his head a little and his Quebec accent surged. "Mon cher, is not at all necessary! We love to make you happy with a little food, a little wine, a nice view," Chef Andre said, waving his arm at the white expanse of Wascana Lake, frozen over now, and the Legislative buildings beyond, snow laced and photo-ready in the dazzling sunlight. He took Freda's mottled hand, sporting an enormous amber ring set in a fanciful swirl of gold, and pressed his lips to her knuckles. "We are at your service, bon appetit!" Chef said before disappearing into the steamy kitchen at the back of the small bistro.

"Children, children, let's have a toast!" They all quieted, lifting their glasses expectantly in Freda's direction. The winter sun bounced sparkling light off the snowy deck outside, throwing bright beams across Freda's face, making her sapphire blue eyes appear lit from within.

"To you, the next generation, to the holidays, and to the New Year," Freda said. They all touched glasses, but before they could drink, she held up her hand. "And one more thing. I want you all at the Italian Club at 11 am on New Year's Day for a special treat. Wear something nice and bring your hangovers, if you have them. There will be hair of the dog!" Freda said, giving a knowing smile to Mickey and Andrew, well known in the family for their love of drink.

By the time coffee and desert was served, Mickey was off on a tangent about how expensive baby things were, and how Sashay could not sleep in her bassinette much longer, so he and Suyin were going shopping for a crib, one of the new types that would convert to a toddler bed when it was time. At this, Suyin perked up and began talking about the Kate Spade diaper bag she wanted. Freda listened half-heartedly, not really caring about such things. It was just baby furniture.

Mickey got up and headed toward the men's room, but paused, squatting between Sophie and Freda, leaning on Sophie's chair arm, into her space, forcing her to bend awkwardly away so as not to touch him.

"Gram, this is so wonderful, isn't it Soph? We just love this tradition of the Cousin's Brunch, right?" he said.

Freda smiled, wondering what the hell Mickey was up to. Sophie was clearly uncomfortable with Mickey's physical closeness. To distract her, Freda asked, "Aren't you all heading out to the Belmont place today?"

"Yeah, we're going to grandma's after lunch and then we'll come back Christmas night," Sophie said. Freda smiled to herself as Sophie, now more at ease, proceeded to give her a rundown of their upcoming visits with relatives and friends.

"Be right back," Mickey interrupted, clearly irritated that Sophie had Freda's full attention. "I just have to visit the men's." As he straightened up, he shoved his hands in his pockets.

On his return, Mickey stopped by the head of the table once again.

"Okay Gram, Suyin and I have to leave. Don't forget to use that nose spray twice a day," he said, bending to kiss Freda's cheek. "Cousins, take care of my Gram, and I'll see you shitheads on Boxing Day!" he said, too loudly for the quiet elegance of the bistro.

Freda's eyes held an admonition, but Mickey just laughed, and pantomimed an "oops" while giving her a mock sheepish look. They all knew it was an act, because Mickey could not care less about breaking the ambience of the other diners. He enjoyed – no, relished – playing the part of bad boy of the family.

As Mickey and Suyin headed for the exit, a red-cheeked young woman, lunching at the next table, noticed Sophie's wallet on the floor. She waved at Sophie and pointed to the floor.

"Sorry, I think you dropped your wallet, there," she said.

"That's weird," Sophie said, stuffing her wallet back into her handbag.

Freda had a flash of insight. Was that why Mickey was lingering around the head of the table?

Surely not. He's just being pesky little Mickey.

As the brunch broke up, Freda said her goodbyes.

"I can't wait to see your shining faces at the Boxing Day Party! It will be so wonderful to have my family all together in just a few days. Until then, drive safe my little ducks," Freda said, kissing cheeks.

Steve offered to walk Freda to her car, and she gratefully took hold of his elbow to navigate the icy parking lot. She was still feeling a bit wobbly.

"Thank you, dear, for helping an old woman cross the frozen tundra. And tell Sophie to double check her wallet when she gets home," Freda said, as she sat heavily in the driver's seat of her car. "Now I must be off," she said, slamming the door in Steve's puzzled face.

As Freda started the car, she began to hiccup. She gulped a lungful of cold air and held it, hoping to quell them. She hadn't even had any wine! And she was so tired. She fingered the bottle of nose spray Mickey had given her. It couldn't hurt. She squirted a round of the oddly-scented mist into her nose and decided, given how she felt, that one of Rita's lozenges and a nap might not be such a horrible idea after all.

By the time she got home, Freda was drowsy and not at all sure she could even park the car in the garage. But she managed. She always managed, didn't she? As she trudged through the snow to the back door, Freda felt the weight of her years pressing against her. She wasn't one to nap during the day, but her knees ached from the barometric pressure swinging down ahead of the coming blizzard, she had a persistent dull headache, and something—maybe that nose spray—had made her so sleepy she could barely stand up.

"Ken, I'm back," she called from the back door.

"In here Mum," Kenna responded from the living room. "How's it going?"

"My knees are killing me today. It's the damn blizzard coming. Be a love and bring my pain patches, would you? They're in my medicine cabinet," Freda said, as she peeled off her gloves and pulled off her boots.

"Okay, just be a minute," Kenna said, and Freda heard her tromping upstairs.

Freda tucked herself into her favorite chair, wrapping the heavy knit throw around her legs and pulling her feet up onto the ottoman to be warmed by the fire. She closed her eyes and was immediately pulled down into the depths of a deep, dreamless sleep. She didn't even feel Kenna pulling up her pant legs to roughly rub an adhesive bandage on each knee.

17

WORKING VACATION

DECEMBER 23

The wind was picking up. Leon read the weather forecast out loud as they sat down to breakfast with Leon's mother, Janice. Nothing fancy, just a typical prairie breakfast: bowls of steaming oatmeal with maple syrup, and a pile of buttered wheat toast alongside a dish of warm, soft-boiled eggs.

"Grandma, this rhubarb jam is amazing," Sophie said around a mouthful of toast and jam.

"We had a bumper crop this year, so take some home with you," Janice said, beaming. "I've got plenty in the cold room."

Camelia's phone buzzed. Byron. She was tempted to let it go to voice mail, but that would just annoy him, so she plastered a smile on her face as she left the table.

"Hey, good morning Byron!" she said, sounding cheerier than she felt.

"Yeah … look, I'm going through the docket …"

"Why're you at the office? Shouldn't you be home?"

"… and you have a hearing on Jan. 4, but you're not scheduled back to the office until Jan. 7, so how is that going to work? And I'm here because we're open when the Courts are open, or don't you know about that?" he said.

Camelia flinched at his sarcasm as her mind ricocheted around looking for clues. She couldn't recall any hearing. But that wasn't what Byron wanted to hear.

"I'm pretty sure we're vacating that hearing, but let me confirm and I'll call you back," she said.

When I figure out what the hell you're talking about.

"Okay, you do that. I'll be here" he said, and hung up.

Camelia closed her eyes and drew a deep breath. Why couldn't he let up for just a few days? But she knew the answer. It wasn't in his DNA. Byron was truly a shark: smart, patient, relentless.

"Everything alright?" Leon asked, but his steely glare said it all.

He was annoyed, and Camelia didn't blame him. They hadn't had one vacation—not one, in all these years—that didn't include work.

"I just need to verify something for Byron," Camelia said. "Won't be a minute."

She grabbed her iPad and logged onto the firm's client management system. When she opened her docket, there it was. *Bergman Temporary Orders Hearing, January 4, 11:30 a.m.* She racked her brain but Camelia could not remember seeing an Order to Appear. Maybe Cate forgot to tell her. But that was unlikely.

Or maybe it was lost in a blackout.

Lately, there had been too many hours lost. Her memory was the one thing she could not afford to lose, no matter how much she craved another glass of wine.

After the holidays, dry January for sure.

Opposing counsel in the case, Daniel Diamant, was not the type to give an extension on the hearing. Hell, he was barely civil. They'd been friendly once, but that was before Camelia stepped back from a too-good-to-be-true offer to join his practice as a partner. In the due diligence, she inadvertently discovered some shady practices, and when she questioned him on it, Diamant transformed from fawning friend to mortal enemy. No, Diamant would not give her a break on the hearing.

If Camelia couldn't make a deal on the temporary orders, she would have to cut their vacation short. She'd need at least two days in the office to prepare. Even then, it would be a tooth and nail fight against Diamant. And Leon would be furious for the lost vacation days. It happened every time they took a trip, and this time it was her own fault. Camelia was having trouble—even more than usual—concentrating on work. Between panic attacks and happy hours that ran all the way to a blurry bedtime, she seemed to always be playing catch up.

Camelia dreaded the thought of calling Diamant because he would make her grovel. It set her teeth on edge to even think of it. She was already banging out an email to her client, hoping she would agree to less spousal support so they could vacate the hearing. She hated herself for bargaining against her own client in order to make a hearing go away, but would hate herself more if she had to tell Leon she was cutting their holiday short.

So these are my life choices now. Screw my client or screw my family and in both cases screw myself if it doesn't work out.

If she could just get this small concession, Leon would never be the wiser, the hearing would be vacated, and Byron would be satisfied.

I really need a drink.

"Hey Cam, almost done?" Leon called from the hallway.

"Yep, just let me finish this email, and I'll be right there," she said.

Camelia could not let this get away from her. Not now. There was no middle ground. She deserved to relax and enjoy the holidays with Leon, but she had to meet Byron's exacting standards if she was going to hold onto her job. And if she was able to meet Byron's expectations to a T, maybe she could still make partner.

The prize was so close she could taste it. But not if she blew this hearing.

18

Tumbling Down

December 24

Freda was of the generation that had their hair styled weekly, always polished and put together, even if the outing was just to the grocery store. Today, Kenna was having her hair done, too, and she hoped Freda would offer to pay since her credit card was perilously close to its limit.

They were due at the salon at 9:30. It was already past 8:30, and Freda wasn't up yet, which wasn't like her. Unless there was a party—when Freda could hang on through the wee hours and then sleep the day away with the best of them—she had always, piously, been up by 6:30, no matter what. Kenna poured a little rye in her coffee and popped half an oxy. She tapped her nails on her cup.

Come on you old bat. We're gonna be late.

The clock on the mantel chimed the hour. It was 9:00 and Freda still wasn't downstairs directing everyone's lives. What if she'd died in her sleep? It wasn't impossible. Kenna smiled at the thought. It would be too good to be true to have Freda slip away overnight, leaving her whole bank account to Kenna. No one would ever know. Except Mickey. But he wouldn't blab.

Kenna climbed the stairs, the pale morning light throwing dim shadows on the thick Persian rugs carefully laid along the long stretch of oak floor. She paused to catch her breath, then limped down the hall, the old floors creaking here and there, as they had since she was a child. Kenna tapped lightly on Freda's door, turning her ear to hear if Freda was up and about. She heard nothing other than a branch tapping the side of the house as the wind gusted.

"Mum, are you up? It's almost time to go," she called out, her voice booming in the stillness of the hall. "Mum! Are you up?" she called out, louder, when Freda didn't answer.

She pushed open the heavy door and confronted an empty bed. Part of her was disappointed. It would have been such a simple solution to find Freda dead, despite the inevitable fuss.

"Mum? Where are you?" Kenna glanced at the bathroom. The door was open, but the light wasn't on. The closet door was shut.

Where the hell is she?

Kenna walked around the bed. Freda was on the floor, lying on her side, her nightgown wrapped around her waist, exposing her fleshy backside. Kenna gasped, clapping a hand over her mouth. At first, she was too startled to check to see if Freda was breathing or not. Instead, Kenna turned away, her hand still pressed to her mouth.

Ohmygod ohmygod ohmygod.

She fished her phone from her pocket, her muddled mind racing in circles.

Okay, think now. Shit shit shit. What's the first thing to do?

Think. Think.

Okay, get a grip.

First things first.

First thing. Is she dead or alive?

Kenna turned back toward Freda and tentatively kicked her exposed foot, pale against the dark red and gold of the rug. Freda moaned and flopped onto her back, startling Kenna.

“Holy shit, Mum, are you okay?” she said, bending over Freda’s legs, gripping her ankles too harshly.

Freda came slowly to consciousness.

“Not … well …” Freda muttered, her words slurred and drawn out.

It was a joke in the family that if Freda was sick, they would all know every detail before her first foot was in the door. But no measly ailment would stop Freda from fully participating in her usual activities. If anything, illness seemed to spur her on, as if it were a personal challenge.

Kenna pulled on her arm, dragging her into a sitting position. “Mum, you have to get up if you want to make it to your hair appointment,” she shouted, hoping to bring some urgency to Freda’s slow rise. “Come on, Mum, you gotta get up off the floor,” she continued, pulling on Freda’s arm more violently than she intended.

Kenna felt her anger rising.

Just get up before this becomes a real emergency.

The last thing she needed was an ambulance showing up, EMTs demanding answers, making a mess of things.

“Help … me … up,” Freda said, lifting her arms.

She looked frail and vulnerable there on the floor, making her pathetic gestures, crepey arms quaking and quivering.

Kenna wrestled Freda up and onto the edge of the bed. Freda’s face was pale with a sheen of sweat, her eyes unfocused and wandering. Her hands fluttered at her side, and her head bobbed on her chest, as if she were falling asleep.

Kenna pulled Freda’s chin up to face her. “Mum, what the hell got into you?”

Great. Just what I needed today.

“Don’t know … so tired …” Freda said, a dribble of saliva running down her chin.

“Well, you need to get dressed cuz Jolene won’t hold your appointment, so come on now,” Kenna said, and clapped her hands. “Chop, chop!”

Freda coughed and pointed at her water glass on the nightstand.

"Water? Here, drink up," Kenna said, handing Freda the heavy crystal glass. "And what are these for?" she asked, holding up the small box of lozenges.

Freda lost her grip on the water glass and it fell, rolling down the front of her, wetting her chest and lap with tepid water before landing on the rug with a hushed clunk.

"Fucking hell, Mum. Are you drunk or something?" Kenna said, although it wasn't a question as much as an accusation. "We gotta get a move on."

Freda rose from the bed, unsteady on her feet, and staggered to the bathroom. Meanwhile, Kenna went into the closet, pulling out clothes. She heard Freda relieve herself. Then she heard her mother gagging, a dry heave.

"Are you puking? Jesus, pull yourself together, Mum. You're acting like an old alkie. How 'bout the red sweater and gray slacks?" Kenna said, tossing underpants and a bra on top of the bed.

Kenna stepped into the bathroom and ran cold water on Freda's wrists. She held a facecloth under the tap and handed it to Freda.

"Mum, hold this cold cloth to your face for a minute. It'll revive you."

Freda staggered out of the bathroom clutching the wet facecloth, and fell onto the tufted bench at the foot of her bed.

"So I guess we're playing Dress The Mum, today, huh? Ready?" Kenna clutched at Freda's nightgown, pulling it over her head. She handed Freda a pair of panties, a bra, a pair of slacks, then a sweater. Freda fumbled with each item of clothing, but managed to dress herself, until it came to the socks. Freda held them out to Kenna.

Kenna knelt in front of Freda, pulling on the socks. "Okay, ready? We need to get going!" Kenna slowly pulled Freda to her feet, ignoring her lolling head and watery, rolling eyes.

Freda stood up, her bony arms reaching out as if to steady herself against the air. Kenna grabbed her by the upper arm and steered her to the hallway, more dragging than assisting, but she didn't care. Freda was alive and upright, so she would get her to the hairdresser and then see where the day took them.

Freda moaned. "Slow down … not well."

Kenna wasn't in the mood to indulge Freda's complaints. She had plenty of her own problems.

"Today we play my way, Mum."

19

SILVER BELLS

DECEMBER 24

Jolene watched the bare tree branches quiver as the wind rattled the front door. The forecast said a blizzard was on its way. She'd hoped to finish up a little early to beat the storm, but the salon was booked solid. She looked up from Jackie O'Malley's foil-wrapped head to see Kenna helping Freda out of her Mercedes sedan.

The car screamed wealth, a concept foreign to Jolene, a single mom with a good enough income from styling hair, but not nearly enough for luxuries like a fancy car or the kind of jewelry Freda wore. Jolene wasn't jealous, though. Freda was an old friend, an entertaining and loyal client, a military widow, and a generous member of the community who had to put up with that miserable daughter of hers. She deserved every penny.

It startled Jolene to see Freda struggling to get out of the car. She had been doing her hair every week for almost 20 years and had never seen Freda like this, unable to get herself up and around. Last week, Freda had come in alone and was her usual self. Brash, full of laughter and gossip, looking forward to the Italian Club Christmas Feast with her beau, Arthur.

"Excuse me, Jackie, I have to see to Mrs. Swenson," Jolene said, snapping her rubber gloves off and rushing to the entrance. She pushed open the glass door against the wind, setting a string of silver Christmas bells jangling.

"Freda, can I help? Everything okay, Kenna?"

"Nah, we're fine," Kenna said, dragging Freda by the arm as she shuffled into the salon.

"Here, Freda, let me get you settled," Jolene said, fear rising in her chest.

This was most definitely not the woman she had seen last week. She helped Freda out of her coat and steered her to her usual chair, near the window.

As Jolene turned away from Freda, she caught Kenna glaring at her mother. She leaned close to Kenna.

"What's going on with your Mum? She was just here last week and she was fine, and today she can barely walk. What happened?" She studied Kenna's face for answers.

Kenna flushed and stammered. "How should I know? She's ancient, in case you haven't noticed. I found her on the floor this morning. Scared me shitless. But she's better now," Kenna said, glancing over at Freda, slumped in her chair.

"This is better?" Jolene spat out, suddenly enraged on Freda's behalf. "She needs to be at Emerg, Kenna, not getting her goddamn hair styled!" Jolene said.

"Really, Jolene? I think you should mind your own business. Mum is fine. And you probably don't know, but she's a total fucking hypochondriac and if I took her to ER every time she complained, that's all we would ever do," Kenna said, then abruptly shifted to a more conciliatory tone. "But yes, of course, I'm taking her to Emerg as soon as we're done because, obviously, this is not normal. She was much better earlier this morning and insisted on having her hair styled, but yeah, she looks pretty tired," Kenna added.

"This is way more than tired. I've never seen her like this. Please, do the right thing, and take her to ER as soon as we're done," Jolene said, turning on her heel.

Kenna saluted Jolene's back. "Yes m'am," she muttered, but Jolene pretended not to hear.

Freda's head lolled on her chest, and she was pale as milk. Jolene was worried Freda couldn't hold herself up well enough to walk to and from the wash station, so she used a spray bottle to mist her hair, just damp enough to allow for a quick set and style. Kenna was now seated with another stylist, Lisa, for her blowout, chattering away like nothing was wrong. But there *was* something wrong. Jolene just didn't know what, exactly.

Working with Freda's hair was an easy meditation for Jolene. Her hair was brilliant platinum, only modestly boosted by a rinse that Jolene applied every other visit. Which would have been today, but Jolene didn't want to take any more time than necessary getting Freda coiffed and out the door. She was tempted to call 911 herself, but it was more than she could face today. It was bad enough to work during the holidays while your kids were sitting at home getting into who-knows-what, but to start a big drama with Kenna was just too much. If she butted in, she'd probably have to tell Kenna she was Freda's newly-named personal representative, and Freda had made it clear she didn't want that information leaked until after her marriage to Arthur.

Jolene let out a sigh and squeezed Freda's shoulders. Freda's hair was styled, but she hadn't said a coherent word during the entire process and Jolene was deeply worried.

"Here you go," Kenna said, handing Jolene a credit card from Freda's wallet.

"Should I put both on this one?"

"Yep. Mum's treat today," Kenna grinned.

Jolene arched an eyebrow at Kenna as she handed her the receipt. She pressed Freda's hands between her own.

"Freda, I hope you feel better. Have a good Christmas and Boxing Day with your family. I want to hear all about it next week, okay?" She turned to Kenna and said, more urgently, "Take her to ER now! Promise me?" Her eyes were tearing up.

Kenna snorted. "Don't be such a Nervous Nelly. I'm sure she's fine, but yeah, I'll take her to ER," she said.

Kenna made a show of carefully escorting Freda out to the car. She turned and waved aggressively at Jolene, who shuddered at Kenna's blasé attitude. She only hoped Freda made it through the night.

With that crazy drunk as her caregiver, how long can she survive?

20

T'WAS THE NIGHT BEFORE ...

DECEMBER 24

The wind was already howling around the eaves as Kenna's phone dinged with a weather alert. The blizzard was arriving, and she still had to pick up a few stocking stuffers, a couple of bottles of rye, and some of her favorite snacks. It shouldn't take more than an hour if she left now, before the brunt of the storm hit.

But Freda was becoming a worry. Rita and Dave were out at the Becker family farm, an hour east of the city, otherwise Miss Smarty Pants Nurse would have been around to take over. She considered calling Rita to come back to town, but thought better of it. She didn't need her sister counting every cocktail and going on and on about Mum's care. It was all fine and dandy for Rita and Ben to second guess how Mum should live, but after the holidays, they'd be off in a hurry, leaving Kenna behind to do all the work. As usual, if Mum needed to be *managed*—and it was sure looking that way now—it would be up to Kenna to decide what was best for Mum.

She walked into the kitchen to find Freda staring into a half-empty cup of tea, her mouth hanging open, eyes glassy.

"Mum, I'm going out to do my last minute shopping. Need anything?" Kenna asked.

Freda mumbled something as her eyes moved slowly to the doorway.

"Wanna go sit in your chair and watch the world go by?" Kenna didn't wait for an answer. She hooked her elbow under Freda's armpit and pulled her to her feet. "Steady now. I don't need you sprawled on the floor."

She steered Freda from the kitchen to the living room and into her favorite chair. As Kenna propped Freda's feet on the ottoman and threw a shawl on her legs, her phone dinged. It was a text from Mickey.

Gram okay today? She was feeling sick

It wasn't like Mickey to be so concerned over Freda's health, but Kenna saw it as a good sign. Maybe someday he would dote on his own mother as much as he did his Gram. Of course, knowing Mickey, he was likely more worried about Freda's money than her health.

Fucking brown noser.

"Mum, Mickey texted to find out if you're feeling better. Looks like no?" she said, mostly to herself, as Freda wasn't saying much. "I'll let him know you're under the weather."

Freda fumbled and patted around her waist.

"What are you looking for, Mum?" Kenna poked her hand into Freda's sweater pocket and fished out a little bottle of nose spray with Chinese lettering, holding it up in her plump fist. "Where'd you get this?"

"Mmm …" Fred mumbled.

"Gotta be from Mickey, because I can't make any sense of all that gobbledygook on the bottle. Probably eye of newt or something. Here." She held the bottle to Freda's nostrils and pumped one spray in each.

"What about these lozenges? Want one of these?" Kenna said, but her voice sounded too loud against Freda's mute gaze. She unwrapped a lozenge.

"Here you go," Kenna said, and shoved the lozenge between Freda's lips. "I'm putting the spray and lozenges back in your pocket. Here's your phone. I'll be back in a bit. Just have a snooze," Kenna said, tossing the words over her shoulder as she left the room.

The front edge of the blizzard swept through the narrow streets of the old neighborhood and rounded the curve at the Crescents, slamming itself into trees, cars, and picture windows. It blasted arctic snow into crevasses and cracks, sealing doors shut, softening all the hard edges. By the time Kenna got home, the driveway was drifted in, and the street was a mirage of grey and white, color drained by the waning light and blowing snow. The wind shoved her sideways as she shuttled her shopping bags from the garage to the mud room.

Kenna flipped on lights as she walked through the back of the house.

Seriously? Is the old bat still sleeping?

Kenna stopped to adjust the thermostat a bit warmer as she headed down the hall toward the living room. She was chilled to the bone and hungry, but Freda clearly wouldn't be cooking tonight. More and more, it seemed Kenna had to fend for herself. How was that at all fair, when she'd been out in the cold all afternoon? The least Freda could do is put the kettle on.

When Kenna entered the living room, she froze. For the second time that day she thought she was witnessing a corpse. Freda's head was lolled to one side, the knit blanket was on the floor, and a wet stain darkened the crotch of her gray slacks.

"Jesus Mary and Joseph."

Then Kenna saw Freda's turtleneck rise and fall ever so slightly.

Kenna wheeled around, back to the kitchen. She didn't want to take care of Freda, nor should she have to. And she certainly wasn't going to clean up pee-soaked pants. She was cold and worn out and ready to settle in by the fire. Kenna desperately needed a drink, so she poured a short rye and Diet Coke, bypassed the ice altogether, and tossed the whole glass back in three gulps.

The rye calmed her. Kenna slowed down and thought things through. Freda obviously needed to go to the hospital, but after that, what? If she didn't take care of Freda, who would? Her siblings sure as hell wouldn't. Not with Rita living in Vancouver and Ben in California. Mickey had his own busy life and barely had time for his own mother, let alone his Gram.

First things first.

Kenna belched loudly and smacked her lips. If she took Freda to the hospital, they would evaluate her. She recalled her own recent stint in the hospital after her accident, the visit from the health region social worker and hospitalist, assessing her ability to live on her own during rehabilitation from her injuries. They might decide Freda couldn't manage by herself and should be in a care home. Kenna wouldn't have to say a word and, even better, she wouldn't have to consult with Rita and Ben. This could actually work out in her favor if they determined Freda was unable to take care of herself. She laughed with relief.

Only one way to find out.

"911, what is your emergency?" the dispatcher said.

"I think my mother had a stroke," Kenna said.

The dispatcher took her name and address, along with Freda's date of birth and symptoms.

"An ambulance will be there as soon as possible but, with the blizzard digging in, there are wrecks all over town, and it might take a bit longer than usual," the dispatcher said.

"I don't need longer than usual, I need faster than usual. She had a *stroke*, for crying out loud. *Isn't that an emergency?*" Kenna said, her voice getting louder as she became more agitated.

"I don't really recommend it, but if you can manage, you can drive her to the hospital yourself," the dispatcher added.

"Are you fucking kidding me?" Kenna said, thinking about the urine on Freda's pants. "How the hell am I supposed to manage that? And in a blizzard?" Kenna shrieked.

"Please try to remain calm. Do you want me to stay on the line with you until the ambulance arrives?" she said.

"No, I don't need you on the line. I need you to send an ambulance right fucking now, because my mother is dying, do you understand?"

"Yes ma'am, they're on their way."

Kenna hung up and shuffled into the kitchen to pour another drink, then stopped. She would be expected to go to the hospital, so she better be sober … and ready to drive. Instead, she nibbled off the edge of an oxy to soothe her nerves. Kenna placed her jacket, boots, and purse in the foyer and texted Mickey.

Called 911 Gram is not well

She heard sirens approaching, as her phone dinged a response.

At in-laws let me know if I need to come

Kenna smirked.

Will do – xoxo

Having first responders in your house sounds like a great idea until they arrive. Four men tromped right into the living room—across the expensive antique rugs and oak floors—in snow and salt covered boots, laden with equipment. They were terse and serious, their eyes conveying a numbed out sadness at all they had seen. They pushed Kenna aside, gently, but forcefully, and went to work on Freda. One started an IV. Another took vitals. The other two got the gurney ready. They spoke to Freda in assertive, firm, loud voices, narrating their every action.

"Ma'am, we are going to lift you up and place you on the stretcher, here, okay? And then we're going to wrap you in a hot blanket and get you into the ambulance, okay? Then we're going to take you over to the hospital for a checkup, okay? You're with the best medics on the prairies, ma'am, and we're gonna take good care of you. Your daughter is right here and she'll ride along with us …" the paramedic said.

"Wait, no, I'll drive my own car," Kenna interjected, as she followed the stretcher out the front door.

"Follow close. The blizzard's picking up," the ambulance driver said.

21

VISITOR'S HOURS

DECEMBER 24

Kenna drove the heavy Mercedes through the snow drifts, trying to avoid the curbs, following the flashing lights of the ambulance. The blizzard had sucked all the light out of the sky; even though it was barely five, it was fully dark. She hunched over the steering wheel, squinting into the blinding reflection of snow in her headlights.

The storm didn't care about Christmas Eve. Weather didn't care about the creatures—both human and beast—who would die tonight as the storm ground everything in its path to frozen dust. The wind rocked the car.

Kenna parked and struggled to get across the parking lot, bent against the wind. She was cold and tired and, well, there was a fair bit of oxy in her system. All she wanted was to curl up on the sofa with her iPad and a rye and DC. Her cheeks were stinging by the time the ER doors whooshed open, enveloping her in warm air. She checked in with the desk, and was directed down the hall, Bed 4.

Kenna glimpsed Freda through the gap in the curtain and quickly pulled it closed behind her. God forbid anyone see her mother in this state. A nurse swished in behind her and grabbed Freda's chart.

"Are you the daughter?" she asked, pulling a pen from her pocket.

"Yes, Kenna Shores," she said, breathless and winded from walking across the parking lot.

"Are you okay?" the nurse asked.

"Oh, sure, just freaking out about Mum."

"The doctor will be …" she started.

The curtains parted again and a young Asian woman flipped a stethoscope into her ears. She brushed past Kenna, pushing Freda's sweater up over her belly.

"This is Dr. Ngo," the nurse said, gesturing towards her, as if introducing a friend at a cocktail party.

Is she even old enough to be a doctor?

Dr. Ngo held up her hand to shush them, listening intently to Freda's stomach and now, her chest. She turned to the RN.

"What do you have?" she said curtly.

The nurse rattled off the vitals. The doctor turned to Kenna.

"What happened?"

"Well, Mum wasn't feeling well, so she took a nap. I went out and when I came back, she'd pissed herself and couldn't wake all the way up," Kenna said. She remembered the nasal spray. "She was using some nose spray, some Chinese herbal thing, for a cold," she continued.

"Mmhmm. Anything else?" Dr. Ngo asked.

Kenna didn't mention finding her on the floor, or the dizziness, or any of the other little complaints. "Not that I can think of. Looks like she had a stroke, huh?"

"It's possible. We'll make sure she's stable and run some tests, but for now that's all we can do until we figure out what happened," Dr. Ngo said. "I'll be around in an hour or so when the results are back." Her white lab coat billowed behind her as she half-ran to the next patient.

"I need a list of Mrs. Swenson's medications. What is she taking?" the nurse said.

"I . . . I think something for blood pressure. Not sure what else, but I can check at home."

"Okay, have a seat in the waiting area, and I'll call you when the tests are all done," the nurse said.

It sounded to Kenna like she was being dismissed. She shoved her fingers through her dense, curly hair, pulling her scalp tight.

"You know, it's Christmas Eve and my kids are home, so is it okay if I just come back later? I don't really want to hang out with all the germs out there," she said, slipping the little lie in as easily as a hot knife in butter. After all, it was technically true. Her kid was at home—his in-laws' home—but still, it was mostly true.

"Sure, leave your cell number and we'll call you if there are any changes. I think for tonight we'll mainly be running tests and keeping an eye on her. We'll have your mom admitted in a bit, and then up to a private room. You can call the front desk 24/7 for an update," the nurse said.

Finally, she could get home to a warm sofa and a cold cocktail.

She gave the nurse her best conciliatory smile and gushed, "Oh thank you sooo much. I'm just sick about this. I mean, kids in one place and mum in the other. She lives with me, you know, poor old dear, but I can't leave everyone sitting around the dinner table!" she said, the lies feeling so real, so easy.

Kenna was happy to walk away from all those pathetic souls trapped in the hospital on a blustery Christmas eve night. A handful of staff huddled by the waiting room windows, watching the white-out like a tribe of shamans in dusty green scrubs, calling the storm into being.

The wind groaned and howled around the ER entryway, fooling the automatic doors every now and then. They would snap open, letting a gust of frigid air inside, where a collective groan would go up from those scrunched down into their parkas, waiting.

Waiting for death. Or deliverance. Or both.

22

And All Through The House

December 24

The drive from the hospital to the Crescents house was slow and tedious, even though snow ploughs were already grumbling their way down Albert Street. Kenna had to gun the car to get over the drifts in the driveway, and she felt triumphant when she finally pulled into the stillness of the garage.

She half ran to the back door and collapsed on the bench inside, cold and winded.

What a helluva night.

Kenna took off her coat, kicked off her boots, and made her way into the kitchen to mix a very tall tumbler of rye and DC. She cranked up the fireplace and the furnace was running, but on this kind of night, the old house was no match for the weather. It creaked and moaned in protest as snow drifted up against the west side of the house. On her way to the living room, Kenna grabbed a bag of chips and her phone. She let out a deep sigh as she sank into her corner of the sofa with her iPad and a couple of oxy in her pocket.

Kenna texted Mickey, anxious to unload her news.

Gram admitted @ hospital. Here if you want to come over XO

She waited for a response, but it didn't come. Kenna fumed over the slight but only for a moment. She quickly realized Mickey would only make her feel guilty for not staying at the hospital. As her crossfade of oxy and rye whisky took hold, Kenna texted Rita.

Took mum to ER. Looks like a stroke. They r running tests and will admit her.

As for Ben, Rita could break the news to him if she wanted. Kenna was not in the mood to be her brother's keeper. Or her mother's. Or her sister's. Or her son's. They were all exhausting.

Kenna was barely settled into an online poker game when a man called, asking for Miss Shores. It took a beat to get her mouth working, but even so, she was slurring.

"Thishis MishShores," she said.

"I'm calling from the hospital. We've admitted Mrs. Swenson and moved her to a private room, so you can come stay with her if you want, although the roads are pretty bad right now, so maybe wait for morning?" he said. "Also, we need a list of Mrs. Swenson's medications. We're doing bloodwork and it looks like ER didn't get that information from you," he continued.

"Okay, hang on" Kenna said.

Kenna walked into the kitchen and steadied herself against the counter before reciting Freda's prescribed medications from the bottles on the counter: Simvastatin, Amlodipine, Warfarin, Oxaprozin.

"Oh, and she takes OxyContin now and then when her back is bothering her. I can't find the bottle, but I think it's the 80 mg pills," she said.

After she hung up, Kenna checked her phone again for a response from Mickey or Rita. Nothing.

Mum's on her deathbed and no one is even gonna text me back? Assholes.

She considered calling Rita, worried about the cell service at the Becker farm, but then again, why should she? If Rita and Mickey weren't going to be grownups and monitor their phones, there was no reason for Kenna to do it for them. Besides, her bones were aching and she needed to take care of herself, for once. Kenna poured another drink and jumped into an online poker game.

Finally, just after eleven, her phone dinged.

Sorry didn't see text til now. Going to hosp in a few.

Kenna felt a surge of affection for her son. He was that kind of kid. The kind that would go out in a blizzard to see his ailing grandmother. She felt the satisfaction of having raised a kind boy, a good man, the type of person who looks after others. Unlike her snobby sister, who hadn't even bothered to respond.

Just wait, though.

When Kenna was holding the purse strings—which, by the looks of it, could be any minute now—they would all change their tune.

23

Visions of Sugar Plums

December 24

"Do you really want your mother to be there alone with Gram all night? And what if she dies? You'll never forgive yourself, Mick," Suyin said, stifling a yawn.

Mickey sipped a rum and eggnog and scratched his belly. She was almost right. Even though he was sure he could forgive himself for not being there, his mother would *never* let it go.

"I know, I know, but I was hoping Mrs. Claus would unwrap a little something for me," Mickey said, tugging at Suyin's sweater.

Suyin elbowed him. "Knock it off. I'm serious," she said.

"Okay, okay," Mickey huffed. "We just got home, but sure, I'll go back out in a fucking deadly blizzard and drive all the way across town, probably for nothing."

He got up with a sigh and went to the back door, taking his time putting on his parka and boots, hoping Suyin would relent.

"Text me when you get there," she said, giving him a sideways hug. "And drive careful." Suyin pushed him toward the door.

"Fine. I'm going. I'll be back when I can."

Goddammit.

Forty white-knuckle minutes later, Mickey pulled into the hospital parking lot. He could just vaguely make out the brightly lit EMERGENCY ROOM sign, even though he was only a few steps away. The lot was drifting in, and he regretted the decision to come. If not for Suyin, he would have gladly stayed home, sipping rum and eggnog by the fire. Besides, what help could he be? If Gram was fine, there was nothing to do. If Gram wasn't fine, there was nothing he *could* do. But he was here now, so he might as well make an appearance.

Upstairs, the nurse on duty directed him to Freda's room.

"Is my mum, Kenna Shores, in with her?" he asked.

"No, Ms. Shores had to go home to her children and will be back in the morning," Charge Nurse Gayle Germaine said.

"She what?" he blurted, then caught himself. The nurse didn't seem to notice.

"Sorry, what?"

"Nothing, thanks," Mickey said.

Kenna's lie was a cold slap. She was at home, warm and safe, while he was here, risking his life in a blizzard, and for what?

Mickey smiled at Gayle. "I'll just pop in to say hi to Gram. Merry Christmas," he said as he walked away.

"And Merry Christmas to you as well, but don't be long. She needs to rest," Gayle said.

Mickey quietly entered Freda's room and was shocked by the sight of her. If it weren't for the consistent, slow beep of the heart monitor, Mickey would have sworn Freda was dead. She looked small and old, with tubes in her arms, and an oxygen cannula in her nose. He swallowed hard.

"Gram? It's Mickey, how ya doin?" he stage whispered.

Freda's response was a moan. He leaned over her in the dim light and stared intently at her ghostly white face. Her lips were purplish.

That can't be normal.

Mickey sat down in the bedside chair and watched Freda's chest slowly rise and fall. She would be dead soon, even if it wasn't tonight. He knew he should feel badly about it, but Gram was ancient, like 85 years old. It was time for the younger generation—his generation—to take over, to use all that hoarded wealth on stuff that mattered. Like a new house for his family, for starters.

"Gram, I can't stay, but I wanted to say goodbye in case you don't make it," he whispered. "But you're gonna be totally fine."

He didn't believe that last part. The impending loss of his grandmother was suddenly real. He couldn't breathe at the thought of being the only person in Kenna's life, but then again, there would be all that money.

"I love you Gram. You're the best," Mickey said, clasping Freda's hand.

He thought he felt her squeeze back. At the slight pressure, another rush of thoughts slammed into Mickey's mind. What if Freda *didn't* die? What if she was just like this forever? He didn't know what residential nursing care cost, but he imagined piles of money disappearing into an abyss. His inheritance would evaporate overnight if Gram didn't die.

Talk about a worst case scenario.

He stared at her mottled hand in his, so different from his daughter's plump, smooth fists. Mickey had envisioned Sashay growing up with Gram, as he had. He heaved a sigh. Gram was so much easier to be around than his own mother, but god help them all if Freda lived on for years like this.

Moments later, Mickey slipped out of his grandmother's room and rushed past the empty nurses' station to the exit. As he sprinted down the stairs, he decided coming to see his grandmother had been a good idea after all. He'd satisfied Suyin that he was a caring family man, *and* found out his mother was lying about being here with Gram. He couldn't wait to see the look on Kenna's face when he dropped that little bomb.

As he exited the hospital, Mickey took stock of the howling wind pushing snow over and around the cars in the lot. He'd seen worse. He smiled to himself. He could go home with a clear conscience.

As Mickey made his way across the parking lot, the only other person crazy enough to be out in the blizzard was a woman in a distinctive red

Canada Goose parka. At first, Mickey thought it was Kenna, wearing the parka Freda had gifted to Rita, Ben, and Kenna last Christmas. But it couldn't be Kenna, because she'd given her parka to him when she could no longer zip it up. It couldn't be Rita either, because the woman got out of a big grey pickup, and Rita drove an SUV, not a truck.

Merry fucking Christmas, whoever you are.

24

Kenna's Christmas Miracle

December 25

It had all happened much faster than she expected.

Kenna hung up and rolled over, pulling the fluffy down comforter close. Her bed was snug and warm, while the blizzard continued to howl, slamming the branches of the old elm against the side of the house. Daylight was still hours away, and she wanted to bury herself in a drift of sleep.

But the call had shocked her awake.

Her mother was dead.

There was no time for lollygagging, as Freda would say.

Kenna had to get organized and, despite the lingering fog of her nightly crossfade, she felt more alert and alive than she had in ages. She smiled to herself as she rummaged through the papers on her nightstand, looking for the lists she'd prepared last night. It was going to be a merry Christmas after all.

Kenna arrived at the hospital just after 5 a.m., clutching a rosary and bible, her head and heart pounding in unison. She slipped on the mantle of propriety, saying all the expected things, the proper things, as Freda had taught her children. After firmly declining Dr. Fitzgerald's offer to call the chaplain for last rites, Kenna shooed everyone from the room.

Under the harsh overhead lights, Freda looked shrunken and strange against the faded blue sheets. It frightened Kenna, so she flipped off the lights, leaving only the dim bed lighting on. She drew a deep breath and, with one glittery fingernail, poked Freda's purple-tinged hand. She was cold, but otherwise it wasn't too creepy.

Okay, the worst part is over. Just keep your shit together.

Kenna placed the bible on Freda's chest and carefully draped her mother's elaborate antique rosary over top. She drew a votive from her handbag and lit it, then placed it on the over-bed table.

"Okay Mum, here we go. Hail Mary, Full of Grace, The Lord is with thee. Blessed art thou among women, and blessed is the fruit of thy womb, Jesus. Holy Mary, Mother of God, pray for us sinners now, and at the hour of death. Glory Be to the Father, and to the Son, and to the Holy Spirit."

Kenna hadn't been to mass in ages, but the words came easily, decades of rote repetition taking over. She crossed herself and wedged into the visitor chair next to Freda's bed.

"I can't believe you actually up and died on me. Jesus Christ, Mum. I hope you're enjoying the view from hell because this is the last Christmas you'll be ruining for me."

Freda's sunken cheeks and mottled hands gave no retort, but Kenna was rebuked nonetheless. Her face crumpled as she choked on a sob.

"Oh Mum. I didn't mean it. I didn't want you to die. Not like this. What am I gonna do? What am I gonna do without you?"

Reality was setting in and, even though the day was still new, Kenna was already exhausted. Her whole body ached for alcohol and oxy, but she couldn't rest. Not yet. She'd taken Freda's advice for once and had carefully made notes in preparation for this day. She pulled a list from her handbag.

All I have to do is the first thing on the list. Just the first thing.

Kenna pulled the sheets away from Freda's legs. Her memory was correct. She peeled a patch off Freda's left knee and went round the bed to the other side, but there was no patch on the right knee.

Where the hell is it?

Kenna froze when she heard a rustling at the doorway. The door opened an inch, and Kenna heard someone asking about Mrs. Swenson. The door hastily closed again.

Shit. Not now.

Kenna looked around and, in a panic, hurriedly shoved the patch into the biohazards bin. She didn't know how often the bins were emptied, but surely no one would go fishing around in all that yucky stuff.

She jerked open the small closet next to the bathroom. Freda's pants and underwear were in a plastic bag on the floor of the closet, but her cardigan sweater was hanging up.

There was a tap on the door, and a nurse entered.

Goddammit!

Kenna shut the closet door. They could just throw Mum's clothes away when they cleaned the room. Not like she needed them now.

"Miz Shores? I'm sorry to bother you, but when you have a chance, we'll need to know where to transport Mrs. Swenson," she said.

"I was just going to call Springer Funeral Home, if you'll give me half a minute," Kenna said.

"Of course, and we're right outside if you need anything," the nurse said, backing out of the room.

Okay, second item on the list.

Kenna went back to the bedside chair, looked up the funeral home, and clicked on the phone number. She knew no one would be there, but she got what she needed: the after-hours number. She tapped her pen against her knee, annoyance rising with each ring of the phone. Joseph Alexander, president of Springer Funeral Home, answered after a few rings. Kenna could tell she'd woken him up, but she didn't care.

"I am so sorry for your loss, Kenna. We all loved Freda and be assured we'll help you plan a fitting celebration of life," he said.

"Thank you, Joe. We're all in shock, but Mum's wishes were very clear. I'm her personal representative, and I have to follow her instructions. Like, it's the *law.* Mum wanted to be cremated within 24 hours and no services. That's what she told me," Kenna said.

"My goodness. That doesn't sound at all like Freda …"

"I don't think I can talk about this now," Kenna said, with a flourish of sniffling.

"Yes, of course, all this can wait. I'll call Mitch—our driver—and have him pick up Mrs. Swenson as soon as he can get there, but give him an hour. The roads are a mess," he said. "And bring a copy of the PR acknowledgement. We need it for the file."

"I'm sorry, but I'm …" Kenna sobbed into the phone. "I'm just … I'll wait for your guy by the west exit but I don't have my paperwork."

"Don't worry, dear, we'll manage the details. Sit tight and Mitch will be there soon," Joe Alexander said.

Kenna paced in the hallway, near the exit, waiting for the guy from Springer to show up. It was taking forever, and she was feeling that antsy, itchy need for … something. She peered out the exit looking for the Springer transport van. Nothing.

Kenna paused. She had to be cautious. This was a time for strategic action, not panic, not emotions. She bought a Diet Coke from the vending machine, nibbled a tiny bit of oxy, and let it dissolve on her tongue, swishing it down with the cold soda.

Her phone dinged with an incoming text from Mickey.

On our way in a half hr you up?

Must be nice to sleep in without a care in the world.

Her resentment didn't last. It was actually better that Mickey wouldn't be coming to the hospital. Kenna had too much on her mind and didn't want Mickey or anyone else to know Freda was dead until the cremation was managed, so she texted him back.

At hosp with mum be back in 1 hour

She couldn't do anything until the guy from Springer showed up, but Joe Alexander said they would need some kind of … what was it? Power of attorney? And that meant it was time to call Bob Barrett. She scrolled through Freda's phone until she found the lawyer's private cell phone number.

To reassure herself, Kenna reviewed the list she'd written and revised a dozen times, and carefully crossed off the third item. On the sixth ring, she got Barrett's voicemail.

"Sorry to bother you, this is Freda Swenson's daughter, Kenna. It's an emergency. Call me." She hung up, waited a couple of minutes, and called him again. This time, he picked up on the third ring.

"Hello? Kenna?"

"Yeah, hi. Sorry to call so early but I'm all alone and Mum said to call you if anything happened, and … it's happened." Kenna let out a little sob and blew her nose loudly.

"What's happened, Kenna? Is Freda okay?"

"No, Bob, Mum died this morning. I'm at the hospital now."

"Oh nooooo. I'm so sorry. I just saw Freda at the Italian Club last week, and she was dancing the night away with Art Rossi. This is just horrible, Kenna. What happened?"

"They don't really know. Seems like she had a stroke or something. It all happened really fast. I called an ambulance last night, and they admitted her, but she died this morning, just like that. And now Springer wants a … what was it? … something to do paperwork for the personal representative before they'll take Mum's body and oh my god Bob it's just more than I can bear so I'm calling you because it's a legal thing and I don't know what to do!" Kenna sobbed into the phone. "Please, Bob, I need you to help me."

Silence.

"Bob? Are you there?"

"Yes. Yes, I'm here. But I don't want to talk about this over the phone, Kenna. Can you come to my office tomorrow? We can discuss Freda's estate plan then," he said.

"But Bob, what about Mum? Springer won't take her … her … her body … I need the PR thing," Kenna shrieked between hiccupping sobs.

"It's okay, Kenna, take a deep breath. We'll get this sorted. But the one thing you *should* know, that you *have to know*—Freda revised her estate plan last week. She named a new Personal Representative."

"I know, Bob. Because Jonathan died. She named me," Kenna said.

"No, Kenna, I'm sorry. Freda did not name you as the Personal Representative."

No fucking way. It better not be Rita.

Panic bloomed in Kenna's stomach, spreading an icy tingle to her fingers and toes and scalp. Her pulse raced and her ears burned, her mouth went dry and her vision blurred. She pressed the cold can of soda to her forehead. This could not be true. When had Freda gone to Bob's office? How had that escaped her notice?

"Bob, I don't know what you're talking about. I can't handle this right now. Seriously. For chrissake, I have to take care of my mother and I'm all alone and really … really, Bob, I need this taken care of."

"If you want, I can call Springer and talk to them, or I can call Freda's PR, but it's Christmas morning …," Barrett said, his voice trailing off.

She could tell he didn't want to call anyone and would probably just roll over and go back to sleep as soon as he hung up.

"Who is this secret PR that I know nothing about?" Kenna said.

"Please, can we talk about this in person? I really don't want to discuss the details over the phone when I don't have the file. I'm sure you understand. I want to be accurate, and I would be fibbing if I said I could recall every detail."

Kenna's mind whirled along with the snow devil whipping through the parking lot. She watched it through the frost-crusted window, winding itself up, higher and higher, until it fell apart. That's how she felt. Like she was going to disintegrate from the tension of holding herself together in the face of everything that was happening, with no comfort from her old pals: rye and oxy.

Shit shit shit. What would mum do?

A memory popped into her head, Freda at the head of the table, berating her for something or other. She could almost hear Freda's voice. *When in doubt, think first, act later. Don't be an idiot and answer in haste. You have to think before you open your mouth again, Kenna. Think.*

Kenna had to fend off Barrett for now, to get time to figure things out. She took a deep breath and sat up straight.

"You know what, you're right, I'm sorry. I just need to calm down but I guess I panicked for a minute. I can come on the 27th and we can go over everything. In the meantime, I'm gonna get some rest. I'm so sorry for disturbing you on Christmas. I've been up all night with Mum, and I'm not thinking clearly," Kenna said, marveling at how easy it was to parrot Freda, to sound composed and grown up, without actually saying anything.

She hung up with a smug grin on her face.

I can totally do this.

25

AND TO ALL A GOOD NIGHT

DECEMBER 25

It wasn't lost on Kenna that even she, the runt of the litter as Freda liked to say, could be cool and confident when she put her mind to it. It took nerve, and some practice, but she had family history and money on her side, making everything manageable if she could just stay focused.

Kenna felt a rush of cold air from the exit doors as a man entered. She hoped it was the guy from Springer.

"Kenna Shores?" he asked.

She stood up and stretched. "That's me."

It would be so good to be home, if she could just hold it together for another couple of hours.

Mitch Sanger sent Kenna along ahead of him, explaining he would meet her at Springer in a few minutes. She drove slowly through the snow-clogged streets. She couldn't even tell where the entrance to the parking lot was, so she parked as close to the curb as she dared, the blizzard having obliterated all the markings.

So far, so good.

Now if she could get past the paperwork issue. It was just another stupid bureaucratic formality and, thankfully, it wasn't Joe Alexander she had to convince. Kenna dug around in her handbag until she found her Christmas card for Mickey. She pried one sparkly fingernail under the flap and carefully opened the card, fishing out five crisp $100 bills.

That oughtta do it.

Kenna looked up to see Mitch waving from the front of the building, like a giant toddler in his camo parka and snow pants. She turned off the car and struggled down the drifted over the sidewalk. Mitch held the door against the wind and ushered her to a small chapel. Kenna dropped her parka and handbag on the modern blonde wood pew and thanked him, dabbing her eyes with a tissue for effect. Mitch didn't seem fazed.

"Mitch, did Joe tell you Mum has to be cremated immediately? Like right now? I mean, I don't get it but she was serious about her so-called Viking send-off: no casket, no clothes, just her and her Bible, into the fire, within 24 hours. I think it's awful but she was getting kind of senile at the end. And I'm sorry to make you work on Christmas, but …" she put her face in her hands and let the tears come. "Sorry. I'm babbling. Please, it will give us peace knowing Mum's wishes were honored. And I can pay for your trouble," she pleaded, fingering the bills in her pocket.

"That's not necessary, but thanks. You can square that up with Mr. Alexander. And he said I should get a copy of your PR papers, just so all the paperwork is in order," he said.

"Well, this is your Christmas bonus then," Kenna said, pressing the five $100 bills into his hand. The cash was supposed to be a little surprise in Mickey's stocking, but he wouldn't need it now. "Just take it. And I thought I had a copy of the PR at home, but I can't find it. Seriously, my brain is mush right now, so it's probably right under my nose. I called Mum's lawyer, but you know how they are. He wouldn't even answer the phone, but then again it's Christmas and he'd probably bill me double if he picked up," she said, with a weak smile. "I can bring it over on the 27th if that's okay. You don't have to worry. I have it, just can't put my hands on it right this second."

Mitch ran a hand over his bristle of blonde hair and studied the carpet for a moment.

"Please, really, if we don't follow Mum's last wishes, my sister will kill me and probably you, too." Kenna touched his arm for effect.

"Okay, but I gotta call Joe."

"Oh god no. That poor guy is trying to enjoy his Christmas, and I've already bothered him enough. He and my Mum were old friends, so … I swear. I'll bring the PR day after tomorrow. I already have an appointment with the lawyer to pick up a copy in case I can't find the one at home," she said, dabbing her eyes.

He hesitated, shifting his weight from one foot to the other, and Kenna could see him wrestling with the decision.

"I know it's not by the book, but I know how Joe is. He's old school, and he'll want to honor my mother's wishes. Surely that counts for something, even if the *lawyers* don't approve," Kenna said.

"Yeah, lawyers," Mitch said, rolling his eyes. "I don't want to offend your family or Joe, so … okay, you can pick up the ashes when you deliver the PR papers to Joe. I'll be back in a bit. Oh, and there's water in the hall, but I'm sorry, there's no coffee made," Mitch said, as he moved for the door. "And thanks for this," he said, holding the money up. "Not at all necessary but very much appreciated." He winked.

Kenna gave him a sad smile. "You're the best, Mitch, and I'm going to make sure Joe knows it."

Too fucking easy.

"Miz Shores, your mum is ready if you want to say goodbye," he said, in a voice barely above a whisper.

Kenna startled out of her reverie. She didn't know how much time had passed, and wondered if she'd nodded off.

"That didn't take long! Okay, let's get this over with," she said, but then thought she sounded too callous. "I mean, this is awful and I just want to . . . you know, have the worst of it behind me," she added. She dabbed at her eyes again, even though they were dry. "I still can't believe it," she said.

"Oh, and here's Mrs. Swenson's rosary. It can't go in the crematory, so I thought you might want it as a keepsake," Mitch said, dropping the rosary in Kenna's hand.

She clutched it and squeezed her eyes shut, doing her best to convince Mitch she was a deeply grieving daughter. She covered her face with her hands and took a deep breath.

"Okay, I'm ready," she said.

26

Holly Jolly Christmas

December 25

Mickey was dancing to Michael Bublé's Christmas album when he saw Freda's car pull into the drive. For a moment, he thought Gram was coming home after all. But Kenna and Rita were both the spitting image of Freda, and he quickly realized the bundled up lump behind the wheel was his mother, a shorter, plumper version of Gram.

A few minutes later, Kenna called out from the mudroom and Mickey danced towards her, arms outstretched, a cocktail in one hand. He was already two drinks in and feeling the warm glow of emotional generosity.

"Mum! Finally! I was getting worried. We let Sashay open a toy while we waited, but Santa hasn't arrived yet," he said, making air quotes around Santa. "How's Gram? Can I get you some Christmas cheer?" He lifted his glass.

"I'd love a little cocktail, thanks. And yeah, let's open gifts with my favorite grandbaby, then we can talk about Gram," she said.

He heard the undertone of something serious in her voice. Dread rose in his throat and a chasm opened in his gut. He didn't know what was going on, but Kenna was not usually this somber. She was probably pissed off that he hadn't shown up to the hospital while she was still there. Or maybe she was mad about him spending the Christmas loan on presents instead of necessities.

Or maybe she just needs a drink.

"Sure, whatever you want. But first, a little rye and DC for my favorite Mum," he said.

Even though it was barely 9 a.m., Mickey poured another round of drinks and they settled by the fire. The three adults ooohed and aaahed, helping Sashay unwrap gifts when her little fingers couldn't manage. After Sashay unwrapped the last toy, Kenna stacked Freda's paltry cache of gifts to one side, the most intriguing being a small box from Arthur.

"Whaddaya think this is?" Kenna asked.

"Looks like jewelry to me," Suyin said, leaning closer.

"Everything looks like jewelry to you," Mickey laughed, elbowing Suyin. She glared in return.

"Hey aren't you driving today? Better slow down on the booze," Suyin said.

Mickey was getting pretty buzzed and knew he needed to throttle back, but he also needed a little extra courage to face what he knew was coming: a lecture from his mother about … who knows what. But he might as well get it over with, and he really didn't want Suyin overhearing *that* conversation. No telling what would come out of Kenna's mouth.

"Mum, can you help me for a minute?" he said, gathering up piles of spent wrapping paper as he headed to the kitchen.

"Sure, it's what I do," she sighed.

Mickey was already formulating alibis in his mind. But for which part? The hospital visit? The loan? Or the fentanyl he'd promised but not yet delivered?

As Kenna came into the kitchen, Mickey pulled the door closed behind her and put his finger to his lips. He moved closer and dropped his head.

"What's up, mum? You're starting to freak me out," he said, giving her his most endearing smile. "And where the hell were you last night? I thought you were at the hospital, but no one was there when I showed up."

Kenna put her arm through his and leaned against him.

"Never mind that now. We have a little family problem and I want you to pay close attention to what I'm about to say. It's important we're on the same page," she whispered. "No fucking up!"

27

SUGAR AND SPICE

DECEMBER 25

Rita pulled the last pie from the oven and placed it among the other four on the kitchen table to cool. Two pumpkin, one apple, one rhubarb, one custard. Next up: butter tarts, from Mum's family recipe. Everyone coveted Freda's recipe, which she was infamously stingy about sharing, but Rita had managed to duplicate it perfectly. She never let on that she knew Freda's secret of using butter-flavored Crisco instead of real butter. It made the crust perfectly flaky and unctuous with rich, oily flavor.

Rita blew out a sigh laden with memories and began sifting, measuring, folding, and rolling the dough. In the adjoining family room, Christmas music played softly on the stereo. Her mother-in-law was knitting by the fire, the quiet punctuated by her father-in-law flapping the pages of yesterday's newspaper, sipping Baileys and coffee. Dana was still asleep. It felt peaceful and festive, like the holidays should.

Except for a niggling dread.

Rita shook her head to dislodge the stray tentacles of regret and shifted back to the tasks before her. The Boxing Day party was *tradition.*

And it was her turn to host, which is the only reason Rita was manically baking in her in-laws' kitchen. She shuddered at the thought of the family gathering.

Last year, Kenna erupted in angry sobs over dinner because her ex, Tony, went to Hawaii for the holidays with his wife's family instead of coming to the Boxing Day dinner for Mickey's sake. Dave, emboldened by his third (or maybe fourth) glass of wine, kicked off the argument when he burst out laughing and said, *he's your fucking ex, Kenna. I don't think he owes you every holiday for the rest of his life.* Camelia was quick to throw in her two cents about blended families, then Mickey had to defend his mother, and then Sophie piped up, and it all went downhill from there.

This year was going to be even worse.

As she rinsed her hands, Rita saw Dave outside on the long driveway, struggling with a bag of salt. He was panting with the effort, little puffs of steam escaping his mouth, and she sent up a tiny prayer that he not have a heart attack for his efforts. Rita turned back to her baking. She was cutting rounds of dough when her mobile phone rang, so she let it go to voicemail.

When it rang again a few seconds later, she grabbed a towel and wiped her hands.

"Okay, okay, I'm coming," she muttered.

When she saw the caller was her younger sister, she exhaled and braced herself.

"Merry Christmas, Kenna."

"Not so much, Rita. Sorry to break it to you, but I, uh . . . um, no way to say it but to say it. Mum's dead. She passed this morning at the hospital. I was with her the whole time. It was very peaceful," Kenna said, her voice flat.

Rita sucked in her breath as the kitchen started to spin. She slid down the cabinet to the floor.

"Kenna, what happened?"

"Mum wasn't feeling well, so I called an ambulance and they took her to ER. I think she had a stroke or something. Then she died this morning," Kenna said.

"What did the doctor say? I mean, did they run tests?"

"How would I know? You're the nurse, but you weren't there, were you? Even after I texted you!" Kenna snapped back. "Call the hospital yourself. I'm sure they'll tell you whatever you wanna know."

"Jesus, Kenna, you don't have to be such a bitch."

"Do you want me to tell you what happened or not? Just zip it for a minute. Mum wasn't feeling well in the morning. I went out for some last minute shopping and when I got back, Mum was not any better. In fact, she was worse. She pissed herself in her sleep, and she wouldn't wake up. I swear she had a stroke or something, so I called 911 and the ambulance took her to ER. Must have been around 5:30-ish," Kenna said.

"Why didn't you call me right then? Jesus." Rita closed her eyes and counted, slowly, to ten. She would not let Kenna do this to her.

"I texted you when I got home, and you didn't even bother to text me back. It's not my fault you're a million miles from a cell tower."

"We're in the middle of a goddamn blizzard in case you didn't notice. I just want to know what happened while Mum was in your care, if that's not too much to ask," Rita said, her anger rising quickly in response to Kenna's jabs.

"Well she wasn't in my care, was she? She was at the hospital. They admitted her and were going to do some tests, but I never did find out if she'd had a stroke or whatever, because she just up and died. So, anyway, I'm doing the sisterly thing here, and I really don't appreciate the way you're talking to me. I don't deserve this." Kenna began to quietly sob.

"Okay, okay. What do you need me to do?" Rita said, and her anger settled into its old nest of resignation.

"There's no need for *you* to *do* anything. I've already called the lawyer and the funeral home."

"Wait, what? Why did you call Mum's lawyer?

"I called Barrett because Mum said if anything happened to her, I was to call him. So I did. He's an ass, by the way," Kenna said.

"And you called Springer, right? Because Joe is Mum's friend, and that's where she … who she wants to take care of her," Rita said.

"Yes, I talked to Joe himself. I'm not a moron, you know. So, just keep prepping for tomorrow, because we're still having the Boxing Day party. Mum would totally want us to keep up the tradition."

Rita started to protest, but reconsidered. If there was one thing she was sure of, it was that her mother would expect them to adhere to family rituals, even if she wasn't there. Freda would want the show to go on in her absence and, besides, it would probably be good for the family to be together.

"Anyway, I have a lot of calls to make, so I'll see you tomorrow," Kenna said. She hung up before Rita could say anything more.

Rita dropped her phone on the floor and rested her head on her knees. It was all so surreal: Freda dead; Kenna calmly taking charge; her own heart pounding in her chest, drumming out a conflicted rhythm of relief, sorrow, and resentment for her deceased mother. Freda had been a contradiction of wonderful and horrible, juxtaposed in such a way that only years of calculated separation allowed Rita to feel whole. She watched the butter tarts browning, a lifetime of prickly interactions lifting from her body as tears poured down her cheeks.

Dave came in, kicking off his boots at the back door. His eyebrows were frosted over and his cheeks were red with wind burn.

"Holy shit, it's cold out. Wish that miserable storm would . . ."

When he saw Rita on the floor, tears wetting the front of her apron, he dropped his parka and rushed to kneel beside her.

"Kenna just called," Rita said, her voice full of tears. "It's Mum."

Dave pulled Rita close and wrapped his arms around her. "I'm sorry, sweetheart," he said. "What do you need me to do?"

"Dave, I just …" Rita said, quietly crying.

"I know. It's okay, love."

"Tomorrow's dinner is still on, but then I just want to go home."

Dave kissed her forehead and got to his feet. Rita could hear him quietly telling his parents and his mother's murmured response.

Suddenly, Rita felt relief washing over her as she realized what Freda's death really meant. For the first time, she could have a peaceful holiday alone with Dave, without traveling halfway across the country. They could spend Christmas with just their kids and grandbaby. She could completely avoid the annual festival of bickering with her family.

Rita pulled the tarts from the oven. The sight of them, perfectly golden-brown, plump with raisins, lined up so neatly, made her burst into tears again.

This would be her last Boxing Day party. Ever.

No effing way am I doing this again.

28

A Christmas Story

December 25

The AirBnB was a comfortable haven, even if there were only a few inches of wood and drywall between Camelia and the blizzard. She cranked the gas fireplace up and sipped a mimosa while Leon flipped through channels on the television, looking for *A Christmas Story*. They had prepped brunch and were just waiting for Sophie and Steve to get up. Despite the howling wind, it was going to be a perfect, lazy Christmas day.

And then Rita called.

"Merry Christmas to my favorite cousin!" Camelia said.

She heard Rita's voice break as she tried to speak.

"Hey, hey, Rita, what's going on?"

"Oh god, Cam. It's Mum. Kenna just called. Mum had a stroke or something but Kenna didn't really have much information and I don't ..." Rita blew her nose. "She . . . she died. Early this morning."

"Oh god. Oh *no*. I haven't even seen her. What the hell happened?" Camelia said, before bursting into tears. "I just … I don't …" Leon touched her shoulder.

"Is everything okay?" he whispered, worry sharpening his features.

"It's Auntie Freda. She . . . she died this morning," Camelia said.

Leon's eyes glazed with tears as he sat down on the sofa next to Camelia.

"Do you know anything about what happened?" Camelia asked.

"Not really. Kenna took mum to ER last night, and she died during the night. She thinks Mum had a stroke," Rita said.

"I can only imagine Kenna's reaction. She must be a complete mess," Camelia said.

"As usual, she was short on facts. But she wasn't upset at all. She already called the funeral home and the lawyer. Never thought I'd see the day Kenna had her shit together."

"Yeah, that's a first. Maybe she drank herself numb," Camelia said.

"Maybe. Just caught me off guard. But she also said Mum fell out of bed a couple of days ago, and she didn't even think to call me. On top of that, she *still* took Mum for her hair appointment! Doesn't that seem strange, even for Kenna?"

"Oh my god. Why didn't Kenna take her to ER right then? What the hell was she thinking? I can't believe it. *Fucking Kenna.* That's horrible. I'm so sorry," Camelia said.

"Yeah, the whole thing is horrible. Anyway, I have a long list of people to call, so I'm gonna get back to it. Oh, and the Boxing Day dinner is still on, but I guess it's a wake now. So I'll see you tomorrow?"

"Wow, okay, are you sure you're up for it?"

"Do I have a choice? I am my mother's daughter, and you know Freda would want us to bear down and walk it off," Rita said with a mirthless laugh. "Besides, I have enough food for an army, and it will be good for everyone to clan up and share some stories."

"Yeah, you're right. Is there anything I can do to help?" Camelia said.

"I don't think so. I'm sort of on autopilot because it hasn't sunk in. Right now I just need to tick the boxes and finish cooking."

"Okay, I'm here if you need anything."

"Actually, if you guys can show up a little early tomorrow. I could use the extra hands and a buffer from Kenna," Rita said.

"No problem. We'll be there, and call me if we can do anything to help," Camelia said.

She hung up and sat, frozen in place, as she tried to make sense of the world without Auntie Freda. It didn't yet seem real. Of course, strokes happen and they can take a person down in a blink, but Auntie Freda? It couldn't be true.

She knew she was just being wishful: *wishing* Freda was still alive, *wishing* she had taken more time with her, *wishing* Freda was at home, in her beautiful living room, her feet towards the fire, having a glass of sherry, laughing over a story she'd heard at the Italian Club. Camelia wished for the same thing every person left behind wishes for: *more time.*

Camelia's reverie was interrupted when Sophie and Steve came clattering downstairs a few minutes later, still half asleep.

"Merry Christmas!" Sophie called out. She stopped when she saw their faces. "What's going on?"

At the news, Sophie fell sobbing onto the sofa, while Steve paced in a tight, nervous circle. They asked the same questions Camelia had asked Rita, but there were no details to share.

"Come on, now. We still have to eat. Steve, wanna put on another pot of coffee?" Leon said. "Sophie, come on, kiddo."

Leon and Camelia moved around the kitchen, cooking waffles, pouring coffee, feeding a steady spoonful of normalcy to each other. When they were all talked out and brunch was finished, Sophie and Steve headed upstairs to shower and dress, while Leon mixed Bloody Caesars. Camelia stood at the picture window, staring with unseeing eyes at the neighbor shoveling in vain as bursts of gale-force wind tossed his neat piles back onto his driveway.

Her legal mind had clicked on, despite—or because of?—the deep pang of loss. This detachment, so necessary in her childhood, was a convenient strategy that allowed her to step back from her emotions and survey the facts. Of course, she knew this day would come. After all, Auntie Freda was 85 years old. But she wasn't *that* kind of 85-year-old.

Even in her dotage, Freda was a whirlwind of bustling activity and non-stop judgment for those who failed to keep up. Freda had volunteered at the library, the art museum, and the RCMP Auxiliary; traveled abroad every year with her sorority; baked her iconic butter tarts and lemon bars for special occasions; hung out at the Italian Club with her friends every Friday night; and guiltlessly tossed back expensive wine almost every evening. Freda was, frankly, a role model for how to live a rich, full, long life. And now she was gone. The shock rocked Camelia's precarious emotional balance and waves of anxiety gnawed at her gut.

And, underneath the sorrow and worry, something else began nagging. Something wasn't right. Rita said Kenna had called the funeral home and contacted the family lawyer, even before calling Rita.

Why?

Why would Kenna be so keen to wrap things up? These questions, these little threads, frayed at the edges of her mind all day, even after a double Caesar. And another one.

What happened to make Kenna suddenly so efficient, so organized, so … responsible?

That night, after a subdued dinner of takeout Chinese, spooning with Leon under a cloud of comforter, Camelia sorted through a knot of persistent thoughts. She couldn't put her finger on it, but something was off.

Or am I just being obsessive?

Despite a headache and being bone tired, Camelia's mind took off, working on a timeline. It was an occupational hazard: always looking for the hole in the story, the numbers that didn't quite add up, the little detail that unraveled the whole charade.

She recalled all the cases they had reviewed at firm meetings. In almost every case, some nurse, doctor, or pharmacist had prescribed the wrong thing or the wrong dose, leaving a patient dead or disabled. She wondered what they had given Freda in the ER, and then later when she was admitted. Had anyone checked allergies or contraindications for other meds? The list of possible problems scrolled through Camelia's head and she recalled Byron's cynical words: *There are a thousand ways to die, and most of them are in the hospital.* She wanted an explanation, a way to put this all away in a nice neat box.

The likely causes of Freda's sudden death were stroke, heart failure, or aneurysm. That was easy enough to confirm. But Kenna had put herself squarely in charge, and that was strange. She wasn't the logical one in the family at the best of times, but with her mother not even cold yet, it was inconceivable that Kenna wouldn't be a blubbering mess. And why did Kenna call Freda's lawyer?

Who does that?

It didn't make sense.

Or maybe it makes perfect sense, and I just don't want it to.

Kenna, of all people, wasn't organized or logical. She wasn't the type to figure things out without being told, so who was coaching her? The only person she could think of was Mickey, but he wasn't exactly a genius, either. Camelia went back over it in her mind, considering the possibilities.

This was not the Christmas story I wanted to hear.

Camelia lay awake for a long time after Leon's snores settled into a slow rhythm. She curled into his back for warmth, unable to sleep as memories of Freda kept crowding in. Camelia would need divine inspiration to sort this out.

What would Freda do?

29

Just Like the Ones We Used to Know

December 26

Camelia, Leon, Sophie, and Steve arrived in a somber clump; early, as arranged. Their greetings were subdued as Rita's husband, Dave, hung up coats and patted shoulders and offered drinks. His steady presence was a relief as Camelia was momentarily overwhelmed with memories of past holidays, half expecting Freda to come around the corner any moment. She swallowed the lump in her throat and went to find Rita in the kitchen.

"My friend. I'm so sorry. How you holding up?" Camelia asked after a long hug, her tear-filled eyes searching Rita's.

"You know, it's just weird right now," Rita said. "I mean, it's not real yet. I can't believe Mum's gone, even though we all knew this day would come, sooner or later." She continued wiping down Freda's Royal Albert Silver Maple china. "And you wanna know what's really crazy? After what? Fifty years of being alone? Mum was in love."

"Whaaaat? With who?"

"Arthur Rossi, from the Italian Club. She was going to announce her engagement today," Rita said, shaking her head. "They were getting married on New Years'."

"Holy shit. Auntie Freda told me to bring something dressy, but I didn't know it was for her *wedding*. I don't think I've ever met him, have I?"

"Maybe not. I've met him a couple of times, and he's lovely. Very old school. Perfect for Mum, actually," Rita said, and her eyes filled with tears. "I wanted him to come today as planned, but he didn't feel up for it, poor old dear."

"Oh god. He must be crushed. It was just so … sudden. I didn't even have a chance to see her. And now she's gone." Camelia shook her head as a sob escaped her throat.

"I know it *seems* sudden, but I see this all the time in my work with hospice. Things happen. People die in hospital every day, which is not to say Mum should have …" Rita swiped tears from her cheeks with the back of her hand. "Sorry, I promised not to cry today. It's not like Mum and I were close or anything, but ... I guess I don't really know how to feel," Rita said, taking a deep breath.

"Feeling conflicted is totally normal. Give yourself a break," Camelia said.

"And on top of everything else, I'm not getting any help from Kenna. She hasn't even come downstairs since we got back this morning, which is weird, even for her," Rita said, shrugging.

"You mean she hasn't helped you *at all*?"

Rita shook her head.

"Fucking Kenna."

"Yeah, I'd say it was grief, but she managed to call Mum's lawyer right away," Rita said.

"Yeah, so you said yesterday. What's that about?"

"Her excuse was to get the will read while we're all in town, which sorta makes sense," Rita said.

"Knowing Auntie Freda, her affairs are in perfect order, so there shouldn't be any issues with the estate," Camelia said.

"Yep. When we first got here, Mum told me she had updated her will and her healthcare directives were all in order. It was almost like, I don't know … she was *prepared*." She waved her hand at her brimming eyes. "Okay, I gotta stop this."

"I'm sorry. Look, it's gonna be a rough day, so let's set everything up so you can focus on drinking, as a good Catholic wake demands. What goes where?" Camelia asked, waving her hand over the food and dishes piled on the kitchen island.

"Yep. Deep breaths. I think we should just put everything on the console and sideboard in the dining room. Maybe contain the mess a bit," Rita said.

They moved to the dining room with trays of food and dishes. Rita rolled red linen napkins into enameled rings while Camelia arranged silverware and dishes on the tables. After tucking a fresh garland around the edges of the long sideboard, Rita lit a row of tall red tapers.

"It looks very festive, Ree," Camelia said.

"It does, doesn't it? I think Mum would like it," Rita said, surveying the room.

"Auntie Freda would definitely approve."

"Okay, I think we're done for now. Dinner's in the oven and will be ready in a couple of hours. And I need a pick-me-up. Wanna get a buzz, before the rest of them get here?" Rita said, with a conspiratorial smile.

Camelia raised her eyebrows and grinned. Rita motioned for Camelia to follow her downstairs. Rita paused by the front door and grabbed her medical kit.

"Better not leave this laying around where curious grandbabies can get into it," she said, and headed down the stairs.

"What is it?"

"Oh, just my med kit. Should have left it in Van, but we left straight from work, and I forgot about it being in the car," Rita said. "Now I have to babysit it, because of the meds."

"Oh yeah, I wanna hear about the new job," Camelia said.

As she descended the stairs, she was overcome with memories of their youth, sneaking puffs of weed in the basement rumpus room, blowing smoke out the window, thinking they were so clever. But that was ages ago, before Freda renovated. Now, at the bottom of the staircase, a heavy door opened into a large guest suite, with windows facing the backyard. In front of the windows, two tufted leather wingback chairs invited them to sit.

Rita reached into a sleek travel tote and pulled out a small hand-blown glass pipe and a little case that Camelia guessed held Rita's stash. She smiled to herself. The room was nicer, but some things never changed.

Camelia inhaled deeply when Rita passed her the pipe, the soothing rush of smoke entering her lungs, like falling into a familiar embrace with an old friend. Relaxing into the overstuffed chair, her anxiety melted away.

This is almost as good as Klonopin.

For a little while, it was as if nothing had changed. Rita and Camelia exchanged stories, reminisced about classmates, and gossiped about recent divorces and marriages among the old gang. But, inevitably, the conversation veered back to the present, a place they were both trying to avoid.

"So, what happens now?"

Rita's gaze was fixed on the overcast sky blurring into the snow drifts, a frozen world in a dozen shades of white.

"I guess now we … manage. We can get an estate auction company to come in and sell off Mum's things, and I think she already talked to Jojo's son, Bruce, about listing the house," Rita said.

"What? She was going to list this place?" Camelia couldn't believe Freda would get rid of the family home.

"I know. It rocked me too. But last week Mum said she was moving into Arthur's condo after the wedding," Rita said.

"Well, selling the house will be on hold for now, until the reading of the will."

"Yeah, I suppose so. I need to find out how to ship Mum's remains to the National Cemetery to be interred with dad. There'll be a ceremony there, I'm sure, but I don't know anything about the logistics."

"Surely the people at Springer will know. She can't be the first military widow they've … managed," Camelia said.

"Hey, you don't have to pussyfoot. I'm around death all day, every day. The words don't bother me, you know."

"I suppose not. You'll have services here, too, won't you?" Camelia asked.

"Freda Swenson would not have it any other way! So that's the other thing. We'll have to be in touch with the priest at Holy Rosary for a funeral mass and all that." Rita sighed into her glass of wine.

"There's plenty of time, and we can all help. I mean, it was just yesterday."

"Seems like ages, in some ways," Rita said.

"It doesn't seem real, does it? I keep expecting her to throw that door open and give us what-for about smoking pot in her basement," Camelia giggled. "Remember that time …"

Rita burst out laughing. "Oh my god how could I forget? The look on your face!"

"And yours. Auntie Freda was so pissed off," Camelia laughed.

"She never forgave me for burning that hole in the rug, but somehow she wasn't at all surprised it was from a joint. Turns out, she knew all along!" Rita dissolved into fits of laughter.

"Yeah, no thanks to the snitch!" Camelia said.

"Oh god, that's right. Kenna ratted us out, as usual. What a brat," Rita said.

"She hasn't changed at all, has she? So typical, pretending to sleep in just to get out of helping." Camelia sipped her wine.

"Meanwhile, she's probably upstairs chugging rye and coke, playing games on her iPad," Rita said.

"Kinda hard to keep up the Saint Kenna the Put Upon act when she's half cut and not lifting a finger."

"She's being so … I don't know. Just so not Kenna and yet, completely Kenna. Like, she was her usual martyr self when we stayed over last week. Then, when she called to tell me about Mum, she was super snarky. But, at the same time, she apparently has everything all organized." Rita shrugged.

"When has she *ever* been organized? Think about it," Camelia said.

"Yeah, it's weird that she's pretty much taken over. Whatever. There's no logic. It's Kenna. And here's me … I can't even think beyond dinner," Rita said, blowing out a long trail of smoke. "And don't let Kenna start in on me, or I'll lose it. The last thing I need is to have a screaming fit in the middle of dinner." Rita laid the pipe in a vintage ashtray and stood up.

Camelia gave Rita a quick hug. "Let's go upstairs and have more wine to brace ourselves, because you know Freda would!"

"Mum always loved a good wake. Do you remember Lucky Belmont's? God, we were all trashed by noon."

"How could I forget Leon and all his cousins lining up to sing *Sweet Caroline*?" Camelia said. "Still have no idea what that song had to do with anything, but it was funny!"

They laughed over the memory as they headed back upstairs, where Leon and Dave were hunched over the coffee table, eating garlicky kielbasa and cubes of aged cheddar, talking shop. Sophie and Steve were holding down the other end of the sofa flipping through an old family photo album balanced on their knees.

Camelia plopped into the Bergere chair in the bay window, near the fireplace. It was her aunt's favorite. As she nestled in, Camelia detected the faint scent of Freda's perfume.

"Special delivery, all the way from B.C.," Dave said, handing her a glass of Okanagan pinot noir.

Camelia sniffed the glass and took a sip. "It's delicious, thanks for bringing the good stuff." She tucked her feet under her, pulling a throw over her lap.

Rita sat opposite her in the matching chair, her face pale in the afternoon light. Camelia was struck by how much Rita, her shoulder-length hair now shot through with silver, looked like Auntie Freda.

She held up her glass. "Here's to Auntie Freda. May her memory be a comfort for us all," she said, leaning in to clink glasses with Rita.

Rita took a sip, and Camelia realized her friend was struggling not to cry.

"Now," Camelia said, "tell me all about the grandbaby."

As she told stories about her perfect beautiful genius granddaughter, Clara, Camelia watched Rita's face relax into a smile. Soon they were giggling over new parent foibles and toddler antics.

In the glow of the tree, with the warmth of the fireplace, laughing with an old friend, it almost felt like Christmas.

30

A Boxing Day Wake

December 26

"Here's my favorite family," Kenna said.

The conversation stopped and all heads turned to see Kenna, stuffed into a red and green spangled sweater, limping down the stairs, like some faded movie star making her grand entrance.

Rita caught Camelia's eye, and they exchanged a look. Was it really a coincidence that Kenna had waited until everyone arrived to finally make an appearance?

"Come on, everyone grab a drink and warm up by the fire. Be sure to have some food. Rita's outdone herself again."

Wait. Did Kenna actually just take over Rita's Boxing Day Dinner?

"Come on now, don't be shy. Dave, Ben, can you guys bartend for us? And Ree," Kenna waved her hand over the sideboard, "you'll have to give everyone a tour of the appies. I have no idea what half of this stuff is."

"Looks totally Left Coast to me," Mickey smirked.

"It's all local cheese, sausages, and bread from Lumsden. Living in the prairies doesn't mean you don't appreciate good food, does it?" Rita said.

The air crackled with a snap of tension.

"I don't care where it came from, I'm starving," Andrew said as he loaded a plate. Relief and laughter rippled through the room as the family relaxed, teasing him for his notoriously huge appetite.

Dave, Leon, and Ben—friends since grade school—took over a corner of the dining room, pouring drinks, downing Bloody Caesars, and gorging from the charcuterie board. The kids—all the adult children—formed a knot at the fireplace end of the living room, speaking in low tones amongst themselves. Mickey was the only one who didn't join them, sticking close to Kenna's side instead. The grandchildren—Darren's three year old Clara, and Mickey's two year old Sashay—stomped around the room in their stocking feet with wide eyes and giggles.

Even though people were still filling their plates and moving between the living and dining rooms, Rita tapped a fork on her wine glass.

About time you took over, Ree.

"Happy Boxing Day, and I'm glad you all made it safe and sound despite the weather. Unfortunately, this is no longer a Boxing Day Party, but now a wake, in honor of our matriarch," Rita began, and her voice hitched. "Even though Mum left us yesterday, we definitely feel both her presence and absence." Her eyes glistened with unspent tears. "I know we're all shocked to have lost Mum so suddenly. It's a good reminder that life is short, so we must take care of each other. We can be grateful and comforted that Mum didn't linger, that it was swift and merciful, as she wanted. As she said to me just the other day, she didn't want to end up a drooling bag of bones," Rita said. A small patter of laughter followed her comment. "For our mother, grandmother, and aunt, a lifetime Catholic, please join me in saying The Eternal Rest." She paused and leaned into Dave. "Eternal rest grant unto her, O Lord …" Rita finished the prayer, crossed herself, and took a deep breath.

A chorus of amens responded. The Catholic teachings ran deep in the Swenson family.

"I'm not sure if Mum told everyone, because she wanted to make the announcement today, but I'm sure she asked all of you to bring something dressy to wear on New Year's Day. The reason is that Mum became engaged to be married and her wedding …" Rita said.

Before she could finish, the room exploded into excited questions.

"What? Are you kidding?" Ben interrupted, his voice booming over the room.

"That's adorable," Ben's wife, Norah said.

"Kinda old for a wedding, if you ask me," Rita's daughter, Dana, said.

"So old people can't get married, Dana?" Sophie asked.

"Who on earth was she marrying?" Ben said.

"So that's why I had to pack a sport coat?" Leon said.

"Is this for real?" Ben asked again, too loudly. "Do Harri and Jojo know anything about this?"

"Yes, Ben, it's true," Rita said. "Mum was intending to marry Arthur Rossi, a lovely old gent she knew through the Italian Club. Harri and JoJo think the world of him, by the way."

"Who is this guy, again?" Andrew asked.

"Some old dog from the Italian Club. Probably thought he'd struck gold," Mickey said.

Rita held up a hand. "You would have all met him today, but Arthur was too shook up to come. It makes Mum's death even more sad, because, after all these decades of being a widow, she had finally met her match."

Kenna exhaled in a huff. "Well, the wedding's off. *Obviously*."

There was a lull in the conversation as Kenna's words hit them with the force of finality.

"Duh." Dana rolled her eyes at Kenna. "Does anyone know what happened? Grandma seemed fine at the Cousins Brunch."

"She said she felt a cold coming on, though," Andrew responded.

"Yeah, then Mickey gave her that weird nose spray," Sophie said, throwing a sharp glance in Mickey's direction.

"It's not *weird*. It's Chinese herbal medicine." Mickey's eyes flashed with anger, and he glared back at Sophie.

No love lost between those two.

Camelia raised an eyebrow at Sophie, even though she couldn't blame her for resenting Mickey.

"Okay, regardless of what happened, Mum passed away. Let's share some memories and have a few drinks in Mum's honor before we sit down to dinner. You know how Mum loved a good wake, so let's give her one!" Rita said, invoking Freda's upbeat tone.

Before anyone had a chance to take a breath, Mickey spoke up. "I'd like to start with a story about my Gram when I was about ten …"

It was so typical of him to jump in ahead of Rita, Ben, and Kenna, but Camelia couldn't help smiling. Mickey's story was a glorified, over the top retelling of a childhood event, centering him as the hero of the day.

Camelia thought about what story she would tell. Would it be the time they all went to Toronto for a family vacation? Or that hilarious faux pas at the spa, when she took Auntie Freda to Palm Springs for a girls' getaway with Rita, Dana, and Sophie? Maybe the time Auntie Freda chased a would-be burglar out of the house with a hot iron, only to discover it was her housekeeper's husband, come to deliver lunch? What would capture the inquisitive, sharp-tongued wit of her beloved aunt?

After Mickey finished, they went around the room. Everyone shared a favorite memory, a funny anecdote, a momentary glimpse into Freda's straightforward, no-nonsense world of hard work, charity, and constant social activity. Camelia settled on the Spa Faux Pas as her contribution. When the stories turned maudlin, Rita rang the little crystal bell Freda had always used to summon everyone for dinner.

As the antipasto gave way to sit-down courses, there was a shuffling and arranging of bodies around the cobbled-together tables and mismatched chairs in the dining room. Finally, all of them were crowded around, shoulder to shoulder. Throats were cleared, water sipped, and napkins unfurled in the awkward silence.

Everyone, including Camelia, was waiting for direction. Without Freda at the head of the table, they didn't know how to begin. Camelia wanted to guide the Swenson clan towards closure and a peaceful resolution of Freda's death, in a subtle way. But it wasn't her place. She wasn't a Swenson, even though Freda's household was the life raft that kept her afloat during her lonely, unsupervised childhood. Camelia was nothing more than a second cousin, Rita's best friend, a Freda favorite. No,

Camelia was not in charge here, as much as she wanted to be. But she could give a nudge.

She tapped her glass with her knife and looked to Rita. Rita looked puzzled for a moment and then composed herself.

"Hey everyone, before we eat, it was Mum's tradition to say the Lord's Prayer," Rita said, and they reflexively joined hands. "Our Father, who art in heaven …" she said, and their voices joined, filling the oak-paneled room.

A chorus of amens seemed to have the effect of unleashing their appetites.

"Kenna, Ben, after dinner, we should talk about Mum's arrangements so I can start making calls," Rita said. "We need to pick out her outfit for the funeral mass. Springer should be able to arrange for Mum to be sent on for interment with Dad at the National Cemetery."

Camelia smiled to herself.

Well done, Rita.

Kenna slurped her cocktail and looked at Mickey for a beat longer than normal.

"Well, I don't know how much there is to discuss," Kenna said. "I've already arranged for us to meet Bob Barrett on the 30th for the reading of the will, before you all take off."

"Thank you for arranging that, Ken," Ben said. "But what's the rush?"

"You want your inheritance, don't you? Remember Smitty's family? They couldn't get a dime until the funeral was over and the will was read. I assumed none of you would want to wait that long," Kenna said. "I know I sure don't want to, because I've gotta pay the electric bill on this place."

"Okay, makes sense," Rita said.

"As for picking an outfit, there's no need. I already had Mum cremated."

Holy shit.

The silence following Kenna's bombshell vibrated with tension.

Then Rita exploded.

"Are you fucking kidding me?" Rita shrieked. She stood up, gripping her napkin in trembling hands. "You know damn well Mum was to be interred with dad! When did you even have a *chance* to have Mum cremated?"

Kenna shrugged. "Yesterday, at Springer. Seemed like the thing to do since I'm basically the only one who lives here. I mean, Mum's dead so that pretty much leaves me in charge of *everything*."

"Oh, you are *so* wrong about that, Kenna. You fucking inconsiderate bitch." Rita dropped her fork onto her plate with a clank and stomped across the hall to the living room, slamming the door behind her.

"Really, Kenna? How *could* you?" Camelia said, getting to her feet.

As she left the room, Camelia grabbed Rita's wine glass and her own. Angry voices erupted behind her.

Rita was in the living room, curled up on the couch, staring into the whiteness outside.

"You okay?" Camelia asked, handing Rita her glass of wine.

"Yeah. No. I don't know. I will be. I just can't believe Kenna had Mum cremated," Rita said. She wadded up a damp tissue and reached for another. "I always knew—*we all knew*—Mum was to be sent to Ottawa to be buried next to dad. Cremation was *never* an option. It's a Catholic thing."

"Hell, even I knew Auntie Freda was being buried with Uncle Geoffrey. There's no way she wanted to be cremated. Complete sacrilege in her book," Camelia said. "I mean, Auntie Freda can still go to the National to be with Uncle Geoffrey, and a lot cheaper this way, but still. Fucking Kenna," Camelia said.

"Yeah, *fucking Kenna.* I guarantee Mum would never have authorized cremation because we *literally* just talked about it a few days ago. She said, and I quote, *my burial plans remain the same*," Rita said. "I don't know where Kenna got the idea, or the balls, to do such a thing."

"Has she lost her damn mind?" Camelia said.

"Probably. As far as I know, Mum prepaid her funeral expenses for transport and burial, not cremation. It's just the most inconsiderate, mean spirited… " Rita shook her head. "I don't even have the words."

Camelia could feel the anger pulsing off Rita, but wasn't sure how to comfort her.

"Do you think it's worth asking Kenna why she did it, especially without talking to you or Ben?"

"Why bother? Kenna's never been above lying to save her own skin, so whatever she says now will just be more lies," Rita said. "And they wonder why I never come back here? Jesus."

Rita ran her hands through her hair and dabbed her eyes. "What a mess. But I guess calling your sister a bitch is one way to break the ice at your mother's wake!" she said, rolling her eyes at her own folly. She stood in front of the window and squared her shoulders.

"Actually, I think you said fucking bitch," Camelia snorted, giving Rita a sideways hug. "All this is hard enough without being out here by yourself. Come on back to dinner. This is *your* feast, and you've worked so hard to make everything wonderful. We can deal with Kenna tomorrow," Camelia said.

"You're right. Screw Kenna. I'm going back in there just to watch her squirm. She can stomp off to her lair if she doesn't like it," Rita said.

Everyone stopped talking when Rita and Camelia returned to the dining room. Kenna rose clumsily from her chair and approached Rita. Camelia hovered, not willing to leave Rita on her own. Kenna groped for Rita's hands, squeezing them in her plump palms.

"I'm sorry, Ree. You weren't around when Mum passed, and the hospital wanted a decision, so I just had to take charge," Kenna whispered.

Rita jerked her hands away. "Really? We were *all* here and you knew it," she said and gestured around the room. "The *only* reason we're all here is *for Mum*. But you didn't call when she went to Emerg, and then you didn't even have the decency to ask Ben and me about cremation." Rita's voice was rising, gaining force. "So no, Kenna, you *didn't* have to take charge."

"I texted you, and you didn't respond so what was I supposed to do? It all happened so fast. All I did was come home to …" Kenna began.

"Mum was by herself, in the hospital, and you came home? You left her alone? What is *wrong* with you?" Rita shouted.

"What makes you think Mum was alone?" Kenna asked, glancing at Mickey.

"Yeah, where were *you*, Rita?" Mickey added.

Rita shook her head, but didn't answer, so Kenna continued. "What I *started* to say before you bit my head off is that I texted Mickey to come to the hospital because I had to come home and get Mum's meds. I was going to head back to the hospital, but then they called and got the list of Mum's meds over the phone. The guy said I should stay home because the blizzard was outta control. It was too dangerous. And besides, that bossy bitch of a nurse wanted me out of there. She probably gave Mum the wrong meds!" she said.

Is this Kenna's theory, or alibi, or both?

"I think Mum's right. I saw the nurse give Gram something … who knows what … and you know she was allergic to everything," Mickey chimed in.

"Who said anything about an allergic reaction? I thought you said Mum had a stroke," Rita said.

"That's what they said, but who knows what kind of stuff they gave her after I left?" Kenna said.

"They would have given her whatever meds the doctor ordered, Kenna. *That's what nurses do.* God, you're a dim bulb sometimes," Rita said.

"Oh, I forgot, you're the brilliant one, aren't you? Even if I had been there, what could I have done, other than watch Mum sleep? After all, *I'm* not the nurse in the family!" Kenna sniffled into a damp tissue.

"One more reason you should have called me from ER the minute you arrived. I could have at least asked the right questions." Rita's voice was trembling with rage.

"Get over yourself. No one could have done anything. When I left, Mum was completely out of it, and I don't think she ever woke up. Which, if ya think about it, is a pretty nice way to go, eh?" she slurred. "Better than the old bitch deserved, if you ask me," she said, softly.

Camelia gasped and Kenna glared back at her.

"You didn't know our mother like we knew our mother," Kenna hissed.

"I knew Auntie Freda my whole life, Kenna. She may not have been perfect, but she sure as hell didn't deserve to die alone. Any one of us would have come right away *had we known*." Camelia said, her temper flaring. "But you didn't think of anyone other than yourself. As per usual." Camelia glared right back at Kenna.

"This is none of your business, Cam. This is a *family* matter," Kenna said.

Don't do it. Don't take the bait.

Camelia took a sip of wine and released a long exhale. These people were *her* family, too. Kenna could just piss off with that family matter crap. Sure, Auntie Freda wasn't her mother, but she had stepped in and cared for Camelia when her own mother was absent. Camelia turned away.

"Not today, Kenna. Just stop." Rita returned to her seat at the head of the table.

"If you want another report, ask Mickey," Kenna said, turning to Mickey. "You was the last one to visit Mum, *weren't you*?" Her tone was a little bit mocking, almost threatening.

Mickey's head turned sharply in Kenna's direction, but he quickly softened, pressing his thumb and forefinger to the bridge of his nose. He gave a dramatic sniffle.

"Well, it was either me or Rita," he said, and looked at Rita, unblinking, for a long moment. He shrugged. "Anyway, Gram was sleeping the whole time I was at the hospital, so I didn't really get to talk to her. The nurse came in and gave her some meds in her IV and told me to come back tomorrow . . . because, you know, the blizzard was already bad by then. But there was no tomorrow, because by then, Gram was already gone," he said, shaking his head and pressing his napkin to his eyes. "Who knows what they did to her?"

Jesus, what a drama queen.

"Kenna, what happened *before* you went to ER?" Camelia couldn't stay quiet any longer. "What made you call the ambulance in the first place?" She focused her gaze on Kenna, studiously avoiding the dirty look she could feel Mickey firing in her direction.

"Mum didn't feel well, and she wouldn't wake up all the way," Kenna said. She paused to take a long drink of her rye and DC. "Call the hospital if you're so interested. I'm done being interrogated over the worst thing that's ever happened to me." Kenna covered her face with her napkin and leaned into Mickey as she began to sob.

It was only then Camelia realized the tense exchange had frozen everyone in place. Even the toddlers were shocked into silence. The only sound was Kenna's sniffling.

Camelia saw Andrew quietly trying to sneak another helping of potatoes onto his plate when the serving spoon slipped and clattered into the china bowl. The spell was broken. Everyone went back to eating, talking, and avoiding eye contact with Kenna and Mickey.

Now that Andrew had broken the ice, the family passed platters back and forth, resuming their animated chatter, stuffing themselves with food. Camelia looked around the room and realized half of them were indifferent to Freda's death and the other half were relieved she was gone. But Camelia, who'd felt a bond with her aunt for as long as she could remember, had lost her appetite. She had been just a few miles away as Auntie Freda died in solitude, without anyone there to hold her hand or comfort her as she slipped away.

Camelia felt an indignant fire growing inside. She just wasn't sure where to direct it.

31

End Of An Era

December 26

With full bellies and the soothing lull of Christmas songs on the stereo, they all retired to the living room for dessert while the kids cleaned up. Ben and his son, Andrew, along with Rita's son, Darren, competed for who could eat the most pie, while others were still focused on remembering Freda. It was a wake, after all.

Camelia couldn't help but watch Kenna. Her strangely calm behavior and rush to get Freda's affairs sorted was so out of character, it made Camelia's mind turn in dark ways. She had so many questions, not just about what had happened to Auntie Freda, but what was going on with Kenna and Mickey. They were acting strangely, even for them. They'd been the only ones to see Freda in the hospital, but Kenna wasn't answering their questions. There was nothing she could do about it tonight, but Camelia was going to take Kenna's snarky suggestion and visit the hospital tomorrow, maybe even get a copy of Freda's medical records. She needed to know if there had been a definitive diagnosis, just to put her mind to rest.

Until then, Camelia was enjoying Rita's melt-in-your-mouth butter tarts and trying to lay off the wine. But Dave kept circling with the bottle, and it was warm and cozy by the fire.

"Just a splash, Cam?" Dave cajoled.

"Well, when you put it that way …" Camelia held out her glass, and Dave filled it almost to the brim.

Rita and Kenna had entered into a truce in order to play with the granddaughters, rolling a ball on the floor between them. Before long, Clara and Sashay started fighting over the ball, piercing Camelia's wine buzz with angry shrieks. Suyin and Darren picked up their respective toddlers, wrestling the squirming kids as they defied soothing.

Now that the grandkids had declared war, Camelia wondered who would leave first. She didn't have to wait long. As soon as the kitchen was tidied, Kenna announced she was in too much pain to hang around any longer.

"Mick, help me up, wouldya?" Kenna said, from her perch on the sofa. "All this activity … I have to go lie down, but don't feel like you have to leave on account of me," she said. "Enjoy for as long as you like."

Rita shot Camelia a look. It was as if everything was suddenly Kenna's. *We'll see about that.*

"That's okay, we have to go anyway. Sashay needs to go down for her nap or we'll be dealing with the spawn of Satan," Mickey joked. On cue, Sashay let out a yowl.

"So we're all settled on Mum's services and all the other stuff? I hate to be this way, but if I'm staying on after New Year's, I need to tell my boss right away," Ben said.

"The services are up to you and Rita, because I don't think Mum would want any fuss. But first …" Kenna began.

"Since when would Mum not want a fuss? She was all about the fuss!" Ben said.

"Whatever. But *first* we have to go for the reading of the will on the 31st at Barrett's office. If there's probate, it could take a while to sort things out, but I'll … we'll all have a better idea after the will is read," Kenna said to Ben. She turned to face the rest of the family. "Thank you all for making Mum's wake bearable for me. Now, I'm headed upstairs before my leg gives out. Mickey, give your old Mum a hug."

"Suyin, do you have everything?" Mickey asked.

Suyin tucked her phone in a Kate Spade bag. "Yep, just need to grab the diaper bag on the way out."

"Nice handbag, Suyin. And I hear you got a new Kate Spade diaper bag, too?" Sophie said, with a knife's edge in her voice.

"Yeah, how'd you guess?"

Mickey tilted his head at Sophie and Camelia saw him mouth, "Shut the fuck up."

"Because it turned up on my credit card," Sophie said.

Suyin looked from Mickey to Sophie and back again.

Mickey laughed, but his jaw clenched. "Oh, Sophie, you're hilarious! But you're also a little coocoo bananas. Mum gave us some Christmas money, right Mum?" he said, curling his arm around Kenna's shoulders.

"Yep. But don't get used to it. When the estate is settled, I'm sure all you kids will be getting some cash, so no more handouts," Kenna said, smiling.

"So, when will that happen? Because I'm going to have to call the cops about my stolen credit card, otherwise I'll have to pay off Suyin's new handbag," Sophie said, red splotches appearing on her neck.

Mickey's laugh was brittle and too loud.

"Jeez. Don't be so uptight, Sophie," Mickey said. "If there was a problem with your card, I'm sure it will get worked out."

Sophie stared at him with narrowed eyes, then shook her head, ever so slightly, and turned away.

"I'll deal with you some other time, Mick," Steve said, glaring at him.

As soon as Mickey and Suyin got Sashay tucked into a wad of blankets, they were out the door. Camelia couldn't help but think they were in an awful rush to get away from the conversation about Sophie's credit card.

Was Mickey really that sleazy?

Camelia wondered what had happened, because Sophie hadn't said anything to her about it. She would debrief Sophie and Steve when they got home but, for now, she was far more interested in the new conversations sprouting up.

With Kenna upstairs in her room, the rest of the family erupted into whispers of speculation and accusations against the first responders, the hospital, the nurses, the doctor on call, and even a whiff of anger toward Kenna for not calling *everyone* from the hospital.

Camelia sipped her wine as she listened from Auntie Freda's favorite chair, tucked into the bay window by the fire, taking mental notes. She glanced outside to see Mickey tucking Sashay in the back seat. He was so *adult* all of a sudden, but gratingly so. Mickey had the soul of a huckster, and if he had stolen Sophie's credit card, there would be hell to pay. As she watched, instead of getting in the car, Mickey walked around the back of the house, out of view. Curiosity got the better of her, and Camelia headed to the kitchen. She watched as Mickey unlocked the garage and stepped inside.

What is that little shit up to?

As she drained her glass, Camelia felt the room spin a bit. She couldn't even remember how many glasses she'd had.

"Cam?"

Camelia turned to see Leon staring at her. He tilted his head towards the door.

"Looks like you've had plenty. I think it's time to go."

What's a wake for, if not to toast the end of an era?

32

One Man's Trash

December 27

The next morning, Camelia flat out lied. She wasn't proud of it, but damn, it came easy.

"I'm gonna run over to the hospital and pick up Auntie Freda's medical chart. Rita didn't think she'd be up for it, so I said I would do it. I shouldn't be long. Anything you need while I'm out?" Camelia said to the top of Leon's head.

He looked up from his iPad. "I can drive you over, just give me a half hour to respond to some email," Leon said. He was in work mode.

"I'll be back by the time you're done. So just have another cup of coffee, and I'll be back soon," Camelia said, and headed for the door.

"Okay babe, thanks. Drive careful," he said, without looking up.

At the hospital, the grandfatherly docent at the information desk directed Camelia to the correct floor, and she headed to the elevator bank. The hospital layout was blandly familiar. They all seem to follow the same format, so finding the nurse's station was easy. When the young nurse hesitated in answering her questions, Camelia asked for the charge nurse. Someone with authority.

It's what Freda would do.

She thrummed her fingers on the counter, waiting for the charge nurse to show up, trying to think about anything other than the thirst at the back of her throat.

A few minutes later, a woman who could only be the Charge Nurse squeaked down the hall in rubber clogs with a rolling gait that told of too many long shifts on her feet. She pushed her glasses up on her nose as she approached, and Camelia could feel the sizing up.

"I'm Gayle Germaine, the Charge Nurse. You wanted to see me?" the woman said. Her downturned mouth gave her an air of disapproval.

Camelia softened her expression and brightened up her smile. "Hi Gayle, I'm Camelia Belmont, and my Auntie Freda was here a few days ago, before she passed away. It's been tough, with Christmas and all … anyway, we need some details about Auntie Freda's condition and treatment for the life insurance folks. You know, gotta satisfy their need for paperwork. They want reports on bloodwork and meds, but Francine said I'd need to talk to you." Camelia nodded toward the young nurse seated at the station.

Gayle nodded. "Yeah, I talked to someone about it already. Rita … Decker? Becker? The daughter. She called this morning. I already told her we don't have the blood draws anymore, sorry."

"Oh, I don't think they need the actual blood, although I'd love to drop that off on his desk!" Camelia gave a little laugh. "Can you imagine? Anyway, I think all the insurance company needs is a copy of the chart with all the lab and test reports. They'll look for any angle to deny payment," Camelia said, shrugging. "And it wouldn't have to be such a rush, but one of the grandkids found a screaming deal on a bigger house—they have a toddler and one on the way—but, of course, he can't make an offer until we know whether the insurance benefits are going to come through and … oh, it's all just such a complicated mess."

It all came out in a rush. She hoped she sounded as clueless and bereaved as she felt. It was her best cover. People helped idiots. It made them feel superior. Camelia could see the wheels turning in Gayle Germaine's mind, her eyes narrowing on Camelia's expensive handbag.

"Dr. Fitzgerald was Mrs. Swenson's GP. He's an excellent doctor, so I'm sure Freda received the very best care," Gayle said.

Camelia could see her hackles going up at the hint of wrongdoing.

"Oh, this has nothing to do with malpractice or negligence or anything like that. The insurance company will do anything to avoid paying benefits if they can get away with it, so they'll want to verify Auntie Freda didn't have some disease she hadn't told them about," she continued. "And it's probably for nothing. I mean, 85-year-old women die every day but life insurance companies are such vultures." Camelia shrugged.

"Okay, who's the insurance adjuster? We can send the chart to him directly," Gayle said, doing an end run around Camelia's plan.

Shit.

"Um, you know, I think his name is Benson or Jenson or something like that, up in Saskatoon," Camelia said. She was foundering now, making stuff up as she went along. "And, Rita—she's the eldest daughter that called you—has his contact info, but she's busy arranging the funeral. I'm just the errand girl, trying to do my part for the family," she continued.

Why does it feel so wrong to employ a little white lie – okay, a swarm of lies -- when so much is at stake?

"We don't give out charts to just *anyone*," Gayle said, and glanced at Francine. "You'll need to fill out this form for a copy of the chart," she said, rifling through a stack of folders. "Gotta keep the fellas in legal happy." Gayle's voice trailed off, and she shook her head as she handed Camelia the form.

Camelia grabbed a pen and started to fill it out.

"Damned insurance companies. They're always looking for an angle. Why can't they just accept that people die, through no fault of their own, when their number's up? I mean, not that it was her time, but at least she went peacefully."

Camelia drew in her breath. "Why do you say it wasn't her time?"

"Oh … nothing, I guess. Mrs. Swenson was a ripe old age, after all, but you know, sometimes you just think maybe … I don't know. Then, well, to just be dropped off alone, on Christmas Eve no less," Gayle said. She shook her head and abruptly busied herself with the forms. She seemed embarrassed.

Camelia hoped she was able to mask her shock.

"So, *no one* was here with Auntie Freda when she passed?" Camelia asked, jamming her hands in her parka pockets to hide her trembling.

She was momentarily overcome with grief as she pictured Freda, abandoned, alone. Did she know? Was she aware that no one was by her side? She choked back a sob and dabbed at her eyes with a crumpled tissue from her pocket.

"Well, I was on the floor along with one other nurse and two aides, but no family were here," Gayle said, flipping through Freda's chart. "The ambulance brought Mrs. Swenson into ER around 6 p.m., with her daughter, Kenna Shores—we have her signature on the DNR orders—but she must have left soon after because we called her at home at 7:10 p.m. for a list of meds," Gayle said.

"Why DNR orders?" Camelia's senses were on alert now.

"It's routine, particularly for elderly patients, like your aunt," Gayle said. "Anyway, we logged her meds. Then, a friend popped in around 11:30 p.m., Jane somebody. Cannoli? She was here for about 20 minutes. Right after she left, around midnight, the grandson came in. He was just here a few minutes. The other nurse on duty responded to the heart alarm around 4:40 a.m. Mrs. Swenson had passed in her sleep, and … with the DNR order …" Gayle wouldn't meet Camelia's eyes. "We didn't attempt resuscitation."

"Poor dear," Camelia said, and fresh tears stung her eyes. "Is there anything else you can share with me about her condition?"

Gayle and the young nurse exchanged a quick glance. There was something about the way the two nurses were looking at each other that seemed like a secret neither wanted to share.

Gayle sighed. "Freda was such a fixture in our community for so long, raising money for the new cancer center and such. I quite liked her. She had spunk."

"Please, if there's anything we should know … we don't want to give the insurance company any traction to deny the family's claim. But it's more than that. We loved Freda, and we're all just rattled by losing her so suddenly."

"I … I wouldn't say anything was out of the ordinary, exactly. Not under the circumstances. Mrs. Swenson was not totally coherent, she was in and out of consciousness, but that's typical," Gayle said.

"Typical for what?"

"Her age. Her condition. We didn't get a chance to run all the tests, but her condition was consistent with a stroke," Gayle said.

"What about medications?" Camelia asked.

"They're all listed in the chart," Gayle said.

But did Freda receive something she was allergic to?

"Okay, thanks. And … I'm not sure it's allowed, but may I see Freda's final … can I see her room? I mean, assuming no one's there."

"Her room's still empty, and it hasn't even been cleaned yet," Francine said. "It's the holidays, so don't hold it against us."

"We're always short staffed over the holidays. Big epidemic of Molson Flu at this time of year," Gayle said, with a snort, referring to the popular Canadian beer.

"Plus, it's kinda slow up here over the holidays. All the hubbub is on the ortho ward. Car accidents, slip and fall, that kind of thing," Francine added.

Gayle interrupted. "As a hospital benefactor, Mrs. Swenson had a private room. I'm happy to show you where she spent her last hours."

Gayle motioned for Camelia to follow her.

"If you want to spend a few minutes alone, I'll get the chart copied for you," she said, pushing open the door to the private room.

"Thank you so much."

The nurse pulled the door closed behind her when she left. Camelia surveyed the room. It was large, with a wall of windows on one side, the bed, two side chairs, an ensuite bathroom and closet, and a small bank of cabinets with a sink. Next to the sink, on the wall, hung a biohazard bin and a sharps bin. Underneath was a stainless steel trash can.

She walked to the windows and leaned her head against the cold glass.

God, I need a drink.

The windows looked out onto a small park where dark, naked trees huddled in the center of the snow-covered square. Someone was walking a little dog in the park, both wearing matching plaid parkas. Camelia stifled a laugh.

If Auntie Freda were here …

Camelia closed her eyes and inhaled deeply. She could feel the pulse of cold air coming off the windows and heard the rattle of a cart beyond the door. She slowly exhaled. And inhaled again.

What happened, Auntie?

She wondered about Auntie Freda's last visitors. Were Kenna and Mickey hiding something? What really happened when they were here? And did it have anything to do with the speedy cremation Kenna had orchestrated?

Wispy, vague hunches were swirling around, not fully formed, as Camelia's mind tried to decipher the signposts in this foreign land. Something wasn't adding up, and she could feel her frustration rising. She was used to reading financial statements, not rummaging around for clues as to why an old woman died.

Jesus. What's wrong with me?

Kenna said to contact the hospital for details, and that's what she was doing. She shook her head and turned back to the room.

Time to get busy.

When she opened the little closet next to the bathroom, her breath caught in her throat. The charge nurse said the room had not been cleaned, but she didn't expect to see clothes. Auntie Freda's cardigan, a classic St. John boucle knit, was hanging up. What looked like slacks and a sweater were folded into a clear hospital bag on the floor of the closet. Instinctively, she pressed her face to the cardigan and immediately felt Freda's presence. Her scent—Chanel No. 5—permeated Camelia's senses. Tears filled Camelia's eyes.

Okay, pull yourself together. You've got work to do.

She hesitated a moment, then pulled the cardigan off the hanger, rolled it into a tight cylinder and crammed it into the bottom of her oversized handbag. It might be the only keepsake she would get, and Camelia didn't want the last thing Auntie Freda wore to end up in a donation pile.

Next, Camelia pushed open the trash can. There were a handful of tissues, a burned down votive candle, and several rubber gloves. She pushed against the lid on the biohazards container, but it was locked. Same with the sharps.

Dammit.

It was going to nag at her if she couldn't have a look. For what, she didn't know, but this is what people did when they were investigating, wasn't it? They looked at *everything*.

She stepped out of the room, into the hallway, and down to the nurse's station, where Gayle Germaine was writing notes in a chart.

"Okay, I know this is going to sound completely paranoid, but is there any way I can have a look at the biohazard and sharps waste in Freda's room?" she asked. At Gayle's sharp glare, she added, "I'm just trying to think like an insurance investigator, so I want to make sure I cover every possible contingency. Like, what if there was something in the trash from one of Auntie Freda's visitors that she was allergic to? They might use that as an excuse to deny the family's claim."

Gayle rolled her eyes and heaved a sigh. "Francine," Gayle said, "what's the pickup schedule for sharps and bio this week?"

The other nurse had answered the phone. She held up her index finger.

"As you can see, we're busy, so this might have to wait." Gayle seemed to take pleasure in delivering that news, even as Francine hung up the phone.

"No, it's okay, Gayle, I've got the email right here," Francine piped up. "Says all the sharps and bio were to be picked up yesterday, but with the blizzard and the holidays, we're looking at next week," she said.

"I guess that's good news," Camelia said. "Can I have a look?"

"God only knows what's in there. Probably just old bandages and IV trash. I don't think there will be anything useful," Gayle said, crossing her arms over her chest.

"Yeah, you're probably right. And I wouldn't even know what I was looking at. But I kinda feel like I need to turn over every rock, because if the insurance company doesn't pay out … well, it's going to be so difficult for the family."

There was a long pause as Gayle stared, blinking, at the clock. Camelia could see her mind turning almost as fast as the second hand.

"Well, come on then, let's get to it. I don't have all day. Gloves, please!" Gayle said, as if she might change her mind. She pulled fresh gloves from the bins at the end of the nursing station and marched down the hall to Freda's room.

"Pull the door shut," Gayle said, as she spread a blue surgical chuck on the floor. She used one of the keys jangling from a red wrist coil to unlock the biohazard bin. "Probably not much here, but let's have a look. And brace yourself, it might stink."

Gayle dumped the contents: gauze pads damp with rusty blood, a cough drop, used bandages, and some IV tubing. Camelia spotted the spent syringe at the same time as Gayle.

"What the hell is this doing in here?" Gayle said, her lips forming a thin line of disapproval. "This should be in the sharps bin! And this," Gayle said, holding a bit of IV tubing adhered to a translucent patch. "This isn't even ours. *Jesus.*"

She set the syringe and patch off to one side. The brand name *Duragesic* was printed in white letters across the thin, transparent material.

"I have to look at the chart again, because I don't recall Mrs. Swenson being on a patch," Gayle said.

"So, what is it?"

"It's fentanyl. Usually for advanced cancer patients. I can tell you right now, no one here prescribed this, and from what I saw, there was no need for this level of pain meds," she said, a look of puzzlement on her face, pushing her brow into a striation of concern. "In fact, we haven't used a patch on this ward for weeks."

"Yeah, but couldn't some other nurse have given Freda this?"

"As Charge Nurse, I sign off on controlled meds inventory, so I would know," Gayle said.

"Okaaaay … so what does that mean?" Camelia said.

"It means either Mrs. Swenson had the patch when she arrived, and it was later removed, or someone disposed of someone else's patch in this bin. Since this stuff is counted and controlled at every shift, I doubt if any of my staff would be stupid enough to just toss it without accounting for it. The other thing is, when we administer a patch, we write our initials and the date and time right on the patch. This patch wasn't applied here." Gayle's voice was confident.

"But the patch could have been prescribed by her doctor, right?" Camelia asked.

Her hands were sweating inside the latex gloves and her heart was tap dancing against her ribs.

What the hell is going on?

"Yes, but surely her daughter would have mentioned it . . . then again, sometimes family members don't know what they don't know."

"So, it's likely Auntie Freda was wearing this patch when she came into ER?"

"That would be my guess. Depending on where the patch was placed, and if no one gave ER a heads up, they wouldn't have known about it," Gayle said.

"Would it have shown up in her bloodwork?"

"Sure, if we were testing for opioids, which we weren't. Mrs. Swenson wasn't a pain patient as far as we knew, and she sure as heck wasn't a drug addict, was she?" Gayle said, sharply. She pushed her glasses up and stared at the little pile of waste in front of her, shaking her head. "What a hell of a thing."

"No kidding. I'm glad we looked, because if Freda had cancer or something … that could give the insurance company an out," Camelia said. "So … can I take this with me?"

Gayle looked at Camelia for a long moment.

"I'm just going to step out to the nurse's station. If someone happened to take the trash out, how would I know?" Gayle asked, raising her eyebrows. She looked from the pile on the floor to Camelia and back again. "Your copy of the chart will be at the desk. And be extremely careful because fentanyl can be deadly. Even just handling it … don't take your gloves off, and don't be long." Gayle moved quickly to the door and shut it behind her.

Camelia smiled to herself. Gayle was a reluctant ally against the fictional insurance company. She pulled out a handful of sandwich bags, placing the syringe and cough drop in separate bags. She held the patch up to the light. It was translucent and she could just make out a couple of smudges. She pulled out her cell phone and turned on the flashlight to get a better look.

Holy crap.

Fingerprints. She quickly tucked the patch in a sandwich bag. She wrapped the rest of the items in the blue chuck and stuffed it in the bottom of the trash bag, then tied the bag off in a triple knot and placed it beside the can. Housekeeping would pick it up when they cleaned the room.

No harm done.

With a warm copy of Freda's medical chart in her bag, along with everything else she'd gathered up, Camelia gushed her thanks to Gayle and Francine as she scribbled her name on the release forms as illegibly as possible. Just in case someone checked.

Camelia ran to the frigid car, breathless with cold by the time she got in. She willed the car to warm up as she panted steamy little clouds and her mind roiled with questions. She was surprised at how easy it was to get information—and evidence—from the hospital, just by naming a common enemy. But her heart was racing. Between improvising her role, lying through her teeth, and steeling herself against the nagging urge to have a drink, Camelia was winding up to a panic attack, which she could not afford right now. She leaned her forehead against the cold steering wheel and took slow, measured breaths.

Focus, focus, focus.

Camelia knew she was on the trail of … something. Did someone give Auntie Freda the wrong meds? The wrong dose? Who, besides the hospital, had access to hardcore pain meds and was willing to give them to Auntie Freda? Whose fingerprints were on that patch? Did that person, whoever it was, know it could kill her? Or was this just another stupid medical mistake?

As Byron always said, *doctors bury their mistakes, lawyers litigate them.*

But there was no burial. Only a hasty cremation. Camelia could feel the outline of something very wrong, but the details were fogged over, greyed out, not quite there. Yet.

33

Ashes to Ashes

December 27

As Camelia pulled out of the hospital parking lot, her phone dinged. Leon wanted to know if she was on her way home. She only wavered for a moment. She needed to find out what the mortuary knew and Springer Funeral Home was just a few blocks away. Maybe they could shed some light on Freda's condition when they retrieved her … remains.

It still doesn't feel real.

The thing that kept nagging Camelia was that Kenna, Mickey, and the mystery friend had all been with Freda immediately prior to her death. Byron would say that the three pillars—opportunity, motive, and means—all had to be in place. They all had opportunity. Kenna and Mickey certainly had motive—money. But the means? Auntie Freda likely died of a stroke. So how do you make that happen? And what about the friend? Who is she?

The car was just warming up by the time Camelia arrived at Springer Funeral Home and she dreaded stepping out into the freezing wind again. She paused in the warmth to text an excuse to Leon.

Be there soon – stopped for java

Camelia took a deep breath. This was probably a wild goose chase.

What the hell am I going to say?

For that matter, who was she even going to talk to? She steeled herself and tried to think of how Freda would manage it. And she knew. Freda would draw herself up to her full height, march inside, demand to see the owner, and then proceed to ask for, without explanation, what she wanted. All while flashing her toothy grin. That was her way. Imperious, entitled, and yet, somehow, knowing how to make it all seem like your privilege to serve her needs.

Camelia pulled open the heavy front door and took note of the plaque on the wall:

Joseph Alexander
Owner, Springer Funeral Home
Honorable Order of the Blue Goose
Most Loyal Gander, 2012

What is it with men and their secret animal clubs?

She stifled a laugh and squared her shoulders, taking a deep breath of over-warm air, tainted with an undertone of embalming fluid that could never be fully masked.

The young woman at the reception desk smiled.

"Good morning. Can I help you?"

"I'm here to see Joseph Alexander. He was a friend of Freda Swenson. It's personal," Camelia said, in her best Freda manner.

God I hope he's still alive.

She rested her handbag on the counter, making sure the designer badge was fully visible. It was a cheap move, but status symbols have a subconscious effect on people. A receptionist wouldn't earn enough in a month to buy such a bag, and Camelia knew from her litigation training that most people mistakenly equate wealth with knowledge and authority.

"Um, sure, yep. What's your name again? Ya wanna coffee or cuppa tea?" She spoke like a pure prairie farm girl.

"Camelia Belmont, niece of Freda Swenson. And no, thank you."

Camelia seated herself in one of the plush brown club chairs to wait. She needn't have. Within seconds, a distinguished, slightly-built man with silver temples and a runner's stride came purposefully down the hall.

"Ms. Belmont, Joe Alexander," he said, extending his hand. "I am *so* sorry for your loss. Freda was an old and dear friend and I'm just *terribly* sorry about losing her. She was such a pistol," he said, his voice polished from decades of talking to bereaved relatives.

"Thank you. May I have a moment in private?"

"Of course, please, come on through," he said and gestured for Camelia to go first, his palm up in an old-fashioned way.

Joe Alexander's office was paneled in blonde wood, with an antique partners' desk centered on a thick, navy blue Persian rug. Two dark leather club chairs faced the desk, behind which a Dorothy Knowles landscape of a rapeseed field in bloom dominated the wall, similar to the one hanging in Freda's dining room.

Impressive.

She sat, ramrod straight, and despite her snow boots, crossed her legs at the ankles, as Freda would have. She took a deep breath.

Help me Auntie! I need this guy's cooperation.

"So how can I be of assistance, Miz Belmont? Are you here to talk about a memorial service or …? " he asked, his long fingers templed against his chin.

"Please, just call me Camelia . . ."

"Oh, I remember now. You're the lawyer, from the U.S. Freda spoke of you in most glowing terms. She was proud of you, you know," Joe said. "But please, continue, I'm sorry for interrupting."

"Yep, that's me. But I'm not here as a lawyer (*lie*). And yes, at some point we will discuss a memorial, but not today. I don't even know if you can help, but the family has asked me to run this little errand (*lie*) to find out what we can and dispel any doubts before we present the claim to the life insurance company (*lie*)." Camelia swallowed. Joe nodded slowly, so she continued. "They're all such vultures, and Auntie Freda's death benefit is pretty big (*maybe a lie*), so we're worried the claim will be denied on any flimsy grounds they can come up with. We have the hospital chart, but they don't keep anything like blood samples after a person dies, so I'm just here to find out if your people kept anything. Anything at all, even in the trash or whatever, that might help us get ahead of any questions in advance of the insurance adjuster," she said.

I'm going to be a professional liar by the time this is over.

Joe Alexander's bushy silver eyebrows had risen as she talked and he resembled an owl, wise and curious. She half expected him to let out a whoooo.

"Well, of course I'm happy to help, but I don't think we would have anything useful. Kenna Shores called in the cremation from the hospital, on Christmas morning. I sent Mitch to manage it and he took care of the cremation right away, as requested. I don't think we'll have anything of any use to you, Miss. … Camelia," he said.

"I understand, but …," Camelia dabbed at her leaking eyes. "Sorry."

"Yes, yes, well, Mitch is the only person who might have any information, but it's his day off," Joe said, his eyes carefully mapping Camelia's face. He seemed to be struggling with something. "Camelia, are you aware of your aunt's last wishes?" he asked abruptly.

"Well, um, no, not really. I mean, I know she had a will and such, and we always knew she would be buried in the National Cemetery with Uncle Geoffrey, but she didn't share the details. At least not with me. I think Kenna has a copy of the will because she lived with Auntie Freda for the past couple of years, so she would be the one …" Camelia's voice trailed off.

What is he getting at?

"I see. Well, I'm sure it's nothing, but you know, I knew your aunt for practically my whole life. That's how it is in a small city like this. You run in the same circles and know the same people. I was pretty surprised when

Kenna requested immediate cremation and no services. She said it was a Viking send off and Freda had to be cremated within 24 hours post-mortem," he said, shaking his head. "Have you ever heard of such a thing? That is *not* the Freda I knew. For one thing, Freda's a lifelong Catholic. She was very much a fan of the pomp and circumstance," Joe said.

Camelia could see he was as uncomfortable with the cremation as the rest of them. "A Viking send off? What do you think that means?"

"I wish I knew! But with Miz Shores being the Personal Representative, we had no choice in the matter, you understand."

"It's so confusing. Auntie Freda was not a Viking. I mean, she married one. Uncle Geoffrey was Swedish, but Auntie Freda was Greco-Italian. None of us know anything about this Viking funeral. Except Kenna, I guess," Camelia said.

"Hmmm, it's odd, isn't it? Anyway, Mitch will be back to work tomorrow if you want to come back then," he said.

Camelia knew her face revealed her disappointment. "I'm a bit desperate to make sure I recover anything of Freda's. No offense to your Blue Goose friends, but you know, the damned insurance adjusters … I don't want to fail on my *one little mission* here," she said. She pushed the tissue to her eyes.

"We have clients and we have friends. Freda was my *friend.* What exactly do you *think* is going on?" he asked.

"Oh god, I don't even know. That's why I'm running around trying to find out if there was any cause for Freda to die besides *natural* causes. I mean, did she have a stroke or a heart attack or was it cancer or something else? We just don't know. She wasn't in the hospital long enough for them to diagnose her … condition."

"But what would we have that the hospital doesn't have?"

"Clothing, medication, stuff like that I guess? I don't even know what the adjusters will be looking at, but I know they'll be looking for some underlying cause of death so they can deny the claim. It's a lot of money, so …"

"My dear, Dr. Fitzgerald said Freda died of natural causes, and if he said so, there is likely *nothing* underlying the cause of death other than old age," he said, compassion coating his words.

"I know, but …" Camelia nodded. She could sense an undercurrent in Joe's words. Was it grief over Freda's death or remorse over the cremation? Her head pounded. The thirst was almost intolerable.

"I wish I had been here to help Miz Shores, but it was Christmas morning. Let's call Mitch and see if he can shed any light. It's his day off but I'm pretty sure he's on the sofa watching hockey," Joe said, picking up the phone and dialing as he spoke.

"Hey Mitch, Joe here. Sorry to bother you on your day off, but one of Freda Swenson's relatives is here and she's following up about Mrs. Swenson's demise. Do you mind?" It wasn't a question.

Joe passed the cordless receiver to Camelia and she took it, her hand trembling as she gripped the receiver and repeated her story to Mitch.

"Did you happen to find anything on or with Mrs. Swenson's body prior to cremation?" Camelia asked.

There was a long pause and she could hear him dragging on a cigarette.

"You know, Miss Shores asked that she be cremated with nothing other than her bible, which was easy because she was in a hospital gown. There weren't any other clothes to remove. We always check for jewelry or things that might be um … explosive or melt or somehow damage the … you know . . . the cremation machine," he said.

She knew he was avoiding the word "oven" even though that was the best description. He took another couple of drags on his cigarette.

"Did you remove anything?"

"I mean, I took a couple of bandages off, but other than that, she was au naturel, if you understand," he continued.

Camelia now took her own deep breath, wishing she had a cigarette too. "What kind of bandages, Mitch?" she asked, carefully, as if the question itself would destroy the evidence.

"Just bandages, like from an IV. Oh, and a medication patch. We always remove that stuff. Leaves a residue," he said.

Bingo.

"Do you have a normal place to dispose of that kind of thing?" Camelia asked.

"Yep, for sure. Everything that comes off a client that doesn't go to the family goes in the burn bin. We destroy all that stuff so no one gets infected or whatever," he said.

Camelia heard a lighter and another long inhale. He was chain smoking and it made her itch for a cigarette even though she'd quit ages ago.

"Thank you so much, Mitch. I really appreciate your help today and have a good holiday," Camelia said, handing the phone back to Joe. He spoke briefly to Mitch and hung up.

"So, it sounds like Mitch didn't really find anything of any use. I don't know that we have anything here that can help you, Camelia," he said.

"Well, I think Mitch was very helpful. He said he removed a medical patch from Auntie Freda's … body … and I wonder if it might still be around somewhere, like the burn bin he mentioned." She smiled and looked at Joe hopefully, her eyes searching his for a glimmer of relenting.

He sighed and pressed his lips together, his unblinking eyes focused on Camelia's.

"You're an awful lot like your aunt, you know," he said, barely suppressing a smile. "Alright. Come with me, let's put this to rest," he said, and walked out of the office with Camelia close behind.

As they entered a heavy door marked Staff Only, the smell of embalming fluid immediately overwhelmed Camelia. Joe didn't seem to notice. He led the way down a corridor to another heavy door, glancing back to make sure she was with him.

"This is *never* done, you understand, but for Freda …"

Camelia placed her right hand in the air. "I understand and this is just between us," she assured him. "Scout's honor."

He nodded, seemingly grateful for her promise.

The cremation room was smaller and more cramped than Camelia had expected, but then she realized a larger room was adjacent, where the family would send their loved one off without seeing the actual mechanics of it all. The room was tiled to waist height in a stark white, the walls above painted a pale institutional blue.

She didn't want to actually look at the crematorium, the oven, the agent of reducing people—*ashes to ashes, dust to dust*—but she couldn't help it. The enormous stainless steel machine dominated the room. A narrow stainless steel prep table was to one side, gleaming in the fluorescent lighting. Nearby, a small counter and sink sat atop drawers that Camelia imagined contained instruments of torture or god knows what.

An industrial waste bin in bright blue punctuated the space. Stenciled on the side was "Burn Bin." Her impulse was to rush over and dump it on the floor, but she had to let Joe do the honors. He was the boss here.

He gestured, "Here's what you're looking for, but I honestly don't know if you'll find anything inside. Freda was cremated two days ago and it's possible the bin's been managed," he said, and his voice softened. "But let's have a look, shall we?"

He lifted the lid a crack and peeked inside. "Not much here, but you're welcome to see if this is what you're after," he said.

Camelia propped the lid open but she couldn't reach the bottom of the bin. "Can we dump it out so I can have a better look?"

Joe nodded and grabbed a plastic sheet from the cabinet, spreading it on the floor. "Just in case," he said.

He didn't need to say just in case what. Joe was a fastidious man and Camelia knew that dumpster diving was far below his pay grade. She felt a pang of shame for having demanded this, but then thought of her aunt.

What Would Freda Do? Freda would not let a bit of squeamishness get in her way.

She scanned the contents of the bin.

There it was. A patch: a clear, innocuous looking piece of latex.

Camelia felt the heat rising on her face. These patches could have killed Auntie Freda. If what Gayle Germaine said was true, she could have overdosed just by touching it. If Freda didn't have some hidden ailment that required fentanyl, she could have easily died from not one, but two patches.

So maybe Auntie Freda didn't suffer from a failure of old age. Maybe it wasn't a vessel bursting in her brain, pumping blood into her skull in a flood of devastation.

This little patch could be the killer. But who? And why?

Who had access to this much fentanyl and who would have set out to use it on Auntie Freda? Did she have cancer? It would be uncharacteristic for Auntie Freda to keep that kind of information to herself. She certainly never had before.

Camelia did a mental inventory: four rubber gloves; one medical patch; a dozen or so large gauze swabs that smelled like alcohol; one cough drop; some paper towels; three bandages with white tape; and a balled up piece of paper.

She pulled a Ziploc bag from her purse and stepped to the latex glove dispenser on the wall.

"May I?" she asked. Joe nodded.

It felt official to be snapping on gloves and rooting through the trash in the back room of a crematorium with Joe looking on, his face arranged in professional impassivity that could mean anything. For all she knew he was making a grocery list in his head. He watched her putting the fentanyl patch in a bag, then she grabbed the ball of paper. She began to smooth it when Joe moved swiftly to her side and put his hand over hers. It was a subtle, but authoritative move. It said, *this paper is mine.*

"Camelia, you understand, this might be private, regarding another client," he said, gently prying the paper from her hand.

He turned away and opened the crumpled paper. It turned out to be notes jotted by Mitch regarding Freda's cremation, which Joe handed back to Camelia with an apologetic smile.

"I'm the cautious type," he said.

"Well of course you are and rightly so," she responded. "I so appreciate a man who takes his work seriously," she continued, placing her hand gently on his forearm. "You're a true professional and I admire that," she said, conspiratorially. Camelia knew how to sway a jury, even a jury of one.

Trying to contain her eagerness, she quickly absorbed the contents of the wrinkled page.

SWENSEN
Daughter Kenna Shores
85 yo female dec @ hosp
No clothing
No jewelry
No pacemaker
Hosp gown removed
Rx patch removed
Lozenge removed
PR docs @ cremains pick up
Body prepped for immediate incin
Release signed
Ashes to be urned
MDS

Camelia read the list again, as if the answer were hidden in those few words.

"Joe, what does this mean? *PR docs @ cremains pickup?"*

"Let me see that," he said, reaching for the list. "Good grief. Well, what it means is that Miz Shores didn't bring her Personal Representative documents with her. I'll have to have a word with Mitch about that, as it's our policy to get documents in advance of *any* action by *any* family member. It keeps us out of squabbles, which I'm sure you, as a lawyer, can understand."

Her excitement over finding a potential murder weapon gave way to rage. So Kenna had Auntie Freda cremated with no proof of her legal authority. None of these patches had anything written on them, which the Charge Nurse, Gayle Germaine, claimed was standard procedure. So where did these patches come from? Medical error? Maybe. Purposeful overdose? More likely.

How dare someone do this to Auntie Freda?

"And what about this? It says lozenge removed. Does that make sense to you?"

Joe glanced at the list and back to the trash on the floor. "I hate to be indelicate, but when we prepare the deceased for a final viewing, it includes washing the face and cleaning the mouth. Prior to positioning the body, just as a matter of course. People often have medical items left on or in their orifices at the time of death. Freda apparently died with a lozenge in her mouth, which is fairly common. Patients often have a dry mouth ..." Joe said. He fidgeted with the button on his jacket.

Camelia bent and picked up the lozenge, and stowed it in a sandwich bag. She pulled off her gloves and squeezed Joe's arm. "You sir, are a good friend, and I know Auntie Freda—and all of us, to be honest—are so grateful for your kindness and prompt attention during a very difficult time in our lives. Please know that I will not forget this service to our family," Camelia said.

"Don't thank me just yet. I can't let you leave with that patch. That's a controlled substance," Joe said.

Camelia looked from the bag in her hand to Joe's face and back again. She straightened her back.

"I think these meds are an important part of figuring out if the insurance company has grounds to deny our claim, don't you? I mean, what do you think I would do with it? I'm happy to sign a release or whatever, but I'm taking it with me," Camelia said.

Joe's face registered surprise. Camelia guessed he wasn't accustomed to having a woman talk to him like this.

"But ... it's the law. I would have to report it."

"Isn't it also the law that you need a PR form in order to cremate a body?" Camelia stared at Joe, then began walking to the door. "Besides, what are you going to report? I'm just a family member picking up my aunt's medication from the funeral home. Nothing more."

Joe Alexander ran one bony hand over his tie.

"You'll sign for it, then?"

Camelia walked out of Springer, her designer bag slung over her shoulder, heavy with evidence that could prove Freda's death was anything but natural.

Goddammit I need a drink.

It wasn't until she got in the car that she fully realized the implication of Mitch's list.

PR docs to be delivered when ashes picked up.

Kenna had gotten away with having Auntie Freda cremated without proof of her authority. But why? When she had been so organized with everything else, why wouldn't Kenna have brought a copy of the *one thing* she knew she would need—the document appointing her as personal representative?

34

THE GOOGLE SLEUTH

DECEMBER 27

Camelia returned to a blissfully warm, silent house. Sophie and Steve had gone to a friend's, and Leon was sprawled on the bed taking a nap. The cloudy sky cast a faint, gray glow over the living room where Camelia huddled by the fireplace, wishing she could justify a tall vodka soda. Her head pounded. Maybe just a nip?

Holiday drinking hours apply, and it's 5 o'clock somewhere!

She tiptoed to the kitchen and splashed some vodka in a cup, topping it with cranberry juice. After the first gulp, she drained the glass.

Dry January. For real.

She went back to her corner of the sofa by the fire. In her mind, a tangle of disconnected ideas formed a Gordian knot. Auntie Freda was an elderly woman. A host of things could have gone wrong. Even so, the niggling wouldn't stop. Did Auntie Freda pass peacefully in her sleep, as everyone said, or did someone shove her into the abyss? Why did Auntie Freda's death feel so … off? Sure, Kenna was acting weirder than usual and Camelia had run across some unexplained medication, but so what?

By initiating that quickie cremation, Kenna put herself in this somehow. She was Auntie Freda's so-called caregiver, lived with her, and had plenty of opportunity if she wanted to accelerate her inheritance.

But what was her motive?

Kenna was living a good life under her mother's roof, with minimal expense and almost no responsibilities. She had it all, or so it seemed. And if Kenna was involved, then Mickey had to be in on it, because mother and son were like two rotten peas in a pod.

And what about the mystery visitor?

The nurses on duty?

Dr. Fitzgerald?

Maybe one of them was the culprit. If there even *was* a culprit.

And what if something nefarious *had* happened?

What difference would it make?

Nothing she did would bring Auntie Freda back.

But that wasn't the point, and Camelia knew it.

She couldn't help herself. Three decades of law practice made her mind snap to attention at any whiff of wrong-doing. And justice—that thing she always said she'd devoted her life's work to—demanded *action*, not just lip service.

Her thoughts drifted to her earliest memory of Auntie Freda. She must have been six or seven years old, terrified of the imposing woman standing on the front steps of that enormous house. It was the kind of thing kids had nightmares about, being dropped off in the middle of the night with a veritable stranger.

Her mother had whispered in her ear, "Behave yourself. I'll be back in a week. S*he's not as mean as she looks.*"

She'd shoved Camelia in Freda's direction before driving off into the darkness. Freda had taken Camelia's small, cold hand and dragged her inside, to the kitchen, where the warm scent of hot chocolate instantly perked her up. Fortified with cocoa, Freda carried Camelia upstairs, tucked her into her own massive bed and stroked her hair until she fell asleep. It wouldn't be the last time Camelia found refuge in Freda's home.

There were so many reasons her beloved Auntie Freda should not have died alone. She may have died of a stroke. Or natural causes. Or she may have died from an overdose, or an allergic reaction. Or maybe it was something even more sinister? But regardless of what the truth turned out to be, Freda deserved the honor of a close look. And if it turned out something had happened to Auntie Freda—by mistake or on purpose—justice required a cold appraisal of the facts; no favoritism, no bias. *Everyone* was a suspect.

Was she up to it? She'd only spent a couple of hours running after the facts, and she was already exhausted. And what did she have to show for it? She thought about the little baggies in her handbag.

I have to think like Byron. I have to look for the little inconsistencies.

Camelia started a list of her theories and all the information she would need to confirm the cause of death. There were really only three options. Camelia flipped to a fresh page and wrote:

1) natural causes: stroke, heart attack, aneurysm

2) accidental death: medical error, overdose;

3) intentional death: overdose, or …?

Freda's death pointed to stroke, heart attack, aneurysm, or—based on those fentanyl patches—a possible overdose. But without even a sample of her blood, how would Camelia ever find out the truth? She opened her iPad and started searching. She read about the symptoms of stroke, heart attack, and aneurysm, then moved on to overdose. Those fentanyl patches … Auntie Freda could have overdosed accidentally. Or not so accidentally.

One search led to another, and before she knew it, Camelia was down a rabbit hole of criminal investigation. As she scrolled through pages of hits, key elements jumped out at her.

"If a killer can conceal the DNA of the victim and killer, it's a perfect crime."

Okay, that's not helpful because they're all family members and their fingerprints have been all over Auntie Freda's house for decades.

"Murderers commonly target vulnerable populations."

Auntie Freda was elderly but vulnerable? Not likely. Demanding was more accurate. She did not suffer fools.

"Look for behavioral evidence … hate or anger, lust or jealousy, fear or insecurity, entitlement."

Now we're getting somewhere.

Hate or anger.

Could be anyone, but Kenna is Suspect Number One because they lived together. Familiarity breeds contempt, and who else would hate Freda enough to want her dead? Who else was angry with Freda?

Lust or jealousy. *That seems remote given Auntie Freda's age and her new fiancé, but maybe Arthur is some kinda possessive perv?*

Fear or insecurity. *Kenna? Arthur?*

Entitlement. *Mickey, Suyin, Kenna, who else?*

Camelia kept scrolling, skimming an article on evidence gathering. Auntie Freda was at the hospital when she died, so there wasn't much evidence to gather. She was sure she'd already done as much as possible.

Camelia wrote bold headings on fresh sheets of paper.

Incident.

Evidence.

Pool of suspects.

Testimony.

Hypothesis.

She had to connect motive, opportunity, and means. Given the evidence, pool of suspects, and testimony, what was her hypothesis of who perpetrated the incident? Isn't this where Byron would start? Camelia didn't dare call him given their recent tensions, but she wanted to. She wanted to hear the authority of his experience guiding her in how to proceed. But hadn't she observed enough around the firm to get the gist of it?

If she were truly investigating, she would be looking at browser histories, cell phone records, email threads, social media posts, recent destinations in phone and car GPS nav systems. Other than the social media posts, there's no way she could get access to any of those important pieces of evidence.

Then again, Kenna was sloppy. Camelia walked through Auntie Freda's house in her mind. If Kenna were in the living room, she could easily snoop around Freda's bedroom to see if she had fentanyl or other medications that would point to a life-threatening illness.

She could get away with it, if someone was there to distract Kenna.

Like Sophie.

Just a quick visit would be all she needed.

Camelia placed an online order at Sweetie Pies for pick up the next day at noon.

Just a little something to open the door to Freda's house and Kenna's heart.

35

HOT DISH, COLD HEART

DECEMBER 28

"Leon, Sophie and I are picking up a mac 'n' cheese casserole to take over to Kenna. We won't be long. Need anything while we're out?" Camelia said.

While Leon gave a little smirk at Camelia's sudden interest in being a good cousin, he didn't protest. He knew the protocol. When death arrives, bring a hot dish.

"Yeah. Don't forget to pick one up for us," he said, gesturing at Steve.

"Yum!" Steve rubbed his belly. "And bring cinnamon buns," Steve added, grinning.

It was clear neither Leon nor Steve were interested in doing a grief visit, particularly with Kenna.

"I swear, you two eat like toddlers," Camelia said, laughing.

"Drive safe," Leon added, giving Camelia a peck on the cheek.

Sophie balanced the warm casserole of ham, broccoli, macaroni, and cheddar they'd just picked up from Sweetie Pies on her lap while Camelia drove.

"This smells so good I want to eat it right now," she said.

"Hopefully Kenna will have the same reaction. Now, I brought you along for a reason. Here's what I need you to do. I'm gonna excuse myself for a phone call. Keep Kenna eating and talking while I'm upstairs. When I get back, I'll keep her company so you can go through Kenna's bedroom and bathroom. Look for anything that looks like medication patches. The brand is Duragesic and they look just like clear bandages. While you're there, take something—something she won't notice—that will have her fingerprints. I've got a handful of sandwich bags for you. Whatever you take, put it in a bag and seal it up," Camelia said.

"Oh, Mum. Are you sure we should be snooping? This is like straight out of a movie. What if I get caught?" Sophie said.

"If you get caught, just start crying and say you felt Auntie Freda's spirit. That should shut Kenna up," Camelia said.

"But what if I *do* feel Auntie Freda's spirit? That's gonna shut me up, too!" Sophie said, smiling mischievously.

"Okay Trouble Maker, let's just stick to our plan, okay?"

As she pulled into Freda's driveway, Camelia's throat tightened with tears. This was going to be hard to pull off when she was fighting back a wave of grief along with a ball of anxiety lodged in her gut.

They walked up the icy sidewalk, a steady wind pushing against them and freezing their breath. Kenna was visible through the big bay window, curled on the sofa. Camelia waved and saw a grimace dash across Kenna's face before she plastered a smile in its place. She met them at the door.

"Hey there, Cam, Sophie, what's the occasion?" Kenna said, already slurring even though it was barely noon.

Camelia pushed past Kenna into the entry hall. "The occasion, my dear, is that your Mum is gone, and we need to take care of each other," she said.

"We brought a delicious mac 'n' cheese casserole from Sweetie Pies, Auntie Kenna. It's still warm, so if you haven't had lunch yet …" Sophie held up the distinctive carry-out bag as proof.

"Oh my god, you guys, you didn't need to do that," Kenna said, her eyes tearing up.

Camelia felt a pang of guilt for suspecting Kenna of wrongdoing.

What if I'm wrong?

But *if* she were wrong, that was actually a good thing, because it meant Kenna didn't have a hand in Auntie Freda's death. She blew out a puff of air and put on her most sympathetic expression.

"How're you doing? Are Rita and Dave around?"

Kenna shivered. "Come on to the front room, I've got a fire going. It's cold as hell out here," Kenna said as she walked to the living room. "And no, Rita and Dave went out Lumsden way to see the Hubbards. You know Dave. He knows every farm family from here to Saskatoon and can't wait to go reminisce over old times," she said, rolling her eyes.

"Oh, that's too bad. Would have loved to see them today, but we'll catch up later. We're just worried about all of you," Camelia said.

"Auntie Kenna, looks like you were cozy on the couch, so snuggle back in and I'll get you a tray and be right back. After all you've been through … it's the least we can do," Sophie said.

Camelia had to suppress a snort of laughter. Sophie could lay on the fawning. It was a bit disconcerting to see how genuinely she seemed to be doting on Kenna, even though Camelia knew Sophie wasn't at all fond of her or Mickey.

Duly noted. My daughter is a big faker.

Sophie headed off to the kitchen with the bag of food while Camelia settled into Freda's favorite chair.

"If you don't mind, while you're up, can you pour me another rye and DC?" Kenna called out.

"I'll get it," Camelia said, and grabbed Kenna's cup as she headed to the kitchen.

Sophie arranged a tray with a large bowl of steaming mac 'n' cheese while Camelia filled Kenna's Big Gulp cup with rye and Diet Coke, squeezing a bit of fresh lime into the glass.

"You go ahead," Camelia said.

Sophie gave her a big-eyed grimace, then broke into a sunny smile. "Lunch is served, Auntie Kenna," she said as she walked to the living room.

Camelia waited a beat, then popped her head into the living room.

"Here's your cocktail, Kenna. Bear with me for a minute. I have to call my boss back. You guys dig in and I'll be right back," Camelia said, making eye contact with Sophie.

"Shit, you're working? Aren't you on holiday?" Kenna asked, talking around a mouthful of food.

"I'm supposed to be! But when the boss calls, I have to answer," Camelia said. "I'll just pull the door shut to keep the heat in."

She closed the door behind her, and grabbed her handbag as she passed through the central hall. Camelia quickly climbed the broad staircase, the heavy carpet muffling her steps. When she reached the top, she turned towards Freda's bedroom. Camelia had been swept up in her amateur sleuthing, but now the reality of Freda's death hit her again, hard. Tears burned in her eyes, and her nose began to drip.

Dammit. Not now. This is no time to break down.

She took a deep, shuddering breath and pushed the door to Freda's bedroom open. It was exactly as she remembered, and she had to stifle a sob with her fist.

Quarter-sawn oak planks, the grain deepened by a century of patina, gleamed in the dim light. The oak wainscoting was inset with what Camelia thought of as bordello wallpaper: burgundy red with a narrow, pale cream stripe. The ornate fireplace was cold. Freda's massive four-poster bed was sloppily made, a thick wool blanket had drifted to the floor, and the pillows were all bunched to one side. Freda's housekeeper, Naomi, would surely have made up the bed, had she been around.

So where is Naomi?

Camelia scanned the room, trying to think like a TV investigator, since that's about all she had as a reference. No doubt Byron would have some brilliant insight, but she couldn't ask. Not until she had redeemed herself in his eyes, and that hadn't happened. Yet. She shook her head.

This isn't about me. This is about Freda. Where are the inconsistencies?

She held her hands beside her eyes like horse blinders, blocking her peripheral vision. Starting at the far corner near the ceiling, Camelia swept her eyes across her field of vision for anything that looked out of place. She'd learned this trick from a realtor: to overcome blind spots, to see your house like everyone else does, focus on small bits instead of the whole room. Everything looked normal, other than the unmade bed.

Freda's study—converted from its original purpose as a nursery—was beyond her bedroom, far removed from the living room, so Kenna wouldn't hear her creeping around if Sophie kept up the chatter. Through a set of French doors, Freda's writing desk and a small Tiffany lamp were tucked under a bay window. The desk top was tidy, uncluttered, and held only a blank note pad, a couple of pens, and a card from Arthur that read, "Lady in Red -- You look wonderful tonight."

Awww. He's one of those mushy guys.

An old oak barrister's chair with a leather seat was parked at Freda's desk, so Camelia sat and gently opened drawers. Pens, cards, stamps, fresh envelopes and blank card stock, engraved with Freda's monogram. A small address book got tucked in Camelia's handbag. In the lower right drawer, underneath a pile of new Christmas cards, she found treasure: a folder containing papers with handwritten notes and a sealed envelope that proclaimed, in Freda's hand, Last Will and Testament of Freda Swenson. She didn't have time to inspect any of it, so Camelia shoved the entire folder to the bottom of her handbag. She flipped through the files in the lower left drawer: household bills, receipts for services, letters from relatives, and at the very back, a folder of old photographs and papers. Camelia looked at her watch. She'd been upstairs for six minutes.

As she tiptoed to Freda's ensuite bathroom, her phone rang. Camelia frantically fumbled in her handbag, grabbing her phone to turn off the ringer.

Shitshitshit.

She was supposed to be *on* a call, not *receiving* a call. Did Kenna hear the phone ring? She froze in place, holding her breath, listening. The sound of Sophie and Kenna talking was no more than a faint murmur. Camelia exhaled, silenced her phone, and tucked it in her pocket.

This detective stuff is nerve wracking.

Other than the bronze fixtures and mirror frames, the entire bathroom was shades of white, including Freda's robe. It was all very feminine and clean.

Just like Auntie Freda.

Camelia could smell her perfume in the air. A brass tray held cosmetics, hairspray, brushes and combs, and a variety of pill bottles. She quickly scanned the labels: amlodipine for blood pressure; prescription strength ibuprofen; a reflux medication. In the medicine cabinet, there were the usual things: toothpaste, toothbrush, eye drops, mouthwash, Tylenol, Tums, a box each of BandAids and Salonpas patches. Most important, there was no sign of fentanyl or other medication that would indicate a serious health problem.

Camelia had been gone almost 10 minutes. She noisily hustled back downstairs, and flung open the living room door.

"You know, you'd think that when your boss *knows* you're on vacation with your family he would make it quick, but that's not Byron's way. Sorry about that. Just another glamorous day in the life of a lawyer," Camelia said, the words rushing out to cover for her nervousness. "Hey, any casserole left?" she grinned.

"Tons left and I made a bowl for you. I'll be back. I have to pee like crazy," Sophie said, heading for the stairs.

"Hey, you can use the powder room if you don't want to climb the stairs," Kenna said, slurping her cocktail.

"Nah, that's okay, I'm used to climbing stairs ten times a day at work and I could use the exercise after all that food yesterday," Sophie said, smiling broadly.

Camelia picked at the casserole.

"So, Kenna, how are you doing?"

"I guess I'm as well as I can be given that my body is in constant pain from the accident and all the surgeries," Kenna said. "And now that Mum is gone … there's so much to do."

"I'm sorry. It's gotta be rough. Are you guys gonna have Auntie Freda's services right away?" Camelia said.

"No, Mum didn't want any services. 'No fuss' she told me. But I might do a celebration of life thing in the spring," she said, holding out her bowl to Camelia. "I'd take seconds if you don't mind."

"Oh, sure, I can get that for you," Camelia said, heading to the kitchen. She took a deep breath to tamp down a flare of resentment at Kenna's sense of entitlement. She was her mother's daughter, after all. As Camelia scooped out another helping of mac 'n' cheese, she heard a faint ding and glanced over at the kitchen desk.

Camelia knew she shouldn't … but what would Freda do? She smiled to herself. Auntie Freda would just barge right in. And isn't this what criminal attorneys like Byron did? Poke around in other people's stuff in the pursuit of justice?

It was the Royal Bank of Canada page, open to a message.

TO: KENNA A. SHORES
FROM: RBC Royal Bank
SUBJECT: Your account is overdrawn!
DATE: 27 December 2015 01:27

The following account(s) are overdrawn and your immediate attention is needed.

- Account 08271-8883450

Click here to view your account statement online.
If you require assistance, please contact us at 1-800-796-5522.
Thank you.

There's a big fat motive. But how could Kenna be out of money?

Camelia needed a minute to sort this out. She could almost hear Byron's voice in her ear.

Every piece of evidence is relevant, until proven otherwise.

She pulled her phone out of her pocket and snapped a photo. She didn't know what it meant in the scheme of things, other than proof Kenna could have had a financial motive for … what? It didn't even prove Auntie Freda was killed. All this proved was Kenna couldn't manage her money.

Camelia could feel a headache coming on from the pressure of sneaking around, lying through her teeth and—worst of all—trying not to drink through her grief. Kenna's bottle of rye was on the counter. Camelia waffled back and forth in her mind for a split second before tipping the bottle back for a long drink. The burn was reassuring. It warmed a cold spot inside and calmed her rattled nerves, until a momentary flash of insight hit her in the gut.

Jesus. I'm no better than Kenna, slugging off the bottle in the middle of the day.

She shook her head. Of course that wasn't true. Camelia wasn't lying on her mother's sofa all day, drinking herself into oblivion. But the recognition of their similar weakness allowed her to give Kenna a genuine smile as she returned to the living room.

"Here you go, Kenna! That Darlene, she sure knows how to keep our bellies full, huh?"

"I love her cinnamon rolls. To die for. And her Nanaimo bars. And, just about everything else," Kenna said, around a mouthful of macaroni.

"Then you'll be happy to know there's a little treat tucked in the fridge for later," Camelia said. "And, not to change the subject, but I just want to confirm we're supposed to meet at the lawyer's office on the 31st, right? That's still a go?" Camelia asked.

"Yep. Luckily, Bob was able to clear his calendar for us. It just makes sense to have the reading of the will while everyone's in town, so we can move on," Kenna said.

"I guess so. And then the real work begins," Camelia said, looking around the room. "Have you thought about where you'll live?"

"What makes you think I'm going anywhere?" Kenna asked.

Was it anger that made her eyes narrow and her cheeks redden, or was it the alcohol? Camelia couldn't be sure, and either—or both—was possible.

"Oh, no reason. I just assumed you'd want to downsize given how huge this old place is," Camelia said.

"Well, I gotta live somewhere, but yeah, this house is past its prime. Who knows? I might move closer to Mickey, or I might get a condo downtown. I haven't had a chance to really figure anything out. It's only been a couple of days ..." Kenna's voice trailed off and her eyes filled with tears.

"Of course. There's plenty of time for all the decisions that have to be made."

"You know how Mum was. I'm sure she has everything nicely buttoned up, so I'm not really worried about it. Plus, there's Bob. He'll make sure it's a smooth transition," Kenna said.

"But you're the Personal Representative, right? So that means following up on Auntie Freda's directives will be up to you."

Kenna was shoveling another forkful in her mouth. When she finished chewing, she took a long drink of her rye and DC. She seemed to be considering her words.

"As far as I know, I'm Mum's executor. At least that's what she told me," Kenna said.

Why would she lie about something so easily disproven? Camelia could hear the lie in her words, but she also noted the equivocation: *as far as I know ... that's what she told me.* Typical Fucking Kenna. Camelia was itching to cross examine her.

"As Freda's Personal Representative, you should have some paperwork, an acknowledgement or something like that. Not sure what they call it in Saskatchewan, but a form stating that you're the PR. Do you have that?" Camelia asked.

"It's around here somewhere," Kenna said, not looking up.

"Well, you must have it, because you were able to get Springer to do the cremation. Surely they asked for your authority?"

Kenna's mouth twitched down and her eyes narrowed. "What's it to you? This really isn't any of your business, Cam."

"No, I get that. It's just … as the lawyer in the family, I'm just trying to be helpful, Ken, so you don't get in trouble …" Camelia said.

"Trouble for what? Taking care of my mother through her death and last wishes?" Kenna said.

Camelia could see she was pushing too hard, making Kenna defensive. That's not how to encourage a witness. She switched gears.

"Good point! I mean, you were the one who *finally* noticed Auntie Freda was sick, when no one else did. And that says a *lot* about you, as a caregiver. I'm sure Auntie Freda confided everything to you, since you two were so close. Was something going on with her health that she didn't share with the rest of us?" Camelia asked.

"Cam, Mum was old. She had a stroke and died. At her age, these things happen all the time."

Camelia saw the opening and pushed it wide open.

"Sure, of course. It's just … you told me to ask the hospital for details, so I did. And now I'm wondering why Freda needed fentanyl," Camelia said.

"What the hell are you talking about? What fentanyl?"

"You know, the patches."

Kenna's cheeks were already flushed, but it seemed to Camelia that the color deepened.

"I don't know what you're talking about. Mum didn't … who told you Mum was taking fentanyl?" Kenna's voice held an edge, but of what? Was it fear? Anger?

"The nurse at the hospital. She didn't seem to know anything about the fentanyl patches either, so I thought surely you would know, but apparently not," Camelia said, with a shrug. She couldn't push too hard, or Kenna would turn on her. "Anyway, we need to go. Leon will be wondering where his lunch is. Sophie?"

"I'm in here, cleaning up the kitchen," Sophie responded. "Ready to go when you are!"

"One less worry for Naomi, right?" Camelia said, as Kenna eyed her.

"Yeah, she gets pissy if the house isn't already clean when she shows up," Kenna said. "Yet another thing I have to manage. Naomi will be back next week, but that doesn't help me now." She closed her eyes, shook her head, and heaved a sigh. "Everything is on *me* now that Mum up and died."

Camelia didn't know how to respond without having it out with Kenna, so she called out to Sophie. Kenna didn't bother to get up as they layered on parkas, scarves, boots, and gloves.

"Let us know if you need anything!" Camelia called over her shoulder as Kenna waved from her spot on the sofa.

In the car, Camelia let out a long exhale.

"So? Any luck?" Camelia asked.

"Mission accomplished," Sophie said.

36

Partners In Crime

December 28

As they pulled out of Auntie Freda's driveway and onto the street, Camelia asked again, "So? What did you find?"

"I found some things. Things you might find mildly curious." Sophie wiggled her eyebrows. "Get this. A box of little packets, like those wipes you get with takeout, labeled … hang on" Sophie said, scrolling through her phone. "Duragesic fentanyl. That's what you're looking for, right?"

"Holy shit, Sophie, yes, that's *exactly* what I was looking for. Anything else?"

"Yep. There's a prescription bottle with Auntie Freda's name on it for oxycodone. There were only a few tablets left. I took a pic of the label. And I grabbed an old compact for fingerprints," Sophie said.

"Very good work, Inspector Sophie. So riddle me this: why did Freda need oxy and why would her prescription be in Kenna's room?"

"No idea," Sophie said. "And there was mail on Kenna's nightstand so I took pictures. Just bills, but one was from a mail order pharmacy in the U.S."

"Seems odd for Kenna to be ordering meds from the States when she has free healthcare, but then again, addicts do that. They sprinkle their scripts all over the place so no one knows they're doubling up. Maybe Kenna's worse off than I thought," Camelia said.

"Well, given some of the people you work with, you oughtta know. Anything interesting in Auntie Freda's room?"

"I didn't see anything out of place and Freda's bathroom was … normal. Just blood pressure meds and the usual Band-Aids and stuff," Camelia said. "Nothing that would point to a serious illness."

"Auntie Freda seemed fine at the Cousins Brunch. She wasn't limping or anything, like she was in pain …" Sophie said.

"Oh god, I haven't even had a chance to tell you! The reason I had you looking for patches is because I found two of them yesterday. One at the hospital and one at the funeral home," Camelia said.

"Wait. You went to the hospital and funeral home? What the … Mum! Seriously? Tell me everything," Sophie said.

Sophie's eyes widened as Camelia recounted her efforts the day before.

"So, anyway, the fentanyl patches didn't have anything written on them, and the charge nurse at the hospital said that if it was administered by them, it would have been logged and the nurse who applied it would have initialed it," Camelia said. "I guess they track all the controlled meds, which makes sense. And the one I pulled out of their bio bin had fingerprints on it. The nurse was very clear that those things must be handled with gloves, that's how toxic they are."

"Oookaaay. That sounds super shady. So … Kenna gave the patch to Auntie Freda?"

"It kind of looks that way, doesn't it? When I went to the funeral home …"

"Yeah, what's that about?" Sophie clapped her mittened hands together. "Wish the heater would hurry up."

"Just a hunch that maybe Freda had arrived with, I don't know, something on her body that might give me a clue as to what she actually died from. And that's where I found the other patch."

"You don't think she had a stroke, like Kenna said?" Sophie asked.

"It's possible, but it's also possible it was a medication error. I have a case where the opposing party had a heart attack in Court, but there was a Narcan box on the stretcher when they wheeled him out," Camelia said.

"Narcan? Like for junkies?" Sophie said.

"Narcan, like for *overdoses*," Camelia said. "When I told Rita about it, she said a fentanyl overdose can cause a heart attack, which I never knew. So maybe it could cause a stroke, too, who knows?"

"Google knows. And Auntie Freda's doctor. He would know," Sophie said.

"Good point. I need to add him to my list of suspects," Camelia said.

"Seriously? You think her *doctor* killed her?"

"Not at all. I just know that doctors and nurses sometimes make medication errors."

"Okay, then onto the shit list he goes! So, what did you find in Auntie Freda's room?" Sophie asked.

"I hit the jackpot. For one thing, I found her address book, so we can contact all her people when it's time for a memorial …"

"But, Auntie Kenna said there weren't going to be any services."

"Kenna can do as she pleases. And so can we. No one can stop us from having a memorial if we want to. I, for one, believe Freda deserves a good send off, don't you?" Camelia said.

"Yeah, of course. I just thought it had to be a group project," Sophie said.

"Sure, for *normal* families. But nothing about this is normal, is it?"

"Nope. Totally not normal. Anything else?" Sophie asked.

"I also found a folder with Auntie Freda's will and some notes, so I took that as well. To safeguard it, mainly."

"Shit, don't let dad see it! He'll kill us if he finds out we've been snooping."

"Which is why we're gonna keep our mouths shut when we get home, okay?" Camelia's phone rang. "Sophie, grab my phone and see who's calling."

"It's Byron, do you want me to answer?" Sophie said.

"Crap. Yes, tell him I'm driving and I'll call him later," Camelia said.

Sophie relayed the message to Byron and hung up.

"He sounds grumpy."

"Great, just what I need. A grumpy boss." Camelia shook her head.

"Anyway," Sophie said, pulling Camelia's thoughts away from an angry Byron, "after all this, what do *you* think happened to Auntie Freda?"

"I wish I knew. She could have died from a stroke that just arrived on its own. Or she could have died *accidentally* from a stroke resulting from a medication error," Camelia said.

Sophie snorted. "More likely a Kenna error. She's such a … weasel."

"Innocent until proven guilty, Sophie. We're in the discovery phase of the case and that means we *discover*. We don't make conclusions until the discovery is finished. So yeah, Kenna's definitely a weasel, but she's an innocent weasel, at least for now," Camelia said.

"Yeah, *for now*," Sophie said. "But if she did something to Auntie Freda..." Sophie slapped her fist into her palm. "She's gonna get it."

37

THE WEIGHT OF EVIDENCE

DECEMBER 29

"Is there someone who can help me out with fingerprint matching? I know it's a weird thing to ask, but I kinda need to put two pieces of a puzzle together, and I don't know who else to call," Camelia said, cradling her phone against her shoulder.

She figured if anyone could help, it would be the RCMP Depot. Hell, they'd been training Mounties since the late 1800s, so surely someone over there knew how to run a fingerprint.

The man who answered the phone hesitated. "Well, m'am, it's the holidays so there aren't many people around right now, but I might be able to help. What's the nature of your problem?"

"It's nothing serious, just … I want to match the fingerprints to see which of my aunt's caregivers might have been giving her too much medication. Is that something you can help me with?" she asked, sugar coating each word.

"Well, um, maybe. I guess you can bring it over, and I'll see if someone will dust them for you, see if there's a match. But understand, this isn't a usual service we offer, so I don't even know if the lab will do it or what the fee will be. Hang on a sec," he said. Camelia could hear him talking to someone. "Okay, we close in a couple of hours, and if I'm tied up, you can talk to our senior docent, Chip Conroy," he said.

Camelia gasped. "Did you say *Chip Conroy*?"

The name reached back into her memories. She was 14, at her friend Janet's for a sleepover. They were all set to slather up with baby oil, lay out in the backyard, and get a tan. As they were getting changed in Janet's room, Camelia shrank away, conscious of the fresh welts and bruises on her back and buttocks. But Janet saw the marks before Camelia could pull her bathing suit up. Her friend didn't say anything, but the next day, before Camelia headed home, Mr. Conroy gave her a key to the house on a bright purple ribbon. *Just in case you stop by and we're not around. Consider this your second home*, he'd said, and squeezed her shoulder. That simple act revealed so much: Janet had told her parents, the Conroys were willing to shelter her, and she had a safe haven. She loved them for not making it a thing.

"Yep. He's our senior docent, but he's also retired from the RCMP, so he'll be able to sort this out. When you get to the campus, follow the signs to the Heritage Centre."

Camelia hung up, marveling at the idea of seeing Mr. Conroy again, after all these years. He had to be what, 75 or 80 by now?

As she stood up, Camelia was instantly dizzy and nauseous. Between the tension, grief, and skipping her customary morning cocktail—orange juice and vodka, or coffee and vodka, or a smoothie and vodka—Camelia was getting a taste of detox. She didn't like it, but she didn't dare take a drink.

Focus, focus, focus.

As she dug around in her purse for an ibuprofen, Camelia realized Auntie Freda's cardigan, her will, and the little address book were all crammed into her cavernous, oversized designer bag.

No wonder it weighs a ton.

She pulled the cardigan out and gently shook it. Chanel No. 5 wafted from the cream boucle knit. Camelia pressed it to her chest as a wave of grief raked at her insides. As she squeezed the sweater close, something hard pressing into her stomach.

What the hell?

She turned the cardigan around and held it up. There was a bump in the right pocket, the weight making the pocket droop.

Reaching into the pocket, she found a paper-wrapped lozenge and a little white spray bottle. She pulled her handbag close again and fished out the baggies from the hospital and funeral home, laying them out on the kitchen island.

From the hospital, she had a patch, a lozenge, and a syringe.

From Springer, she had a patch and a lozenge.

Her head was pounding. Camelia took a long drink of water to wash down an ibuprofen.

Then she carefully unwrapped the lozenge from its paper. Orange. Just like the other two. The wrapper was from a popular brand of over the counter cold remedy, containing zinc, Vitamin C, and Echinacea. It wasn't proof, exactly, but to Camelia the lozenges all looked the same.

The little bottle of nose spray had a handwritten label in Chinese characters, which meant nothing to her. It could be anything. But recalling what Sophie had said at the Boxing Day dinner, she knew it had to have come from Mickey, which made her automatically suspicious.

Camelia had *someone's* fingerprints on at least one of the patches, but whose? Sophie had done her part, copping a compact from Kenna's bathroom, so they could at least rule Kenna out. Or not.

She also had the nose spray, lozenges, and syringe to be analyzed for ingredients. If she could get the fingerprinting done, maybe she could also get the Mounties in the lab to do a chemical analysis. But even so, did any of these things contain something so toxic to Auntie Freda's system that it killed her?

Camelia had plenty of time to get to the RCMP depot and, hopefully, get a match on the fingerprints, because Leon was out with Dave Becker at a curling tournament all afternoon. Just one hitch: Sophie and Steve had the rental car. They were due back soon, but Camelia was pacing the floor, impatient, restless.

She texted Sophie, who responded immediately.

On our way now just leaving The Keg

Camelia exhaled and tried to ease the anxiety gnawing at her, bringing back her thirst with a vengeance. She eyed the bottle of vodka on the counter, its clear shimmer taunting her.

Just one to steady the nerves.

No, no, no.

She was headed to the RCMP Depot, and the last thing she needed was to show up smelling of booze. She washed down a Klonopin wafer, and impatiently waited for her daughter and son-in-law.

Within minutes, Sophie and Steve banged in the back door, bringing a rush of cold air with them.

"Mum, we're back!" Sophie called.

"In here, kids," Camelia called from the kitchen. "I need to take the car and head out right away, so I hope you didn't have plans."

"Where to? Something fun? Should we come along?" Sophie said.

"I have this evidence," Camelia stole a look at Steve, not sure how much Sophie had shared with him. "And I need to run an errand before I can decide if it's important or not."

"Mum, I told Steve about our visit to Kenna, so you don't have to tiptoe." Sophie said.

"Cam, she sang like a bird," Steve said, with a smirk.

Sophie rolled her eyes and elbowed him. "What's the errand?"

"I'm going to the RCMP Depot to get a fingerprint match on the patches and that compact you lifted from Kenna. And I'm going to find out if they can do a chemical analysis on the other items to find out what they contain," Camelia said.

Steve looked at Sophie and back to Camelia. He pressed his lips together and blew out a little *wheeeew*. Camelia could see he was steeling himself to disagree with her.

"It's not my family or anything, but … are you sure you want to go down this road? It's not like a couple of fingerprints are going to resolve much, right?" Steve asked.

"It won't necessarily resolve *anything*, but it's another piece of data. My question is, why would *anyone's* prints be on a medical patch, when you're supposed to be gloved to apply them?" Camelia said.

"It's a fair point, Steve," Sophie said.

Camelia didn't know how long a fingerprint would last. Did they eventually fade out or did they last forever? She would have called Byron, but she was purposefully giving him space and time to forgive her. He had been abrupt and irritated in their last call, and she knew better than to push him. Even though he would be able to answer the question in five seconds, she couldn't approach him with … what was this? Her suspicions and, frankly, not much more.

"Do you *really* think Auntie Kenna did something to Auntie Freda? She's dumber than dirt. I think if anyone has the murder mojo, it's Mickey," Steve said.

"Well, sure, Mickey's a jerk, but let's not jump ahead. Besides, why would he want to kill Auntie Freda? Unless he knows what he's going to inherit," Camelia said.

"Why would he inherit anything? I mean, wouldn't all of Auntie Freda's stuff go to her kids?" Steve asked.

"Auntie Kenna is definitely alive and kicking, so Mickey wouldn't get a dime. It would all go to Rita, Ben, and Kenna, right?" Sophie said.

"We can speculate all day, and that's one of the reasons I want to get these prints checked. Facts, people! I need *facts*, and I only have a short window before the Heritage Centre over at the RCMP Depot closes, so I need to get going," Camelia said, clenching and unclenching her hands.

Her patience was wearing thin, a sure sign a drink was in order. The sooner she got this chore done, the sooner she could celebrate. Although it seemed like everything was a celebration lately, an excuse to toss back a couple of drinks or a bottle of wine. The thirst nagged in the back of her throat. Klonopin only made her want more. Movement would help. For a while. She pulled on her coat and grabbed the car keys from the console by the door.

"Hey, how about if I drive you? The roads are pure shit," Steve said.

Camelia was grateful for the offer, but it sort of felt like cheating if she dragged them along on her wild goose chase.

"Yeah, Mum, you don't need to be driving in this weather. Let us take you," Sophie said.

"Really? I have plenty of experience driving in this kind of weather," she said.

But even as she said it, she knew it wasn't true. She'd been in Arizona a long time, where winter was a non-event, but there was something else in Steve's tone that troubled her. Maybe he didn't want her driving under the influence and this, of all days, when she was achingly sober.

"Well, okay, since you offered," Camelia said, handing Steve the car keys. "Let's roll."

38

Father Christmas

December 29

Steve followed the signs on the RCMP campus to the Heritage Centre, and parked on the curb. Sophie and Steve waited in the car while Camelia made her way inside, where a young man with a high and tight haircut was helping two women with tickets for the museum. She looked around. An older gentleman in a red volunteer vest approached Camelia.

Wow. He looks really good for his age.

"Oh my god. Mr. Conroy? I can't believe it." Camelia held out her hand. "Camelia Belmont. I was a close friend of Janet, back in high school," she said, grinning.

His face lit up, and he opened his arms for a hug. "Well, I'll be damned. Look at you! All grown up but not aged a day. Of course I remember you. How could I forget the 16 year old kid that threw up all over me when I dragged you two out of the Rusty Nail?" he laughed.

Camelia felt her cheeks flush. The memory of that smoky bar reminded her how much she wanted a drink.

"Oh dear. Misspent youth and all that."

Conroy laughed and waved it away. "Ancient history. Does Janet know you're in town?" he asked.

"I haven't had a chance to call up all the old rabble rousers yet. We came in a few days ago for a family Christmas and … it's been a rough holiday," Camelia paused.

"Oh?"

"My auntie Freda, Freda Swenson, you know her, right? She passed away a couple of days ago, quite unexpectedly," Camelia said.

"Oh, no. I'm so sorry. I hadn't heard. I know Freda pretty well from her work on the Auxiliary. A tireless volunteer if ever there was one. Bless her. What happened?" Conroy said, shoving his hands in his pockets.

"Well, that's just it. We're not sure. There seems to have been a discrepancy with medications and so on. And that's actually why I'm here," she said.

"Wait, are you the fingerprint lady?" Conroy said, planting his hands on his hips. Camelia read it as a hostile move.

Great. Dudley Do-Right is gonna screw up my whole plan.

"Um, well …" Camelia's phone buzzed in her pocket. "Excuse me, sorry," she said, saw it was Byron, and declined the call. "Sorry about that, anyway …"

"So it *is* you. Allow me to escort you over to the lab, Miz Melia," Conroy said. The childhood nickname made her nostalgic for things she'd never had.

"That's very kind of you, as usual," Camelia said. A wide grin filled Conroy's furrowed cheeks.

"It's not generally for the public, but under the circumstances . . ." he said, a twinkle of mischief lighting up his gray eyes.

Camelia glanced outside. The wind was picking up, and it was cold as hell out there.

"How far to the lab, do you think? It's pretty awful out," she said.

"Well, it's a fair walk, but I have a utility cart out back if you'd rather ride."

"How about the back seat of a nice warm car? My son-in-law has the heater running on the curb outside" she said.

"Hey, now there's an offer I can't refuse! Let me grab my coat," he said, and turned to the young man behind the counter. "I'm going to the lab for a few minutes, so man the fort, Heinrich!"

Camelia could tell by his excited demeanor this was as much an adventure for Chip Conroy as it was for her.

When they got across campus, Conroy pointed to a parking area near the front door of one of the historic clapboard buildings, its windows lit from within.

"We'll wait here," Steve said.

Sophie glared at him. "No, *you'll* wait here, and I'll go with Mum," she announced. Steve shrugged. He knew how to pick his battles.

Camelia and Sophie followed Chip Conroy down the snow-banked walk. It had been precisely shoveled and salted, no doubt by a squad of new recruits. Inside the vestibule, the scent of old wood and disinfectant encircled them. They followed Chip down a central hall to a large open room, brightly lit by humming fluorescent lights. A stainless steel counter ran down the center of the room, cluttered with microscopes, bottles of various sizes, glove and mask dispensers, paper towels, and clipboards. None of it looked up to date and there wasn't another soul in sight.

Conroy gestured for them to sit at a small table off to the side. "So, what's this all about? Really." Conroy said, his voice suddenly serious.

"I'm not sure, but … like I said, my Auntie Freda died and there's not a clear cause of death," she said, glancing at Sophie.

"What does the death certificate say?" Conroy interjected.

"It says natural causes, but her death was sudden …"

"As so many are. Why do you think the attending physician would risk his medical license by falsifying a legal document?" Conroy asked.

Camelia's palms began to sweat. He was interrogating her.

"Just … a totality of the circumstances. Auntie Freda was fine…"

"I was with her on the 22nd and she seemed okay," Sophie added.

"Then she went into the hospital on December 24. Her daughter, Kenna Shores …" Camelia began.

"Wait, Kenna Shores of the infamous drunk driving incident that damn near killed her and three other people and took out the power grid for half of the south end? *That* Kenna Shores?" Conroy asked.

"One and the same. She's my second cousin. And Freda's youngest daughter."

"I had no idea they were related. Go on," Conroy said.

"Anyway, Auntie Freda died within hours of being admitted, so they didn't really have a chance to run tests or get a good diagnosis. Then, on the same day—*Christmas day*—Kenna had Auntie Freda cremated without even asking the rest of the family. So when I went asking at the hospital …"

"Have you been playing detective, Cam?" Conroy's good natured twinkle had returned.

"Maybe a little bit. But somebody has to! I found a syringe, fentanyl patches, and a throat lozenge in the trash at the hospital, and another patch and lozenge at the funeral home," Camelia said. "I also found a nose spray and more lozenges in Auntie Freda's sweater."

"Wow. Not sure how you managed all that, but well done to you," Conroy said.

"Mum can be pretty darn persuasive," Sophie said, grinning.

"That's a whole other story. Anyway, the lozenge and nose spray sort of make sense because Auntie Freda reported she was coming down with a cold. What doesn't make sense are fentanyl patches. No one seems to know why she was receiving such powerful pain meds," Camelia said.

Her phone buzzed again. She glanced at the screen. Byron. She declined the call, again.

This can't be good news.

Camelia continued. "The charge nurse at the hospital said the patches weren't administered by them. Kenna claims to know nothing about them, but she had a box in her bathroom. So here we are. I just want to know if Auntie Freda died of a medication error or accidental overdose or if she had a serious illness and didn't tell anyone or … I don't know what."

"So you want fingerprinting because ...?" Conroy asked.

Camelia's nerves had steadied as they talked, and she knew she could trust Chip Conroy with her suspicions.

"To find out who handled these patches. Because I think Auntie Freda overdosed, and I want to know who was responsible. And, I guess I want to know what's in the nose spray and the lozenge, because another possibility is that Auntie Freda had an allergic reaction to something."

Conroy rolled his shoulders, reminding Camelia of his younger days, her friend's dad, handsome and commanding in Red Serge and tall boots, his posture as upright now as ever.

"Okay, a coupla things. First, you know the RCMP won't just offer up its services because a family member feels suspicious," he said. Conroy leaned back and gestured to the empty lab. "Second, in case you can't tell, our forensic analysis lab was shut down a while ago. Everything goes to Edmonton, Vancouver, or Ottawa now," Conroy said.

"Well, shit. Oh, sorry," Camelia said. He was still Mr. Conroy, after all.

"I can do the fingerprinting on my own, but the other things are out of my hands," he said. "And understand, I'm *only* doing this as a favor to you. Nothing official about it. It won't take long to compare the two sets of prints and tell you if they match, but I can't tell you who they belong to, because even if the prints were in the national database, I don't have access to it anymore. Since I retired," Conroy said.

Camelia chewed the inside of her lip. She would have to figure out something else for the chemical analysis.

"It's actually three sets of prints. Two on medication patches and one on a cosmetics compact," she said.

"Okay, a bit longer, then," Conroy said. "I have to get back to the Heritage Centre, so how about you leave this stuff with me, and I'll call you tomorrow when I'm done?" Conroy said.

"Is that okay? I don't want to cause a problem for you," Camelia said.

"Are you kidding? This is the most fun I've had in ages," he said, a mischievous grin lighting up Conroy's face.

Camelia dug a paper bag out of her purse and dumped it on the counter: two patches; one nose spray bottle; Kenna's compact; three lozenges; a syringe.

"Here's what I have. And I guess never mind these," she said, scooping the syringe, nose spray, and lozenges back up. "What I'm really worried about is that my aunt may have OD'ed on these damn patches," Camelia continued.

"Interesting. Okay, I'll do this first thing tomorrow, and I'll call you as soon as I have the results," Conroy said.

Camelia handed him her business card. "My mobile is at the bottom. You have no idea how much I appreciate this, Mr. Conroy. And is there a fee? Because I'm happy to pay."

"Nah, this one's on the house. Consider it a little Christmas gift," Conroy said.

"That's very kind of you. Thank you, really."

"Hey, don't mention it. No, really *do not* mention it!" Conroy said, laughing at his own joke. He looked at his watch. "Okay, let's scoot, ladies!"

Progress. Finally. Maybe this would answer at least one question: who handled the patches. Or so Camelia hoped. But what was she going to do about the nose spray and lozenge? She was tempted to just toss them and forget about it, but that's not what a real investigative attorney would do. As Byron often said, *there is no such thing as irrelevant evidence.*

When Camelia and Sophie got back to the car, Steve had the heat cranked on high, which helped calm Camelia's shaking hands. As soon as she was buckled in, Camelia grabbed her phone and scrolled to her assistant's direct line.

"Hi Cate. I need a favor. Can you please send a FedEx label to my email for that private toxicology lab Byron uses? I need chemical analysis on a couple of things. Can I have it by tomorrow morning, please?" Her assistant promised it would be in her inbox within 15 minutes.

"And Camelia, don't forget about that hearing in Bergman. It's on the 4th and I still don't have a signed stip from opposing counsel to vacate the hearing," Cate said.

Shitshitshit.

Camelia had completely forgotten about it.

Thank all the goddesses for perfectly organized Cate.

"Cate, I … we've had a bit of a family emergency here. My Auntie Freda died a couple of days ago, and it's a mess. Please call the Court and Diamant's office for an extension, because I might have stay here longer than planned." She hated herself for playing that card, even though it was true.

"Oh no. I'm so sorry, Camelia. Are you guys okay?" Cate asked.

"As well as can be expected, but I don't have much spare time," Camelia said. "And do you know why Byron's blowing up my phone?"

"Byron's just being Byron. He's all amped up because Ashcroft is pushing for an investigation into Suzanne Anders. Ashcroft's claiming she tried to kill her husband," Cate said. "And he's noticed us on a deposition."

Camelia could feel her heart tap-dancing in her chest, getting warmed up for a full speed panic attack. She took a deep breath.

"Cate, Suzanne Anders hasn't retained us. All I did was show up for her initial hearing. I didn't agree to represent her," Camelia said.

"I know that, and you know that, but Suzanne seems to think we're on board. She asked to come in to sign her fee agreement and leave a retainer deposit. What do you want me to do?" Cate asked.

Camelia heaved a sigh. "I *really* don't want her case. It's going to be a complete shit show."

"With Anders and Ashcroft on the other side? They'll eat us alive," Cate said. "But Byron is chomping at the bit."

"Yeah, he would be. I don't want to make an enemy out of Suzanne. She's well connected and could send a lot of business our way, so set an appointment for a couple of days after I get back and I'll let her down easy. And hey, thanks for the heads up and let me know when you get the extension." Camelia hung up and leaned her head against the cold glass of the car window.

Goddammit.

Just one more thing standing between her and a much needed drink.

39

Fa La La La Fingerprints

December 30

"Okay, I'll start with the bad news."

Camelia held her breath. She'd been eager to take Conroy's call, to find out the results of his fingerprint analysis, but now she wasn't sure she wanted to hear what he had to say.

"It looks like we have a crime on our hands," Conroy said.

"Oh? How so?" Camelia asked, tentatively.

"Cam, these patches have been tampered with. And that presents a problem," Conroy said, his voice lowering. "It isn't visible to the naked eye, but both of these patches had puncture marks. That usually means someone has drawn off most of the medication with a syringe. They're police evidence now."

"I'm not sure I understand. How is that a crime?" Camelia said.

"It's not a crime in isolation, but it's evidence of criminal activity. Junkies draw off the fentanyl in the patch for injection. Really popular with heroin addicts. With the Patch for Patch program, you can't get a new patch until you turn over the old one, so these could be black market.

People make a *lot* of money selling used and fake patches for addicts to game the trade in program," Conroy said.

"But the two I gave you for fingerprinting were in the trash. If they're so valuable, why did someone throw them away?" Camelia asked.

"Obviously, nurses aren't trading them in. But you're right, whoever threw them away could afford the loss," he said.

Camelia recalled Gayle Germaine's displeasure at finding the syringe in the biohazards bin instead of the sharps disposal, where it belonged. She could feel her antennae perking up.

"Okay, I'm still not sure I understand the crime aspect, but more importantly, what makes these two patches *police* evidence when there's been no crime that we know of?" Camelia said.

"No crime that *you* know of. I'm sorry, but I had to turn these over to the RIDU," he said.

"The what?" She sucked in her breath, her mind scrambling to catch up.

This can't be good.

"Regina Integrated Drug Unit. It's a task force with the RCMP and Regina Municipal Police. They're the team working on the opioid problem, and they collect evidence of trafficking," Conroy said.

Jeez. Did he have to be such a hardass?

"Mr. Conroy, I appreciate your work, but I don't know how this indicates trafficking. I'm not 100% convinced it's a criminal matter, but I do see potential for a civil case for wrongful death or medical malpractice, or even abuse of a vulnerable adult. I think I'm entitled to safeguard the evidence I'm gathering to support the family's claim to the insurance company for her death benefits. And I need those patches as part of the evidence I'm compiling," Camelia said.

"I think we're going to have to disagree on that, Cam. Chain of custody requires that it be logged and held by the RCMP. But there is some good news. The patches both have one set of prints, and those prints match the compact you provided. All in all, you've done a good job detecting," Conroy said. "Any idea who this person is?"

"Yeah, I know who it is," Camelia said.

Her heart was thumping. Was she prepared to hand Kenna over to the cops? Suddenly, all the ramifications of her actions came skidding into focus. "But I'm not ready to disclose that information just yet," she said.

"The guys at RIDU already ran the prints," he said. "So, you're not breaking a confidence if you decide to make a statement."

Holy shit.

She wasn't sure what the cops would do, or how quickly they would act, but this could screw everything up. In her idealized version of this fiasco, she would gather all the evidence, put all the pieces together, and present a nice little package to … who? Rita? Bob Barrett? The cops? Now she saw the flaw in her half-baked plan. She hadn't anticipated anything past her own 'aha' moment.

Even though Camelia had done a far better job at gathering evidence than she expected—and better than anyone would ever give her credit for—she'd failed to plan for *every* contingency. She never considered for a moment that she would actually uncover a *crime*. Medical malpractice? Maybe. Hospital error? Sure. But drug trafficking? That scenario hadn't occurred to her.

Doubts began creeping in. What if it was just her own preconceived notions making Freda's death seem like foul play? What if it was an accident? Was she just trying to pull off a Sherlock Holmes move to prove something to Byron? What if she really didn't have a clue what she was doing?

Her hands were shaking.

Camelia's stomach rolled itself into a tight ball.

Breathe. Breathe. Breathe.

"Are you there?" Conroy asked.

"Yeah, sorry. That sorta threw me for a loop."

"They matched the prints to a female in the database for impaired driving. Sound familiar?"

"Yeah, it does. I guess I didn't anticipate you would turn everything over without even talking to me," Camelia said.

"It's *evidence*. I appreciate that you trusted me with your suspicions about Mrs. Swenson's death, but you must realize I'm RCMP first. Sure,

I'm retired from the job, but you *never* retire the oath. I turned the two patches over, as I'm obligated to do. I expect you would understand that, as a lawyer," he said.

There was a long pause as Camelia processed what he had just said. In family law, her evidence was *hers* until she disclosed it. But if she had been thinking like a *criminal* attorney she would have known Conroy would turn over anything that looked like evidence of a crime.

I gotta quit thinking like a divorce attorney!

Camelia took a deep breath. Did it even matter if she had the patches or not? After all, an answer as to whose fingerprints were on those patches was what she had gone in search of. Now she knew. Kenna had handled the fentanyl patches. Not that she'd necessarily intended to put Kenna in the spotlight. Kenna did that herself.

"So, what now?" Camelia asked, desperately trying to modulate the panic out of her voice.

"Now? Nothing, unless someone in RIDU contacts you for a statement. It's out of your hands now, Cam. And mine," Conroy said. He let out a long exhale. "Sorry."

Camelia's mind was churning. What else could Conroy give her?

"Just one more thing. I don't understand why these tampered patches would be on Auntie Freda's body at the time of her death. It doesn't make sense."

"I considered that, too. One possibility is that the suspect—sorry, the person who administered the patches to your aunt—didn't know they'd been tampered with. You can't really tell by looking. Mrs. Swenson wouldn't have received the full dose, but surely enough to sedate her, especially if she didn't have a tolerance for the drug," Conroy said.

"Got it. Thank you, for your time, even though this wasn't really what I had in mind," she said.

"I'm sure. But if you have anything else in your possession, or if you know of someone else who has something like this in their possession, don't sit on it, Camelia. Turn it over. We have an opioid crisis on our hands, and whoever supplied these patches is part of the problem," Conroy said. "People are dying from this crap every day."

In that moment, Freda's voice came through: imperious, demanding, and wholly obeyable. "You cannot possibly think my Auntie Freda—or her family—is somehow involved in tampering with fentanyl patches."

"I'm not the one making the accusations. That was you. But someone supplied these patches, and you know how the dots connect. From user to dealer to supplier. It's serious stuff, Cam, and the RIDU guys won't back down. They'll be all over this," he said. "Don't get caught holding anything back, okay?"

"Thanks for the heads up," she said.

Camelia hung up and slumped to the floor, leaning against the bedroom wall. Her breath was coming in gasps.

"What the fuck have I gotten into?" she whispered.

40

Blue Christmas

December 30

Camelia was outwardly silent as she navigated the icy roads, but her mind was chattering nonstop.

"Everything okay, hon?" Leon asked.

"Oh, yeah. Just thinking about a work thing. And before you say anything, I know, I know. We're on vacation," she said, as they pulled into the parking lot.

Leon was off for an afternoon of billiards and beer with some old buddies, while Camelia went shopping the after-Christmas sales. Or, that's what Leon thought she was doing. In reality, while Leon was sipping a pint, she would be trying to track down Auntie Freda's health history.

Some vacation.

"Don't blow our retirement fund at the mall! See ya later, babe!" Leon blew her a kiss as he slammed the door.

Camelia gave Leon a weak smile, guilt ridden at her parade of lies. As she drove north, back through the Cathedral neighborhood, Camelia ticked off the list of people she had to talk to before the RIDU team swarmed:

Arthur Rossi, Freda's lifelong friends, Harriet and Josephine, and Auntie Freda's doctor, if she could get in to see him. What did they know? She would start at the Italian Club, where she might be able to find Arthur, Harri, and JoJo all at once. She had no idea if they would be there, but it was near the vacation rental and certainly worth a stop, since it was their favorite haunt.

The winter sun was blinding, bouncing off the snow and ice, boring a searing trail into her head, turning up the volume on her thumping headache. Camelia pulled into a parking space near the front of the Club and checked her lipstick in the rearview mirror. She looked like hell and didn't feel much better, but now that Conroy had turned over the patches to the drug team, she didn't have much time to figure out what happened to Auntie Freda. Camelia knew, once the RIDU stepped in—if they were anything like the Arizona cops—she would be sidelined while they criminalized everyone in sight.

Camelia crossed the freshly plowed parking lot to the entry, the Christmas décor looking tired and unremarkable in the bright light of day. As she entered the Club, a rush of warm air greeted her with the scent of garlic, basil, and lemon. Delicious with a glass of wine, nauseating on a stomach full of coffee, nerves, and ibuprophen.

She paused to unbundle and get her bearings, taking in the notable local Italians on the wall of photos to her left. Mostly old guard who were probably long since dead, by the looks of it. As she folded her gloves into her pockets, she turned, and was shocked by her aunt's toothy grin. A memorial of sorts, on an antique console: a large framed photo of Freda with a dapper looking gent, their arms around each other, beneath a bower of pine and twinkling lights, beaming into the camera. She didn't recognize the man, but he was distinguished in a Christopher Plummer sort of way. Old school. And clearly smitten, as his gaze was on Freda, not the camera.

Hello, Arthur Rossi.

The Club had the hushed atmosphere of old elegance. The thick carpets were deep carmine, with gold and green acanthus leaves woven into the border. Ornate chandeliers hung at intervals along the corridor, punctuated by arches and heavy glass-paned doors on either side. Strains of soothing jazz music completed the effect, lending an ambience of elegance, hushed conversations, tinkling crystal. Camelia could imagine Freda in this environment, her old fashioned formality meshing perfectly with the intended mood.

She followed discreet signage to the cocktail lounge, hoping to find her aunt's girlhood friends enjoying an aperitif before lunch. Or better yet, Arthur Rossi drowning his sorrows.

Beyond a dark oak arched doorway was a cozy, wood-paneled room with a blazing fire at the end. A massive antique bar took up the entire wall to her right, while floor to ceiling bookshelves filled the space between tall windows looking out onto a frozen garden. Leather wing chairs and small tables scattered here and there gave the impression of a private library, the sort of place you would find at your grandfather's Tuscan villa. Or so she imagined, having never been to Tuscany.

A bleached blonde in her forties was behind the bar, slicing lemons. As Camelia approached, she glanced up and plastered a fake smile on her face.

"Good morning, can I offer you a drink?" she said.

I thought you'd never ask.

Camelia hiked herself up on a barstool and read her name tag. "Thanks, Beverly, I would love a short vodka soda," Camelia said, without a moment of hesitation.

She badly needed something to take the edge off. As Beverly poured, Camelia pulled out a twenty and pushed it across the bar.

"Anything else?" Beverly asked.

"Yes, I'm looking for Arthur Rossi," she said. "He was my Auntie Freda Swenson's fiancé."

"Your aunt?" she said. "I heard … I'm so sorry for your loss. And Arthur is heartbroken, poor thing. He's here, you know. In the dining room, taking his lunch like he always does," Beverly said.

Finally, a bit of luck.

"Which way?" Camelia asked as she grabbed her drink.

Beverly waved her arm to the right. "Go back to the main corridor. The dining room is two doors down, on the right."

Camelia followed the corridor to another arched doorway. A handful of patrons huddled over menus. Seated by the fire, an older man in a tweed jacket and turtleneck leaned back in his chair, staring absently out the window, his plate barely touched.

Camelia recognized him from the photo in the lobby, but today he looked older, less alive. As she approached his table, he turned.

"Yes, dear?" he said, a trace of his Italian native tongue coming through.

Camelia stepped forward and held out her hand. "Mr. Rossi? I'm Camelia Belmont, Freda's niece," she said. His eyes immediately reddened and filled with tears as he stood. He took Camelia's hand in both of his, cocooning it in his broad, warm palms.

"My dear, I've heard so much about you. I was hoping to meet you … under happier circumstances," he said, choking a bit on the last words. "Please, sit with me," he continued, gesturing to the chair at his left.

"Mr. Rossi, I am so, so sorry," Camelia said, placing her hand on his forearm. He bowed his head and pulled a linen handkerchief from his breast pocket, dabbing his eyes and rubbing his aquiline nose.

"Yes, yes, I'm sorry too. Freda was truly my soul mate. After all these years of being friends, after my Abby passed, we discovered something else in each other," he said. "And now she's gone, and I don't even know what happened," he continued, not meeting Camelia's eye. "Rita called to let me know, but she didn't have any details. I left a message for Kenna, but she hasn't called me back. I know Freda passed in the middle of that horrible blizzard, but I would have made my way to her side, had I only known. I didn't even have a chance to say goodbye." He pressed the handkerchief to his eyes.

"Mr. Rossi …"

"Please, dear, call me Arthur. We were almost relatives, after all," he said.

Was this really the kind of man who would kill his fiancée? Maybe Arthur Rossi was broke and marrying Auntie Freda for her money. But then, he sure as hell wouldn't kill her before the wedding. For now, he was off the list of suspects.

"I would have gone to be with Freda, too, had I known. It was just so … sudden. You knew her better than any of us. Did she seem sick to you?"

Arthur fidgeted with his cup of coffee. "Yes, maybe. Something odd was going on. Freda was woozy the night of the Feast of the Seven Fishes. She actually fainted when I announced our engagement at the party, but I thought it was just … I don't know, the wine, the excitement, the dancing."

"Did she mention anything before that? Had she been to the doctor?"

"No, but you know how she could be. She claimed it was just a bit of lightheadedness," Arthur said. "Not that it will bring my Freda back, but I would love to know what the devil happened." His deep set brown eyes glistened with unspent tears.

"I would too. I loved her, and I feel robbed." Camelia fingered the turned edge of the tablecloth and wondered how much more to say. Based on nothing more than her gut feeling after a few minutes of conversation, she felt Arthur could be an ally. But still … who knew? She thought Conroy was an ally, too, and look where that got her.

"I should have insisted that we go immediately to the hospital. How could I have been such a fool?" Arthur asked.

"You can't blame yourself, Arthur. There was no way to predict this outcome. But … some things aren't adding up. Do you know of any reason she would be on pain medication?"

"Her arthritis was a bother in the cold weather, but she seemed to manage well enough with some ibuprofen, a bit of arnica, and a drop or two of port in the evening," he said, and his eyes glazed over, as if recalling just such an evening.

The expression on his lined face made Camelia uncomfortable, as if she were witnessing a private pain too deep for strangers. She drained her drink and waved her glass at a passing waiter. She knew it was a bad idea to have a second, but goddammit, she needed a little fortitude.

"Arthur, I'm curious to know if Auntie Freda was using more potent pain meds. Fentanyl, oxycodone, that kind of thing," she said.

His shocked face said it all. He wasn't faking it. If Freda had been using pain medications, Arthur knew nothing of it.

She plunged on. "In all seriousness, it's possible Auntie Freda died of an accidental overdose. It could have been caused by a medical mistake. You know, wrong medication or wrong patient or both. Or … there may be another explanation I haven't thought of."

"*Madonna mia*," he whispered. "There is no chance Freda was taking fentanyl or oxycodone."

The waiter set Camelia's second vodka soda on the table and she took a long sip.

"Are you sure? Maybe she was covering up a serious illness?"

"No. Freda is … was … allergic to opioids. She couldn't take that kind of thing. She even had an allergy alert on her keychain. You know, in case she was in a car accident or …" Arthur pressed his handkerchief to his eyes. "She was the definition of stoic. Oh god, I wish I knew …"

Camelia doubted Auntie Freda was as tough as Arthur thought, but she was definitely a prairie woman: practical, forthright, strong-willed. And no one had mentioned an opioid allergy until now. Not the hospital and certainly not Kenna.

"Yes, Freda was a prairie woman, through and through. And we may never know what really happened, what with Freda being cremated …"

His head snapped up and his eyes turned dark. "What? Freda was *cremated*?" he growled, his voice cutting through the low chatter in the room.

People nearby turned to stare. Camelia nodded.

"Those were *not* her wishes, I can tell you that for certain," he said, jabbing his finger into the tabletop for emphasis, rattling the silverware on his plate. "We discussed these things. At length. She was to be buried beside Geoffrey, just as I intend to be buried beside my Abigail," he said.

Camelia leaned in, aware they were now the center attraction in the dining room. "Her daughter, Rita, intends to have Auntie Freda's ashes interred with Uncle Geoffrey, so her wishes will still be honored."

"I see. But still … my poor, dear Freda," Arthur said, shaking his head, and dabbing his eyes.

Their waiter approached. "Mr. Rossi, may I bring you anything else?"

Arthur looked up. "I'm so sorry, my dear, I seem to have lost my manners. May I offer you some lunch?" he asked.

"Thank you, no, I have to run," she said. Camelia looked longingly at her half-full vodka soda as she pulled a business card from her handbag. She slid it toward him. "Please, call me day or night. I would be happy to hear from you any time."

Arthur rose from his seat as she did. Camelia gripped his hands, and turned to leave. As she walked away, he spoke her name. She turned back to see Arthur standing beside the table, backlit by the fire, his image fierce and tense.

"Camelia, find out what happened. Freda deserved to die in my arms on our 20th anniversary. She must be avenged."

This man is a warrior.

He said something in Italian.

When he saw her puzzled look, Arthur said, "It means, there is no greater torment than to be alone in paradise."

41

A Prescription for Pain

December 30

Without waiting for the car to warm up, Camelia drove out of the Italian Club parking lot. She was sick at the thought of someone giving Freda a drug she was allergic to. If it was true, it meant the cause of Auntie Freda's death was anything but natural.

Could it have been an accident? Just another medical mistake? It was the holidays, after all. And there was that horrible snow storm. And they were short-staffed. Could one of the nurses have mixed up the meds? Or even Dr. Fitzgerald?

Or maybe someone closer.

Goddammit, could it really be Kenna?

Her fingerprints were on the patches. She had unlimited access to Auntie Freda. And, based on her bank account, she was broke. Maybe desperation for money drove her to accelerate her inheritance.

If it was Kenna, she was snug at home, thinking it was all wrapped up in a tidy package. The perfect crime. Except she hadn't counted on Camelia.

There wasn't enough hard proof for Camelia to turn over to the RCMP, so it was still up to her to close the loop. As it stood right now, she knew they would laugh at her paltry so-called evidence. She pulled over by the Legislative Building and dialed Rita.

"Hi, how are you doing?"

"Oh, you know, reeling from all this shit. What's up?" Rita sounded impatient.

"Well, I have a couple of things to run by you. My lawyer brain has been on high alert, so I went to the hospital and talked to the Charge Nurse, and it seems like Auntie Freda had a fentanyl patch removed, which she says wasn't administered by them," Camelia said, leaving off the bit about rummaging through the biohazard waste. "So then, on a whim, I went over to Springer and talked to Joe Alexander. And guess what? The guy who cremated Auntie Freda removed a fentanyl patch from her . . . "

"Cam, what the hell are you doing?"

"Well, I'm poking around, trying to make sense of Auntie Freda's death. I don't want to wonder my whole life if there was a medical mistake or if something else happened. Something on purpose," Camelia said.

Rita heaved a sigh. "I get it. I really do. But why do you think it's sinister that Mum was on pain meds? She was 85 for crying out loud! Lots of old people are on a cocktail. It's not unusual," Rita said. "You can't believe the laundry list of meds some of these seniors are taking. I see it every day in hospice."

"But is that really how Auntie Freda was? I get that overmedication is rampant, but I met Arthur Rossi today, and he says she was allergic to opioids. So why did she have fentanyl patches? Doesn't that seem unusual?"

There was a long pause and Camelia knew Rita was going into RN mode, just as she had gone into lawyer mode. She would be calculating weight and dosage and so on. As she should. Freda was her mother, after all, despite their difficult relationship.

"Okay, that's definitely weird. I guess I'd forgotten about the drug allergy. Not like it was something Mum talked about in casual conversation. But it could have been someone else's patch. And I know where you're going with this, Cam. You think Kenna offed Mum. Which makes no sense. She had everything handed to her on a platter, so why kill the golden goose?" Rita said.

Camelia saw her logic, but she also knew something Rita didn't: Kenna was broke.

"I don't know the why. All I know is I'm following a thread. It's nagging at me day and night, and I thought I should keep you in the loop," she said.

"Camelia, *please*. Let it go. Nothing will bring Mum back, and all this is just too upsetting," Rita said. "And sorry, but Kenna's my sister. Regardless of what else she may or may not be, she's family, and I don't feel good about dragging her through the mud just because she didn't do things the way you or I would have. Just leave it alone. It's Christmas, for crying out loud. Why don't you just go have some holiday cheer and relax?"

Tears strained Rita's voice, a sure sign Camelia had pushed her friend too far. She had intended to ask Rita a lot more questions about Auntie Freda's health, but she didn't dare. Not now.

"Got it. I won't bother you with my paranoid fantasies. I'm sorry I upset you." Camelia's own voice hitched with tears. "Anyway, I guess we'll see you and Dave tomorrow night? What time do you want to come over before we go out? We can order takeout," Camelia said, hoping to smooth the rough waters between them. She loved Rita and didn't want to hurt her more.

After ending the call, Camelia pulled out of the park, and headed for the vacation rental. As she drove, she ticked off all the ways she could confirm drug allergies. She remembered that Auntie Freda always used the pharmacy on South Albert, whether it was cotton balls, hairspray, or a prescription, it was her go-to. On a whim, Camelia turned around, hoping she could find a kind soul willing to help her out. She had nothing to lose.

In the parking lot of the drugstore, Camelia hesitated, not wanting to step back into the freezing cold now that the car was finally warm. But, it was her second-to-last stop before heading back to the house, so she pulled her scarf tight and, head bent against the prevailing wind, scurried inside.

The pharmacist was a fastidious 40-something man with a barrel-belly straining against his white tunic. As she stepped toward the counter, Camelia clasped her hands to keep them from shaking. It was nerve-wracking to be an actress all day. She wished now she had stayed at the Italian Club with Arthur long enough to finish her second vodka soda.

"I hope you can help me out. My aunt, Freda Swenson, got her prescriptions here, and—god rest her soul—she passed last week. We're just tying up loose ends for the life insurance company, and I need a list of my aunt's medications and drug allergies. Would you be able to help with that?" she asked, applying her sweetest intonations.

She felt like a fraud and a cheat. The room tilted a bit. She realized she hadn't eaten.

"Oh, I'm very sorry. That's a bit of a shock, eh? She was just in a couple of weeks ago, and she looked hale and hearty! Missus Swenson was such a dear. But that's how it is sometimes, eh? And yes, I can help. Since Mrs. Swenson is now deceased, and you're a close family member, I'll just need you to fill out a form, then I can disclose her records." He handed Camelia a form, then looked at her more closely. "Are you alright? You look a bit pale," he said.

She wasn't alright. Camelia felt sweaty, nauseous, and shaky. She desperately needed something, *anything* to take the edge off. But this was just nerves. It couldn't be that she *needed* a drink. She'd just had a vodka soda half an hour ago.

I'm not that far gone, am I?

"I'm a bit wrung out from losing my aunt, but I'm sure I'll be fine. Probably just need a nap and a cup of tea," she lied, as she filled in the blanks on the form.

"I'll be right back with a copy of Mrs. Swenson's prescription history," he said, and turned away.

Camelia waited, fidgeting, sweating in her parka. She dug around in her handbag and found some gum. In a few minutes, the pharmacist returned with an envelope.

"Here's what we have. First page is known drug allergies, and the second page is current medications. I hope it helps," he said.

"Perfect. Thanks, and happy new year," she said.

Camelia rushed through the store, out the doors, welcoming the cold blast on her sweaty face. She gulped the air and swallowed the burst of saliva that hit her mouth. Inside the car, she leaned her head on the steering wheel, its icy cold numbing her skull. She sipped at a nearly frozen water bottle, sighing when the cold liquid hit her stomach, quelling the urge to throw up.

Gotta get home, eat something, and get my own pain medication: a tall vodka.

42

BEDSIDE MANNERS

DECEMBER 30

Before Camelia could head back to the vacation rental for some respite, she needed to check the last item off her list. She had to talk to Dr. Fitzgerald about why Auntie Freda had fentanyl patches and a script for oxy. The pharmacy records said Freda was allergic to opioids, and there were no prescriptions listed for either drug.

Dr. Fitzgerald's contact information was on the printout as the prescribing physician, so Camelia punched in the number on her phone. Her hands shook from the cold, nerves, and, well, maybe from a lack of alcohol. It rang three times before it went to a recording.

"If you need to reach the on-call nurse, please press 4 now," a homogenous female voice said. Camelia pressed 4 and waited as the car heater began to thaw her feet. She heard the clicking of the call being forwarded.

"Dr. Fitzgerald's office, this is Rachel Bonhomie, how can I help you?" she said, her French-Canadian accent showing up in the pronunciation of her name.

"Hi, I'm sorry to bother you, but I'm trying to reach Dr. Fitzgerald regarding my aunt. She was a patient of his," Camelia said.

"I'm sorry but Dr. Fitzgerald is out for the holidays. Can I help?"

"Maybe. My aunt—Freda Swenson—died on Christmas morning and I think Dr. Fitzgerald was there?"

"Yes, I'm so sorry for your loss. Dr. Fitz told me she'd passed. Is there something I can help with?" Bonhomie said.

"It's about her meds. I'm trying to tie up loose ends for the life insurance people. From what I understand, Auntie Freda had a prescription for OxyContin, and she had fentanyl patches at the time of her death, but they aren't listed on her prescription records and she was allergic to opioids. I'm just following up to make sure there wasn't a medication mistake or something at the hospital," Camelia said. "Not that Dr. Fitzgerald had anything to do with that, but there might have been a mix up that could really screw up the life insurance."

"Hmm. Okay. Let me pull up Mrs. Swenson's file. Who am I talking to again?"

"Camelia Belmont. I'm Mrs. Swenson's niece."

Bonhomie put her on hold and Camelia was jolted by the abrupt segue to loud country music. A few minutes later, Bonhomie was back.

"Okay, I'm looking at Mrs. Swenson's list of medications and she was prescribed Oxaprozin, Simvastatin, Amlodipine, and Warfarin. Dr. Fitz has not issued any prescriptions for opioids of any kind and her file is flagged. Mrs. Swenson is . . . was … allergic. Are you *sure* she was given OxyContin and fentanyl?" Bonhomie said.

"Well, not 100% sure, since she was cremated, but the hospital records say …"

"Okay, well, someone needs to answer for that because there's no way Dr. Fitz would have prescribed it." She was suddenly defensive. "Perhaps in the emergency room …" Bonhomie didn't finish her thought.

"I would really like to have a conversation with Dr. Fitzgerald about all this. Do you think you can get him on the phone?"

"Well . . . ordinarily, I would say no, since he's supposed to be having some R and R over the holidays, but I think he'll want to clear this up. Hang on a minute," she said, and put Camelia on hold.

The jangling country and western music was back, sawing away at Camelia's nerves.

Sweet Jesus. I need a drink just listening to this music.

Minutes passed before a man's voice interrupted Merle Haggard.

"James Fitzgerald here. I understand you have some questions about Freda Swenson?" he said.

"Dr. Fitzgerald …" she began.

"Please, just call me Fitz. Everyone does."

"Thanks. I'm Camelia Belmont, Freda's niece. I appreciate you taking my call. I won't take much time. I just have a few questions about how my Auntie Freda died. Or should I say, the life insurance people are going to have questions, and I'm trying to be fully prepared," Camelia said.

"I'm sure you are. You're the lawyer from the States, aren't you? Freda mentioned you were coming for the holidays," he responded. "Fire away, counselor!"

"Oh, it's not like that. I'm just trying to get a handle on things. I know Auntie Freda wasn't really in the hospital long enough for many tests to be run, but surely you have a sense of what took her so quickly?"

"I don't have her chart in front of me, but you know, sometimes …" Dr. Fitzgerald said.

"I actually have a copy of her chart and that's why …" Camelia said.

She heard his quick intake of air. "Ooooh, so *that's* why you're calling. You've seen the tox screen," he said, interrupting her.

The resignation in his voice, and the way he assumed she'd seen something put Camelia on high alert.

What the hell is he talking about?

She flipped through the photocopied pages, her hands stiff with cold. There was no toxicology report within the meager stack of pages, and she felt confident she would recognize one, given how many she'd reviewed in her family law practice. She replayed the moments of receiving the copy of the chart, knowing she hadn't misplaced anything because it hadn't left her handbag until now. What had she missed?

Suddenly, she knew. It happened right under her nose. The glances between Gayle Germaine and the other nurse, Francine. Gayle's smile as she handed over the copy of the chart, folding a sheet of paper into her pocket.

"Look, I …," Fitz began. Camelia thought she heard him mutter *fuck* under his breath. "Do you have time to meet? I think this is better discussed in person."

"Oookay. I'm on South Albert now. Where do you want to meet?" Camelia said.

"If you're already out … do you mind coming to my house? I'm not far, just a couple of streets over from Freda's place, in the Crescents," he said, and rattled off his address.

"I'm on my way Dr. … Fitz," Camelia said, and pulled out onto the ice-rutted street. Her mind was whirling, but decades of legal training had created muscle memory. She wouldn't tip her hand. She would let Dr. Fitzgerald believe she had the tox screen. Let him talk. Let him hang himself.

"So what about this toxicology report is so important that you can't talk about it over the phone?" Camelia said. Her hackles were up. Or maybe she just needed a drink.

There was a long pause, then a heavy sigh, as Dr. Fitzgerald ran his hand over his chin. He had a couple of days' stubble, and looked tired, but beneath that were the remnants of a kind, handsome face.

"Look, this was a one-off for me. I ordered the tox screen post mortem. Because I've seen this before. Not with Freda, of course, but others. The confusion, lethargy, sudden onset, the purplish hue," he said, and his voice cracked. "I never meant …"

He stood up and walked to the window, his hands shoved in the pockets of his jeans. An image of Aaron Anders being wheeled out of the courtroom arose in Camelia's mind. The purple cast to his lips and skin.

Rita was right.

"You think she overdosed?" Camelia asked.

Dr. Fitz took a deep breath and blew it out, audibly. "Yeah. I do. I mean, just look at the tox screen," he said, nodding his head.

"And you say this tox screen was in Auntie Freda's hospital chart? Because I have a copy from the charge nurse right here," Camelia said, waving the thin sheaf of papers, "And there's no tox screen," Camelia said.

Dr. Fitzgerald looked confused for a moment. Then he seemed to realize his mistake, as a hint of grin appeared. He shook his head, just enough for Camelia to catch it.

"God, I'm an idiot. You got the chart from Germaine?"

"Yes, Gayle Germaine gave me a copy after I filled out about twelve pages of forms. Like I said, I've looked through it all, and there's no tox screen."

He nodded. "Right or wrong, she's protecting me. And the hospital. Obviously, I would make a lousy criminal. Look, before we go any further, I assume I'm going to need a lawyer."

"Not on my account. We're waaay out of my jurisdiction. And if it's any consolation, it's actually a *good* thing to be a lousy criminal, you know," Camelia said, shifting to face him. "I'm not out to get you. I just want to know what happened. My aunt was allergic to opioids, but at least one fentanyl patch was attached to her body at the time of death. And when I reviewed her chart, in the notes under existing medications, it says *Oxy Prn.* So how did that happen?"

"Let me see that," he said, holding out his hand for the chart.

Camelia handed it to him.

"Okay, that's poor penmanship," he said as he ran his finger down the page. "It's *Oxaprozin.* That's an NSAID I prescribed for Freda's arthritis. As for the oxycodone and fentanyl, it wasn't me. I don't know where Freda came into contact with the stuff, but by the time I saw her, she was gone."

"My fear is someone gave my aunt those meds on purpose, to intentionally harm her," Camelia said, tasting the metallic power of her words as they left her mouth.

On purpose. With intent to harm. That's murder.

Dr. Fitz cocked his head.

"You didn't see Freda when she was admitted?" Camelia asked.

"No, I wasn't at the hospital until much later. I'd volunteered to be on call since the wife and I weren't leaving town for the holidays. Then we get the blizzard of the decade. Lucky me, huh?" he said, pacing in front of the window. "The doc who was supposed to be on shift was snowed in, and they called me in around 2 a.m. I was covering ER when Germaine called my mobile. I think it was around 5 a.m. She didn't know I was already downstairs, in the ER," Dr. Fitzgerald said.

"Why would she call you?" Camelia asked.

"Oh, as Freda's GP, to sign the death certificate," he said. "It's a whole process. Anyway, when I saw her—Freda—I knew something wasn't right. So I pulled a blood sample and walked it to the lab myself."

"But . . . when you signed the death certificate, you wrote . . ." Camelia started.

"I know, dammit. I know. I just . . . look, Freda has been my patient for the entire time I've been in private practice. Almost 30 years. She's a fixture in the community. I know it's just little old Regina, but people like her are our royalty. I didn't want her legacy tarnished, and I sure as hell didn't want her family and friends to think she overdosed like some kind of junkie. She was anything but. And then there's the life insurance. They sure as hell won't pay out on an overdose of pain meds with no MAID forms on file . . ."

"Any what?" Camelia asked.

"MAID forms. For medically assisted death."

"Right," Camelia said. Rita had jokingly called it Maid Service.

"Which didn't happen, in any event. Anyway, I know it was not my finest hour, but in my defense, she did die peacefully, in her sleep. Just not as naturally as I would have wished," he said, his voice low, almost a whisper.

"Did Auntie Freda have any underlying conditions or an illness or something that would have caused her to die suddenly? Or did she have a massive stroke or something like that?"

"That's the $64,000 question, isn't it? Your aunt didn't have an acute or terminal condition, or an advanced disease, that might result in sudden death. But she had high blood pressure, and had for years, no thanks to all that good wine, rich food, and a bit of a fiery temper," he said, with a raise of his eyebrows. "So, if she received a medication she was allergic to, like fentanyl, it's certainly feasible it could have created a hypertensive crisis which, in turn, could have led to a major stroke. Based on her chart, her presentation at ER was consistent with stroke. They didn't get a chance to run an MRI because of the blizzard. ER was overrun with more than a dozen trauma patients from a pileup on the Number 1," Dr. Fitzgerald said. "I ended up working on a couple of those patients all night."

"So the fentanyl could cause a stroke?"

"It could."

"Okay, between fentanyl patches and oxy, which one would more likely have caused this hypertensive crisis?" Camelia asked. She might as well depose the witness since he seemed willing to talk.

"Honestly, either or both. Patches are potent, but they're more of a slow release, by design, and the levels in Freda's system were pretty high, like I would expect to see from an injection, or tablets, even lollies."

"I still don't know who would do such a thing. The RCMP guy I talked to said the patches were tampered with, so now the cops have the fentanyl patches. They're going to investigate," Camelia said.

"Look, I don't want any more trouble than I'm due, but of course I'll cooperate. It's about time for me to retire, anyway," he said.

The resignation in his voice pierced Camelia's armor. Tears sprang to her eyes. Camelia could see how a doctor—by all accounts a very good doctor—could get caught up and lose everything. All because he was trying to be a good friend, instead of a by-the-book medical officer. She busied herself by putting the chart back in her bag so he wouldn't notice her tears.

"Just so you know, I have no intention of throwing you under the bus. But be prepared for an awkward conversation about the death certificate if you have to testify as to how you found fentanyl in Auntie Freda's system. From my point of view, you acted as a loyal friend. Nothing more," Camelia said, and rose to leave.

"Thank you for that. It's small comfort, but I'll take what I can get. The guilt has been driving me nuts," Dr. Fitzgerald said.

"You didn't kill her, Dr. Fitz."

"But if I understand what you're getting at, I may have covered for someone who did. And that's almost the same."

43

Suspicious Minds

December 30

"Anybody home?" Camelia called into the house. She desperately wished for silence, to be alone for just a couple of hours, but no such luck. Voices drifted into the back entry from the living room.

"In here, Cam," Leon responded.

Camelia stepped into the living room to see Ben pacing, swigging a beer, and Leon perched on the edge of the sofa, tapping a coaster. Leon would drum on anything, with anything, when he was impatient or irate. By the looks of things, he was both.

Great. Now I get to manage these two.

"Hey Bennie, how's it going?" Camelia said, giving him a sideways hug.

"*Not well*! Not well *at all*! Do you have any idea what Kenna's been up to?" Ben sputtered, his face red.

"Hang on, let me get a drink before you dive in. Looks like you guys got a head start, huh?" Camelia said, nodding at Ben's beer.

"I'll get it so Ben can fill you in. I've already heard it," Leon said, rolling his eyes in Camelia's direction.

"Thanks, hon. Ben, what's going on?" Camelia said.

"Leon, you can blow me off if you want, but I'm telling you, something's going on. And Kenna's behind it, if you ask me," Ben shouted after Leon.

"Okay, what *exactly* do you think is going on?"

"Mum was fine when I talked to her the other day, I think it was the 22nd or 23rd. Then, just like that, she's dead and cremated on the same day? Are you fucking kidding me? Rita and I tried to plan a funeral mass, but Kenna won't even talk about it. I went over there this morning, to try to talk some sense into her, and she was literally tearing Mum's room apart but wouldn't say why," Ben said. "It really makes me wonder about her. I don't even want to say it out loud but ... Kenna drinks *way* too much." Ben's eyes filled with tears. "What if she accidentally … I don't know what."

"Just because Kenna is acting fishy doesn't really prove anything. I mean, if you were to call the cops …"

"Nobody said anything about that," Ben interjected.

Leon handed Camelia a glass of wine. Gratefully, she took a long gulp.

"But if you did call the cops, Ben, what would you say? My mum died of natural causes per the death certificate, and my sister is super efficient and had her cremated?"

"But my question is how did Mum *actually* die? Because natural causes means nothing, really. And when have you *ever* known Kenna to be super efficient about *anything*?" Ben's reddened eyes bored into Camelia's.

He was voicing exactly the same suspicions she felt.

"All good points, but it doesn't prove anything Ben."

"Maybe not, but I asked Kenna why she had Mum cremated in such a hurry and you know what she said? She said you have to bury the body before you can inherit. Seriously, she's an idiot. And that's the other thing. Did you guys get the call from the lawyer's office? We have to be there tomorrow for the reading of the will. So I guess Kenna will get her money, and then she'll be happy," Ben said.

"Yeah, we got the call. Maybe when Kenna gets her inheritance she'll be ready to talk about Auntie Freda's services. Do you know who Freda named as executor?"

"How should I know? You're the fucking lawyer! All I know is this whole thing stinks like something dead in Denmark."

Camelia bit her lip to keep from laughing at his mixed metaphor.

"Have you talked to Rita?"

"I tried, but Rita's no help. I mean, yeah, she thinks we should have a mass and all that, but as for the rest? She actually defended Kenna. Then Dave butted in and said I should just leave it alone. They're staying out of it. Which is just so typical, isn't it?" Ben said. "If the kitchen's too hot, get out of the fire, am I right?"

Ben's metaphors were sometimes hard to follow, so Camelia nodded and took another mouthful of wine.

Sweet Jesus. Just what the doctor ordered.

"Well, I think Rita's pretty upset over all this ..." Camelia said.

"Oh spare me. None of us could be in the same room with Mum for more than an hour without tearing our hair out. Well, except Kenna, but that's only because she was mooching off the old lady like the leech she is. Not that I blame her. Take it where you can get it, I guess. Don't get me wrong. Mum wasn't all bad, she was just a cantankerous old bat *half* the time. What I'm saying is, Rita's not all peaches and fucking cream, and I doubt she's grieving all that hard," he said, draining his beer.

Camelia wasn't surprised at Ben's assessment. He'd always strained against the three women he'd grown up with. She thought about letting Ben in on what she'd discovered, but she had to be careful. Leon was not in the loop yet, so she didn't want to spring it on him and start a fight in front of Ben. Plus, if there was an argument between the siblings, Ben would spit it all out in a fit of pique.

Leon scrolled through his iPod and selected an old Tragically Hip album, while Ben popped a fresh beer.

"Ben, here's a question for you. Do you know if Auntie Freda had any allergies?"

He studied his beer cap for a few seconds. "I don't know, really. She had that bad reaction to Vicodin a couple of years ago. Remember, when we were in Hawaii for Mickey and Suyin's wedding? After that, she didn't take anything stronger than over-the-counter."

"We weren't at Mickey's wedding, remember?"

"Oh, right. Well, Mum hurt her back on the Jeep tour, and they gave her a dose of Vicodin at Urgent Care. That's how Mum found out she was allergic. Thank god they held onto her, because she had a bad reaction right there in the clinic. Why do you ask?"

"I don't know. Just thinking out loud. Maybe she was over-medicated," Camelia said. She didn't like keeping information about his mother from him, but she also couldn't risk Ben bumbling his way into her … investigation. Is that what this was? At least he confirmed that Freda was allergic to opioids.

So why was there a fentanyl patch in her hospital room and at the funeral home?

"I think she took something for arthritis, but probably just ibuprofen or something like that. And blood pressure meds, but that's about it," Ben said, shrugging.

"Hey, guys, can we talk about something not so … dark? We're all sorry to lose Freda, but this rehashing isn't helping. At least it's not helping me," Leon said, giving Camelia a little stab with his eyes.

But this isn't about you, is it Leon?

Camelia swallowed her words with another mouthful of wine. There was no point getting into an argument. Camelia's phone rang. When she picked it up, she saw Byron's name on the screen.

"Hey, gotta take this. Sorry," she said, and headed for the bedroom. "Hi Byron, what's …"

"I thought we agreed you would draft a settlement agreement in the Forman case, but I don't see it on the server. So where is it?" Byron said.

Camelia muttered her apology.

"I hope you haven't forgotten our conversation, Camelia. I know you're on vacation, but our cases don't stop for holidays," he said.

"No, Byron, it's not that. My favorite aunt passed away suddenly on Christmas day, and it has been a challenge, to say the least," Camelia said.

"The infamous Auntie Freda? Damn, I'm so sorry. That's gotta be tough."

He actually sounded sympathetic.

"Yes, the one and only. And I think I've spent too much time with you criminal types, because everything about her death looks pretty suspicious, and it's driving me crazy trying to figure out what happened," she said.

Byron chuckled. "Uh huh. That's how it starts. And then it becomes an obsession. But what makes you suspicious?"

"My aunt was allergic to opioids and died of an overdose of fentanyl. Kinda suspicious, if you ask me."

Byron let out a low whistle. "Are the police involved? Or is this more of a wrongful death situation?"

"Both. The cops are involved because of the fentanyl, but there's no body to examine. My aunt's remains were cremated on the same day as her death, which is also suspicious. But given that there's no way to do a post-mortem, I don't think there's enough evidence to prove murder," Camelia said.

"Some vacation, huh? This business with your aunt sounds interesting … sorry. I don't mean to be a ghoul, but you know what I mean. The death is a tragedy, and the circumstances are intriguing. Send over the Forman agreement as soon as you can, and keep me posted about your aunt," Byron said.

Camelia made her promises and hung up.

Shitshitshit.

How could she have forgotten about the Forman settlement? Even so, it sounded like she'd earned some points with Byron. Or at the very least piqued his interest. On the other hand, Leon was going to be furious about her working during vacation. Again.

Camelia gulped the last of her wine and pulled a pillow into her lap, hugging it against her belly. She had until tomorrow to put together the settlement agreement, but it could wait for morning. Right now, she just needed to hold herself together long enough to call JoJo, which she'd been meaning to do before she was sidetracked by Ben.

Camelia thumbed through her contacts until she found Josephine's number.

"Auntie JoJo? It's Camelia, how are you?"

"Oh, hello dear. I guess I'm as well as can be expected given that my lifelong friend has died and left me in charge of the planet," she said. "I'm actually sitting here with Harri right now. We're drinking scotch and reminiscing. Having a bit of a wake. And you? How are you and Leon managing?"

"We're okay. Upset. Confused. And maybe in shock a bit, too. It's all so sudden," Camelia said. "I'm trying to put all this in perspective."

"Hang on. I'll put you on speaker so Harri will stop nattering at me." Camelia could hear Harriet scolding Josephine in the background. "There, now we're all here."

"Hi Auntie Harri. I know you two must be heartbroken, as am I. And I can't help but wonder if Auntie Freda seemed okay or if she was sick. Maybe with something serious?" Camelia said.

"Hello Cammy, Harri here. Isn't this just the worst? We were with Freda on … what day was it, JoJo?" Harriet said.

Camelia felt a rush of affection as Harriet included her in their little club.

"The 20th. For Christmas Tea," Josephine said.

"Yes, that's right. We saw Freda on the twentieth, and she was just fine. We had a lovely time and talked about our estate plans and her engagement," Harriet said. "Little did we know …"

"If she was sick, serious or otherwise, she would have told us. But it was the opposite. Freddie was in high spirits, looking forward to her wedding," Josephine added.

"So you didn't notice anything out of the ordinary before Christmas eve, when Freda went to the hospital?" Camelia prompted.

"Well, she fainted at the Italian Club the night of the Feast, whatever day that was," Harriet said. "But we'd all had scads of wine, and it was hot as blazes in there with all the dancing, so …"

"That was the nineteenth, Harri. And don't forget, she was proposed to! That would make a person faint, wouldn't it?" Josephine said.

"Yes, too much excitement could make her faint. But I was thinking of closer to the twenty fourth," Camelia said.

"I called on the twenty third to meet for brunch after her hair appointment, but Kenna answered. Said Freddie was getting her hair done and couldn't talk. Which is ridiculous, because *of course* she could talk and have her hair styled at the same time. I called again that evening, and it went to voice mail. But, she didn't call back …." Josephine said.

"That was such a worry. We always took each other's calls no matter what. We learned that the hard way. At our age, when a friend calls, you answer, just in case it's the last time you talk to them," Harriet said.

"So if no one talked to Auntie Freda on the 23rd, maybe she was already not feeling well. You two knew her better than anyone. What you do think happened?" Camelia said.

"I think it was just her time, dear. None of us can predict …" Harriet said.

"Oh for Chrissake, Harri. You saw her. She was over the moon about Arthur, giddy like a schoolgirl. So no, it was not Freddie's *time*."

"She was worried about Kenna though …" Harriet said.

"She wasn't *worried*. Freddie knew Kenna was gonna have a hissy fit about selling the house, but Freddie could handle her. It's been a rough couple of years for Freddie, with Kenna under her roof," Josephine said.

"That's not very kind, JoJo. Kenna's had her own struggles. I mean, that horrible car accident …" Harriet said.

Josephine interrupted. "You mean the car accident she caused because she was double the legal limit on top of oxy?"

"Well … besides, Freddie was in the hospital when she passed, and you know how dangerous that is for us women of a certain age," Harriet said. "It's so scary to know you can get run over by a bus right in front of a doctor, and if you're over 70, they'll say, oh, she died of old age. Just because you're old when you die, doesn't mean you died of old age."

"Okay, that part is true," Josephine conceded.

"And then to skip the rituals? It's so typical of Kenna to just ignore the things that aren't important to her, even though ceremony and ritual meant everything to Freddie," Harriet said.

"True. Our Freddie was a stickler for protocol. Like a wake, a funeral mass, the usual things that normal people have when they die. Honestly, I'm so furious with Kenna right now …" Josephine said.

"They apparently had a little squabble because Freddie wouldn't elope to Hawaii like Kenna wanted her to, so maybe that's why Kenna is being such a little snot," Harriet said. "And Freddie told her she was going to sell the Crescents house, too."

"Wait until Kenna finds out about the new estate plan," Josephine said, with a short laugh that sounded like a goose honking. "That's gonna light her up, for sure."

"How so?" Camelia asked.

"We were sworn to secrecy, Cammy. But you'll find out tomorrow when Bobby reads the will. It's a delightful surprise," Harriet said.

"That sounds intriguing and I can't wait to hear the secret," Camelia said. "I really should go since Ben's here for a visit, but let's get together," Camelia said.

They made a date to meet for brunch at one of Freda's favorite bistros the following week, and Camelia hung up. Their affectionate banter reminded Camelia of her own fragile alliances. She thought of Rita, their lifelong friendship, and how meaningless their little tiffs were in the scheme of things. She vowed to be a better friend.

I could lose her, too, in the blink of an eye.

44

Camelia Comes Clean

December 30

Just as Camelia hung up from her call with Josephine and Harriet, Leon came to check on her.

"Cam, what's going on? Ben's about to leave, the kids just got back, and … are you going to join us?"

"I … I … sorry. Just got off the phone," Camelia sputtered. "Be right there."

"It's kinda rude to just leave Ben hanging. He's on his way, so come say goodbye," Leon said, his words bristling with resentment.

Camelia got up and ran her fingers through her hair. "Yep, you're right," she said, as she followed him to the living room.

"Everything okay?" Ben asked.

"Yeah, sorry, I'm fine. Just had a call from work, then JoJo called," she said.

"No worries. Norah's waiting outside in the car, so I gotta go," he said, and started pulling on his snow boots. "You know, I've been the man in the family since 1971, but you'd never guess by the way Rita and Kenna walk all over me. But now that Mum's dead, it's time for me to step up, starting now," he said.

Camelia hugged Ben. "Wait until you're sober, bro."

He laughed. "I'm not likely to be sober until we get back to California, so …" Ben shrugged. "See you guys tomorrow, I guess." Ben waved and slammed the door behind him.

"So what did the office want?" Leon asked.

Camelia took a deep breath. The weight of holding secrets from Leon was more than she could carry.

What would Freda do?

For one thing, she wouldn't care what anyone else thought. She followed her own instincts, listened to her own inner wisdom, and didn't let the criticism of others slow her down. If she were here, she would just barrel ahead. So that's what Camelia decided to do.

"Sophie? Steve?" Camelia called.

"In the kitchen, Mum," Sophie said.

"Family meeting," Camelia said, pressing her fingertips to her burning eyes.

Leon flung himself on the sofa and raised his eyebrows at Camelia. "Great. Am I gonna need another beer for this?"

"Probably. Sophie, bring the wine," Camelia said. "And a fresh beer for Dad."

When the other three were settled, Camelia laid it all out. Her initial suspicions about medical mistake, her discoveries at the hospital and funeral home, her concerns about Kenna, snooping at Auntie Freda's house with Sophie's help, the meeting with Mr. Conroy and his fingerprint analysis, her visit with Arthur, the report from the pharmacy, and—finally—Dr. Fitz's bombshell.

Steve stared intently into a glass of Guinness. Sophie chimed in, adding her own impressions. And Leon was stone-faced, jaw clenched, his beer untouched on the table.

"Are you done? Because this … this business of fake drugs and fingerprints and all that, it's over the top, even for you, Cam," Leon said.

"But is it? Dr. Fitz said …" Camelia said.

"I know what he said. And it's sad and wrong that Freda died alone in the hospital but she was, after all, 85. Shit happens when you're old. Including sudden death. It didn't *have* to be a drama but you've certainly made it that way. And now you've involved, of all people, the RCMP?" Leon said.

"It's just Janet's dad. I've known him forever," Camelia said, and heard the defensiveness in her own voice.

"*Chip Conroy?* He's not just *Janet's dad*. What were you *thinking*?" Leon said, and dragged his hands down his face.

"Why do you say it like I've done something wrong?" Camelia asked.

"You *know* why," Leon said, and tapped his phone. He swiped and tapped a couple of times and began to read. "Charles Chip Conroy retired as one of the RCMP's finest forensic investigators, etcetera. Retirement a dozen years ago. Colleagues say he knew every whorl and swirl of a fingerprint and could piece together partials all day long without fail. Conroy received blah blah commendations, and so on. I've actually cited his work in a couple of my white papers on cybercrime."

Camelia shrugged. "He's always just been Janet's dad to me. Besides, he's retired. He's just a docent now."

"Regardless, he's an *expert*, and he's still attached to the RCMP, Cam. Freda is dead and nothing—not even a conviction, even if you could actually prove anything—will bring her back. At this point, I'm ready to get on the plane, go home to Phoenix, and forget all about this stupid mess," he said. "But since that ain't happening, I think I'll order Thai food and have something a little stronger than beer."

Leon rose and started gathering their empty glasses. Camelia reached for his hand.

"Don't," Leon said, under his breath. Camelia withered under his icy glare.

Rita, Chip Conroy, and now Leon.

Not to mention Byron, with his own version of the sword of Damocles swinging over her head. Regardless of what happened at work, she couldn't let her marriage fall apart, too. Camelia had to find a way to make up with Leon, if for no other reason than to keep from ruining the holiday for the kids. She thought back to her own difficult family holidays, bristling with angry barbs between her parents. She'd vowed to never create that kind of memory for Sophie. Camelia would have to be the one making the peace offering, though, since she'd created all this conflict, despite knowing how Leon would feel if she barreled ahead. She'd done it anyway. By demanding answers, looking for the truth, Camelia had managed to piss off pretty much everyone.

But what if she was right?

Would that convince them she wasn't a crackpot, just rocking the family boat for her own aggrandizement?

Or have I already gone too far?

45

Eye Witness

December 31

Camelia pulled up to the salon and parked, nosing the rental car into a snowbank. She'd booked a morning at Freda's salon for some girl time with her aunt, away from the rest of the family, but that was before Auntie Freda died. Camelia was exhausted from trying to figure out why her aunt had died so suddenly so, instead of canceling the appointment, she decided to bring Sophie along. At least they would get a little quiet time together before the reading of the will that afternoon.

The salon was in a thoroughly bohemian heritage home that had been a fixture in the area since the early 70s. Sure, the interior had been overhauled every decade or so, but the vibe remained: warm, funky, dependably familiar.

When Jolene Jarvis saw Sophie and Camelia arrive, she rushed to hug them. Jolene offered all the usual small talk—so great to see you, how long are you in town, gosh your hair has grown—then looked at them expectantly.

"So? How's Freda? Is she coming separately? We were so worried about …" Jolene stopped when she saw the stricken look on Camelia's face and Sophie's eyes filled with tears. "Oh no … don't tell me," Jolene said.

Camelia nodded, her lips pressed tight to hold in a sob. "She passed Christmas morning. We didn't even get to see her," she said.

"Follow me," Jolene said, leading the two through the salon to two chairs near the expansive front windows.

"Please, sit down, and tell me everything. And I'll try not to cry too much," Jolene said, pressing a tissue to her nose.

While she expertly painted highlights onto Camelia's hair, Camelia gave the abbreviated version of events. She didn't know much, so it was a short story. Lisa, the stylist next to Jolene, was mixing purple dye for Sophie's hair and waved her comb at Jolene.

"Jolene, tell them about Kenna," she said, her perfect eyebrows punctuating her lowered voice.

"What about Kenna?" Camelia asked. Her lawyer mind was listening intently.

"Well, you know, I've been doing Freda's hair for … I don't know …," Jolene said.

Lisa interrupted her. "Pretty much since you started here, and that's been over 20 years."

"God, has it really been that long? Anyway, I've been doing Freda's hair every week all those years and . . ." Jolene paused, and her bottom lip trembled. She took a deep breath. "Freda just wasn't herself when she came in last week. Not herself at all, you know. She couldn't even hold her head up, and she could barely talk. If I didn't know better, I would have said she was stoned or drunk or both," she said, shaking out a fresh towel and draping it over Camelia's neck. "This will have to sit for a few minutes." She prodded the foils into a pile on Camelia's head.

"But tell her about Kenna," Lisa said, nodding for emphasis.

"Oh, right. You know how Kenna's a total hypochondriac and always running to the doctor for every little thing, right? Well, here's her old Mum, barely able to stand up, and she just goes, like, pfft, no big deal, eh?

It was frickin' weird as hell if you ask me," Jolene said, her prairie accent winding up.

"Did she say anything about why Auntie Freda wasn't feeling well?" Camelia asked.

"No, she didn't seem to know. Kenna said she'd fallen that morning, and I thought that was pretty weird too, eh? Like, why wouldn't she have taken Freda right to Emerg? I told Kenna she should take Freda to the hospital instead of getting her hair styled, and she about bit my head off," Jolene said. "Are you gonna want a trim today, too?"

"Sure," Camelia answered, holding her fingers just a bit apart. "Not too much," she said.

"That's the god's honest truth. Witnessed the whole thing," Lisa added. "Kenna was not the least bit worried, as if it was the most normal thing in the world to have to drag the old bird down the sidewalk," she said, then clapped her hand over her mouth. "Sorry, I'm so sorry. I didn't mean to call your Auntie an old bird," she said, and blushed to the roots of her hot pink hair.

Camelia waved it off. "No worries, I mean Auntie Freda was, in fact, an old bird. A grand old bird. She deserves better."

"Oh, for sure she does, and I can't imagine what happened, poor old dear. I mean, she was on the floor when Kenna found her that morning …" Jolene said.

"Wait. What do you mean she was on the floor? You said she fell but …" Camelia said, craning her head around to face Jolene.

"Didn't Kenna tell you? She found Freda barely conscious on the floor of her bedroom that morning. Like she fell out of bed or something. Kenna thought she'd had a stroke," Jolene said. "I can't believe … well, yes, on second thought, I *can* believe she didn't tell you."

"Holy shit. And she brought her *here* instead of going to the ER right away? What on earth was she thinking?" Sophie said.

"No idea, but she wasn't thinking about Freda, that's for sure," Jolene said. "I called Kenna the next day to check on Freda, but my call went to voicemail, and she still hasn't called back. I didn't want to nag, what with everyone being busy over the holidays."

Camelia's synapses were firing in twelve directions at once. So maybe Freda had a stroke? Or a bad fall that caused a head injury? And if Kenna found her on the floor, why the hell didn't she call 911 right then?

Camelia realized she was already compiling deposition questions. She needed a pad of paper to start jotting notes: all the possibilities, all the various angles of the case and, most important, the big holes in her theory. What part of all this wouldn't hold up to scrutiny?

Their hair styled, Sophie and Camelia moved to the nail area and reclined in side-by-side pedicure chairs. Camelia furiously scribbled notes on the backs of crumpled receipts she was digging out of her oversized handbag. There, at the bottom of her bag, the folder she'd taken from Auntie Freda's bedroom.

How the hell did I forget about this?

A little flash of panic darted across her mind. Camelia was forgetting a lot of important details lately, and she wondered if all the anxiety meds were giving her brain fog. Not that it mattered, since she couldn't really function without them. But what if she couldn't function *with* them?

"Oh my god. I just realized I've been carting this file of Auntie Freda's all over town," she said.

"What is it?" Sophie asked, as Camelia pulled the contents out of the big manila envelope.

"It's Auntie Freda's will, and some other paperwork," Camelia whispered.

"So, let's have a look," Sophie said, leaning over to see.

"I don't have time to read every word, and not sure I should, but I have to know who Auntie Freda's executor is, because that person—whoever it is—should be looking at the wrongful death aspect of all this. It could bring a big settlement to the estate, if I can prove it, and there might also be a life insurance inquiry," Camelia said.

The thick monogrammed paper was marked with Freda's looping script. Camelia was surprised when she saw the date: December 20. Freda must have written this will immediately after her engagement with Arthur. She flipped to the first page, looking for the clause about appointment of a Personal Representative. When she saw it, she sucked in her breath.

"What?" Sophie said.

"Holy crap. Auntie Freda named Jolene as her executor," she let out a short laugh. "This is kind of a big deal. And motive, if Kenna knew about it," Camelia said.

"Why would Auntie Freda … wouldn't she name Rita? She's the eldest," Sophie said.

"Yes, she is the eldest, but that's not always the best choice for PR, because just think of the backlash. Especially from Kenna. But Jolene? I'm surprised, but I think it's *genius*. Jolene won't take any shit off anyone in the family, which is probably why Freda chose her," Camelia said.

As if on cue, Jolene came over with two glasses of champagne.

"Care for a little holiday cheer?" she said, holding the flutes out by their stems.

"I thought you'd never ask," Camelia said, with a sad smile. "And, it's none of my business, but are you Auntie Freda's personal representative?"

"Well, she asked me if I would, and I said yes. I had no idea …" Jolene said.

"Have you talked to Bob Barrett?"

"Yes, he called. I'm supposed to go to his office this afternoon for a meeting about the will. I figured it was to sign the acceptance documents," Jolene said, her brow furrowing. "He didn't tell me Freda had passed. He must have thought I already knew."

"No, it's not a *meeting about the will*, it's the *reading of the will*, Jolene, and you have to be there," Camelia said.

Jolene shook her head. "Ya know, sometimes, I can't hear a thing in here, with all the blowdryers going. Oh man, Kenna is going to be *pissed*," Jolene said. "Sorry, I have to run." Jolene gave a little wave as she left to greet her next client.

"I have to get this over to the lawyer pronto," Camelia said, looking up Bob Barrett's website on her mobile phone. When it loaded, she tapped the phone icon and spoke to the receptionist.

"Yep, it's for the Swenson estate, and I'll drop it off in about twenty minutes," Camelia said and hung up.

She hurriedly pushed the handwritten pages back into the envelope. There was resistance and, when she peered inside, Camelia saw a collection of letter-size envelopes in the bottom. She didn't have time to look at them, as her pedicure was complete and they were on a tight schedule. She folded crisp $50 bills into the tiny tip envelopes at the front desk and waved at Jolene as they left.

"Okay, Sophie, next stop, Barrett's office to drop this file off," Camelia said, turning the defrost to high. They'd only been in the salon a couple of hours, but the windshield was already frosted over.

"Better step on it, because you know how dad and Steve will be if we're late to pick them up. And whaddya think about Kenna bringing Auntie Freda here when she was so sick? Honestly, Mum, I know you don't want to hear it, but Kenna's just *horrible,*" Sophie said.

"You're my witness," Camelia said and held up her right hand. "I swear, if Kenna did something to Auntie Freda, I *will* get to the bottom of it."

This was Camelia in fight mode: fiercely focused, bullheaded, and looking for justice. The difference was that this time it was family. Was she really up for a holy war with the Swenson clan over the death of Freda? Not to mention the friction it was causing between her and Leon. She didn't want to create more hurt for everyone, but she knew there would be no peace, at least in her heart, until she found out who was responsible for harming her beloved aunt.

Camelia drove as fast as she dared to Bob Barrett's office to drop off the original will. She'd lost track of time in the soothing hum of the salon, and they were due back at Barrett's office in just over an hour for the reading of the will, so there was no time to spare. Luckily, Regina is a small city, so getting from the salon to his office was just a few minutes' drive.

"Jeez, Mum, you better not get pulled over for speeding, or Dad will never let you live it down," Sophie said, holding onto the door handle as Camelia rounded a corner.

"I know," Camelia said, with a grimace.

As she pulled up in front of Barrett's office, she realized she needed a record of the delivery. It wasn't that Camelia didn't trust Bob Barrett, it's just that she knew better than to deliver anything to anyone without a record. She'd been burned before. She began pulling items from the envelope and snapping photos with her phone.

"Mum, do you really need a pic of *everything*?" Sophie asked.

"Yeah, I do. I'm making a record of what I delivered. I don't want to be accused of withholding legal documents," Camelia said.

Camelia put the documents back into the envelope and sprinted out of the car, into the law office. She dropped the envelope on the reception desk with a smile and a wave, then ran back to the car. She was headed toward the rental house when she realized she had completely forgotten about dropping the nose spray, syringe, and lozenge at the FedEx office for overnight delivery to the tox lab in Ohio.

Shit. That's the third thing I've forgotten.

"Goddammit, Sophie! I forgot about dropping the FedEx package, so hold on and buckle up. This has to get sent out today, or I'll never get the results back before we leave. Find a FedEx shop for me, please."

"Oh god, mum. We really don't have time, but okay," Sophie said, frantically typing on her phone. "The nearest FedEx office is straight up Albert. And Jesus Christ be careful," she said, as Camelia spun the tires on the icy street, the back end of her car fishtailing wildly across the intersection.

46

The Reading of the Will

December 31

Robert Barrett placed his file on the table and rolled his shoulders. His neck popped, which he took as a good omen. Considering the meeting he was about to have, Bob needed all the good omens he could get.

He glanced at the seating chart Natalie had prepared. From his right, Jolene Jarvis, Naomi Brazda, Arthur Rossi, Harriet Johnson, Josephine Danchuk, Kenna Shores, Mickey Shores, Dave Becker, Rita Becker, Leon Belmont, Camelia Belmont, Norah Swenson, and, finally, Ben Swenson at his left.

As he stood quietly at the head of the conference table, the murmurs stilled and all eyes focused on Bob.

"Welcome, and thank you for coming on short notice," he said, and settled into his chair. "I realize you're all grieving your wonderful Freda—we all are—she was quite a woman, and I'm so sorry for your loss. My understanding is that services have not yet been arranged, and I know it's tradition to read the will and begin distributing bequests immediately after the funeral. But that's just *tradition*, not the law. Under the circumstances, it makes sense to read the will while you're all in town, and then you can make arrangements for services and for the transport of Freda's remains."

Rita and Ben exchanged a look, and they both glared at Kenna, who was concentrating on shredding a tissue.

Bob looked at his notes. The only sound in the room was the rustle of human fidgeting and Kenna's sniffling. Mickey had his arm around her and was stroking her hand. Bob had *specifically* asked that the second generation—the grandchildren—refrain from attending, given the size of his conference room, but Mickey was here in spite of it. He'd insisted his mother was too fragile and heartbroken to attend without him at her side.

"I know this can be a difficult time," Bob said, nodding at Kenna. "And yet, the business of life goes on. And I'm here to help you accomplish the tasks that must be done now that Freda is gone."

"I have a question," Mickey said. "Why are they here?" he asked, pointing at Naomi Brazda and Jolene Jarvis.

"Yes, yes, I'll get to that shortly. But first, some background. In the province of Saskatchewan, we have two forms of valid will. The first is the type you're probably all familiar with: the formal, witnessed will," Bob said, reading from his notes.

Kenna pulled a spiral bound sheaf of paper from her lap and laid it on the worn oak conference table.

"This is Mum's will. It's the one you prepared for her, Bob. It's witnessed and everything," Kenna said.

"Yes, quite right." Bob nodded, and returned to his notes. "And the other type of will is the holographic will. Now, the reason we have a law that allows a holograph, is because of a man named Cecil Harris from Rosetown, up Kindersley way," he said.

Bob felt scholarly, his voice moving down in register as he warmed to his oration. It was a rare moment that Bob had the confidence of an expert, but this was one of those times. It brought a bright energy to his words and his back straightened. Then Mickey interrupted.

"What the hell is a *holograph,* and what the hell does it have to do with us?" Mickey asked.

"You're ahead of the game, Mickey," Bob said with a tense smile. "A holograph means a hand-written document, signed by the testator. It does not require a witness," he said.

Bob could hear his own impatience, but he didn't really care. It annoyed him that Mickey—who wasn't even supposed to be here—wouldn't let him finish. It showed in the flare of Bob's substantial nostrils.

"And?" Mickey said. There was a challenge in his voice.

"And everyone should fully understand what a holograph means," Bob said, his annoyance rising. "Now, Mr. Harris, a farmer, was pinned under his tractor, and scratched out his will on the fender as he lay dying. And our courts said, well now, Cecil Harris made his intentions known and he signed this fender, and that's darn sure good enough." Bob chuckled.

He caught himself and cleared his throat. His hand strayed to his tie, adjusting the knot in a nervous tic. Mickey huffed and looked around the table.

"Paid by the hour, are you, Bob?" Mickey smirked. "We don't really need the history lesson."

Bob turned to Mickey, his eyes narrowing.

What a rude little shit!

"Actually, I don't charge for reading the will. And I am getting on with it, but I think it's important to understand the law," he said.

"Bob, we appreciate the background. Please, we're all interested to hear what you have to say," Camelia interjected.

"Thank you …" he consulted his chart. Camelia Belmont. She was the lawyer. At least one person in the room understood. Bob began again. "At any rate, because of the Harris case, a testator is allowed to handwrite their will …"

"What does this have to do with my Mum?" Kenna blurted. "She has a real will. It's right here!" Kenna stabbed the document in front of her with a glittery fingernail.

"What it has to do with Freda, and with all of you, is that Freda issued a holographic will on December 20, which supersedes *all other instruments*. Including the will you brought with you, Kenna. And *that's* why I wanted you to understand the law," he said, annoyance creeping into his voice.

He flipped open his file, pulled out the original handwritten will, and held it up.

"This is Freda Swenson's last will and testament," he said, waving it with dramatic flair.

Bob imagined himself as Perry Mason producing the smoking gun and, on cue, a gasp rippled through the over-warm conference room. There were murmurs and under-the-breath whispers and even a chuckle or two, but it was Kenna's reaction that caught everyone's attention. Her face drained of color, her chubby hands gripped into fists, and she glared at Bob.

"That's a fucking lie! I have Mum's *real* will right here. What are you trying to pull?" she screeched, shaking the will in Bob's direction. "Camelia, you're a lawyer. Speak up! Tell him! This is Mum's real will!"

"Hey now, there's no call for cursing. And I'm not trying to pull anything. I am honoring my client's wishes, *to the letter*," Bob said. "I know it must be surprising …"

"Surprising? No, it's a joke, a stupid lie. I can't believe you're sitting here telling us Mum wrote a will and didn't tell me. Or anyone. Do you even know if it's real?" Kenna said, bursting into a fresh round of sobs. "I've been through so much and now this." She buried her face in her hands.

"Freda told JoJo and I she was revising her estate plan. We discussed it at our Christmas brunch. What day was that, JoJo?" Harriet said.

Josephine tapped her smart phone a couple of times. "Right. We discussed Freda's new estate plan on … here it is … December 20. She went straight home and wrote her new will, just as she said she would."

Camelia audibly blew out a heavy sigh.

Mickey whispered into Kenna's ear.

Rita dabbed her eyes and exchanged looks with Dave.

Jolene stared at her lap.

Ben and Norah leaned into each other.

Arthur Rossi, seated next to Jolene, nodded to himself, his eyes glistening with tears.

Harriet and Josephine, dressed all in black, clasped each other's hands and whispered to one another.

Naomi Brazda, Freda's longtime housekeeper, rubbed a rough spot on the edge of the table.

Bob took a deep breath. He took off his glasses and ran his hands over his face. This was a rough meeting and made him acutely aware of his shortcomings. Bob was not an eloquent speaker or fastidious researcher. He wasn't sure he fully understood all the nuances of the law, but he understood the basics, and Freda's handwritten will was valid. Sure, it had to be presented to the Court for affirmation, but there was no doubt in his mind that would be nothing more than a formality. He had already compared the stationary and handwriting to that in his files, and it was definitely Freda's.

That wasn't the issue. The problem for Bob was that he hated this kind of scene, and had never developed immunity to such openly confrontational people. Kenna and Mickey were acting so uncouth. Thank god Freda hadn't made *him* the executor. He cleared this throat.

"As I was saying, Mrs. Swenson had every legal right to make her wishes known in either a formal will, such as the one Ms. Shores has in her possession, or a holographic will, such as the one Freda wrote on December 20." He raised his hand as he saw Kenna prepare to speak. "And if you'll bear with me, I will now read the will, so the suspense will be over. After I'm finished reading Freda's will, we can go around the room and answer questions, okay?"

Mickey whispered to Kenna and she nodded. Bob looked around the room as a low hum of yeses accompanied nods of agreement.

The will was written on Freda's personal stationary, thick cream linen paper with her monogram at the top; the same paper she used for all her correspondence. The same paper Bob had seen at least a dozen times over the years. And he had no doubt it was Freda's handwriting, her right-leaning cursive, loopy and full of flourishes. An old-fashioned penmanship style, befitting of Freda.

"Good. Here we go," Bob said, and read from the document in front of him.

December 20

I, Freda Agnes Swenson, nee Corelli, of Regina, Saskatchewan, born December 30, 1935 ...

Harriet gasped.

Bob Barrett paused.

"Oh my goodness, we'll have to cancel Freddie's birthday party," Harriet said, turning to Josephine.

"But Freda's birthday would have been yesterday," Bob said.

"Yes, but Freddie liked to celebrate at the end of June, away from all the holiday hoopla. This year we were cruising down the Rhine," Josephine said, dabbing at tears.

"Sorry, Bob, please go on," Harriet said.

"Where was I? Oh yes ..."

I hereby proclaim this holographic will as my last Will and Testament. This Will provides my wishes and intentions for the disposition of my estate upon my death. This document voids any other Will I have previously signed. I am of sound mind and body.

I appoint Jolene Jarvis, my wonderful friend and hairstylist, as my executor.

There was a bang as Kenna brought her fist down on the table.

"Are you kidding me? Her goddamn hairdresser? Well, good for you, Jolene. I guess you poisoned my own mother against me," Kenna wailed.

Jolene's face flushed as she looked from Barrett to Kenna and back again.

"Mrs. Swenson asked me a couple of weeks ago if I would be her executor, and I said I would. Obviously, I had no idea ... Bob, is there something I need to sign?" Jolene asked, avoiding Kenna's glare.

"Yes, Natalie has the paperwork ready to notarize when we're all done here," Bob said. "Now, if I may?"

My heirs as named in this will are as follows.
I have three living children, namely:
Rita June Becker
Benjamin Isak Swenson
Kenna Anne Shores

I have five living grandchildren, namely:
Darren Becker
Dana Becker
Andrew Swenson
Cassandra Swenson
Michelangelo Shores

I have two living great-grandchildren, namely:
Clara Rose Becker
Sashay Suyin Shores

Of my living friends and extended family, I name:
Arthur Rossi
Harriet Johnson
Josephine Danchuk
Camelia Porcher Belmont
Sophie Belmont
Jolene Jarvis
Naomi Brazda

My primary checking account is with RBC at the branch on 2002 11th Avenue, Regina, opened on December 21, 2020. The account number is 671258349.

"Hold on, Bob. What was that account number again?" Kenna said.

"Kenna … Ms. Shores, there is a second account that Freda mentions next. That's the one you're on as the beneficiary."

"Okay, good. Because I don't recognize that account number, and I'm on *all* Mum's accounts," she said, loudly blowing her nose.

"Is that so?" Ben said, glaring at Kenna.

"Correction. You're on *one* of the *three* RBC accounts," Bob said, a bit too harshly, he realized. "Let me finish, and then I'm happy to answer questions."

My primary savings account is at the RBC branch on 2002 11th Avenue, Regina, opened on February 2, 1977. The account number is 671258350.

My secondary checking account is a joint account with Kenna Shores at the RBC branch at Golden Mile on Albert, and she is entitled to the balance upon my death. The account number is 671259241.

Kenna smirked and nodded at Mickey, apparently satisfied to have inherited the entire account. Bob continued reading.

My safe deposit box is also at the RBC branch at Golden Mile on Albert, and contains Geoffrey's medals, my mother's diamonds, my father's cufflinks and pocket watches, and some loose stones Geoffrey gifted to me on our fifth anniversary. The medals, cufflinks, and pocket watches go to Ben. The stones are to be divided among Rita and Kenna. The remainder is to be liquidated.

From my primary RBC account, I bequest the following:

To Clara Rose Becker and Sashay Suyin Shores, the sum of $50,000 each for their college education, to be held in trust by their maternal grandmothers.

To Darren Becker, Dana Becker, Andrew Swenson, Cassandra Swenson, Michelangelo Shores, and Sophie Belmont, *the sum of $25,000 each. I hope you use it for travel. I've always enjoyed the Maritimes and the Mediterranean.*

My real estate holdings are the Crescents house and a five-acre lot at Long Lake, Regina Beach. The lot is co-owned with Harriet Johnson and Josephine Danchuk, with right of survivorship. I do hope Harri and JoJo enjoy a few more picnics at the lake before they join me in the Hereafter.

The Crescents house is to be listed for sale 30 days after my death. Therefore, all bequests of personal property must be accomplished promptly. No lollygagging!

I direct my daughter, Kenna Shores, to vacate the Crescents house within 30 days of my death.

I further direct my daughter Rita Becker and my son Benjamin Swenson to remove all of their memorabilia and other personal effects from the house within 30 days.

As of Day 31, I direct Jolene Jarvis to oversee cleaning and staging, before placing the residence on the market for sale with Bruce Danchuk, realtor.

Kenna's wailing interrupted Bob.

Mickey's face was flushed in anger. "Unbelievable," he muttered.

"I can confirm Freda gave Bruce the listing details about a week ago, as Freddie was planning on moving in with her new husband," Josephine said, reaching across Harriet to squeeze Arthur's arm. "Bruce will be ready to begin marketing the house as soon as Jolene signs the listing contract," Josephine said, nodding in Jolene's direction.

"Oh I'm sure he's looking forward to that fat commission, too," Mickey retorted.

"Again, these are Freda's wishes, and it's important that we all honor them as directed," Bob said. "Now, please, let's get through this and we can discuss logistics."

My remaining personal property, besides the bank accounts and safe deposit box, consists of the furnishings of my home, my jewelry, my personal effects, my car, my life insurance policy and some investment accounts.

To Arthur Rossi, I bequeath first choice of anything you may want to remind you of me. I love you with all my heart, dear Arthur, and I will meet you on the other side. I particularly think the Dorothy Knowles landscape titled Yellow Flowers, hanging in my dining room, would be splendid over your sofa.

To Harriet Johnson and Josephine Danchuk, my dearest friends in this lifetime, I bequeath second choice of anything you may want as a reminder, including my jewelry. You have been the absolute best companions on this journey of life, and I am so happy to have had you near all our lives.

To Rita Becker, my first born child, I bequeath all of my cookbooks, the Royal Albert Silver Maple China set, all the good knives and pans, and anything else from my kitchen you want. You are a wonderful cook and I hope you continue to prepare feasts for the family long after I'm gone.

To Benjamin Swenson, my first born son, I bequeath all of Geoffrey's military memorabilia, his uniforms, and so on, which are in the two large wooden trunks in the basement storage. Your father's regimental sword is hanging over the fireplace in my bedroom, and should also be yours. Your father loved you very much, and he would be proud of the man you are today.

To Kenna Shores, my last born child, I bequeath my collection of Folmer Hansen pottery. He was a dear friend and your "Uncle Fol" for many years. I also forgive the loans you made on my RBC account. I hope you spent the money wisely.

"Are you fucking kidding me?" Kenna screeched.

Mickey's eyes were wide and his mouth was open. "What the hell, Bob?"

Bob leaned back in his chair and stared at the ceiling, wishing he could just quit, right now, close up shop and get on with retirement. He shut his eyes and pictured a day on the lake, ice fishing and drinking expensive Scotch, trading stupid jokes with his pals, maybe even catching a walleye for dinner. But not yet.

"I'm not sure what you were expecting, Kenna," he said.

"I was expecting you to honor Mum's wishes, just like they're written in here," Kenna said, shaking her envelope at Bob. "This says I'm getting a third of everything, with the rest to Rita and Ben. I can't believe our mother disinherited us all!" Kenna looked to her siblings for support.

"We weren't disinherited, Ken," Rita said. "We're getting what Mum wanted us to have, and that should be enough."

"Easy for you to say," Mickey hissed.

"No one asked you, Mickey. It is what it is," Ben said, with a shrug.

"Rita is correct. No one was disinherited and now, if I may …" Bob said.

To Camelia Belmont, my favorite lawyer (no offense to you, Bob), I bequeath all of my amber jewelry. I know you love the mystery of it as much as I do and will cherish it. Please pass it down to Clara and Sashay, and any other female grandchildren, in your will.

To Jolene Jarvis, my friend and Personal Representative, I bequeath my Mercedes Benz car so you can ride to work in reliable luxury. In addition, I bequeath $50,000 in cash because that bloody car is a gas hog.

To Naomi Brazda, my friend and housekeeper, I bequeath the silver set you've polished all these years. It consists of a setting for 20, serving spoons and forks, tea set, 4 trays, and a set of 6 candlesticks. Thank you for your years of faithful and patient service to my home and family. Please sell the silver — it's worth a small fortune and I don't want you to spend the rest of your life polishing it.

I direct my Personal Representative to hire Gardener's Estates to liquidate the remainder of my household goods, furniture, bric-a-brac, collections, art, and anything else in the house via auction.

I direct Arthur Rossi, Harriet Johnson, and Josephine Danchuk to arrange my funeral mass at Holy Rosary with a memorial celebration at the Italian Club. Make it festive! You know all the things I love, so put on a spread and open the bar. All costs are to be paid by Jolene out of my account.

I will be interred with my deceased husband, Geoffrey, as planned. The arrangements were prepaid and I've enclosed the contract.

The remainder of my estate, consisting of the balance of my primary bank account, the proceeds of sale of my real estate, and the proceeds of sale of my personal property, shall be donated to the Italian Club Foundation as a legacy gift for the sole purpose of constructing a Garden Pavilion in my name and Arthur's. Our names shall be on a prominent plaque . . .

Kenna's audible gasp stopped Bob. Again. At this rate, they'd never get out of here.

"I can't believe Mum would give a fortune to the Italian Club. What a waste. How do we stop this? Bob, can't we protest or fight it in Court or something?" Kenna said.

"I can answer questions when I'm done, but the short answer is no, you cannot stop Freda from bequeathing *her* money to whomever she pleased. Let me finish reading, if you will," Bob said.

Our names shall be on a prominent plaque at the entry to the Freda Corelli Swenson & Arthur Rossi Garden Pavilion. Do make certain they include my birth name as a nod to my Italian heritage. Please have them plant one Freda Clematis for each of my heirs. They can't survive our harsh winters, but will thrive splendidly in the Pavilion. I've left a scribble of my plan for the Pavilion with Arthur, so he can direct the construction. I know Arthur will make my vision a reality.

I assure you these are my wishes and no one forced me into any of it. My children have no need of my money and are entirely too privileged as it is. I will not ruin my grandchildren's ambitions by giving them a windfall.

As for my great-grandchildren, I am providing for their college education because I am not altogether certain their parents will think that far ahead.

None of you have been disinherited although from time to time I have certainly considered doing so; however, if any of you dare to contest this will or threaten to have it invalidated for any reason, you shall be immediately removed from the will and shall have no claim whatsoever against my estate. And remember, it is MY estate to do with as I please, and my intentions as set forth please me very much.

My attorney, Robert Barrett, will have received this in the mail and, if you're reading the handwritten version, it means I have passed prior to having a chance to do a proper witnessed will. Do not give Bob a hard time and follow Jolene's directions to the letter.

Farewell, family and friends. Enjoy your lives and don't waste a second bickering over this.

Freda Agnes Corelli Swenson
from my home in Regina, Saskatchewan.

Bob picked up the document, tapped the pages on the table, and pandemonium broke out.

47

Out With The Old

December 31

Driving through the rutted, icy streets, Leon was reminded of why he would never live in Regina again. No, for him, the relentless heat of Phoenix summers was a small price to pay for not grinding through endless frozen, gray days.

In the passenger seat, Camelia was quietly staring out the window, but he could hear her mind turning. It never stopped. He really wished she would give it a rest. Even on vacation, she was constantly chewing on some problem or other. And now, she was hell bent on proving Auntie Freda died from something other than natural causes.

It hadn't always been this way, or at least he didn't recall it being so. She changed in law school. It was like they taught her to hunt, without any clear guidance on what to look for, so her busy mind constantly scanned the horizon for threats that weren't even there. Sure, the law school experience honed her critical thinking and gave her a career, but it also dialed up her anxiety. Coupled with the stress of her job, the combination had become toxic.

He rolled his shoulders. They ached from being clenched throughout the tense meeting at the lawyer's office, and being hunched over the steering wheel made it worse. All he wanted right now was to sit by the fire with a Black Russian and the spy thriller he was halfway through, but Rita and Dave were coming over before they all headed out to the Trianon for New Year's Eve, and they had to prep.

Leon pulled up to the garage at the AirBnB and waited for the door to lift. He hadn't even shut the engine off before Sophie and Steve were standing beside the car. Leon didn't often take time to consider his daughter and her husband, but all this somber business of death and estates made him introspective as he watched the pompom on Sophie's toque bobbing as she detailed their plans for the evening.

His baby girl. He knew he didn't have to worry about Sophie and that was a huge comfort to a father. She was an accomplished professional in a seemingly happy marriage with a guy he was comfortable around, and that's all he could hope for. Well, grandkids, maybe, someday, but he wasn't going to say that out loud. He didn't want his head bit off for being, as Sophie would say, a puppet of the patriarchy. He smiled to himself. She was her mother's daughter.

"So, anyway, we gotta go, but was there anything interesting in Auntie Freda's will?" Sophie asked.

"Oh, Baby Bear, it was all interesting. But we need to get ready for Auntie Rita and Uncle Dave, so I'll tell you all about it tomorrow. The short version is that you're getting $25,000," Camelia said.

"Wow! That's unexpected!" Sophie said. "But honestly, I'd much rather have Auntie Freda."

"Yeah, it's nice that we're getting money, but *the way* we're getting money sucks," Steve added. "Soph, we gotta get going."

As Sophie and Steve drove away, Leon and Camelia shuffled into the house. The warm stillness billowed around them; it instantly made Leon sleepy, but there was no time for a nap. Camelia changed into her New Year's Eve outfit, while Leon pulled on jeans and a black western style shirt with white trim.

"So, any thoughts about today?" he asked

"In what way?" Camelia brushed plum eyeshadow on her lids.

"You know, the will. Weren't you shocked that Freda left her entire estate to the Italian Club?"

"Oh, the will, yeah, a bit surprising. But not crazy. Auntie Freda was a member her whole life and, like JoJo said, she wanted to leave a legacy that would reach beyond the family. For the community. Personally, I think it's a very civic-minded thing to do, and I applaud it," Camelia said.

"Really? You aren't disappointed you aren't getting a cut? I mean, we could use a little extra …" Leon asked.

"Oh Christ, Leon. Even if Freda had divvied up the estate, I wouldn't be getting anything. I'm a second cousin, remember? I'm grateful to even be *mentioned* in her will. I didn't expect to receive anything, so it's a wonderful surprise. She knew I loved her amber pieces, and now I'll be able to wear a bit of her every day."

"Yeah, I s'pose. No one besides Kenna, obviously, really seemed bothered by Freda's bequest. Arthur Rossi seemed really happy about it, actually," Leon said.

"He seems like a sweet guy. I think it made him happy that she put him in charge of the pavilion project. That will give him purpose. At least for a while," Camelia said, fluffing her hair.

"True," Leon said, and looked at his phone. "Okay, we've got about a half hour, so what do we need to do to get ready for Dave and Rita?"

"Not much. We're gonna order pizza for dinner, so we just need to put some snacks in bowls, throw on some music, set out the liquor, and have a look at the board games in the front closet. I guess if there's nothing there, we can always just play cards until it's time to leave for the Trianon," Camelia said.

"Do you really think they'll want to play games after today? Rita will probably want to rehash everything," Leon said.

"Maybe, but I wanna at least give them the opportunity to put it all aside for a couple of hours. Let's put some games out, and we'll play it by ear. They might welcome the diversion," Camelia said.

Camelia and Leon poured chips and nuts into bowls and lined up bottles of wine and alcohol on the kitchen island. The bottle of vodka was almost empty. The *second* bottle. They'd only been in town ten days, and the second bottle only had an inch or so in the bottom.

"Do we have another vodka? This one's almost done," he said.

"I don't know. Steve put all the liquor in that pantry cupboard," Camelia said. "And if there isn't another one, I'll text Rita to bring a bottle."

"Two bottles in 10 days? And who drank all that vodka, Cam?"

"I don't know. I guess *all* of us?" she said. He caught the note of defensiveness in her voice.

Leon opened the cabinet and took a deep breath. There was another bottle of vodka. And it was already open. As he stared at the bottle, a wave of fear washed over him. He'd been picking up—and just as quickly dismissing—all the cues. At home, he didn't keep a running tally of the bar, because why would he? It was only here, in a strange environ, that he was able to do the math, and it all added up to his wife being a … lush? Or worse? He couldn't bring himself to give it a name.

He didn't know what to say, how to open the conversation, but certainly now was not the time. Not with Rita and Dave on their way. Leon knew, though, that a reckoning was coming, and he was terrified of what lay ahead.

In the back seat of an Uber that smelled of new car and wet wool, Rita gripped a box of baked goods in her lap. She was relieved to get out of the house where the tension was so thick you'd have to cut it with a chainsaw. After the reading of the will, Kenna was viciously angry and blaming everyone—including Rita—for Freda having revised her will.

Rita didn't know why Kenna thought she had anything to do with it, but it was typical. Kenna always blamed everyone else for everything. Nothing was ever her fault. It had been that way her whole life. Rita was overwhelmed and exhausted, and she had no patience for Kenna's self-indulgent ranting. The good news, if there was any, was that Rita didn't have to put up with any of it. With Freda gone and the executor responsibilities with Jolene, Rita was free. Finally, she could live her life as she pleased and to hell with anyone who didn't like it. Including—no, especially—Kenna. Rita blew out a long exhale.

"We could have canceled, you know," Dave said.

"No, we couldn't. I had to get the hell outta there. Fucking Kenna," Rita whispered.

"Don't get me wrong, I'm glad we're going out instead of locking ourselves in the suite until the storm passes," Dave said.

"Kenna's outta control, and I'm sick of hearing it. Apparently she thought she was going to inherit everything."

"She should have known better. An inheritance is never a given," Dave said.

"I never counted on anything from Mum, so it doesn't sting. Much. Still, I would have loved the opportunity to own the house ..."

"Really? It's not like we're ever moving back," Dave said.

"I know but … that house is … I don't know, it's just so special," Rita said.

"As houses go, it's grand. But it's also old, and the foundation is shifting, and it's huge. Way more than we could manage from afar," Dave said.

"You're right. I'm just feeling sentimental about it. And tomorrow I have to see about renting a trailer to haul my stuff home," Rita said. "What a nightmare."

"Okay, but for tonight, let's just enjoy our friends and drink some of this good wine, and relax, okay? You've been through a lot …" Dave said, reaching for her gloved hand.

Rita looked at him with teary eyes. "So have you."

Camelia fussed with the alignment of cheese on the plate and dumped crackers in the center. Finally, a relaxing night with friends. Or so she hoped. The reading of the will had amped up her anxiety—so much drama!—and Camelia was eager to unwind with a stiff drink. Anything to take the edge off.

Of course Leon had to be the one to discover the last bottle of vodka had been opened. Camelia couldn't quite recall why she'd opened it before the second bottle was empty. Maybe that's how sneaking worked. She was sneaking sips behind everyone's back, but lately it was sort of behind her own back, too, because she often didn't recall if she'd had a nip, or not. Which was troubling, because if she couldn't remember having a drink, nothing stopped her from having another. Just thinking about it made her want a vodka soda, *right now*. Instead, she poured half a glass of wine and tossed it back, then filled her glass.

"There's not much here, Cam. Mostly kid games," Leon said, his voice muffled inside the closet. "Wait, I found a tile rummy set and a cribbage board. That's the best I can do," Leon said.

Camelia carried a tray of snacks to the living room as Leon placed the games on the dining table. "Works for me. I always kick your ass in tile rummy!" she laughed.

"Very funny. And tonight, please don't start up about Freda overdosing or whatever," Leon said.

Camelia shook her head and sighed. "I won't. But what do you expect me to do if Rita brings it up?"

"Change the subject. I really don't want to rehash all this again. I heard enough of it from Ben, and I just want a normal evening with friends, okay?"

This was so Leon. He liked his world tidy, orderly, in smooth rows and clean lines and as little conflict as possible. That's why he was so comfortable in his world of cybersecurity. He was able to line up all the code and make it perform as demanded. Everything was predictable. Unlike humans, who were messy and, sometimes, just batshit crazy.

They'd managed to avoid the elephant in the room through cocktails, takeout pizza, and into a round of tile rummy, when Dave cleared his throat.

"So. I don't wanna be the one to bring it up, but …" he said, and looked around the table.

"What's on your mind, Dave?" Camelia responded.

"Oh god, Dave, do we have to? Feels like this so-called vacation has already lasted a year," Rita said, and reached for the bottle of wine.

"Yeah, it's been a rough week," Leon said.

"I know you don't want to talk about it, but I'm just wanna hear Camelia's take on the whole handwritten will thing and …" Dave said.

Leon gave Camelia a look that said, *don't bite*. Not that it would stop her.

"My take? First off, Auntie Freda did an incredibly generous and civic-minded thing. But I'm sure it's a surprise for you guys," she shrugged. "Second, a handwritten will is completely legal, and it sounds like Auntie Freda talked it all out with Harri and JoJo beforehand. And third, I can't believe how damn old Bob Barrett looks," Camelia said, with a shake of her head.

"So you don't think it's weird, *at all*, that she left literally millions of dollars to the Italian Club and basically nothing to her kids? Because let me tell you, a certain person named Kenna is well and truly pissed off," Dave said. "She's having a freakin' meltdown, blaming us, ranting about how unfair life is. As if *anyone* could have told Freda what to do, let alone us."

"She didn't handle it very well at Barrett's office, so I can imagine how she unraveled at home," Camelia replied.

"Yeah, that was pretty over the top, even for Kenna. Obviously she wasn't expecting that outcome. On the other hand, the Italian Club board of directors must be beside themselves. I bet they haven't had that much in the coffers in the entire history of the Club, combined," Dave said.

"Dave …" Rita said, putting her hand on his shoulder.

"What? It's weird, that's all," he said.

"This whole situation is weird," Leon said.

"Guys, it's not that weird. I've only been working in hospice a couple of months, but this doesn't even approach weird. A bag lady—sorry, unhoused woman—was admitted with end-stage dementia. When they unpacked her shopping cart, they found two dead cats sealed in plastic bags with duct tape and about three hundred *thousand* in cash. Now, *that* was weird," Rita said.

"Wow," Camelia said, as she reached for more shortbread to go with the Zinfandel. "You know what else isn't weird? This wine. Damn. Thank you, this is so good," Camelia said.

"Drink up! Everybody was chugging the hard stuff on Boxing Day, so we have tons of wine left," Rita said.

Camelia glanced at Leon. His quick wink told her she'd done the right thing, at least in his opinion, by trying to change the subject. But Dave wasn't about to let it go.

"But you gotta admit it's weird that Kenna had Freda cremated. She had a burial policy, and she was Catholic. Kenna knew better. And all it did was complicate things for Jolene because ..." Dave said.

"Dave, seriously, I don't want to go over all this again." Rita got up from the table. "We need to get ready for the concert. Cam, where's the washroom?"

As soon as the door to the hall bathroom closed, Dave leaned in.

"Look, I don't want to upset Rita any more than she already is, but I don't know who else to tell about this," Dave said.

"Okay ..." Leon said.

"Last night, late, middle of the damn night, I heard a car door slam. I look out the window and what do I see, but Mickey going into the garage. At like 3 a.m.! What the hell's that about?" Dave asked.

"I saw him do the same thing when they left the Boxing Day wake," Camelia said. Leon shot her a look. "Who knows? Maybe he stores ... something ... I don't know what, in Freda's garage," Camelia said.

"There's not much you can store in a garage in the middle of winter except popsicles," Leon said.

The bathroom door opened. Dave straightened up.

"Anyway, we need to suit up because I just got notice our Uber is on the way," Dave said, and headed for the entry.

It was after 2 a.m. by the time Leon and Camelia got home from the Colin James New Year's concert. They tidied up and fell into bed, happy-tired and a little tipsy.

"Thanks for keeping the conversation light tonight," Leon said, pulling Camelia close.

"Just following orders! But this thing with Mickey. What the hell is he up to?" Camelia said.

"Why? Just because he's breaking into the garage in the middle of the night? Oh, I'm sure he's got a *perfectly* good explanation. That little ass has always been up to no good, and I'm sure nothing's changed."

"Wow. How do you really feel?" Camelia said, poking Leon in the ribs.

"I just never had a good feeling about him. Even when he was a little kid. There's just something off. The only word I can think of is devious. He always seems to be trying to get one over on people and lying his ass off about it," Leon said, and yawned. "But whatever the little shit is up to, it has nothing to do with us. In a few days, we'll be outta here, thank god. What time is it? I'm dead tired, Cam."

"Good god, it's almost 3. I need my beauty sleep. What time are the kids due home?"

"They'll be home when the party's over, whenever that is. Happy new year, love," Leon said, and planted a kiss on Camelia's shoulder.

He rolled over, his breathing already beginning to slow. As she began to drift off, she made a mental note to have a look in Freda's garage. Mickey was up to something. Otherwise, why was he there in the middle of the night? Although, just because he was in and out of the garage at all hours didn't mean he was a suspect.

Or maybe it did.

48

Kenna's Plight

December 31

Kenna had to think quick. She chewed her lip, trying to calm her mind. After the bombshell announcement at the lawyer's office, a cold reality was setting in.

Her mother had betrayed her.

Barrett—that traitor—had turned on her.

That conniving bitch Jolene had stabbed her in the back.

Despite receiving Freda's bank account in the will, Kenna would eventually run out of money, no thanks to her mother's stupid idea—more likely Arthur Rossi's idea—to give everything to the Italian Club for a greenhouse.

In the middle of the Canadian prairie. Such bullshit.

She had come straight home and, even though she desperately wanted to wallow in her warm bed, Kenna knew she had to work fast. Rita and Dave hadn't shown their faces yet, but they could come upstairs from the guest suite at any moment. She was pretty sure, if she acted now, she could secure the most valuable things for herself. She hoped Rita didn't catch her in the act, but even if she did, so what? Who would even know the difference? After all, there was no inventory, and she wasn't about to let Jolene in the house to do one.

Kenna went through Freda's room first, grabbing her mother's best pieces: the diamond drop earrings, an old Art Deco necklace and bracelet set that had been her grandmother's, two diamond cocktail rings, a string of vintage South Sea pearls. She shoved the jewelry in a makeup travel bag and threw it under the sink in her bathroom.

Downstairs, she gathered up a few smaller pieces of art, including a hideous Remington bronze that weighed a ton. Freda had often bragged that it was a signed original and, while Kenna had no idea what it was worth, it had to be a lot if it was based on weight.

Between the money from Freda's bank account, and what she would get from the sale of these bits and pieces, Kenna was sure could buy a brand new house in one of the city's new, exclusive developments. She might even have enough to loan Mickey a down payment for a new house, too.

Kenna was caught up in her fantasy now, living in her rightful neighborhood, with Mickey nearby to help out when she needed it. She would have a place at their table every night. She would be an integral part of their circle, along with their young friends. She would be the cool mom. She would be included.

Kenna was contemplating how to get the Dorothy Knowles landscape down from the dining room wall when the doorbell rang.

What now?

She ran on tiptoes to the door, hoping Rita and Dave hadn't heard the doorbell.

She flung the door open to two uniformed officers: one RCMP, one Regina Police. They handed her a flyer from the Regina something-or-other drug unit. She could barely hear them over the sound of her own heart pounding in her ears.

"So, m'am, we're not trying to scare anyone, but we've got an opioid epidemic on our hands, and we're asking good citizens like yourself to keep a watchful eye for anything suspicious," the RCMP officer said.

"Like what?" Kenna asked, her eyes flitting from one face to the other.

"Well, like if you've got a prescription for opioids and it goes missing, or the pharmacy says you've already filled it, when you know you haven't. Things like that mean someone has targeted you and might be using your identity to buy drugs online or in multiple pharmacies," the Regina Police officer said.

After what seemed like an eternity of going on and on about fentanyl and oxy, and the dangers of both, the cops finally left. They'd cost her valuable time. Even as she locked the door behind them, Kenna couldn't recall everything they said, because she was too busy freaking out. She frantically lugged her loot upstairs and shoved it all in the back of her closet, sweating with the effort.

Now she was back in the kitchen, dripping Diet Coke everywhere, trying to hit the almost full glass of rye on the counter. An oxy was melting down her throat and her face scrunched up at the bitter aftertaste. Her breath came fast and there was a sheen of sweat on her brow.

Fucking cops.

What were they up to, asking about prescriptions and wanting to know if anyone in the house had access to opioids?

What if … what if someone knew?

Rita? No, she'd barely been around the house since they arrived.

It had to be Camelia, such a know it all, fucking lawyer, so arrogant, waltzing around with her designer clothes and fancy pocketbook and tropical vacations. That bitch hadn't been around other than Christmas or summer vacation for years—no decades—and yet she acts like she's entitled to … everything. As if she's one of us.

She needs to be taken down a notch.

Kenna perched on the edge of the little French settee in the kitchen to catch her breath and tried to retrace the conversation, to cement it in her memory, so she could recount the whole thing to Mickey. The RCMP guy,

Sgt. Bernard, was kinda handsome in a straight arrow sort of way. He said they were doing a routine neighborhood canvas because of the opioid crisis and wanted citizens to be aware for New Years' Eve.

But then he asked about Vicodin and oxy and fentanyl, so Kenna played dumb. That was her advantage. People always underestimated her. The Regina cop asked if anyone in the household used opioids for pain and that's probably where she blew it. She said yes. If he checked, he would find out she didn't have a real prescription. But Kenna had to say yes, because what if she said no, and was found with oxy or fen? She would be in an even bigger mess. Then Sgt. Bernard went on and on about safeguarding medications. What an idiot.

She tipped the tumbler back and drained half the drink, letting a long belch rumble off her lips in satisfaction.

This is the worst day of my life, and I shouldn't have to face it alone.

She texted Mickey.

Something happened. Pls come asap

Slurping her rye and DC, Kenna could feel the oxy starting to do its magic. Her legs felt warm and spongey. Her belly still felt a little jittery, but the drink would smooth that over soon enough. The stream of oxy reached her hands and she rubbed them together, the tingling warmth steadying them. All she wanted was to crawl into bed and watch a movie, but she was sure Mickey would show up any minute.

As she waited for Mickey, Kenna looked around the kitchen. It was a mess. With Freda gone, and Naomi on holiday, there was no one to clean up the dishes stacked in the sink. No one to wipe up the spills on the counter. No one to take the stinking garbage out. She wanted to leave it until tomorrow, but she had to keep up appearances for Rita and Dave, and whoever else might randomly show up at the door. She loaded the dishwasher and ran a moldy-smelling sponge over the counter.

God I can't wait for everyone to get the hell out of town so I can have some peace and quiet.

Kenna finished tidying up and heaved into the chair in front of the kitchen desk, tapping the keyboard. She wanted to see what that Remington was worth on eBay. She was blown away when she saw a similar signed bronze listed for $125,000, and that was in US dollars. She started tallying up the horde she'd stashed in her bedroom closet and a slow grin played across her face. She was smarter than any of them gave her credit for.

Kenna logged onto the RBC banking site, seeking the reassurance of counting all the money that was now hers. After a few seconds of reading and re-reading the screen, Kenna let out a shriek.

Holy mother of god.

Her heart sank into the knot forming in her stomach.

Her eyes blurred staring at the screen.

Pure fear seeped out of her pores in acrid sweat.

Mickey would know what to do. He would manage all this as soon as he got here. Kenna dug her phone out of her hoodie pocket. Her hands shook as she texted him.

911 Not kidding

Ok – be there couple of hours

How about right now? Need you here

Can't come now but be there soon

Whenever that is.

Kenna needed to slow down and figure out what happened to the bank account—*her* bank account—but her mind was reeling in fear, with the rye and oxy competing for attention.

This was obviously a mistake.

Then she remembered her mother's words, in the reading of the will just a few hours ago: *I also forgive the loans you made on my RBC account.*

Freda must have discovered Kenna's crime. And now, from beyond the grave, she was punishing her in the harshest way possible.

Kenna grabbed a half-eaten bag of potato chips from the counter and was on her way to her room when Rita called out to her.

Shit. Almost made it.

"Everything okay up here? I heard you yell. Are you okay?"

Kenna stopped and turned as Rita came into the main hall.

"I'm fine. Just saw a spider," Kenna said.

"Since when are you afraid of spiders?" Rita asked, one hand on her hip.

"I'm not. It startled me is all," Kenna said.

Jeez. Mind your own business, Rita.

"So do you have plans tonight?" Rita asked.

"Mickey and Suyin and the baby are coming over to ring in the New Year," Kenna said, although Mickey had not actually confirmed that plan yet. "And you?"

Rita glanced at her watch. "Yeah, we're going with Cam and Leon to the Trianon tonight for a New Years' concert party. But first, Dave and I were gonna haul my school stuff down from the attic and sort through it," she said, and paused. "If you're going up for a nap, I can do that tomorrow."

Kenna waivered for just a moment. Let Rita work around her for once. "Yeah, I'd rather you weren't stomping around right over my head because I'm exhausted and need to lay down. There's plenty of time for getting rid of stuff. What time are you guys going out?"

"Around 4:30 or so. We're meeting at their place first, then on to the Trianon. I can't believe Cam got tickets. Colin James is playing!" Rita said, excitement lighting up her face.

A wave of anger rolled over Kenna. "Well la-di-fucking-da. It must be nice to have a social life and go to parties and just move on like nothing happened. Your mother died less than a week ago, and you're out partying? Don't you have any feelings at all?" she said, her face red with indignation.

Rita's face flushed. "Losing Mum has nothing to do with enjoying my life. In fact, I'm pretty sure Mum would approve. She loved a good party," she said.

"Well, since you know so much about Mum, maybe you're the one who put the fucking stupid idea in her head to disinherit all of us." Kenna was warming up to the fight. "She left me fucking *pottery*!"

Rita sighed. "Kenna, I had *nothing* to do with Mum's decision …"

Kenna wasn't finished though. "Really? Because she was talking to you about her will the minute you walked in the front door …"

"Holy shit. Were you eavesdropping?" Rita asked.

"And what if I was? My whole fucking life I've had to take a back seat to you, putting up with your crap, your West Coast bullshit. Miss Fucking Know It All Nurse. Well, look at the mess you've made. You got us all disinherited."

Kenna continued hurling accusations and insults at Rita that had been simmering for decades.

Rita crossed her arms and listened, a faint smile on her face.

Dave pounded up the stairs and stopped just inches from Kenna's face.

"Kenna! Stop screaming! What's got into you? Calm down, already," Dave shouted over her.

"Hey Dave, how about if you just shut up and fuck off. This is family business," Kenna shrieked.

"Okay, that's it. We're done here. Say what you want. Believe what you want. We had *nothing* to do with any of Mum's plans, so just stop your damn ranting," Rita shouted back.

"Whatever helps you sleep at night," Kenna said, leaning on the wall for balance as she climbed the stairs. Mickey would be here soon. He would stick up for her.

"And what helps you sleep at night, Kenna? Is it the rye, or the oxy?" Rita yelled at Kenna's back.

Kenna slammed her bedroom door just to let Rita know she didn't get the last word.

Several episodes of *Friends* and *Grey's Anatomy* later, Kenna heard Rita and Dave leave. Deep shadows and the blue gloom of night spread through the house, even though it was barely 5 p.m. The wind was picking up, whining around the back door like an anxious puppy. She hated the creaking, groaning, popping sounds the old house made. It scared her. She knew it was silly, but she had always believed those noises were ghosts. She wondered if Freda would haunt the house now, too.

And what would Mum's ghost sound like? More nagging?

Kenna rolled out of bed and turned on her stereo to the 80s station. Loud.

No one here to bitch about my music, now!

After a hot shower, Kenna applied evening makeup and pulled her new party top out of the closet. She went downstairs, ready for New Year's Eve with Mickey, Suyin, and Sashay. It was just after six, and still no sign of them. That's how it was with them. They were always late, but she expected them to show up within the hour.

Kenna was starving, and she knew it could be a while before the kids arrived and they ordered dinner. She poured a stiff drink and foraged through the fridge for a snack. When she was satisfied with her selections, Kenna took the plate of cheese and sausages, leftover from the Boxing Day feast, to the living room, where she settled in. As she waited, she nibbled the edge of another oxy and tried to breathe away the fear lodged in her belly. But she was getting impatient.

Where the hell are they?

The wind made it seem even colder in the drafty old house, so Kenna cranked the fireplace up, and propped herself into the corner of the sofa with one of Freda's thick hand knit blankets. She'd been enjoying rye and oxy all afternoon and had to will herself to stay alert, especially in the warm glow of the fire.

As she drifted in and out of sleep on a cloud of chemicals, Kenna considered her situation with a jaundiced eye. This was all Mickey's fault. He needed too much. He wanted too much. And she indulged him, as she always had, in order to keep him close. Mickey was her baby, after all. What else could she do, but help him out now and then? Otherwise, his loyalties would surely shift to his father, or Suyin, or who-knows-who. The boy with the mischievous grin and clever ways had grown into an expert on how to get his way with Kenna. It wasn't that hard, she had to admit, because she rather liked having him around, scheming and plotting his next big victory. Kenna didn't push back because she loved the attention.

Sure, it cost her more than she could afford, but love often did.

49

Prodigal Son

December 31

Mickey sprawled on the settee in the kitchen, watching hockey on the little tv, flicking cigarette ashes into an antique blown glass candy dish. Freda would never allow him to smoke in the house, but she was dead now, no longer around to complain, and he knew Kenna wouldn't care.

He swished a cold beer around in his mouth, trying to rinse off the bad taste he imagined to be there, but it wasn't something you could swallow. No, in Mickey's case, the bad taste was rage, and it wasn't going away anytime soon. It was just biding its time, waiting for Mickey to step into his own, releasing his toxic vitriol into the world. So many people had so much coming to them.

Starting with Mum.

If it wasn't for Kenna, he was certain his grandmother wouldn't have disinherited him. What the hell good was twenty five grand gonna do him?

He drained the beer and called out to Kenna again, jabbing his cigarette out in frustration. It had been fifteen minutes, and his patience was wearing thin, but he knew better than to wake up a sleeping bear. He figured the smoke would wake her up, so Mickey fingered another cigarette and tapped it against the pack. He lit the cigarette and walked across the center hall to the living room. Kenna stirred.

"Mum, are you up now? Mum?"

"Oh, hey. What do I smell? I musta dozed off. Give me a minute, just gotta run to the can," she said.

Mickey grabbed the remote and turned on the stereo to the New Year's countdown station. A few minutes later, Kenna plopped down beside him on the sofa and pulled the hand-knit throw over her lap.

"So we're smoking in the house now?"

"It's freezing out, Mum. And with Gram gone, well …" Mickey shrugged.

"Yeah, whatever. Jesus Christ, it's after 10. Where's Suyin and Sashay?" she asked.

"Home. Sashay was fussy, so Suyin didn't want to bring her out, especially if we stay up to ring the New Year's bell," Mickey said.

Having a kid made that kind of lie so easy. He didn't have to explain that Suyin wasn't with him because they'd spent most of last night and today fighting about money.

Kenna fingered the edge of the afghan and relayed the story of the RCMP visit earlier in the day.

"Okay, Mum, here's the thing. They don't have a fricken thing. It was a routine visit. So they asked about scripts? So what? What difference does it make?" he asked.

But he could see the fear on his mother's face, and it worried him. He couldn't afford to have her panic-talking.

Mickey headed to the kitchen, waving his beer bottle at Kenna. "Want anything?"

Fucking Rumps. They were fishing.

"Sure, love, I'll have a rye and DC. There's a bottle of Coke open in the fridge," she answered.

Mickey returned with Kenna's cocktail and another beer.

Kenna took a sip. "Thanks, Mick, that's a sassy drink!"

"I figured you need a double after today, am I right?" he said, teasingly, giving Kenna a crooked grin. He touched his finger to the tip of her nose. "I think I know my Mum," he said. Kenna burst into giggles.

"Well, you got me there! After today, I need at least two!" she laughed.

Mickey figured Kenna had been drinking steadily all day; she was pretty far gone at the moment. At least she wasn't ranting about the will. He took in Kenna's full makeup, her hair pulled up high in a clip, and her glittery gold top over dressy black slacks.

All dressed up and nowhere to go.

"So where are Rita and Dave?" Mickey asked.

She rolled her eyes. "Miss Know It All Nurse is out with Miss Know It All Lawyer. The four of them went to the Colin James New Year's party at the Trianon. Must be nice."

"I take it you weren't invited?"

"No, and even if I was, I wouldn't go with those bitches," Kenna said.

"Just wondering, since you're all dressed up," Mickey said.

"Hey, I dressed up for *you*, Number One Son!"

She has no friends.

"I mean," Kenna was saying, "it's New Year's Eve and we might as well party down, right?" Kenna snapped her fingers and wiggled her shoulders to the music.

It reminded him of those first years after the divorce. Mickey was just a kid, but they'd play Cocktail Party. They would get dressed up, and Kenna would lay out snacks—all the good treats, too, not just healthy crap—and Mickey could have all the soda he wanted while Kenna drank wine. They would dance around the living room to music on the stereo and, later, play cards. Mickey sort of missed those times, when he was the center of Kenna's attention. These days, she was off in her own problematic, shit-faced world. She barely seemed to notice him.

"So why were the fuckin cops here, if they don't know anything? Like, that's unusual as hell, and it really has me rattled, Mick," Kenna said, swirling the ice in her half-empty glass.

"Who knows, Mum? Just don't get all bent about it. Besides, what difference does it make? You haven't done anything wrong. Right?"

Kenna pulled a little nub of oxy out of her pocket and swallowed it. Mickey gave her a sidelong glance and realized Kenna had almost finished her drink. He knew, suddenly, that his mother was no longer a lush. She had graduated to full blown alcoholic and oxy addict.

"And if you don't slow down on the painkillers …" he said.

"What? Ya gonna turn me in to the cops?" Kenna gave him a sharp look.

None of this should have surprised him. He'd been watching Kenna have her little cocktails his whole life. To him, she'd been just like all the other moms, pouring wine out of their thermos at soccer games, slipping a shot of vodka into their sodas at play dates, and hovering over the adult table at birthday parties. It's what moms did. They drank. And they managed everyone's lives. Except their own.

Mickey felt another rush of impatience as he observed Kenna, slurring, repeating her story again (for the third time now) just to rub the sore spots. He watched her chewing her words and it disgusted him. The way she smacked her lips as she spit out all the delicious details of the RCMP visit—as if she were literally feeding on the danger—made him sick.

Mickey's anger was rising, the heat of it on his face a comfort.

Why did she always have to hog the spotlight, centering herself in the middle of every little drama storm? He realized she was actually *enjoying* this.

Mickey set his empty beer on the table and grabbed his phone. "Well, I guess I better get going."

"You just got here! What about New Years?"

"Mum! I have to go home. I have a family, remember?" Mickey said.

"Oh, Mick, can't you just stay a while longer? It's creepy being in this house alone," she whined.

"If you don't like living here now that Gram's gone, then move out! You've got plenty of money now, right?" he said.

The implication was clear. He expected her to take care of herself. He wasn't going to look after her like she had cared for her own mother.

Kenna's eyes filled with tears. "Is that any way to treat me, Mickey?"

"How am I treating you? I came over, didn't I?"

"Fine. Go back to your Oriental..." Kenna paused, looking sideways at Mickey before letting loose with the slur on her tongue.

"Mum! Please. I'm not kidding. Don't *ever* call my wife *anything* other than Suyin again," he said. "Ever."

Mickey was not about to listen to his mother go on a racist tirade. Sure, he might sometimes argue with Suyin now and then, but he was not a bigot.

"Whatever. I'll take care of myself." Her face was splotchy and her nose started to drip into the crevice above her lip.

Mickey stood and pulled his eyes away from her bloated face, walking swiftly to the front hall. "And for fuck's sake, don't talk to any more cops. I don't need the stress!" he said.

Kenna limped into the hall, looking up at him, her eyes watery and unfocused.

"It's not even midnight! We haven't rung in the new year!"

"Yeah, but I can't just leave Suyin at home all night with a screaming kid, can I?" Mickey said. "We've had our toast and now I have to ... I *want* to go home, to my wife and my daughter."

"Okay, okay. But before you leave, there's something else. I don't even know how to tell you," Kenna said, her eyes filling with tears. "It's way worse than the cops being here, and I know you'll help me figure it out, but I'm seriously gonna puke if you can't. It's the bank account," she said, sobbing now. "It's all gone."

"What are you talking about?"

"The joint account. The one I inherited from mum. It's pretty much empty." Kenna hiccupped and blew her nose.

Mickey paused. He wasn't sure he was hearing this correctly.

Less than two weeks ago, Kenna had loaned him $20,000 from Freda's account. When he'd peered over her shoulder as she set up the transfer, there was over half a million dollars in the account.

So how could the account be empty? Maybe Kenna had made a mistake.

"Okay, Mum, you're not making sense. Let's look at the bank account right now and clear this up, okay? Where's your iPad?"

They went back to the living room, where Kenna opened the RBC app on her tablet and handed it to him. When he looked at the screen, he was confused.

On December 21, $525,000 was transferred out, leaving just a little more than $12,000.

"So … that half a mil went *where*?" Mickey asked. "Did you do something when you were half in the bag?"

"God, you're an idiot. Don't you see, by the $525,000 it says *branch transfer*? That means Mum went to the branch and took the money out. *She took it all out.* Which is why she knew there was 80 grand missing. Remember her words in the will? 'I forgive the loan'? So that money is *gone.* You're *welcome.*" Kenna spat out the words.

Mickey's face flushed to the roots of his receding hairline. She never talked to him like this, at least not since he was a kid.

"Whaddya mean *you're welcome*? If there's $80,000 gone, and you loaned me $20k, then you have 60 grand, am I right? *You're* the one that took the money! I can't help it if *you stole from Gram* to give me a loan!" Mickeys' survival instincts emboldened him.

"Oh, I see. Is that your story?" Kenna said.

"Yeah, I thought I would go with the truth," Mickey retorted.

"That's a first. No one will recognize you."

"Really, mum? Sixty grand? *Where the hell did the money go*?" Mickey said, his indignation taking root.

"This and fucking that, and it's none of your business. I have expenses," Kenna said. She gulped the last of her drink and wiped her lips on the back of her hand.

"Like what? Cases of rye? Diet Coke? Fake oxy scripts? Or maybe that little online poker habit?"

Mickey's initial hurt quickly tapped into his well of anger. She had a lot of damn nerve.

"Talk about the pot calling the kettle black. You're such a little piss ant. You have no right to talk to me like that," Kenna sniffed. She held out her hand for the iPad. "So, remind me, when are you going to repay the 20 grand I loaned you?"

Mickey handed her the iPad, inspected a cuticle, bit off a chunk of skin, and spit it on the floor. He had to think this through.

"I asked you a question, Michelangelo. I'm gonna need that money back right away," Kenna said, fixing her reddened eyes on Mickey.

Instead of answering, he stood, stretched, and walked to the kitchen where he could think for a minute without Kenna screeching at him. He could repay Kenna out of Sashay's college account, but why should he? Things were different now. It was every man for himself and besides, Kenna was receiving a nice, fat disability check every month from her government job, on top of the alimony she still received from his father. He wasn't sure exactly how much that came to, but it was damn sure more than he had coming in right now.

Mickey looked through the fridge for another beer, but there weren't any, so he poured three (or was it four?) fingers of rye in a glass and added a couple of ice cubes. His thoughts were skittering around trying to gather up the details of what had happened.

He would have killed Freda with his bare hands had she appeared in front of him right then. Now, he wouldn't be able to count on Kenna as his safety net, granting him little loans here and there. Hell, at this rate, he'd end up having to help Kenna out. Not that he would, but still. It was an epic fuck you from the old bag, and one he didn't deserve.

Hadn't he always been Freda's favorite?

Hadn't he been the one to show up and shower her with compliments and put up with her stupid advice and listen to her go on and on about the Italian Club or the Mackenzie or whatever else she was up to?

Hadn't he helped both Kenna and Freda more than they had ever helped him?

Mickey's resentment was rising and, as this injustice took hold, he was becoming more agitated. How much had he given up so those two could be happy? He was sure to visit them at least once a week, taking time away from Suyin, Sashay, and his friends. He was on call if either of them needed an errand run or something heavy lifted at the house. He was the man of the family, and those two owed him.

I'm the reliable one.

It was infuriating that Freda had moved the money, but even more frustrating that his drunk mother hadn't seen it coming. Did she really think she would get away with blowing Freda's money like that? How could she believe Freda would never check her accounts? He would have handled it a lot better, but it was too late now. Now, it was all about recovering as much as he could before the estate appraisers came around. He could at least snag some jewelry to pawn, if he could get past Kenna.

Mickey took a long swallow of his drink as Kenna limped into the kitchen.

"Enjoying my booze? We have a problem on our hands, Mick. Any bright ideas about how we're gonna get out of this mess?" Kenna said. She blew her nose and opened the refrigerator. "And since we're obviously not ordering dinner, I'm gonna have some leftover mac n cheese. Cam brought it over the other day. Want some?"

"No thanks, I already ate."

Kenna shrugged. "Of course you did." She scooped a mound of casserole into a skillet and turned the gas burner on high.

"You're frying it?" Mickey said.

"Just heating it up. It's better than the microwave," Kenna said, stirring the still-cold pasta around in the pan. "So about my money … you need to come up with a way to pay me back, and it needs to be soon."

"Mum, I can't pay you back until I get some sales this spring. You know that, right?" Mickey said, keeping his voice low and even, trying to slow the tide of anger between them.

"I can't wait that long, Mick. I'll be out of cash in a couple of weeks," Kenna said, not looking at him.

"For real? Mum, there's still $12,000 in the account. How can you spend that much in a couple of weeks when you don't have *any* expenses? You're still getting alimony from dad, you're getting disability, and …" he said, his anger surging again. How could his mother be so thick-headed? "Are you gambling that much? Because if you are, you need to stop. And what about all the under-the-table oxy and fen I've been giving you? What's that worth?"

Kenna was silent as she poked at the sizzling macaroni. She dropped the spoon in the pan and turned to face Mickey, her eyes blazing in her blotchy face.

"How dare you. I was looking out for *us*, as *usual.* I did nothing wrong," she hissed. "The only thing I did was help my son have a nice Christmas and my mother overcome the pain of old age."

"Oh, *right.* Is that the story you're telling yourself? You fucking poisoned Gram with one of those fake patches, didn't you?" Mickey said, plunging the accusation into Kenna like a shiv.

"What do you mean *fake*? I asked you for help getting meds because I didn't want to go through all the red tape with my doctor. If there was a problem with those meds, that's on you, Mickey, not me."

Mickey laughed. "I only did as you asked. I got you extra oxy like you wanted. And, when that wasn't enough for you, I even got you fentanyl. How the hell do you think I came up with all of it? I couldn't exactly waltz into London Drugs and ask for a bag of fen, now could I? I put my own safety on the line for you and your drug habit. And now you're calling the loan? Where am I supposed to get the cash?"

"I told you, I have expenses, and it's none of your damn business how I spend my money. *My* money, not *yours.* We agreed it was a loan, right? Well, time's up. I need my money back. And don't you dare tell me you've already spent it all on handbags for your goddamned chink!" Kenna yelled, moving close, pushing her index finger into Mickey's chest for punctuation.

Her insult against Suyin landed squarely.

A jolt of rage surged through Mickey, lighting up his senses with adrenaline and cortisol.

Before he knew what he was doing, he had shoved Kenna back, hard, his palms smacking against her shoulders, pushing her off balance. His fists grasped the thick fabric of her top.

She fell back, the skillet clattering on the stovetop.

Kenna's elbow landed in the open flame of the gas stove, protected, momentarily, by her anger and her sleeve.

Mickey didn't notice as he held her there, his eyes bulging in rage, his hands full of Kenna's glittery sweater. He was growling, like an animal, unable to form the words to express his desire to kill her, to shut her up, to stop her incessant screeching.

"Get the fuck off me, Mick!" Kenna screamed, trying to push him back, but he was far too strong. "Get off me you little shit."

The glaze in her eyes and the slur of her words only infuriated him more.

His mother was a drunk and a drug addict, and she had screwed them all over by stealing from Freda and now, here she was, demanding that *he* suffer so she could cover her crimes.

In an instant, with a little whoosh, Kenna's top was in flames.

She screamed in pain as the gas flame melted the synthetic knit to her arm and back, the flames leaping up, toward her hair.

Mickey stepped back and, reflexively, tossed his drink towards the burner. The flames flared as he realized, too late, the liquid in his glass was almost entirely alcohol.

Kenna lost her balance trying to get away from the flames singeing her back, and fell to the floor, her screams turning to sobs.

"Mickey! Help me! Mickeeeeeeeeeeee …"

But Mickey wasn't helping.

He was running.

Just like he'd always done in a crisis.

Just like he'd done that summer when Dana fell into Wascana Lake and almost drowned.

Just like he'd done when the police caught up to Andy Yin.

Just like he'd done when Suyin's water broke.

Just like he was doing now.

Mickey ran to his car and slammed the door.

In the numbing cold, he dropped his head, pressed his hands to his face, and let out a long, heavy exhale that carried his incendiary rage into the night.

Let it go, Mick. Let it go.

50

Hot Mess

January 1

Despite a bit of a hangover, Camelia was energized after their fun New Year's Eve with Rita and Dave. For a few hours, it was almost as if Freda hadn't died, leaving the family in a shambles. Leon and Dave were joking around like teenagers, Rita relaxed with the music, and Camelia leaned into the comfort of their easy friendship. It was a great way to start the New Year, and now she was looking forward to a lazy day in the company of Leon and the kids, drinking mimosas by the fire.

Leon was cooking bacon, humming along to the stereo.

"Good morning, babe," she said, planting a kiss on his neck. "It's still morning, right?"

"Close enough. Happy new year to my lovely bride. How about a cuppa coffee? We've got Bailey's or Kahlua," Leon said.

"Coffee straight up, but I wouldn't say no to a mimosa," Camelia said. Today really was shaping up. "Kids awake?"

"I think I heard them rustling around upstairs, but I don't ask questions," Leon said, and laughed.

They both turned as Sophie ran down the stairs clutching her phone, Steve on her heels.

"Mum, Dad, Auntie Rita's trying to get in touch with you," Sophie said. "Where's your phone?"

Leon and Camelia exchanged a look. "My phone's in the bedroom, Cam, can you grab it?" Leon said, as Camelia ran out of the kitchen.

Camelia returned, white-faced.

"Holy shit. Kenna's in the hospital. We gotta go," Camelia said.

"What happened?" Leon said.

"Rita said there was a kitchen fire, so who knows? Let's get a move on!" She said as she ran back to the bedroom.

Camelia pulled on jeans, a sweater, and thick socks. She twisted her hair into a ponytail and patted a tinted moisturizer on her face. But when she came back into the kitchen, Leon was still in his pajamas, turning the bacon.

"Leon, what the hell. We gotta go."

He took a deep breath. "Cam, hon, we haven't even had breakfast. And there's literally nothing we can do at the hospital but sit around and stare at each other," he said.

"Don't you think we should be there to support our family? Because I guarantee they would be there for us," Camelia said.

"Yeah, I know, but Jesus. It's been one thing after another, and we haven't had a minute of down time. And on top of that, I promised my new client I would install some security software today. Start the year out fresh, and all that," he said.

Camelia started to make a snide comment about him working on vacation, but she didn't want to start a fight. She knew he was putting in the extra effort because his company was a fledgling startup and he needed some traction, but still. Every time *she* worked on vacation, he railed at her for having no boundaries and being a pushover for the firm. Yet here he was.

"So, you want me to go *alone*, then?" Camelia asked.

Sophie looked up from her cup of tea. "Mum, I can go with you. The boys can stay home and play with their computers," she said.

Steve smiled at her. "I like how you think. Because no, I'm not really up for hanging out at the hospital either. Too much like work," he said.

"Give me five minutes, Mum," Sophie said, and ran upstairs.

It was the garage door closing that put the notion in Camelia's mind. Dave mentioned seeing Mickey going into the garage in the middle of the night, and she'd seen him do the same on Boxing Day. It might be her only opportunity to have a look on her own, without anyone else around.

"Okay, bear with me. I just want to swing by Auntie Freda's place before we head to the hospital. I want to have a look in the garage," Camelia said.

"Oh Mum, what are you up to now?" Sophie said.

"Something is going on with Mickey. With the house empty, it's my chance to see what he's been doing in Auntie Freda's garage, without anybody wondering what I'm up to. Won't take but a minute."

When she turned into the Crescents, Freda's driveway was crowded with cop cars. Camelia's heart leapt to her throat.

Just how bad was this kitchen fire?

She parked as close as she could get. Police officers had taped off an area around the back door, now covered with foam and ice. An officer was sitting in a patrol car by the back gate, keeping an eye on things. Another cop was herding curious neighbors off the driveway and onto the sidewalk. Camelia approached the nearest cop.

"Excuse me, I'm Freda Swenson's niece. I heard about the fire. How bad is it?"

"I'm sorry, your name?" the officer said, her gloved thumbs hooked in her coat pockets.

"Camelia Belmont, I'm visiting for the holidays, Officer … Gallagher," she said, reading the police officer's name tag, velcroed to her parka.

A man approached and interrupted, "Hey, Camelia? Everyone get out okay?"

"Hey Jeff …" Camelia said, reaching out to pat him on the shoulder.

"And you are?" Officer Gallagher asked.

"Jeff Berenchuk. I live just over there," he said, pointing. "I just wanna know if Kenna and Mickey are okay," he said.

"Sir, all I can say with certainty is that Ms. Shores was taken to ER. She was the only one in the house," Gallagher said.

"Well, if you say so," Berenchuk said.

"What makes you think Mickey was here last night?" Camelia asked.

"Because I saw him. He came up the alley around 10 p.m. but not sure when he left because we went to bed. Next thing we know, there's fire engines rocking us outta bed," Berenchuk said.

"He must have left before the fire," Camelia said, and turned to the police officer. "Do you know what time the fire was reported?"

"All I can tell you is that the 9-1-1 dispatch was around 11:30 p.m. The fire department arrived a coupla minutes later," Gallagher said. "Ms. Shores was the only person here when we arrived on scene."

"How long until this," Camelia gestured with her gloved hand, "is all sorted?"

Gallagher looked around. "We would have been done already, but last night was pretty busy. Lots of action on New Year's Eve. The investigation team is just gonna finish up and we're outta here."

"Investigation team?" Camelia looked at the old house and felt the stab of loss.

"It's standard. Gotta figure out what caused the fire," Gallagher said.

What the hell did Kenna do?

51

The Vigil

January 1

Camelia waved goodbye to Jeff Berenchuk and walked quickly back to the car, slapping her hands together to keep warm.

Sophie was straining to see what was going on.

"What the hell, Mum? I thought it was just a little kitchen fire!"

"I know. It looks pretty bad, doesn't it?" Camelia said. "And, obviously, I can't go poking around in the garage with a bunch of cops watching, so off to the hospital we go," Camelia said.

During the few minutes it took to get to the hospital, Camelia relayed to Sophie the sparse details she'd learned.

"That's it?"

"Maybe Rita knows more. We'll find out when we get to the hospital," Camelia said.

"Honestly, our family puts the fun in dysfunctional," Sophie said, rolling her eyes. "And Steve was worried about being bored out of his mind. Ha! No such luck."

By the time she parked the car, Camelia's head was pounding and she felt shaky. She needed a double shot of espresso with a double shot of vodka to match, but that wasn't on the menu in the hospital cafeteria, and she'd left her coffee sitting on the kitchen island.

In the lobby, Sophie and Camelia stopped at the coffee kiosk for two large lattes, then found their way to the Burn Unit, where the Swenson clan had taken over the waiting room. Rita, Ben, Norah, and their families, all eight of them, were lined up on the blue vinyl chairs.

Camelia rushed to Rita's side.

"Rita, what the hell happened?"

"We're not done with our bad luck, apparently. All I know is Kenna was cooking something on the stove and got her sleeve in the flame, and poof! Synthetics. They don't even really burn. They just melt. They've knocked her out for now, and we're waiting for the Burn Specialist. I just hope he isn't hung over like the rest of us," Rita said.

Camelia looked around the waiting room again. "Where's Mickey?"

"No idea. I've been calling him every half hour since around three this morning, but he's not picking up," Rita said. "He was supposed to be at the house last night with Suyin and Sashay for New Year's with Kenna, but they must have been a no-show."

"No, Mickey was there. Or that's what Jeff Berenchuk said."

"When did you talk to Jeff?" Rita asked.

"Just before we came. I swung by the house …" Camelia said.

"Did you talk to Dave? He stayed behind to make sure the house got closed up properly and to call the insurance adjuster, while I came over here," Rita said, as her phone dinged. She swiped the screen. "Dave's on his way now. What a shit show."

"I didn't see Dave, just a few cops, then Jeff showed up. Anyway, he said Mickey got there last night around ten, but Jeff didn't know when he left," Camelia said.

"They must have left before Kenna set herself on fire. She was probably piss drunk," Rita said, shaking her head.

"Kenna's gonna be okay, right? I mean, these aren't life-threatening burns, are they?"

"No, she'll be fine, but the burns will take a while to heal," Rita said. "Nothing to do right now but wait for the Burn Specialist. And try to stay awake."

Camelia hoped Rita had informed the nurses about Kenna's drinking habits but didn't want to ask. Kenna might survive the burn, but would she survive without a rye and coke drip? Camelia felt horrible for thinking it, but it was also a real concern. Alcoholics couldn't just go cold turkey without consequences. Camelia knew this too well, having watched her own father go through the DTs when he was hospitalized with his first heart attack. It was like watching a fish gasp for water, and all you want to do is throw it back into the lake and watch it swim away.

She walked around the lounge, pausing at the bank of windows. The cold was seeping in around the metal frame and snow was falling once again, blanketing the city in blue-white. She turned back to the room, where Rita was sipping tea and flipping through a magazine, her eyes unfocused on the pages. Camelia picked up the blue canvas satchel in the chair beside Rita.

"This yours? May I?" Camelia asked.

"Oh yeah, here," Rita said, taking the bag from Camelia and stuffing it under her chair. "My med kit. As soon as there's a siren, I go into work mode."

"Muscle memory, yeah? How you holding up?"

Rita shrugged. "Okay, I guess. I mean, Christ. I'm worried about Kenna, and I'm dead tired. Dave and I got home at what? Two? We arrived to emergency vehicles at the house, so we still haven't been to bed."

"Jesus, Ree, you shoulda called me."

"I know, but really, why keep *everyone* up all night? It's not like you could do anything. That's why I didn't text until ten. Figured I'd let you sleep a bit," Rita said.

"Sorry, we turned our phones to silent when we went to bed. Some cockamamie idea about sleeping in," Camelia said.

"Wouldn't that be nice? I'm so damn tired."

"No rest for the wicked, apparently. And I'm worried about Kenna, too. Partly because, you know, she drinks quite a bit, so …" Camelia said.

"You mean, like everyone else in the family?" Rita said, raising her eyebrows.

Camelia winced. "Ouch. But no, what I mean is that if you're used to having alcohol regularly, wouldn't it be a problem to suddenly have none at all?"

"Of course. But do you really think Kenna's that far gone?" Rita said.

Camelia was taken aback for a second. Wouldn't Rita, a medical professional with decades of experience in ER, recognize alcohol and drug abuse when she saw it?

"Hate to say it, but yeah, I think she has a serious drinking problem. But you're the nurse. What do you think?" Camelia said.

"I don't know what to think, but you're right, going cold turkey could be so much worse for her recovery … I should say something, I guess," Rita said, in a voice laden with sadness. "How on earth did it come to this?"

Camelia put her arm around Rita's shoulders and pulled her close. "Kind of a hot mess, isn't it?"

Rita leaned away, leaving only a shift of the air in her wake. "It's worse than a mess. My mother's dead. My sister almost burned the house down and herself with it. Oh, and the RCMP have been sniffing around, no thanks to you. I'm just kinda done," she said.

"What do you mean the RCMP are sniffing around?" Camelia said, gently removing her arm.

Jesus, Mary and Joseph.

Fear ran up her spine and sweat sprung along her hairline. Camelia's mind was turning in on itself. Chip Conroy said he'd turned the tampered fentanyl patches over to the drug unit, but she didn't think …

Sonofabitch.

Of course they would investigate, and she'd just brushed it off, not wanting to follow the thread of inevitability. The cops had identified the fingerprints, and found Kenna in their database, with a prior. The uncomfortable truth was nipping at Camelia's heels.

My skin's gonna have to get a lot thicker if I'm going to be any good at this.

"That's what they do when people start giving them ridiculous ideas about elder abuse and overdoses, Cam, and you know it. What's done is done, but I hope now you can back off. I just need to focus on Kenna right now."

"Right. Focus on the family. And speaking of family, still no word from Mickey?"

"He's not answering his phone or texts and neither is Suyin. They probably shut their phones off to sleep in, too. But they ought to be answering, because I guarantee Sashay is up by now," Rita said.

Camelia thought about it for a moment, then leaned in to whisper, "Do you want me to go to Mickey's and roust him?" she said.

"That would be a big help. No need for Suyin and the baby to come, but Mickey will be upset if he's not here for Kenna …"

"No problem. I'll go check on Mickey," Camelia said, even though she didn't want to drive halfway across town. "On the way back, I can pick up some food from Sweetie Pie's. Want anything?" Camelia offered the promise of food as an olive branch.

"Did someone say Sweetie Pies? I'm in!" Ben's eldest, Andrew, was suddenly wide awake.

Camelia smiled. If there was anything that could bring the family together, it was Darlene's famous cinnamon buns. Everyone seemed to perk up.

"Can you grab something for the staff? They'll appreciate it," Rita said, pressing a $50 bill into Camelia's pocket.

"Stop it, I got this," Camelia said, and held the bill out to Rita.

"Okay, I'm too tired to fight. Drive carefully," Rita said.

"Sophie? Shotgun?" Camelia said.

"It's about 50 below and snowing like hell, but sure, I'll come along."

In the car, as they buckled up, Sophie said, "Mum, where's Mickey? That little rat isn't even here, and Kenna could die!"

"First off, Kenna's *not* going to die," Camelia said. "And Rita's been trying to reach Mickey and Suyin, but she thinks they might have their phones off to catch up on sleep. That's why we're going to their house," Camelia said.

"Oh, I didn't hear that part," Sophie said.

"I just wish the Burn Specialist would come around so we can find out how bad it is," Camelia said.

"Well, after all his time in the fire department, Steve would say *every* burn is a bad burn," Sophie said. "Seems like karma, if you ask me."

"Unusually fast for karma, but you never know," Camelia said. She fiddled with the defrost. "I wonder if Kenna will need surgery, or rehab, or whatever, which means she probably can't be on her own. At least not for a while,"

"She's got Mickey. I mean, he's a dick, but he's close with Kenna," Sophie said. "Not that Kenna deserves all this attention, but whatever. I'm not ever going to forgive her for what she did to Auntie Freda."

Camelia agreed, silently. If anyone played a role in Freda's death, she was going to find out. Auntie Freda deserved to be avenged, and if that meant taking Kenna and Mickey down, then so be it. Or maybe it was all Mickey? Her mind began churning out theories.

"Come on, Soph. That's enough speculating. Let's go roust Mickey so we can get to Sweetie Pies before they sell out of cinnamon buns!"

52

MISSING IN ACTION

JANUARY 1

Camelia and Sophie pulled up to Mickey and Suyin's house, a pretentious McMansion on the east side of the ring road, crammed in with dozens of others just like it. The walk hadn't been shoveled, but there was a narrow tamped down path leading to the front door.

How can they afford this much house?

Camelia took a deep breath of the warm air in the car, steeling herself for both the cold blast of Saskatchewan wind and the equally frosty welcome she'd no doubt get from Mickey. But this was family, and he needed to know his mother was injured.

"Looks like Mickey is doing alright for himself," Sophie said, looking around at the houses. "So why is he stealing credit cards?"

"You know, I didn't get the full story on that. And I thought Steve was going to rip his face off at the Boxing Day dinner. Did Mickey *really* steal your credit card?"

Sophie's cheeks flushed with anger. "Do you think I'd lie about it?"

"Of course not. I just wonder how you can be so sure it was him," Camelia said.

"Okay, Miz Prosecutor, I *know* it was Mickey because he was going on about Christmas shopping at the Cousins Brunch. Couldn't shut up about it. And Suyin too. Her and her Kate Spade frickin diaper bag. *Really*?" Sophie huffed. "Then some woman tells me my wallet is on the floor, *right after* Mickey was leaning all over my chair talking to Auntie Freda. I hadn't even opened my purse the whole time! When Steve walked Auntie Freda to her car, she said I should check my wallet when I got home. But when I looked in my wallet, my credit card was there, so I didn't think anything of it. About three hours later, I got the fraud alert from my bank. So yeah, Mum, Mickey fucking stole my credit card. I don't know if he took a picture of it, or what, but he used my card to buy a bunch of designer crap for Suyin. And I'm pretty sure he lied to her about it, because I honestly don't think she had a clue by the way she acted at the Boxing Day thing." A red splotch had crawled up Sophie's neck as she ranted.

"I see. And you told the credit card company what happened?"

"Of course I did. But it's the holidays and they're busy, and they just said they'd take it off my bill. Which means Mickey got away with it. So excuse me if I don't go in with you, because I'd probably slap the smile right off his face," Sophie said.

"I get it. You have a right to be angry. Wait here, and keep the car warm. I'll be right back," Camelia said.

"Don't have to ask me twice!" Sophie responded.

Out here, on the edge of town, there was nothing to break the wind. It pulled at Camelia's scarf and nipped at her face as she waited on the front step. After a couple of minutes, she rang the doorbell a second time.

She heard Suyin's high voice, in a sing-song, "Be right there!"

Camelia tried to smile despite the freezing wind.

Suyin appeared shocked to see Camelia at her door, panicked even, her eyes darting from Camelia to the curb and back again. She held the interior door open, but when Suyin didn't open the glass storm door, Camelia pulled it open and moved to enter.

"Hi Suyin, can I come in? It's so cold out! Is Mickey home? Rita's been trying to get hold of you guys for hours!" she said, the words rushing out in a wave that pushed Suyin back into the hallway.

Suyin pulled her cardigan close and crossed her arms against her narrow waist.

"Um, Mickey's not here right now," Suyin said. A howl came from the back of the house. "Hang on, I have to make sure Sashay doesn't tear the kitchen apart." She trotted away and Camelia followed. The kitchen was littered with toys, clothes, newspapers, magazines, and dirty dishes.

"Uh oh, someone's got a full diaper," she said, to Sashay's angry face. "Be right back!"

As Suyin took Sashay out of the room, Camelia's eyes fell on a stack of magazines on the counter, and she flipped through them as she waited. In the stack was a worn copy of *Canada Today* and the cover story was *Ordering Deadly Drugs from China is Easy*. She was so engrossed in the article, she didn't hear Suyin return.

"So, anyway, Mick's not here."

Camelia looked up. "Canada Today. I haven't read one of these in ages. May I?" Camelia asked, holding the magazine up.

"Sure, those are ready for recycling, so help yourself," Suyin said, as she hiked Sashay onto her hip.

Camelia slid the magazine into her purse.

"Say hi to your auntie, Sash," Suyin cooed, and Sashay hid her face in Suyin's shoulder. "Sorry, she's at that stage of making strange. Anyway, what's up? Why is Rita looking for Mick?" Suyin's voice was friendly, but her body language was defensive.

"There was an incident last night, a kitchen fire at Auntie Freda's house, and Kenna was injured. She's in the burn unit. When she couldn't reach Mickey this morning, Rita got worried," Camelia said.

"Oh my god, that's awful," Suyin said. "Mickey must be at work if he's not picking up, but I have no idea exactly where he is, you know, out showing houses, he could be anywhere. When I got up this morning, his car was gone, but he usually leaves for work before I'm up," she said.

"Mickey's at work on New Year's Day? Hmmm. The neighbors saw Mickey at the Crescents house last night, so …"

"What are you talking about?" Suyin said, a wave of color rising on her wan face.

"We just need to find Mickey. Kenna's in bad shape, and she's going to want him there when she comes to."

Suyin's eyes widened. "What do you mean she's in bad shape? How bad? Like, is she gonna die?" Suyin said.

"No, I don't think it's life threatening. But the whole family is wondering where Mickey is, and I know he'll want to be there for Kenna, so we just need to track him down," Camelia said.

Suyin pulled her phone from her cardigan pocket. "Sorry, my phone was off." She'd barely turned it on before it began to ding insistently with incoming messages. "I'll text Mickey 911. That's our code for something important, and he wouldn't *dare* ignore me," she said, staring at her phone.

Sashay happily chewed on a ring of measuring spoons.

"Thanks Suyin," Camelia said, and walked to the door, Suyin trailing behind her.

"He'll be there as soon as I find him," Suyin said, her small nostrils flaring. "It's not the first time he's passed out at Danny's. Or Andy's. Sonofabitch," she said, and slammed the door.

"So? Was Mickey sleeping it off?" Sophie said, as Camelia put her seatbelt on.

"He's not home. Suyin said it wouldn't be the first time he passed out at his friend's house. It was just *weird.* Like she tried to cover for him, but then basically admitted he didn't come home last night, and she has no idea where he is," Camelia said.

"Which friends?"

"She just said Danny or Andy. Do you know them?" Camelia said.

"Andy Yin is Suyin's cousin, and they're all tight. Danny is a guy they hung out with in school. Danny Whitehouse. His dad used to be a big deal with the tribal government. I heard Andy went to jail for dealing, but he must be out now, if Mickey's hanging out with him," Sophie said.

"His friend Andy went to jail for dealing what, exactly?"

"How would I know? I can Google him, if you want," Sophie said.

"Nah, it doesn't matter. Hopefully by the time we get back to the hospital, Mickey will have turned up," Camelia said, turning up the heater fan.

"He'll just make it all about him, anyway. As usual," Sophie said. "I really don't want to see him. Ever."

"I get it. And I need to get some work done, anyway. Tell you what, text Rita to let her know we're picking up the order from Sweetie Pies, and I'll wait on the curb while you deliver everything up to the gang, then we'll head home, deal?" Camelia said, but she was already distracted by the tasks lining up in her head.

"I hate that you and dad are spending your holiday working, but if it gets me out of listening to Mickey go on and on about his stupid life, I'm all in," Sophie said.

It was just a short drive to the hospital from Sweetie Pies. As Camelia nosed the car up to the curb her phone dinged. It was Mickey.

Heard you were looking for me. What's up?

Camelia showed Sophie her phone. "So I guess Suyin didn't tell him what's going on, and he hasn't read any of his messages. Seriously?" She thumb-typed a response.

Check your messages. Kenna in Burn Unit 6 floor at hospital. Come ASAP.

"I'll be right back. Keep the car warm," Sophie said, and kneed the car door shut, her arms laden with bags of sandwiches and cinnamon buns.

Camelia leaned against the headrest and closed her eyes. She'd been blaming Kenna for Auntie Freda's death, but Mickey was the one creeping around the garage and hanging out with criminals. Even so, would he really hurt Freda? Or Kenna? It might just be an odd coincidence that he was at the house right before the fire started. Or was Mickey responsible for the fire? Camelia shook her head. No, Mickey was devoted to Kenna.

Nothing was making sense anymore.
I need a long, tall drink and a short, sweet nap.

53

Happy New Year

January 1

Mickey showed up a couple of hours later to find Rita and Dave alone in the hospital lounge. His heart was beating a little too fast from the bump of meth he'd had with Andy earlier. He'd only meant to smoke enough to clear the cobwebs of last night's oxy and boilermakers, but maybe he went a bit too hard on the pipe. His jaw hurt from clenching his teeth, no thanks to the meth.

An itchy ring of sweat broke out around his armpits when Mickey saw his reflection in the glass doors to the waiting area. His eyes were bloodshot, underscored with dark circles, his face was pasty and puffy, and his hair was plastered to his head. He looked down at his wrinkled clothes. Mickey didn't want to get too close, especially to Rita. She always stared at him too intently, like she knew what he'd been up to. He lifted his chin in greeting as he walked past Rita and Dave to the entrance of the burn ward, pushing the swinging doors open with both fists.

"I'm here to see Kenna Shores," he announced loudly to no one in particular.

Rita rushed up behind him.

"Hey, Mickey, keep it down, okay? Kenna's in number 4, just over there, but you'll need to gown up to go in and …," Rita sniffed the air and recoiled. "Wow, rough night? You stink to high heaven." Her pursed lips were their own chastisement.

"For fuck's sake, Rita, back off. I'm here for Mum, not you," Mickey said, his anger pushing Rita back a step.

She raised her hands, palms facing Mickey. "Well excuse me. We've been here for hours waiting for you to show up, so please, take over with my blessing," she said. Her eyes summed him up before she turned on her heel.

"Dave, we've been relieved of duty. Let's go." Rita grabbed her parka, slung her kit over her shoulder, and walked out of the lounge.

Dave gave Mickey a piercing stare, then followed Rita down the hall to a bank of elevators.

So there's the truth of it. Rita wasn't actually worried about her sister, she was just there to show off and rag on him. Someone touched his elbow as he stared after Rita and Dave. He whirled around, startled.

"Sir? Can I help you?"

"Yeah, I'm Mickey Shores, and I'm here for Kenna Shores," he said, covering his mouth too late, as a cloud of foul breath landed in the space between their faces.

"Yes, we've been expecting you. I'm Allison Foster, and I'm your Mum's nurse today. There's a cloak room right there where you can stow your parka, and you'll find gowns, masks, gloves, and shoe covers in the bins on the counter. Wash your hands thoroughly, then gown up, and I'll meet you back at the nurses' station in a few minutes," she said.

"Really? Is that necessary?" Mickey said.

"It's absolutely necessary if you intend to see Ms. Shores. Otherwise, you can wait in the lounge. It's your call," Foster said, without hesitation.

"Okay, okay, calm down. I'll glove up for you," he said, leering.

"You're not doing this for me. It's for your mother. Or you're not going in. I don't care either way," Foster said, as she walked away. Her tone was flat, unmistakable. She'd caught the innuendo and was having none of it.

Mickey's cheeks flushed with embarrassment, which only made him angry.

Fucking chicks have no sense of humor any more.

Mickey donned the disposable gown, cap, booties, gloves, and mask, snapping the cuff of the gloves as he returned to the nurses' station. Foster looked up from the notes she was entering on the computer. She pulled on a fresh set of gloves and donned protective gear.

"Ready? Keep in mind, Ms. Shores is in a lot of pain, so we have her sedated. Most of the burns were on her back, which is why she's propped on one side," she said, as she pushed open the door to Kenna's room.

Mickey gagged at the smell as he entered the room.

"Everything okay?" the nurse asked.

"Yeah. Why wouldn't it be?" he said, pinching the mask close to the bridge of his nose to avoid the stench coming off his mother's burns.

The nurse shrugged as she checked the IV bag.

Kenna was hooked up to an IV and a couple of monitors. It made Mickey feel a little woozy.

"Mum, can you hear me?" he said, leaning over the bed rail.

"Mr. Shores, no touching, please. Your Mum is at high risk for infection. She may not wake up, but she can hear your voice," Foster said, and left the room, pulling the door closed behind her.

Mickey waited for her to leave before turning back to his mother. He pulled the room's lone chair closer to the bed and slumped into it, exhausted and hung over.

"Mum, what the fuck? You almost burned the damn house down! I called it in, by the way, otherwise you wouldn't even be here. So, you're welcome. But, you *stupid cow*. Jesus Christ."

Mickey couldn't tell how serious this actually was, but it frightened him. What would happen if Kenna couldn't live by herself? Would he be expected to offer Kenna a home, even temporarily? If he even mentioned it, Suyin would kill him. No, Suyin would *leave* him, and that was worse. She would never allow his racist mother to live under the same roof. But

Kenna had blown all her money, so how would she afford a private care home, or even a home nurse? The questions rolling around in his head were taking their toll.

"Mum, for real, we gotta sort some stuff out. I gotta put you on notice. Like, you can't go panicking every time a cop comes to the door. And you gotta quit the casino and those online games. With Gram's money gone, we just can't afford it, ya know?" Mickey ran his hand over his face. "And you're gonna get better, you really are, but you might have to stay in rehab until the burns heal up. I mean, I'd 100 percent have you come home with me, but … shit, you burned that bridge with Suyin." Mickey's eyes burned with tears. "Christ, Mum, you made a big fucking mess of *everything*, but I'm here, *as usual*, to help you clean up."

Mickey leaned back in the visitor chair. He wished he'd eaten something because his guts were churning.

"Look, I was up half the night with Sashay, so I'm just gonna catch a few winks. Looks like that's all you're gonna do too, so wake me up when it's time for dinner," he said, and laughed at his own weak joke. "And happy fucking new year."

54

RUN, RUN, RUDOLPH

JANUARY 1

The shift nurse was just logging out of the computer when Sgt. Bernard approached.

"Good afternoon, I'm Sergeant Major Bernard, RCMP, and I have a few questions about a patient, Kenna Shores." He held up his badge.

"Hi, I'll be right with you. Just have to finish this up," she said. She typed as he drummed his fingers on the counter.

"Okay, how can I help you?"

"I'm with RIDU, and I've got a limited warrant," he said, passing a folded document to Foster. "We're investigating Miz Shores for a potential connection to an illicit drug operation. You'll see the scope at the bottom. To be clear, she could be a victim or involved in some other way."

"Okay, just let me get a release form," Foster said. She rifled through a file drawer until she pulled out a sheet of paper. "Here we go, sign here," she said, pointing to the bottom of the page. "And I'll need a copy of your I.D."

As he signed, Sgt. Bernard said, "Kenna Shores was admitted, correct?" He slid his I.D. across the counter.

"Yes. She's in Room 4," Foster said, stapling the release to the Warrant. She put his I.D. on the photocopier.

"Details?"

Foster grabbed the I.D. and photocopy, and pulled a chart from the wall. She flipped through a couple of pages.

"Miz Shores was brought to emerg before midnight, admitted around 2 a.m. with third degree burns to her left torso, buttock, and the back of her left arm. She has two fractured ribs, also on the left. The paramedics believe she accidentally started a grease fire in her kitchen, then fell as she tried to put it out. On top of that, she has some pre-existing conditions secondary to an auto accident, according to her medical records. She's in pain, but it's not life threatening. She'll recover," she said, slipping the Warrant, release, and copy of Bernard's I.D. into Kenna's chart.

Sgt. Bernard scribbled notes.

"Tox screen?" he said.

"Yes, hang on," Foster said, as she rifled through the pages and scanned with her index finger. "She was positive for alcohol, OxyContin, ibuprofen, and trace amounts of fentanyl," she said.

Bernard's head popped up from looking at his notes. "Fentanyl? How much?"

"Not much. Looks like she was way over the limit for alcohol, at 1.73. The level of oxy suggests she had at least 80 mg and maybe more in the 6-8 hours prior to testing. As for the fentanyl, metabolites show a trace amount, which could mean she had ingested some up to 36 hours prior."

Bernard nodded slowly. "Would she have that level of fentanyl in her system from handling it?"

"Maybe, hard to tell," the nurse said.

"Who's been here today?"

Foster rattled off the names of everyone who had registered as a family visitor. "And her son got here a little while ago. He's in with her now," she said.

Bernard pulled an evidence bag from his pocket and held it up in front of her. "Ever see these around?" he asked.

Foster took the bag from him. "Sure, fentanyl patches, but they didn't come from a medical facility because there's no date, time, or initials. You know the protocol."

"You have any go missing recently?"

"Not in our unit. We don't use them. Those are usually for terminal cancer patients, that kind of thing. Our patients need something that works way faster," she said.

"Got it. Hey, I don't wanna suit up, so can you let Mr. Shores know I wanna talk to him about the fire?"

"Sure, and you can use the staff lounge, it's empty right now," she said.

"Mr. Shores, there's an RCMP sergeant here to talk to you about the fire. He's in the staff lounge at the end of the hall," Foster said.

Mickey was startled awake. "Jesus," he said, running his hands over his face. "I nodded off there for a minute. Thanks, where again?"

She pointed to the left.

"Just go left, straight down this hall. It dead ends at the staff lounge. Can't miss it."

"Got it. I'll just stop at the men's and … what's the guy's name again?"

"Um, I think he said Bernard. Don't forget to suit up again when you come back," Foster said, pulling the door closed behind her as she left the room.

Mickey's mind whirled. Why would the RCMP want to talk about a house fire? That was a city cop's job. And that name, Bernard, sounded familiar.

Was it … no way.

Mickey grabbed his phone and looked up Andy's trial. The Leader-Post had run a story about it. He scrolled through the article looking for witnesses. There it was. Bernard was the goddamn Rump who arrested Andy. Was he also the RCMP officer that Kenna was ranting about yesterday? He couldn't recall their names, but if Bernard was one of them …

Mickey needed to get home. Now.

He opened the door a crack and looked up and down the hall. No sign of the RCMP or the nurse. Mickey tiptoed into the cloak room and grabbed his parka, then sprinted to the right, to the exit stairwell. Inside, he tore off the protective gear and tossed it on the landing, donned his parka, and ran down six flights to the lobby level. When he got to the bottom, he stopped to catch his breath. He ran his hands through his hair and headed out of the stairwell, walking nonchalantly to the exit nearby.

Catch me if you can.

Mickey pulled into his garage and paused to corral his thoughts, which were racing around like monkeys behind his hangover. He needed to be careful and logical, but that's not how he felt. No, he was agitated and wanted to punch something. He left his keys on the seat of his car, and pulled his boots off at the door, but left his parka on. He would be leaving right away and couldn't waste time. The house was quiet.

"Su! Suyin! Where are you?" he called out in a loud stage whisper, as he rounded the corner into the family room.

"I'm right here, Mickey. And keep it down. I just got Sashay down for her nap. So? Where the fuck were you all night?" Suyin said, from her perch on the couch. She tossed her magazine aside.

"The Rumps are after me, Su. Get Sashay, and go to your parents' house. I'm headed back to Andy's. I just stopped to grab something," he said.

"Oh, so you *were* at Andy's all night? And here I thought you were going to your mother's. I guess Andy doesn't have cell service at his house anymore? And why are the cops looking for you? What have you done?" Suyin said, hands on hips, and a steely glare in her eyes. "And no, I am *not* going to my parents' house. I haven't done anything wrong, so I don't need to hide out. And what about tonight? I thought we were going out for dinner?" Suyin hissed. "What have you done, you stupid shit?"

Mickey didn't have time to argue. He plunged his arm into the freezer and pulled out a Ziplok bag the size of a Cornish hen, and a smaller one, like a pound of butter. He shoved them into a grocery bag.

"Do you *always* have to be such a bitch? Our babysitter is in the fucking burn unit, so no, we're *not* going out for dinner. *Jesus.* Do what you want, but don't say I didn't warn you. I'm outta here," he said as he headed back to the garage, grabbing a ball cap from the mudroom. He slammed the door on Suyin's protests.

Mickey jumped into Suyin's SUV. As he backed out onto the street, he pulled the ball cap low on his head and drove slowly down his street, cautiously coming to a full stop at the corner. Instead of heading straight to Andy's, he drove south, towards Freda's house.

It was a gray afternoon, and night was seeping in from the horizon. He flicked on the headlights and drove to the Crescents, hoping the cops were no longer lurking around Freda's burned out house. It should have been *his* house, but the old bitch had disinherited all of them. What had he *ever* done to deserve Gram's wrath?

Mickey pulled into the alley, and stopped a few houses down from Freda's. By the time he parked and pulled on his gloves, Mickey's rage at the injustice of Freda's bequest was blooming. It was a good thing he'd been smart enough to look out for himself instead of counting on anyone else to do right by him. Mickey tucked the grocery bag into his parka. He looked over his shoulder as he scurried along fences and under bare branches, his boots crunching in the packed snow.

When he got to Freda's garage, he leaned against the door and removed his glove to punch in the key code. The garage door began to open, spilling light onto the frozen drive. When it was a few feet open, he ducked inside and ran to hit the button on the wall, bringing the garage door back down. Even though he had every right to be here, at his mother's home, he didn't need to be seen poking around.

Kenna's Volvo and Freda's Mercedes were parked neatly, side by side. Storage cabinets at the front of the garage were closed, but not locked. Mickey went straight to his hiding spot: a box labeled KENNA MISC. He'd put a false bottom in the box and stacked Kenna's paperwork on top so anyone looking would think it was just a box of old files. He smiled to himself.

Smarter than Andy and Danny, put together.

Mickey had always been able to spot a hot business opportunity and, when Andy got out of prison, Mickey saw his chance. He knew Andy would need to be cautious, so Mickey offered to help his friend out for a piece of the pie. But he wasn't a dealer. That was Andy. Mickey was just a shrewd business partner, making sure goods were delivered and fees collected, on time.

He fished out the packages from his parka, and tucked the larger one under the false bottom. Opening the smaller one, crammed with cash, he took out a stack of twenties—just a loan, Andy would never know—and closed the bag, before tucking it in with the rest of the stash.

No one suspected he was using the garage at the Crescents house to hold his stash between deliveries. Besides, once the cops backed off, he'd be making a delivery and this would all be gone. Not that they had anything on him. And he wasn't actually doing anything *wrong*, just helping a friend, but still ... no need to tempt fate. He didn't need his good name getting linked to anything *shady*.

He closed the cabinet and exited the side door of the garage. Night had fallen. No need to risk opening the overhead door and shining a light on himself. He was almost home free.

Back in his car, Mickey let out a long exhale. The only evidence was well hidden from his wife, his mother, and the cops. Suyin was mad at him right now, but he knew she wouldn't blab. Kenna was sedated and wasn't talking to anyone today. Once she woke up and he could talk some sense into her, she'd realize this was all her own fault. If she even remembered anything.

Now all Mickey had to do was warn Andy off but, since he wasn't answering his phone, Mickey would have to head over there in person. It seemed low risk. With the holidays and all, no one would notice an extra car at Andy's house.

Mickey drove down the dark alley, headlights off.

He didn't notice Jeff Berenchuk, sipping eggnogg, watching from his kitchen window.

55

Secret Santa

January 2

Camelia was perched on the edge of the sofa, clutching her iPad in one hand and a vodka soda in the other, alone in the comfortably silent house. She dialed Byron's mobile, sipping at her drink. She realized she wasn't supposed to be drinking, and put it on the coffee table, as if Byron had some sort of sixth sense.

"Hey Byron. Happy New Year!"

"What's up?" The terseness of Byron's response told Camelia all was not forgiven.

"I've got a bit of a problem on my hands and wanna ask you a coupla questions, if you've got a few minutes."

"It can't wait?" Byron said.

"No, I'm sorry, but I won't take much of your time. It's not work related, though. It's about my aunt. No one seems interested in the sudden death of an 85-year-old woman, but the cops are very interested in the fact that she had some fentanyl patches on her body at the time of death that were not prescribed."

"I'm sorry to hear that. And?"

"I'm trying to put together a little package of evidence for the RCMP, but I'm not the nationally recognized criminal law expert that you are. How would you proceed?" she said, hoping her bit of brown-nosing would smooth his jagged edges.

"I'd need more details, and now's not really the time. Look on the firm database for a file called Evidence Organization for Capital Cases. When you've read that through, I can answer questions, but not today, okay? Trying to have a little quality time with the wife, if you don't mind," he said. "Oh, and Cate got a continuance on your hearing because you said you had to stay on up there, so don't make a liar out of her."

"Got it, thanks," Camelia hung up and downloaded the file.

She tapped the file open on her tablet and scribbled a list as she scanned the contents.

Draft a timeline in chron order
Match events to evidence & suspects
ID motives and opportunity for each suspect

How would she ever track all the events and movements of all the people around Auntie Freda? How could she find out every opportunity there was for someone to poison her? As for motive, it could be anyone who would inherit—or *thought* they would—but of those, who was the most likely?

Kenna, of course.

Besides money, though, what else was there to gain? People kill each other for all kinds of reasons: lust and love, money, revenge, self-defense, power.

Camelia crossed lust and love off the list. She just couldn't see Arthur Rossi as the killer.

Same for power and self-defense. Freda didn't wield any power outside the family. While she was influential, she wasn't a politician. She certainly hadn't attacked anyone.

Revenge was harder to eliminate because how would Camelia know if someone's rage had been on a slow simmer?

Still, money seemed to be the most likely motive. Sure, Kenna was living in the lap of luxury, even if it was all technically Freda's. But she was also overdrawn on her bank account. Kenna was receiving disability benefits as a result of her car accident, and Tony was still paying spousal support, so where was all that money going?

Camelia tapped her pen on her notebook. She didn't have all the information. She wasn't omniscient. All she could do was organize the timeline of events as she knew them. She drew a chart on her notepad and started filling in dates.

She let her mind wander as she sipped her cocktail and watched the fire. She was missing something, but couldn't quite grasp what. The only hard evidence she had at the moment were two fentanyl patches. Really nothing concrete, just a bunch of circumstantial things that might—or might not—point to a crime. Even the items she'd sent off to the lab—the syringe, nose spray, and lozenges—were probably nothing, but she'd find out for sure when the lab results were posted.

Something was missing. It was just the smoke of an idea, as easy to grasp as the shimmer coming off the fire.

Auntie Freda died of an overdose, that much she knew. Kenna was involved somehow, but what about Mickey? They both could have money as a motive. They both had ample opportunity to dose Auntie Freda. And the means? She really needed the lab results.

There was one other missing piece.

Who was that mystery visitor?

She poured another cocktail and logged into the toxicology website again.

The results were posted.

Finally!

But instead of relieving her mind, now she had a whole new problem. Camelia was suddenly facing two more pieces of disjointed information that sizzled with their own questions.

The lozenge was sugar, zinc, echinacea, Vitamin C, artificial orange flavor, food coloring. Just a cold lozenge.

The nose spray contained saline, xylitol, echinacea, and a low dose of OxyContin. *Sweet Jesus, what kind of Chinese medicine was this?*

Finally, the syringe contained propofol and sufentanil. Not fentanyl. So that syringe wasn't used to draw off fentanyl from the patches.

But what are these drugs for?

Camelia typed the words into her tablet and read the descriptions of the drugs. She couldn't figure out why a spent syringe with drugs used for surgical anesthesia would be in in Auntie Freda's room, when she hadn't had surgery. And it wasn't even in the sharps disposal, but in the biohazard waste. It didn't make any sense, unless Freda was being prepped for surgery when she died. No one had mentioned anything about surgery, though.

But it certainly answered the question as to why Auntie Freda died quickly, in her sleep. She was loaded up with drugs deadly to her system. Just one of them—the fentanyl patch or the nose spray—would likely have been sufficient to induce a stroke, according to Dr. Fitzgerald.

If someone gave her an injection of these other two drugs, death would have been swift. That wispy trail of an idea was just there, just out of reach.

Still, why would Mickey pass Freda a nose spray he knew could kill her? Who put those fentanyl patches on her? Given the lab results, everyone was, once again, a suspect. She went back over her notes.

Kenna had means and opportunity, but what was her motive? She might have freaked out if she learned of Freda's plan to sell the house, but was it enough to inspire her to murder?

There was one tiny detail that stood out from the reading of the will. In her bequest to Kenna, Freda forgave "the loan".

What loan?

And, more importantly, how much was this loan? If Kenna had borrowed a substantial amount from Freda, maybe that was motive enough.

Camelia recalled the overdraft notice on Kenna's account. At the Boxing Day wake, Mickey said Kenna loaned him some money. Did Mickey lie? Because where did Kenna get the cash to loan to her son if she was broke?

The way Kenna acted with Freda, according to Jolene, was also out of character. Kenna was a hypochondriac, who wouldn't let so much as a hangnail go without medical attention, so why didn't she get help for Freda as soon as she noticed something wrong? And how long did Freda languish before Kenna finally called an ambulance?

Kenna should have taken Freda to the hospital when she found her on the floor the morning of her hair appointment. But she didn't. She dragged Freda to the salon and back home again, and didn't call an ambulance for another 32 hours or more.

Camelia shuddered at the thought of Auntie Freda suffering for hours, even days, without the medical attention she needed. It made her feel sick to her stomach, imagining Freda's confusion and fear, knowing that something was wrong, but not knowing what.

And then it was too late.

Then there were Sophie's photos of the bills in Kenna's room, including one from a U.S. mail order pharmacy. Camelia had noticed Kenna's behavior—how could she not?—and it reeked of addiction. She already had a DUI conviction for a serious car accident a couple of years ago, so substance abuse was established. Then came the post-accident surgeries. It was an easy ride from necessary pain relief to full blown addiction. The mail order pharmacy was all the proof of addiction Camelia needed, because Kenna was obviously going to great lengths to obtain oxy and fentanyl. Otherwise, why would someone covered by provincial healthcare need to order meds online from the U.S.?

But how did Mickey fit into that equation?

Having Auntie Freda cremated the same day as her death was another red flag that Camelia couldn't ignore. It precluded any post-mortem and screamed guilt. According to Ben, Kenna believed no one could receive their inheritance until after disposition of the remains. If the family had to wait around for a funeral mass, especially at the holidays, when the Diocese would be packed with activities, it could take weeks to arrange a high profile funeral like Freda's. Maybe Kenna couldn't wait that long. Why was she so desperate to get her hands on Freda's money? Did she think she could keep the house if Freda was gone? Or did she just need more money for drugs?

And then there were the fingerprints on the fentanyl patches. One of the patches was on Freda's body when she arrived at Springer. Camelia had no idea why Kenna would have put a fentanyl patch on Freda, but regardless of the *why*, Kenna had means. She had opportunity. Clearly, it wasn't a crime of passion. Poisoning takes time and patience—not a hot head—even when using a drug Freda was allergic to.

Mickey's motives were less clear. He may have pressed his nose spray on Freda without knowing about her allergy, but that seemed unlikely since—again, according to Ben—Freda's opioid allergy was discovered during Mickey's wedding trip. Surely something like that would be locked in his memory?

Unless Mickey didn't know there was oxy in the nose spray.

Whoever compounded the nose spray may not have disclosed all the ingredients. Or maybe it was accidentally contaminated? But what if Mickey knew, and gave it to Freda on purpose? Why? Was it on behalf of Kenna? Maybe he was sympathetic to his mother's money woes and decided to help her come into her inheritance. Or maybe Mickey thought he would be inheriting a little pile of his own. Camelia had seen his home, and it was clear to her he was living way beyond his means; otherwise why would a guy with that address have to borrow money from his mother and steal his cousin's credit card? By the way Suyin was dressed at the Boxing Day wake, she enjoyed nice things. Like designer handbags. How could Mickey keep up if he didn't have a steady income?

If money was tight, Freda's decision to list the house with Josephine's son could have given Mickey motive. Sale of a home like that would bring a hefty commission. Was it possible Mickey found out about her intentions and turned on Freda for her betrayal? When Camelia thought about it, it wasn't surprising that Freda wanted to list her home with Bruce, but until the reading of the will, who—besides Bruce and Josephine—knew about it?

Camelia grabbed her tote and dug out the magazine she'd pilfered from Mickey's house. With everything else going on, she hadn't even had a chance to look at it yet. It was a little surprising that *Canada Today* would even run such a sensational lead story: *Ordering Deadly Drugs from China is Easy*. She flipped to the article and skimmed it. The article listed a dozen or more sources to purchase fentanyl via the internet, primarily from China. Someone—Mickey?—had scribbled some numbers in the margin beside *Lucky Golden Life BioTechnology Co.*

Could it really be this simple? Did Mickey just order fentanyl off the internet? Maybe it was just a matter of observing the obvious. Even so, why would he dose Freda with fentanyl? Unless he'd taken the timing of his inheritance into his own hands.

Ben wasn't a suspect at all, since he and Norah didn't even arrive from San Diego until the morning of Boxing Day. Camelia was grateful for that. At least one member of the family wasn't a potential killer!

Rita … it couldn't be Rita. Not her lifelong friend. She was a nurse for Chrissake. Then again, she was a hospice nurse, now, with ready access to the means. If she were at work.

But Rita didn't have much of an opportunity, given she was only under Freda's roof for one night before they left for Dave's family farm. And, Camelia couldn't think of a motive.

Why would Rita do anything to harm Freda, especially now? The old wounds still itched, but that wasn't an exclusive club. Most families held tight to their rusted-out tensions and worn-through resentments. She was dutiful in her monthly phone calls, cards and gifts for special occasions, and the annual holiday gathering; but otherwise, she rarely interacted with her mother. It didn't make any sense for Rita to hasten Freda's demise. Especially if money was the motive. Rita and Dave had a comfortable life in Vancouver. They certainly didn't need Freda's money.

As for the other grandchildren, Camelia ticked off the list as she considered each of them and, just as quickly, dismissed them. Other than the Cousins Lunch, none of them had been around Freda except Mickey. And it was Mickey who offered Freda the tainted nose spray.

Harriet and Josephine were out of the question. And, from what she could surmise, Arthur was, too. If Arthur was marrying Freda for her money he sure as hell wouldn't kill her before the wedding.

And then there was the mystery visitor at the hospital. Who had Kenna notified? Camelia went back to her notes. Gayle Germaine said the visitor was Jane Cannoli, but she didn't sound completely sure. Camelia flipped through the medical chart to the visitor sign-in. The only signature she could readily decipher was Kenna's. Of the other two, she guessed one was Mickey's because it looked both childish and masculine.

As she stared at the other scribble, she squinted and held the page closer, then further. Camelia put her drink down. Maybe she'd had too much to drink. And she'd been staring at her tablet all afternoon. She pulled a bottle of eye drops out of her purse and squirted some in each eye. She blinked away the drops and looked again.

Yes, she'd seen that name before.

Her breath caught in her throat.

It couldn't be.

It just *couldn't.*

But the dots were connecting, arcing across her brain like lightning on a prairie summer afternoon.

Flash. Boom. *Shit.*

Jane Cannoli, the charge nurse, Gayle Germaine, called her.

But it wasn't Jane Cannoli.

It was *June Corelli.*

Rita June Corelli Becker.

56

The Stash

January 3

On the drive to the Crescents house, Camelia steeled herself for the coming conversation. Her dear friend, her lifelong friend, could *not* be a killer.

There had to be some other explanation. But why would Rita lie about not seeing Freda and even go so far as to argue with Kenna about it on Boxing Day? She thought back to the argument and tried to recall if Rita had actually denied seeing Freda or … no, she hadn't denied anything. She'd just deflected. Even so, Camelia was sure Rita was innocent. She had to be, but how to bring it up? Being a lawyer didn't help, not when it was her friend and the question was so … indelicate. Years of dealing with people misbehaving had roughed up Camelia's smooth edges, making her often seem too blunt, too direct, too … honest.

But now that the idea had lodged in her brain, Camelia had to know the truth. She needed Rita to tell her she was crazy. She needed Rita to tell her what really happened: something so obvious and innocent that, as soon as Camelia heard the explanation, it would make perfect sense. She'd realize she should have seen it for herself. All she had to do was find the perfect words so Rita wouldn't hate her for thinking she could have killed her own mother.

Camelia parked the car and gave a little wave to Dave, who was shoveling the driveway along the side of the house. She took a deep breath and braced herself. She had to act normal, and not let the panic gripping her by the throat show itself.

"Hey Dave! You shouldn't be doing this. Doesn't Auntie Freda have a snow service?" She hoped he didn't hear the stress in her voice.

"Hey Cam! They won't be here for a couple days, and I figured this would burn off some of the cookies I've been pounding down," Dave said.

She hesitated.

Camelia couldn't face Rita. Not yet. She had to come up with the words, somehow, to convey her concern and not come off as an accusation.

But maybe what she needed was in the garage. Something that would answer all of her questions about Mickey. And Kenna. And turn the spotlight away from her friend. Dave had seen Mickey going into the garage in the middle of the night, and Camelia had seen him do the same at the Boxing Day wake. Now was as good a time as any.

"So what's this about? Is this from you?" Camelia said, pointing to where the snow was trampled in front of the garage door.

Dave gave her a sly smile. "No, but I think we both know who was in and out of here lately."

"What would Mickey be doing in the garage?"

"There's only one way to find out. I'll go get the key. Be right back," he said, handing Camelia the shovel.

While he was gone, Camelia used her phone to snap photos of the footprints around the garage door, even though the wind had erased anything that might be identifiable.

As Camelia slipped her phone in her pocket, Dave jogged back with a sparkly pink heart-shaped keyring, which had to be Kenna's.

He fumbled for the light switch, flipped on the lights, and started to enter, but Camelia put her hand on his arm.

"Hang on, my eyes need to adjust and I don't want to miss anything," she said. Then, after a few seconds, "Okay, let's be careful."

They stepped into the garage, which felt comfortably warm compared to outdoors.

"Now this is better," Dave said, shoving his gloves into his pockets. "A heated garage is the way to go in this climate." He clapped the snow off his mittens and stamped the snow off his boots.

Camelia looked around until she saw telltale puddles along the wall, in front of the storage cabinets.

"Dave, snow melt." Camelia pointed to the floor in front of the storage cabinets.

"Yeah, or a roof leak."

She looked at the ceiling and pointed to the pristine white drywall above them. "Does that look like a leaky roof to you?"

"Okay, good point, Sherlock. Kenna hasn't been in here for days, so there shouldn't be water on the floor."

"Right. Unless Mickey or someone else was here," Camelia said. "So what's in those cabinets?"

"Let's have a look, shall we?" Dave said, and stepped to the cabinets where the majority of the water had pooled on the floor. He opened the cabinet doors to reveal rows of file boxes neatly stored inside. "What are we looking for, again?"

The interior of the cabinets was dark, so Camelia tapped the flashlight on her phone and shone the light over Dave's shoulder.

"Who knows? But whoever was here last doesn't have OCD," she said, shining her light on a file box labeled KENNA MISC, shoved haphazardly on the top shelf of the cabinet. All the other boxes were shoulder to shoulder. "Can you pull that box down?"

"Sure," Dave said, swinging the box onto the trunk of Kenna's car. "Not much in it if we go by weight," He pulled the lid off. "Just some paperwork."

Camelia reached to the bottom and pulled out the stack of files.

"Old tax returns and such. Wait. Dave, this doesn't look right." Camelia compared the outside of the box with the inside and realized it was too shallow by several inches.

"You're right," Dave said. "False bottom. That's why it's light."

When Camelia pressed down against one corner of the box, the whole bottom tipped up to expose what was below. Dave let out a low whistle at the sight of a bundle of cash underneath the false bottom.

Dave started to reach into the box, but Camelia quickly grabbed his wrist.

"Holy shit. Don't touch anything with your bare hands, okay?" Camelia said. She lifted the false bottom out. "And what have we here?"

Camelia dipped her gloved hand into the box and pulled out a plastic freezer bag stuffed with small blue tablets and a second bag containing boxes labeled Duragesic Fentanyl. Her heart pounded and her palms were sweating inside her gloves.

"So what's all this?" Dave asked.

"Pretty sure it's black market fentanyl, and we need to call the cops," Camelia said.

"So, is this Kenna's dope?"

Camelia raised her eyebrows at Dave. "Dude. Nobody says dope anymore. And I guess it could be Kenna's stash. I mean, it's in *her* file box, in *her* garage," Camelia said.

"Yeah, but Kenna's been in the hospital for …" Dave counted on his fingers. "About 36 hours. So that water on the floor isn't from her tracking in snow. It has to be …"

Their eyes met.

"Mickey," they said in unison.

"Let's just leave everything right where it is, and I'll call the cops to come get this stuff," Camelia said.

"Oh god, really? If you do that, it's gonna be a whole *thing*. I say we just put it back and leave well enough alone," Dave said.

"I can't, Dave, you know that," Camelia said, softly.

Dave dropped his head, let out a long exhale, then looked at Camelia. "I guess I should've kept my mouth shut, huh?"

"Maybe. But we both know it would eat away at you. And besides, I saw Mickey come in here, too. On Boxing Day," Camelia said. She took a deep breath. "The thing is, we're not criminals, Dave. We're not drug dealers. But whoever put this stuff here *is* a drug dealer. This shit is killing people all over the country. We can stop this shipment from hitting the streets. We still have a little bit of honor left, don't we?"

Dave tried to smile, but it was a lopsided, sad attempt. "Yeah, and honor requires us to do the right thing. Might as well make the call, Cam."

Camelia was almost glad they'd found this stash because it meant confronting Rita—the very idea of which made her feel panicky—would have to wait.

57

BUSTED

JANUARY 3

Sgt. Bernard, RCMP, and Det. Johnson, Regina Police, arrived about 20 minutes later, their faces grim and serious as badges were flashed and introductions exchanged.

"Show us what you've got," Bernard said.

Dave opened the garage door, and Camelia pointed to the box on the trunk.

"How'd you find it?" Bernard said.

"We were outside and noticed footprints around the garage door. We were worried about a break-in, because the house has been empty a lot lately. Dave and I had a look, to see if anything was missing. There was a puddle of water, snow melt, in front of this cabinet," she said, pointing, "and this box was on the top shelf, but it was askew. You can see for yourself what's inside," Camelia said.

A muffled knock on the garage door startled them. Camelia started to step to the door, but Johnson blocked her way and swung the door open quickly. Jeff Berenchuk stood there, hands deep in his pockets, looking surly.

"Hey Jeff!" Camelia called out.

"Did you guys have a break in? Something happen?" he asked.

Talk about Mr. Nosy Neighbor.

"We're figuring that out now, why? Did you see something?" Johnson asked.

"Yep. Mickey Shores was here last evening. He parked about three houses down, walked over here, and went in the garage. Then he drove away with his headlights off. That's all I saw, but it's pretty damn shady if you ask me," he said.

"Can you show me where you saw him, exactly?" Det. Johnson said, and followed Berenchuk back outside.

Sgt. Bernard took a dozen or so photos with his phone before putting the lid on the box. "We're taking all this in as evidence, and I'll send a team over to fingerprint the cabinets and the doors. We'll need a formal statement from both of you, but you can follow me in your own cars," he said.

They instinctively tucked their heads when a blast of cold wind rocked the three of them as they left the garage. When the gust of wind passed, Camelia looked up to see Freda in the kitchen window. She staggered back at the vision. Blinking to clear her eyes, Camelia looked back toward the house. But that wasn't a ghost staring out at her. It was Rita, and Camelia's heart seized at the raw grief on her friend's face.

Following along behind Dave to the Regina Police station, Camelia wondered what the hell was going on with Mickey and Kenna. Would this secret stash be enough to charge … who? Mickey? Kenna? Or both? Her stomach quivered in fear.

What have I started?

Camelia imagined the various ways her actions would be scrutinized, criticized, second-guessed, and outright mocked by members of the family. Leon was going to be furious. Rita might never speak to her again.

At the station, she paused long enough to text Leon that she would be another half hour or so, and trotted across the parking lot to catch up to Dave.

"Hey, everything okay with Rita?" Camelia asked, recalling her friend's expression out the kitchen window.

"Whadda you think? She's exhausted from losing her mother, running back and forth to the hospital to see Kenna, cleaning up after the fire, dealing with the insurance people and the contractors, sorting out all the stuff in the attic, and now this. She's been hit with crisis after crisis, when what she really needed was a vacation," Dave said. "But hey, we're gonna be upright citizens, right?" He rolled his eyes.

They gave their names to the desk sergeant and had no sooner taken off their coats than Bernard came for Camelia. She followed him through a rabbit warren of hallways to an interview room where Johnson was waiting.

The two cops gave her the usual spiel about her statement and pushed a pad and pen across the table.

"We'll be back in a few minutes," Bernard said, and they left.

Camelia knew her role here was to give clear, concise, accurate information about finding Mickey's stash. Nothing more. This was not a time for conjecture about … anything. She only knew three things for sure: 1) she saw Mickey go into the garage on Boxing Day; 2) Dave reported seeing Mickey go into the garage in the middle of the night on December 30; and 3) she and Dave found the box in the garage today.

Stick to the facts, m'am.

She wrote it all out, slowly, trying to make her lawyer scrawl as legible as possible. As she reviewed her statement, there was a light rap on the door and Chip Conroy entered.

"Mr. Conroy. I didn't expect to see you here," she said.

And not sure I want to see you.

"Hello Cam. I think they're just humoring an old man, but because I brought the case to their attention …" he said.

"Yeah, about that. I shouldn't have involved you. I understand why you turned over the patches and, while it made things pretty tense in the family, I get it. That's why I'm here, by the way. We found …" Camelia said.

"I know. Bernard told me. And no need for an apology. If anything, I should apologize for not giving you fair warning. I'm retired almost ten years now, but old habits …" Conroy said, shaking his head. "So, Bernard said I could get you up to speed. I thought it might make you feel better to know that the evidence you brought in is tied to a much bigger case," Conroy said.

"Oh? How's that?"

"First off, that was a sizable haul you turned over. But even without that evidence, we had some questions for Mickey. They tracked him down at the hospital, but he gave our guys the slip. Didn't matter though, because we … they caught up to him last night," Conroy said.

"Was he at home?"

"No, they picked him up outside Andy Yin's house," Conroy said. "He was holding some fentanyl and oxy, along with a wad of cash. They also found some interesting stuff at Yin's that will land them both in jail for a while," Conroy continued. "They're charging Andy and Mickey with drug trafficking."

"Holy crap. I mean, I know you're not kidding, but Mickey? I just can't imagine him as a drug lord," Camelia said.

"Oh, he's not. But he's a good little foot soldier with an airtight cover," Conroy said.

"How do you mean?"

"He's a realtor who apparently shows a *lot* of houses, but doesn't make any sales. The RIDU guys were baffled as to how deliveries were happening because they weren't seeing drops between Yin and his cronies. But that's because Mickey was doing all the deliveries. Mickey was just scheduling property showings with Andy's street dealers. He had access to empty houses, and no one questioned the so-called clients he was showing around. It's actually a pretty clever scheme," Conroy said.

Camelia knew Mickey was a slimy little thief—after all, he'd stolen Sophie's credit card—but she couldn't believe he was stupid enough to add drug dealer to his resume. But apparently he was *exactly* that stupid. It was only a matter of time before he was busted, but Camelia wished she wasn't getting credit for it.

"I'm shocked that he would put his family in such danger, not only from the drugs, but from the criminals he's associating with. But, I guess if he's dealing, he's getting what he deserves," Camelia said, with a sigh. Mickey would not do well in prison. "The whole family seems to be falling apart now that Auntie Freda's gone."

"Unfortunately, there's more. Bernard went through Kenna Shores' browser and phone history …"

"They got a warrant to look into Kenna?" Camelia said, her voice coming out in a squeak.

"Yep. Because of Mickey's frequent visits at all hours and the circumstances of her car accident. Turns out Ms. Shores has a bogus prescription for fentanyl patches. We already know the patches she had were tampered with. We're … they're pretty sure it's black market resale. She also had half a dozen fake prescriptions for oxy, so looks like she's got a raging addiction. Along with all the fake fentanyl in her garage, she's getting charged for possession, at the very least," he said. "As soon as she's out of the Burn Unit."

Mickey arrested, Kenna facing charges; Auntie Freda's death seemed to have brought down the House of Swenson. Or maybe it was karma, making a quick U-turn, barreling through the cosmos to avenge Freda. That would be fitting, in Camelia's mind. Let those two pay for what they did.

"Mr. Conroy, I had no idea this would be such a mess. My only concern was about how Auntie Freda died. I didn't intend to bring all this … trouble." Camelia felt a wave of regret wash over her, along with a persistent thirst that wasn't going to go away by itself. She sat on her hands to keep them from shaking.

"I guess it depends on your perspective, Cam. From our … from the RIDU perspective, the team's really glad you poked around. Just getting that stash of fen off the streets is a huge win," Conroy said.

"I suppose." Camelia paused, not sure she should ask the question that had been on her mind. It might be her only chance, so she plunged ahead. "I have a question. Did Mickey or Andy have any syringes on them?"

"I don't know exactly what he was holding, but I can find out. Is it important?" he said.

Camelia nodded. "Yeah, it is kind of important just … you know how it is. You told me the fentanyl patches had puncture marks so … I need to be able to cross all the Ts."

"I get it, and I'll find out. Anyway, I thought you'd want to know what went down and that RIDU was pretty happy with the outcome," Conroy said, and stood. "Now, I can take that statement from you and walk you out, if you're ready."

Camelia said goodbye to Conroy and walked to her car. She didn't feel the elation she expected from solving the puzzle. But maybe that was because she still had to confront Rita about her hospital visit, a chore she dreaded.

It was also, she decided as she pulled out of the parking lot, a chore that would keep.

Auntie Freda's celebration of life was in a couple of days, enough time for Conroy to get back to her about the syringes. If she approached Rita now, without that piece of information, she might be starting something when she didn't need to. Plus, it would be awkward as hell if Rita wasn't even speaking to her at Auntie Freda's services. Yes, the Rita Talk could wait until after the memorial. The pressure would be off. They would have time to really talk it all through.

What couldn't wait, wouldn't wait, refused to wait, was this itching thirst at the back of her throat.

Camelia drove past the Crescents, south on Albert, and pulled in at the Rusty Nail, her father's old haunt. It had been Bobby Porcher's favorite watering hole, his retreat whenever he was fed up with Camelia's mother, or his job, or who knows what. He had a long list of complaints. When she got her learner's permit, Camelia's mother routinely sent her out to fetch her father at closing time. She'd sit outside in the parking lot, waiting for him to come out. He would emerge, sooner or later, shitfaced drunk, singing Goodnight Irene. As long as he was singing, everything was okay. It was when he stopped singing and started shouting that the trouble started. Was it any wonder this was the bar where Mr. Conroy caught her and Janet drinking under age? It was as much her haunt as her father's. She parked and walked across the almost-empty parking lot. As soon as she pulled open the door, the smell—stale cigarettes, old beer, and wet wood—assaulted her senses. Her thirst surged.

Just one, for old time's sake.

58

Remembering Freda

January 5

Freda would have approved of the traditional fresh rosemary mourning wreaths on the front doors of the Italian Club, but the sight of them caught Camelia by surprise and fresh, hot tears filled her eyes.

Inside, the vestibule was warm and bright, with an easel holding an enlarged photo of Auntie Freda from the Christmas dinner dance, looking radiant and happy, her blue eyes twinkling and a bloom on her cheeks. She held a champagne flute aloft and seemed to be cheering Camelia on. A sob bubbled out of Camelia's throat. It was altogether unfair that her beloved Italian Club, the venue for Freda's wedding, was now the place of her memorial.

Camelia arrived alone, ahead of the services, to meet with Arthur, Harriett, Josephine, and Rita. Not exactly a rehearsal, but a quick review before everyone gathered. She followed the discreet signs to the Botanico Milan room and pushed open the heavy door, steeling herself. She didn't know how Rita would react toward her after Mickey's arrest and with charges being laid against Kenna.

Inside, Freda's fiancé, best friends, and eldest daughter formed a small huddle with a woman Camelia didn't recognize.

She quietly joined them at the table, murmuring an apology for being late. They exchanged subdued hellos and introduced Carla Redmond, the event manager. Arthur Rossi was pale and his backbone seemed to be fused with grief. Harriet had taken charge, with Josephine at her side, nodding in agreement. Rita was withdrawn, her expression grim and determined.

"Okay, where were we?" Carla asked, consulting her clipboard.

"The pianist? Where will he set up?" Rita asked.

"He'll be over there, in the corner, and we'll keep the mic volume low," Carla said.

Arthur walked to the tall windows overlooking a frozen landscape where, in a few months, they would break ground on the Freda Corelli Swenson & Arthur Luca Rossi Garden Pavilion. After a pause that felt like an eternity, he walked slowly back to the table. Camelia could almost see the aura of his sorrow draining the light around him.

"Do you think we need to add a few tables to the room? I expect there to be more people than we … " he took a deep breath. "Than anticipated."

Carla looked around the room and consulted her clipboard. She explained where they could place some additional tables, motioning with her hands like a flight attendant pointing out the exits.

They all nodded in assent.

"Is there anything I can help with?" Camelia asked.

"Actually, yes, we need an emcee, and none of us are up to the task," Rita said. "You're used to talking to a room full of people."

"Someone has to take charge, or we'll have pandemonium," Harriet said.

"You don't have to do anything other than invite people to share their memories of Freda. And try to keep the windbags from taking up too much time," Josephine said.

"God knows we're way too old to be standing that long, so we need you, Cammy. It shouldn't be left to chance," Harriet said. "And it shouldn't fall to Rita, either. She's been through enough."

“Yes, of course. I can do that,” Camelia said, offering a weak smile.

Rita looked at her watch, “I think we should leave Carla to finish up. We’re supposed to start in a just about an hour, so …”

“It’s going to be a long evening of reminiscing about my dear Freda,” Arthur said, his voice breaking as he said her name. “We should fortify ourselves in the bar.” He pressed his handkerchief to his nose, reddened from stifled tears.

Josephine and Harriet exchanged worried glances, before busying themselves with leaving.

“Good idea, Arthur,” Camelia said.

A double vodka would help her concentrate and hush the quivering in her belly.

Guests began showing up well ahead of schedule, and it wasn’t long before the Italian Club lounge was full of chattering mourners. The mood seemed festive, almost; no one other than their small circle seemed terribly stricken by Freda Swenson’s death.

But then, most were Freda’s contemporaries, gamely celebrating every day above ground as a bonus. They seemed accustomed to this type of affair, but Camelia didn’t know if she would ever get used to losing people she loved. She’d only had two close losses in her life so far: her father and Freda. Losing an estranged father wasn’t that much of a loss, it turned out. But Freda … Camelia sipped her drink, trying to swallow the lump at the back of her throat.

The five of them—Arthur, Josephine, Harriet, Rita, and Camelia—were crammed around a cocktail table, sharing a plate of bruschetta.

“Are we all set? I’m having a case of nerves,” Rita said.

“Let’s have a shot of courage, then,” Josephine said, signaling a passing waiter. She waved him in, pulled him close, and whispered an order in his ear.

“I assure you, it will be a beautiful remembrance, dear,” Harriet said.

"The family should go first, then Harri and Joey, then me, I think," Arthur said.

"Oh, sweet Arthur, in Freda's heart you were first, but I agree," Harriet said. "Everyone will want to hear from the children. Well, at least the children who are *able* to attend."

"Harri, we aren't going to talk about any of that today," Josephine said, shaking her head slowly. "This is Freda's day."

Rita heaved a sigh.

Carla Redmond approached the table. "You're welcome to go back to Botanico Milan, now. It's all set up," Carla said, and stepped aside for the waiter, who began unloading shot glasses from his tray.

"What's this?" Rita asked.

"It's ouzo dear. A shot of courage," Josephine said, grabbing a glass. "To Freda!" She tipped her head back and tossed the liquid down her throat in unison with Harriet and Arthur.

Rita lifted the shot glass. "To Mum!" She tossed it back with a grimace.

Camelia also tossed hers back, welcoming the warm burn, just a little something to beat back the panic lurking near the surface. But not nearly enough. As their little group wound their way through the crowded lounge to the banquet room, she slipped a Klonopin wafer under her tongue.

When Camelia entered the Botanico Milan Room, she caught her breath. In less than an hour, it had been transformed. The massive chandeliers were dimmed, and the twinkling golden lights in the snow-covered garden glowed through the windows. Dozens of candles shimmered on tables draped in black and cream. Soothing notes of jazz from the baby grand piano gentled the somber purpose of the occasion.

Bouquets of fresh flowers—those Freda had selected for her wedding—were on every table. A garland of greenery and blooms was strung across the wide, ornate podium at the front of the room. Behind the podium, a parade of smiling Fredas flashed across a huge screen as if marching through time: Freda as a child, a teen, in her 20s, at her university graduation, at her wedding with Geoffrey, pregnant, smiling with a baby in her arms, at parties, with Harriet and Josephine in Rome, Paris, and

London, at a picnic. Freda's toothy grin reminded everyone of what had been lost.

Camelia turned and took in the room, empty now, but not for long. The Klonopin was taking effect, and the serenity and calm she longed for filled her belly as she breathed in the scent of flowers and rosemary, the herb for remembrance and mourning.

This was a moment to hold, to remember, to cherish. She gripped the page of notes she'd made. This wasn't like a trial, where she had facts, evidence, witnesses. This time, her words had to capture the culmination of a life. But the photos, the speeches, the tearful memories weren't Freda's life at all. Her *real* life—like everyone's—happened elsewhere, outside the range of the camera lens, in all the little daily habits and routines that, stacked together, created Freda.

Camelia wondered for a moment what her own life would look like in retrospect, but she couldn't go down that path. Not now.

Arthur, Harriet, and Josephine were settling at a table in the front, near the windows. Rita had located Dave, and they were now at the same table. Camelia counted chairs and realized there would only be enough room at their table for Ben and Norah, so she dropped her handbag on the next table and draped four napkins over the backs of the chairs, one each for her, Leon, Sophie, and Steve.

Her phone buzzed. Conroy. She let it go to voice mail.

The doors swung open and a rush of people entered, clamoring for seats near the front, rupturing the solitude. As Camelia watched for Leon, she noticed the glances. Camelia could feel their stares and hear the whispers. It seemed as if everyone was carrying a rumor on their tongue.

Did you hear the latest? What on earth do you think happened? Did you hear about the youngest daughter? The grandson was arrested for dealing drugs, you know.

Camelia's moment of peace flitted away, like a small bird.

She waved at her family, standing tentatively at the doorway. Sophie was holding two glasses of wine; she handed one to Camelia as she gave her a one-armed hug.

"Everything's so pretty," Sophie said, her eyes filling with tears.

"Come on now, let's get seated and, Steve, let's save those seats for the cousins," Leon said, pointing to the chairs next to him.

Camelia checked her phone. Just a few minutes until the memorial was to begin. She glanced at the next table. Rita caught her eye, and nodded. It was time.

Camelia squared her shoulders and stepped up to the podium. She took a deep breath and tapped the mic.

Freda was still here, all around her, in the glow of candlelight, in the soaring notes of the music, in the warm chatter of old friends, in the heart of her favorite niece: the essence of Freda.

This is all for you, Auntie.

Camelia had been on her feet for hours, introducing family and friends, inviting the guests to share a short memory, tactfully interrupting those who began to ramble, and keeping an eye on the clock. Her feet were killing her, and she was starving. When the queue of eulogists began to peter out, she stepped back to the podium to close out the memorial.

"Thank you all for sharing such wonderful memories of Freda. If you knew my Auntie Freda, then you know she left an indelible mark on the Queen City. From Albert Park to Regent Park, from the RCMP Depot to the University of Regina, and everything in between, every corner of the city has benefitted in some way from Freda Swenson's influence. Freda's devotion to her community hasn't ended though, because soon, with the help of her beloved fiancé, Freda's spirit will live on in the new Freda Corelli Swenson & Arthur Luca Rossi Garden Pavilion, which will be built right outside," she said, and gestured out toward the windows.

An excited wave of murmurs rose from the room. She was encouraged by dozens of nodding heads.

"The moments at the *end* of our lives are often deemed worthless, disposable," Camelia said, pausing for emphasis. "At the *beginning*? That's the precious part. Every milestone charted, photographed, Instagrammed, and bragged over. Today, that seems a bit backwards, because I would give anything to have just one recent photo of Freda and me together. When we're young, we have millions of moments ahead of us and most of them will be *firsts*. But it's near the end, the season of *lasts*, that we should be memorializing in journals, celebrating each sundown with champagne toasts. Instead, we look away, avert our eyes from the realities of aging. But, old age will come to each of us, if we're lucky."

Camelia paused. "And now, as we send off our dear Freda, I want to leave you with a *mission*. Don't waste another moment. Take those selfies! Live as Freda did: to the hilt," she said, and lifted her wine glass as she turned to the larger-than-life photo of Auntie Freda behind her. "To Freda Agnes Corelli Swenson. Salute."

A loud chorus, "To Freda" and "Salute" rolled over her, followed by a round of applause. Camelia turned back to see old friends embracing and clinking their glasses in Freda's honor.

With everyone brought to tears and to their feet, Freda's sendoff was complete.

59

Marital Mayhem

January 5

As soon as she was able to extricate herself from well-wishers, Camelia retreated to the Italian Club dining room. It was late, she was tired, she desperately wanted to take her shoes off, and she was ravenous.

Sophie and Steve had already left, and Leon was surrounded by old friends, so she staked out a table in the corner by herself. With it being so late, she ordered an antipasto platter—one of the few things still available from the kitchen—and wine. The heady Italian red was smooth and fruity. And it went down way too easily. Camelia had drained the bottle into her glass and ordered a second by the time Leon joined her, 45 minutes later.

"Finally tore yourself away from the Berenchuks, I see. Want something to eat?" Camelia said.

"Yeah, well, you know how chatty they are. Good call on grabbing something to eat even though … Jesus it's almost 11. I guess we're on the Late Night Bites," Leon said, eyeing the menu and peeling a round of salami from the antipasto platter.

"Yeah, sorry. I couldn't wait. I was starving."

"Well, you worked hard the last few hours and, Cam, you did a great job. Not a dry eye in the place," Leon said.

"Aww. Thanks, hon. But all I did was wrangle everyone to just a few minutes," she said.

"Like that guy from Springer. Pretty sure he could have gone on all night."

"Joe Alexander was an old friend of Freda's, so he had a lot to share," she said.

Leon glanced at the bottle of wine. "So now that the memorial is over, what are we celebrating?" he asked.

"I'm celebrating my dear departed aunt. I'm celebrating the fact that this memorial is behind us. And I guess I'm celebrating a potential career pivot. Regardless of how you may feel about it, I worked hard to find out what happened to Auntie Freda. I didn't quite get all the answers, but I did get a ton of dangerous drugs off the street. It's made me think about changing my practice area from family law to investigative law," she said, and filled her wine glass.

"Hmmm. That's quite a shift. Have you talked to Byron about this?"

"No, but I think he'll be impressed that I was able to give the Mounties enough for at least two arrests. And I really enjoyed it. Pretty sure this will put me back on track for partner," Camelia said. She raised her hand for a high five, but Leon didn't reciprocate.

"I thought you were already on track for partner."

"I mean *more* on track," she said, realizing her mistake. "And don't be Mr. Buzzkill. We're finished with all this, which is what you wanted, right?"

"Of course it's finished, because you wouldn't leave it alone. I wanted it to be finished before it started. This mess has alienated everyone, Cam. I'm not convinced it was worth it," Leon said, his voice full of accusation.

"Catching two drug dealing killers? That was definitely worth it to those of us who value justice," Camelia retorted.

"Right. Because you're the only one who wants justice." Leon stopped talking when their waiter approached. He ordered another antipasto, along with a second wine glass. When the waiter left, he continued. "Don't you see? *There is no justice* because *none of this* will bring Freda back. But maybe that's just my opinion," he said.

When she didn't answer, Leon also remained quiet. Their irritation silently simmered, but neither of them seemed up for a fight.

"I really don't want to start a round of marital mayhem in the middle of the Italian Club, so, not to change the subject, but can we please change the subject?" Camelia said, after a few minutes of stony quiet.

"Fine. What do *you* want to talk about?"

"Tell me who you saw today that you haven't seen in a while," Camelia said.

Leon began telling her about the old friends he'd connected with. By the time the waiter appeared with Leon's food, he'd begun to relax. He forked roasted peppers, salami, and olives onto his plate.

"What about you? Who did you see?" he said.

Camelia rattled off the names of half a dozen old acquaintances of their parents' generation, along with a couple of their mutual high school friends. "And did you see Lars and Debbie? Haven't seen them in for*ever*," she said. "And if it's any consolation, you look at least 10 years younger than him."

"Thanks, I think. He's recovering from stomach cancer, so Lars is setting a low bar," Leon said.

"Oh, no, I didn't know that. In that case, he looks amazing."

Leon was looking over the tab their waiter had dropped on the table. "Crap. Unless you drank an entire bottle of wine by yourself, they've double charged us." He started to wave the waiter over.

"Wait, let me see," Camelia said, as she looked at the bill. "Yeah, that was me. But who's counting?" She knew it sounded defensive and childish.

"I am. At $50 a pop, $100 of this bill is wine. Don't you think that's a bit much? Even for you?"

Camelia cringed. "Holy shit. I wasn't paying attention. I had no idea the wine was that expensive. What a rip off."

"Well, yeah, the prices are a rip off, but Jesus Christ, Cam, you drank a bottle and a half *by yourself*. I thought we were trying to dial back our discretionary spending. At least until I have a steady client roster. Unless wine is no longer optional." The implication was painful.

Camelia's head had begun to pound as Leon harped on about the bill. All she wanted was to crawl in bed, away from Leon's nagging and her own relentless guilt.

"By the looks of it, we need to leave anyway. They're wiping down the bar," Camelia said, her tongue feeling thick in her mouth.

Leon shook his head and waved over their server to pay the bill. Camelia was relieved that Leon wouldn't look her in the eye; she knew what she would see. Disgust.

On the cold walk to the car, she tallied the demons looming over her. Work, of course, and Byron's incessant demands. The constant cycle of pressure from clients, opposing counsel, judges, all the way through trial and beyond. That unrelenting stress fed the panic attacks, which were like a dark cloud following her around. And that uncertainty led to self-medicating: drinking and drugging, crossfading herself into oblivion every day just to make it through to the next round of crises.

Given the weight of her challenges, Camelia felt she was due some credit for being as capable as she was. But then again, careening from vodka to Klonopin to wine and back again was no way to live.

I think they call this phase 'functional alcoholic'.

This holiday, this so-called *vacation* had only made things worse. Auntie Freda was gone, and god knows she was irreplaceable. Everyone was mad at Camelia for rocking the boat, including Leon. He was usually on her side, but he was upset about the rift in the family, blaming Camelia for airing all the dirty little secrets. But wasn't that better than covering everything up? What kind of family depends on lies as their foundation?

Far too many.

Camelia didn't want any part of that kind of family, and she was disappointed in Leon for just wanting to get along, instead of supporting her mission for justice. She wondered how he would have reacted had it been his own mother, although she already knew: he would have been outraged.

The fact that it was Auntie Freda—that imperious, demanding, sharp-tongued matriarch—somehow made it okay with people, as if she deserved her end. But she didn't, and it was repulsive to think Kenna and Mickey had taken matters into their own hands. Of course, she hadn't proven anything yet, but Camelia did not for one minute believe they were innocent. For all she knew, they premeditated Auntie Freda's murder by overdose, thinking their share of her estate would fall into their laps. Or maybe it was just a dumb, drunken mistake on Kenna's part. No matter what actually happened, Freda didn't deserve to have her last few years with Arthur taken from her.

They drove back to the house in silence, classic rock playing on the radio, reminding them both of an earlier time, when they were teens, cruising Albert on a Saturday night in Leon's souped-up GT. It made Camelia wistful, or maybe it was the booze. She reached for Leon and, without glancing at her, he clasped her gloved hand.

"Cam, I …" Leon looked over at her. "Sorry I snapped at you about the wine. It's just … some days it seems like I'm losing you to … something, not sure what."

"I'm right here, babe. You're not losing me," Camelia said.

But am I losing you?

She wanted to tell him about Byron's ultimatum, the increasing panic attacks, the drinking, all of it. But now was not the time. It would wait until they were home in Phoenix. She'd let things settle down a bit before she dumped all her worries in his lap.

They tiptoed through the quiet house, careful not to disturb their daughter and son-in-law, tucked in upstairs. When they finished washing up, they fell into bed. Camelia pressed herself against Leon's warm back. It was a place she felt safe. Safe from Byron's demands. Safe from the family's criticism. And safe from the past that periodically kicked her down the stairs, leaving her in a breathless panic.

Safe. At least for tonight.

Camelia was drifting off, images from the day floating through her mind: the music, the flowers, the candlelight … the phone vibrating in her pocket. Her eyes flew open. Conroy's call. She moaned quietly. The bed was so cozy. The message could wait until tomorrow. But her mind was already alert, her body tensing with nervous anticipation. She wouldn't be able to sleep until she knew why Conroy had called, so she rolled out of the warm bed and tiptoed down the hall to the kitchen.

"Hey Cam, Chip Conroy here. You asked about whether we found syringes on Mickey Shores. We did not. I hope that helps. Take care, now."

Camelia put the phone down.

Shit. Now I have to talk to Rita.

60

TRUE CONFESSIONS

JANUARY 6

They were settled in Freda's living room, probably for the last time. Rita was snuggled into Freda's favorite chair by the fire, and Camelia and Dave were seated at either end of the sapphire blue sofa. Camelia was treading carefully, stalling, putting off the inevitable. But now they'd rehashed the memorial service, shared anecdotes about this old friend and that long lost relative, and marveled at Freda's ongoing involvement in the community. The conversation was winding down.

"More wine?" Dave asked.

Camelia smiled. "A tiny splash."

"So, you guys are leaving tomorrow?" Rita said.

"Yeah, in the wee hours of the morning." Camelia's belly was knitting a ball of dread. But her suspicions were like a thorn, working their way to the surface, tender to the touch. She had to dig it out. Camelia knew Rita wanted the whole mess surrounding Freda's death to be in the past, tucked safely away. But it wasn't done. Not yet. Not for her. All she could think about was that syringe. "Which is why I wanted to … I was going to talk to you when I came over the other day, but Dave and I got sidetracked," Camelia said.

"That's one way to put it," Rita replied.

"Yeah, that was awkward," Dave said.

"Awkward is an understatement. My own sister, my idiot nephew … I just can't." Rita shook her head.

"They made some bad choices and had to know there was a chance they'd get caught," Dave said. "I just wish we didn't have to be involved in it."

"I'm not sure either of them considered the consequences. Not really. People tend to think they're the exception to the rule," Camelia said. She realized as she spoke that her observation applied to Rita, too. And maybe to her. "Have you talked to Kenna?"

"I tried. She was not exactly gracious. She still has it in her head that I talked Mum into changing her will. I think her exact words were 'go fuck yourself all the way back to Vancouver and don't ever call me again'."

"Suits me," Dave said.

"She's not your sister, Bug." Rita picked at a hangnail. The fire crackled. "Anyway, they've transferred her to rehab, so hopefully she'll come to her senses," Rita said.

"That's the best thing that could happen to her." Camelia paused, putting off the inevitable. "I know I made things more difficult for you, and … can we move past all this?"

"I hope so. This—Mum dying—was never going to be easy. I know your heart was in the right place, but Jesus, Cam. What's with the Miss Marple act?"

"I was just … I was blindsided by Auntie Freda's death, and everything about it screamed suspicious. I know I didn't go about it very tactfully, but I just thought I could … I don't know … get some justice for Auntie Freda," Camelia said. "And on that note, I have one more question." She stared intently at Rita, searching her face for signs of truth.

"Oh crap, Cam," Rita said. "What now?"

"I'm sorry, but I have to ask. Are you …" she took a deep breath. "Are you completely sure you didn't go to the hospital on Christmas Eve?"

"Why would you ask me that?" Rita said, her eyes shifting away.

"Because the charge nurse said a Jane Cannoli showed up to visit Auntie Freda. I think she was mistaken. I think she meant *June Corelli*."

There was a long pause. Rita's face flushed red. She and Dave exchanged a look, but Camelia couldn't decipher the message in their eyes.

"What are you getting at?" Rita said.

"There are some things that aren't adding up, and that's why I'm here. I know you'll have a perfectly good explanation, and I want to hear it so I can put my mind at ease," Camelia said.

"What kind of things aren't adding up?" Rita glanced at Dave again, then back to Camelia.

"Okay, I'll lay it out for you, and you can tell me where I'm wrong." She took a deep breath. "Here goes. I was looking for motive, means, and opportunity. As for means, you're a hospice nurse. You have your mother's healthcare power of attorney. You brought your medical kit from Vancouver …"

"That was totally by accident!" Rita interjected.

"… and I know you had the kit with you on Christmas Eve, because when you and I went downstairs on Boxing Day, before everyone else arrived, you grabbed your kit from the front entry. That meant you hadn't left it here when you went to the Beckers, otherwise it would be downstairs in the suite."

Rita just stared blankly back at her.

"At the Boxing Day wake, when you and Kenna got into it, you never *denied* receiving the text from her. You just didn't comment. Then you said something about Auntie Freda dying alone in the hospital, but how would you have known she was alone unless you were there? Then Mickey said he thought he saw you at the hospital."

"Wow. You really have been watching my every move, haven't you?" Rita said.

"Not just you, Ree, and not on purpose. You know how I am. I notice stuff, and it nags at me until I unravel it," Camelia said.

"Like a dog with a bone. Is there more, or are you done?" Rita snapped.

"There's a bit more … you signed in as June Corelli, but the charge nurse mispronounced your name, which threw me off. Then I found a syringe in the biohazards bin with traces of …. Hang on." Camelia pulled a notebook from her purse and read aloud. "Propofol and sufentanil. Which really confused me. I couldn't figure that one out because Freda hadn't had surgery, but when I looked up the MAID protocol, it all made sense." Camelia drew a ragged breath. "You had the means, you had the opportunity, and now I think I understand your motive. Compassion."

"Goddammit Cam, what the fuck?" Dave said, glaring at Camelia.

"Give us a minute, okay?" Rita rose from her chair and grabbed Dave's elbow. "Come here, hon," she said, as they stepped into the front hall, closing the door behind them.

Camelia could hear their muffled voices, but not their words. Her palms were sweating, and she felt like a traitor. Rita and Dave were her lifelong friends.

Did I really just accuse Rita of killing her mother?

She braced herself for the worst as Rita and Dave came back into the living room a few minutes later, their faces grim and sagging with grief.

"Do we have attorney client privilege?" Dave asked.

Camelia paused. It seemed like an odd question, but then again, it might be exactly the right question to ask. She wasn't sure about the privilege because she didn't know what the ethics rules would say about a lawyer out of her jurisdiction, and way out of her depth, talking to an old friend and family member about matters that may or may not have included a crime.

"I guess so? Maybe? I mean, I'm not positive," Camelia said. "Regardless, it's me. I will carry your secrets to the grave."

"I hope so. Because …" Rita's lower lip trembled. She sat back down in the favored chair, clutching an envelope.

"Let's just get it over with," Dave said.

"Right. Kenna texted Christmas eve around 9:30, said Mum had a stroke and was in ER. I tried texting Kenna back, but our cell service was crap because of the storm. It didn't matter, because we drove into town …"

"You drove in that in that godawful blizzard?"

"I borrowed Dad's farm truck," Dave interjected. "No way our car could handle that kind of snow."

"I *had* to go, so I could see Mum one last time, just in case she didn't make it. I didn't admit I'd received the text because, well, fuck Kenna. What kind of person sends that news in a text? Anyway, I expected Kenna to be at the hospital so I could tell her off good, but Mum was alone."

"Okay, but you signed in as June Corelli," Camelia said.

"No, I signed *out* as June Corelli. When I arrived, there was no one at the nurse's station. Somebody coded down the hall, by the sound of it. So I just went to Mum's room without signing in." Rita grasped the stem of her glass, although she didn't take a drink. "I wasn't going to sign *out* either, because by then … I didn't want to be found out. But," she lowered her voice, "Gayle Germaine wasn't going to let me get away with that. So, when she put that clipboard in front of me … I just needed to get out of there, and my middle name was the first thing that came to mind."

"But later, why wouldn't you just admit you were there?" Camelia asked, dread pooling in her stomach.

"Because … you know why. We swore we would never say a word … sorry, Bug." Rita shook her head at Dave. "When I got to Mum's room, her chart was right there. Of *course* I read it. As soon as I saw the CT scan report, I knew she'd had a *massive* stroke. It's what I'd been dreading all the way in from the farm. I've seen it a thousand times and the end is never easy. There wasn't going to be any upside," Rita said as she blew her nose. "Assuming she lived through the night, that is."

"Oh god. That bad, huh?" Camelia said.

"Yeah, the stroke was catastrophic," Rita said, and pressed her fingertips to her swollen eyes. "Cam, what was I supposed to do? Mum's brain was badly damaged. I could see her future."

"I cannot even imagine what you were going through," Camelia said.

"I knew what Mum, and the whole family, was in for. It was heartbreaking, but there was no way I could get the MAID paperwork, because Mum was too far gone to sign anything. And if she physically survived the stroke? Based on the CT scan, she would almost certainly be paralyzed, not be able to speak or eat, and possibly even have shut-in syndrome. The last thing she wanted was to be dependent on anyone. Do you have *any* idea what it would do to her emotionally? This was the *exact* situation she feared the most."

"I know," Camelia said in a whisper.

"I guess it was kismet that we left Vancouver in such a rush, because my medical kit was still in the car when I picked Dave up from work. After thirty some odd years of grabbing that kit when I'm headed to the hospital … it's second nature. That night was no different," Rita said. She looked to the ceiling and let loose a sigh. "After I saw Mum's chart, I went back to the truck for my kit … even though I wasn't sure I could go through with it," Rita said.

"And I couldn't let Rita do this on her own," Dave said.

"If I was going to break the fucking law, it should be just me," Rita said. "There's no way I would want to implicate anyone else, especially my husband."

"Jesus. That's a lot for one person to hold," Camelia said.

"Exactly why I refused to stay in the truck. I went back up with Ree. I couldn't leave her alone with this," Dave said.

Rita and Dave exchanged a look full of love.

"So, I took a syringe from my kit and went back into the hospital. I wasn't completely convinced I'd actually need it. But when we got back to Mum's room, I knew." Rita took a long gulp from her glass of wine and set it back on the table. "My mother asked me for *one* thing. You know how she was. She *never* asked for help. But this time, she asked me for this one *huge* important thing. I wouldn't turn down a total stranger, so how could I refuse comfort to my own mother?" She covered her face with her hands, as if hiding from the truth.

"So it was your syringe I found in the biohazard waste?" Camelia asked.

"Oh god, yes." Rita shook her head. "I injected the compound into the IV, which is standard protocol, but then I kinda fell apart. I was crying, and a nervous wreck, and I just shoved the syringe in the right hand bin.

As soon as it dropped, I realized their sharps were on the left, not the right. But there was no way to retrieve it," Rita said.

"And the compound includes propofol and sufentanil?"

"Yeah … but, how did you figure that out?"

"I had it analyzed," Camelia said. "I wish you'd just told me."

"You're a lawyer, Cam. But even if you weren't, there was no way we could tell you. Or anyone. We swore that night it would be just between us." Dave said.

The reproach in his voice stung like a slap.

Camelia's heartbeat throbbed in her ears. The wine had gone sour in her mouth.

"When we got back to the room, Mum's eyes were open, and she was mumbling to herself, but she wasn't fully conscious," Rita said, pressing a tissue to her nose. "At least we were able to hold her hand and kiss her goodbye."

"She was in rough shape …" Dave said.

"As soon as I asked … Mum and I had a code. I asked if she was ready to go home. Tears were rolling down her face, but she was looking *right at me*, then she blinked, twice. She was giving consent, no question. As soon as I injected the meds to the IV, Dave went back downstairs …"

"You can't leave those diesel engines off for long in that kind of weather or they freeze up," Dave explained.

"I wanted so badly to stay there with her, to see her off. I hung around a little while, but I didn't dare stay because I knew it would only be a matter of minutes before her heart monitor went off, and she'd be swarmed by the staff. Then, I wouldn't be able to leave. So I said my goodbyes and walked out." Rita silently wept for a moment. "Cam, it was the hardest thing I've ever done in my life."

"Oh, honey, I can't even imagine." Camelia took a deep breath. She'd been right. There was a perfectly logical explanation. But who else knew? "Do you think anyone suspected?" Camelia asked.

Rita shrugged. "I don't really know."

"Other than Mickey?" Dave said.

"Yeah, he saw me, or thinks he did," Rita said.

The three of them sat in silence, contemplating the ramifications of Rita's confession.

"Dr. Fitzgerald was suspicious and ran a tox screen …"

"Oh shit," Dave said.

"That path leads straight back to me," Rita said. "Obviously. Because here you are."

"He ran the tox screen anonymously because he knows the symptoms of fentanyl overdose, but he didn't want to risk Auntie Freda's reputation. That's why he said natural causes on the death certificate. Then I found your syringe in Auntie Freda's biohazard waste, which also contained a used fentanyl patch that didn't come from the hospital. And that nose spray just happens to have oxy in it," Camelia said.

Rita's face paled. "All that was in the bin?" she said.

"Yep. Mickey gave Auntie Freda the nose spray. The fentanyl patches came from Kenna. Had her fingerprints all over them."

"What the hell?" Rita asked.

"And now I can account for the syringe," Camelia said. "Dr. Fitz believes the initial doses of fentanyl and oxy, even though they were minimal, created a hypertensive …" Camelia began.

"*Hypertensive crisis.* Of course," Rita said, slapping the arm of the chair for emphasis. "That's what brought on the stroke."

"And it explains why she was so groggy at the salon. A normal person might have been loopy for a few days but would have recovered. But not Auntie Freda. She reacted, and it caused a stroke," Camelia said.

"Holy shit," Dave whispered.

"So … do the cops know all this?" Rita said.

"The cops know, but honestly, they're way more interested in fentanyl dealers than one old woman who died of a stroke in hospital," Camelia said. "They have their arrests, and they seem satisfied to leave it at that."

"Of course they are. Otherwise, they'd have to do some actual investigating, even though you did all the work for them. Did Mickey spike that nose spray? Or did Kenna … do you think she did something intentional?" Rita asked.

"The cops aren't interested in the nose spray. Small potatoes. Mr. Conroy said they took Kenna's statement in the hospital, but are holding off on charges for now," Camelia said.

"*That's it?*" Dave said. "Did she have an alibi?"

"According to Conroy, Kenna started off by throwing Mickey under the bus, then she started bawling and said she'd made a mistake with Freda's arthritis pain meds," Camelia said.

"Mum has … had arthritis in her knees," Rita said.

"With the blizzard coming … the change in barometric pressure can really amp up arthritis pain," Dave said. "But what was the mistake?"

"The mistake being, Kenna apparently slapped a couple of mostly-used fentanyl patches on Auntie Freda when she complained about her knees aching. Kenna *says* she mistook them for Salonpas patches—you know, the over the counter stuff—but they look nothing alike. I think she's full of shit, but we'll never know," Camelia said.

"She was probably half in the bag and couldn't tell the difference. She's always got a rye and diet Coke in her hand," Rita said.

"Maybe it *was* an accident, but if so, it was a deadly one," Camelia said.

Dave shook his head. "You guys are being way too generous. I think Kenna was doing whatever she could to get that fat inheritance," Dave said.

"Maybe, but Mum got the better of her after all." Rita got up and went to sit by Camelia on the sofa as she handed her the folded page. "You know the letters we got from Mum at Barrett's office? This was in mine."

It was Freda's handwriting on an official-looking government form: Saskatchewan Health Authority Medical Assistance In Dying. She turned the page over to see Freda's loopy cursive:

If my death is imminent, and there is no chance of recovery, I elect to terminate my suffering by use of medication. If I am unable to speak, I will indicate my consent by blinking my eyes twice in response to the question: Are you ready to go home?

Camelia looked from Dave to Rita and back again.

"She knew?" Camelia said.

"Maybe she knew something was going on. Or maybe she was just planning for the worst, because she left the date blank. Either way, Mum covered for me," Rita said. "And, obviously, Kenna knew nothing about it."

"So, then, you understand, you did nothing wrong," Camelia said. "You did what your mother asked of you."

"I still used a controlled substance to send my mother to her grave without signed consent. Yes, I was doing what she wanted. It may be legal, but it doesn't make me feel good about what I did." Rita fell against Camelia's shoulder as fresh tears poured down her face.

Auntie Freda was still gone—nothing could change that—but Camelia could finally grieve without the shadow of suspicion. Tears of relief, fatigue, and now, acceptance, rolled silently down her cheeks as the dark secrets evaporated in the light of truth.

61

THE DEATH CARD

JANUARY 8

It was a cloudless morning, the sun arcing through the turquoise Arizona sky, streaming through the French doors in Camelia's bedroom. The fierce light warmed a patch on the polished concrete floor where two matching fuzzy mutts sprawled, paws twitching in secret dreams.

Dust motes waltzed in lazy circles as Camelia's head pounded in time with her pulse. Her eyes burned, her throat was parched. She was dehydrated and hungover from yesterday's long travel day and too many cocktails on the plane, but she didn't have the luxury of a day in bed. She had a long list of things to do before returning to work tomorrow, but it was early yet, a long time until noon, and a little holiday day-drinking was allowed, wasn't it? Camelia popped a couple of ibuprofen and swished them down with vodka and orange juice.

Hair of the dog, and all that.

She pulled on jeans, sucked in, and zipped them up. She frowned at herself in the full-length mirror and poked at her tummy bulge. Note to self: cut out carbs along with the alcohol for dry January, which starts …

tomorrow. She was still on vacation today. She threw the jeans aside and stepped into a pair of yoga pants.

Camelia loaded the washing machine, tucked their suitcases into the back of the closet, and made a grocery list. She could see Leon through the kitchen window, skimming the pool, and felt a surge of affection. Camelia was, for the first time in a long time, hopeful.

She'd helped solve the puzzle of Freda's death, hadn't she? Sure, she couldn't talk about Rita's role, but she could tell the story of Kenna and Mickey, and how she'd gathered evidence of the illicit drugs. Maybe that bit of investigative work would earn her some points with Byron. And she'd been sober for days—okay, mostly sober. But was it enough to put her back in the running for partner?

Her phone dinged. Time to leave for her therapy appointment.

Camelia ran through the events of the past couple of weeks for her therapist, including her revelations about Auntie Freda's death. But now, with the clock running down the hour, she needed help pulling herself together. She needed to be grounded before she faced Byron and the January avalanche of divorce work but also, and more importantly, Camelia needed a strategy for getting promoted.

"How about we spend a few minutes talking about why it's so important for you to make partner," Carlos Chavez said, pen poised above his notebook.

Carlos' large eyes were his burden baskets. All the sorrows of his clients were contained there, in those brown eyes. But all of his compassion was there, too, and sitting under his gaze was soothing all by itself.

"Gee, I don't know, Carlos. How about the money?" Camelia said, sarcastically, and instantly regretted it. Carlos was her safe haven, so why was she acting like this? He was the key to her ability to function well enough to make partner and Camelia desperately needed his help.

"Okay, let's go with money. What about the money is important? How will that extra money make your life better?"

The morning light flattered him as he shifted in his chair. Carlos was attractive, well-groomed, and dressed like the movie version of a psychologist.

Or maybe that's how they're taught to dress?

Marsha Brady, his chubby corgi therapy dog, sighed in her sleep, and stretched. Camelia chewed the inside of her lip.

"I don't know if the money will make my life really *better*, but it *never* hurts to have more money," she said, even though she didn't completely believe it. You always had to trade something for the money: time, energy, peace of mind.

"Do you want to draw a card?" he asked.

Carlos was a Jungian therapist, and tarot was one of his favorite tools for getting her to talk. He shuffled the deck and fanned it out on the massive coffee table between them.

Camelia closed her eyes, pulled a card out of the set, and held it like a talisman. She breathed deeply twice, three times—was she supposed to make a wish?—then opened her eyes and turned the card face up on the table.

Death.

"Well, that's depressing," she said. "Pretty sure I've had all the death I can stomach for a while."

"Let me read the narrative that goes with the Death card and no, it doesn't mean you're going to die. It's way worse than that, Camelia. It means you're going to change," he said, smiling through his sad eyes.

"So Death is coming, and there's no way to stop it, right?" she said.

"The only constant is change, so you have to decide whether to embrace it or resist it. And with change, old things have to fall away to make room for new things, right? Let's apply that to making partner. In order to be promoted, you'll have to leave some things behind. Have you identified what those might be?"

Camelia tried to think about what she might have to let go of, but her mind was wandering. The bouquet of flowers on Carlos' desk was a cluster of pale shades of yellow. They matched the sunlight.

What would she have to give up?

All the good stuff, most likely.

"The partners get a share of the profits, but are responsible for things like capital improvements, overhead, that kind of thing. I think it could be a wash. I'll be leaving a bit of freedom and flexibility on the table. I'll be expected to be a rainmaker. Eat what you kill. So that's a down side."

"How will that increased responsibility impact you? There's the time commitment, for one thing. Where will you be able to scavenge time from your calendar? Will it take away from time with your family?" Carlos asked.

Camelia was quietly wadding up tissues in her lap.

She could feel the bedrock of her marriage crumbling a bit, day by day, but it was still solid. Wasn't it? They had their tiffs, Leon and her, but they were still able to laugh it off. But lately she'd seen something different in his eyes.

Camelia already spent less time with her daughter and son-in-law than she wanted now that they lived in Toronto, but wasn't that normal? Didn't all parents want just a *bit* more than was rational? Or healthy? She wondered if they missed her as much as she missed them.

Her mother wasn't a concern. She was happily ensconced in her retirement village, and barely had time for Camelia between her boyfriend, senior yoga, art tours, happy hour, theme dinners, and on and on.

Then there were her friends and her book group, those priceless jewels of heartfelt support and raucous laughter. A couple of outings a month was all she could manage now. How much worse would it get? She knew, before long, she'd be bowing out of those precious gatherings in order to meet a client or work late.

Camelia knew the commitment of becoming partner would extract a price of time and energy when she already felt stretched to the limit on both.

Could she really put herself out there even more?

Did she really have the energy to spend a couple of nights a week wooing clients on top of her case load and pro bono work?

"The thing is, I want the title, and I think I've earned it," Camelia said.

"How long have you been at the firm now?"

"Just over six years."

"Is that the usual time frame for making partner?" Carlos asked.

"Yeah, it's about average. But I've been practicing for almost 30 years in five different firms. I've done my time in the trenches. Paid my dues and then some. I should've been made partner a long time ago."

When she said it out loud, it infuriated and humiliated her. So many of her law school classmates—even the mediocre ones—had long since moved to the corner office, been appointed to the bench, made full professor, and were miles ahead of her in the tooth and nail competition for success. Meanwhile, Camelia had barely moved up the ladder.

"You'll have to figure out for yourself if feeding your ego is what's best for your mental health," Carlos said. He began writing notes. "Here are some questions for next week. How can you allocate your time to make it work both professionally and personally? What are the new stressors that come with partner, and how will the extra pressure impact your anxiety? Is being a partner in the firm really good for you, or is it just what you've been told to expect?"

Camelia scribbled the questions in her therapy journal.

"There's one other thing. A big fat wrinkle that might make all this moot. Byron put me on notice that I have to stop drinking by the end of the month. All because that dick opposing counsel, Spencer Ashcroft, spread a rumor that I smelled of alcohol when I had that panic attack, right before the holidays," Camelia said.

"That sounds serious. Had you been drinking?"

"No. I mean, not at that moment. It was an 8 a.m. hearing," she replied.

"I know you're aware of this, but you're at high risk for substance abuse. It's part of the lawyer package, but also a big part of your genetics. And drinking on top of these meds is really bad for your liver," Carlos said. "Did I mention it's horrible for anxiety, too?"

If he only knew.

But if Camelia had talked about it—fully admitted the volume and frequency—Carlos would never let it go. And she'd have to face that dark thing, lurking around the corner, threatening to expose her.

"Yeah, so I hear. Anyway, dry January for me, now that I'm home."

Carlos raised his eyebrows and looked like he was going to say something, but didn't. Camelia glanced at the clock beyond his shoulder.

"Looks like we're out of time," Camelia said. She waved the Death card at Carlos. "I guess me and my pal death will be on our way."

"Actual death? It will come to all of us, eventually. Cam, I know losing your aunt the way you did has been a shock to the system," Carlos said. He closed his notebook. "Today, it's Freda's story, not yours. Use this grief to make positive changes in your life. That's how you write *your* story. You get to decide how it ends."

Camelia stood and gave Carlos a brief hug.

"Happy new year, Carlos. I'll see you next week."

As she walked to her car, Camelia replayed Carlos' words.

What could she afford to give up in order to make partner? Was it even worth it? What would she actually gain? A new business card? A whole lot more stress?

She got into her car and turned on the air conditioning.

Jesus. Almost 80 degrees in January?

Camelia wondered how it would be to chase a criminal and come up with nothing. She knew it happened. What if she hadn't found Mickey's stash in the garage or Kenna's fingerprints on the patches? They would have walked. Even though there was no justice for Auntie Freda's death, at least they were charged with the drug offenses. But was it worth the aggravation?

And not just the aggravation. Not everything was cut and dried. What if someone with good intentions committed a technical crime, like Rita had done? Where would she stand on those types of cases?

What she'd learned is that no one really knows what they'll do until a difficult situation—like Auntie Freda's—comes along. Nothing was black and white. No one was completely innocent. And yet, the thrill of searching for and finding clues to Auntie Freda's death had energized her more than she'd been in years.

Camelia headed home, Camelback Mountain glowing pink in her rear view mirror.

Maybe Carlos is right. Maybe it's time I wrote my own story.

THE END

Turn the page for **Helpful Links**, **Author's Note**, and a sneak peek at **Death At the Crossroads**, the second book in the Camelia Belmont Mystery Series.

HELPFUL LINKS

For help with an opioid addiction:

In Canada: https://www.camh.ca/en/health-info/mental-illness-and-addiction-index/opioid-addiction
In the U.S.A.: https://www.hhs.gov/opioids/treatment/index.html

For help with alcohol and drug addiction:

Alcoholics Anonymous: https://www.aa.org/
Narcotics Anonymous is available here: https://www.na.org/

To learn more about the general warning signs of stroke:
https://www.cdc.gov/stroke/signs_symptoms.htm

For information about warning signs of stroke specific to women:
https://www.healthline.com/health/stroke/symptoms-of-stroke-in-women#womens-symptoms

For help with anxiety, panic disorder, addiction, and other mental health issues:

In Canada: https://cpa.ca/public/findingapsychologist/
In the U.S.A.: https://www.findapsychologist.org/

For attorneys who need help with addiction and other mental health issues:

In Canada: https://www.cba.org/Sections/Wellness-Subcommittee/Resources/Wellness-Links
In the U.S.A.:
https://www.americanbar.org/groups/lawyer_assistance/resources/covid-19--mental-health-resources/

AUTHOR'S NOTE

This is my first work of novel-length fiction and Camelia Belmont's virgin voyage into sleuthing. I hope you enjoy her origin story enough to come along with me for the whole series, as Camelia drags herself from rock bottom to the top of her profession as an investigative attorney. We're just getting started!

When I started writing this novel, no one told me it would take a village. In the birthing room of this story are all the people who inspired me along the way: from elementary school teachers, to writers, to random people I've met. These are but a few to whom I owe an abiding debt of gratitude.

First, my family.

Brian Donison, my husband, my anchor, my VP of IT, and my champion; and

Stacie Elliott Donison, my daughter, my Bunny, and travel buddy, and our PSIL, **Scott Elliott**.

My critique partners (all *amazing* writers, by the way), without whom this book would be a hot mess.

Deepthi Atukarola
Leina Pauls
Cormac O'Reilly
Martin Crosbie

The dearest cheerleaders a person could hope for (alphabetically). Thank you all for your encouragement, faith, tolerance, and beta reading!

Rhonda Berg
Shannon Bradley
Barbara Evans-Levine
Brooke Gaunt
Jana Gill
Sharon Hansen
Lisa Martin
Sarah Matheson
Heather Pollock
Allison Whiteside

Truth or fiction? Obviously, this is a work of fiction, but there are some real life people and places I want to acknowledge.

- ❄ The setting of Regina, Saskatchewan is very real, and is etched onto my life as a formative character in my personal history.

- ❄ Sweetie Pies Bakery Café in Regina is real, founded by the very real, larger than life Darlene "Dee" King.

- ❄ The Italian Club, as represented here, is pure fiction. There is an Italian Club in Regina and, to all of its members, I say *cin-cin.*

- ❄ Both the Cathedral Neighborhood and the Crescents are real, but the homes and residents portrayed are fiction.

- ❄ The MacKenzie Art Gallery, and artists Dorothy Knowles and Folmer Hansen are real.

- ❄ *Canada Today* is not an actual magazine, but the article is real. https://www.ctvnews.ca/health/ordering-deadly-drugs-from-china-is-easy-ap-investigation-reveals-1.3144008

- ❄ The Royal Mounted Canadian Police Depot and the RIDU in Regina are real; however, Chip Conroy and the circumstances portrayed are fiction.

- ❄ The Superior Court in Maricopa County is real, and I've spent many hours there over the course of my legal career; however, the attorneys, clients, and scenarios portrayed are fiction. Likewise, the law firm of McCaffrey, Rhodes & Rodriguez is fiction.

- ❄ Addiction, substance abuse, and mental illness are rampant within the legal profession. Coupled with the intrinsic misogyny within the field, women are even more severely impacted, both personally and professionally, by these challenges. My own insights on this problem are here: https://bit.ly/DonisonOC

About The Author

Pamela Donison, JD, has been a writer in one iteration or other her entire life. Currently a practicing attorney, she is a former award-winning military journalist, and acquisitions manager for a division of Harcourt Brace. Her work has been published in numerous legal periodicals, as well as chapters in three legal anthologies. Her short fiction has been published by The Dillydoun Review, Drunk Monkeys, and an upcoming crime anthology through Sisters in Crime, Canada West Chapter.

Her first full-length novel, **Death Comes For Christmas**, is a soft-boiled murder mystery set in Regina, Saskatchewan, and the origin story for an aspiring female investigative attorney. Pamela writes under the pen name PJ Donison, and is currently working on the second in the Camelia Belmont Mystery series, **Death At The Crossroads**.

Pamela is a member of Sisters in Crime, Crime Writers of Canada, and the Pacific Northwest Writers Association, as well as a member in good standing of the State Bar of Arizona. Pamela and her spouse, Brian, live most of the time in Delta, BC, the traditional and unceded territory of Coast Salish Peoples, specifically the Kwantlen, Katzie, Semiahmoo, and Tsawwassen First Nations.

hello@pjdonison.com

Enjoy this excerpt from
PJ Donison's next novel

DEATH

AT THE

CROSSROADS

A Camelia Belmont Mystery

3

The Client

Suzanne stepped out of her vintage baby blue Mercedes in front of the oncologist's office and squared her shoulders. She took a deep breath and walked resolutely into the lobby, her Fendi bag and Burberry jacket quietly announcing her status. Not that any of that mattered today.

She was ushered into an exam room after just a couple of minutes, a testament to the efficiency of Dr. Baum's practice. Or maybe it was a personal favor. They'd been neighbors for years, and their kids had gone to the exclusive Rancho Solano Prep School together. Now he was her doctor, and it scared the hell out of her.

Suzanne settled in one of the exam room's molded plastic chairs, taking measured breaths to slow her heart rate. A quick tap and Richard Baum, M.D., entered the room with a practiced smile.

"Suzanne," he said, and held his arms wide. After a brief hug, he sat in the chair next to hers. "First off, don't be intimidated by all the mumbo jumbo I'm about to throw at you."

"Thanks, Rick, but I'm a nurse, remember? Just spill it," Suzanne said, with a weak smile.

"Yep, I figured you'd want to jump in," he said. Dr. Baum heaved a sigh as he flipped open her chart. "So, we got the labs back, and we have the MRI, and to be blunt, it's concerning. You've got a mass on your left ovary and a lesion on your liver. I'm going to biopsy everything, of course, but on first glance, you should know I'm looking for ovarian cancer. As for the spot on your liver, if the mass is cancerous, it's possible it's metastasized. I'll know more when we finish the biopsies today, but I think we're going to be scheduling surgery and chemo," he said.

The room tilted and Suzanne felt nauseous. A shimmer of sweat broke out around her hairline. Ovarian cancer was bad enough, but *metastasized?*

That kills people.

"I see. Is there any … I mean …" She paused. She knew there wasn't a mistake. "Right, so let's get those biopsies before we start planning my funeral, okay?" Suzanne gripped her own fingers.

"Hey, none of that. But I would like to get some history. Have you had any bloating, difficulty eating, or feeling full quickly?"

"A bit, I guess. It's hard to know, exactly," Suzanne said. What had she missed?

"Any abdominal pain? Urgent need to urinate? Fatigue?" Dr. Baum looked at her expectantly.

"You know these are all things I've experienced my whole adult life, at one time or another, right?"

"Let me put it another way. When did you first decide something was wrong?" Dr. Baum asked.

"Over the summer, I had some intermittent cramps and constipation, but nothing earth-shattering. Then, around October, I started feeling fatigued and noticed I had lost some weight. In November, when I went for my annual, my OB/GYN ran the bloodwork. And here I am," she said.

"Well, I think it's been with you for a while. Not that you're to blame for not being here sooner, because it's a sneaky bastard, hard to diagnose. We'll know more when we get the biopsy results, so I'll need you to change into a gown. Jordan will give you a little sedative, and I'll grab those biopsies, okay?" Dr. Baum got up to leave, and paused at the door. "We're gonna take good care of you, Suzie. Be right back."

Suzanne's mind was spinning, but social graces took over. "Of course, Rick, thank you so much. I'm sure it will all be fine."

But she wasn't the least bit sure. After changing into a rough cotton gown, Suzanne picked at a loose thread as she went back over every twinge. Every headache, back ache, little stabbing pain. When should she have noticed? When did the bloating start? Suzanne thought back to last summer, but she couldn't recall if it was before or after that bit of post-menopausal bleeding.

That should have been my red flag.

Three days later, the verdict was in: Stage 4 ovarian cancer.

The clump of rogue cells was bound and determined to kill her. Not *if*, but *when*. While Dr. Baum broke the news in his quiet, contemporary office, she gripped her elbows with white knuckles, willing herself to pay attention. Suzanne nodded at all the right places as he laid out the treatment plan.

"And Suzie, you know I'm going to do every damn thing in my power to make sure you dance at your grandkid's wedding, right? I will do *whatever* it takes," Dr. Baum said, his eyes shiny with compassion. "You're my friend first, my patient second, and you have my mobile. Consider me to be on call from now until … from now on."

"Rick, you're so kind. And yes, of course we're going to fight the good fight. But I do have one big favor to ask," Suzanne said, staring down at her Gucci heels. She could feel a blister rising on each of her baby toes.

Why do I even wear these damned uncomfortable shoes?

"Name it."

"You can't tell a soul. Not the kids, for sure. And under *no* circumstances can you tell Aaron, understood?" She stared into his droopy brown eyes for emphasis.

"Suzanne, I think that's a mistake. You're going to need their support …"

"No, I won't. I'm not going to lean on them. I have girlfriends for this. Women who have been through cancer treatment and all the shit that goes with it. I don't want my kids worried sick, hovering over me. And I don't want Aaron distracted from running the firm. He has so much on his plate already. I mean it. You will not say a *word.* Promise me." Suzanne grabbed his hand. "Shake on it, Rick."

He took her hand in both of his and squeezed. "I don't like it, but I promise."

Suzanne drove from Dr. Baum's office in North Scottsdale to the hillside home she shared with Aaron in Paradise Valley, craving her cool, dim bedroom. Coming into the mudroom from the garage, she kicked off her shoes and looked down at them.

No more uncomfortable shoes.

She started to toss them in the trash, but Suzanne didn't come from the kind of people who threw away perfectly good shoes. She put them in a shopping bag instead, eventually donating the Gucci heels and another thirty-three pair of ridiculous shoes she'd never wear again.

She sprinted up the stairs to her bedroom—her sanctuary, the place she could cry in private—and bolted the door. She needed time to process before … what? Aaron wouldn't be home any time soon, if at all. The housekeeper had already come and gone. And the kids were … grown. Gone. Living their own busy lives. Suzanne was truly alone.

She took a deep breath, studying the carpet for insight. The diagnosis didn't just confront her with all the vapid clothing choices she'd made over the years. It forced Suzanne to look at her entire life with a new lens. The lens of not much time left. The lens of how can I pack all my living into one year?

Or less.

Suzanne paced the floor, vibrating with the tense energy of a finite life suddenly brought into sharp focus. She rummaged through one of the purses in her closet and found a pack of cigarettes. The wine and coffee bar in the corner of her expansive bedroom was well stocked, so she grabbed an open bottle of pinot noir and poured a tumbler full as she lit the cigarette. She flung open the sliding glass door to the veranda, and plopped down in one of the chairs overlooking the swimming pool. Beyond the pool was the casita, where Aaron had been living for the past several months. She counted on her fingers … eleven to be exact. Ever since the blowup last Christmas over his *femme du jour*. That time, he'd humiliated Suzanne in public—breaking their uneasy truce—by showing up for happy hour at El Chorro with a willowy brunette.

She pointed her middle finger at the casita.

Screw you, Aaron.

In that moment of clarity, Suzanne knew she would divorce Aaron. It was over. She would take her half of everything and live her last days fast and hard. And first class all the way.

She walked inside and grabbed the notebook and pen from her bedside table. She had to start planning. There was so much to organize, to arrange, to schedule.

The first step was to get a good divorce attorney who could settle it all quickly. Assuming she could find one to take her case, given that Aaron would be on the other side.

In her notebook, she scribbled a list of every attorney she knew on a first-name basis, who she felt could be trusted. Just as quickly, she scratched through all but one of them: Angela Laurent at Shipman Wright. The others all belonged to Aaron's circle: golf partners, law school buddies, and a bunch of back slapping favor granting corporate attorneys. They would never break the code to go up against Aaron. She needed an attorney who had nothing to lose by making Aaron angry. And he was guaranteed to be angry.

She tapped on the contacts in her phone and called Angela. The stylish blonde had taken care of her friend's divorce last year—Julia never even had to show up in court—and even if she wouldn't take the case, Angela knew people. But she didn't seem optimistic about Suzanne's options.

"I mean, Suz, really, I don't know who would want to go toe to toe with Aaron. He's got quite the reputation, ya know," Angela said.

"Which is exactly why I need someone like you," Suzanne said.

"I don't have the staff to manage it and, even if I did, I'm not sure I would want the headache. It's nothing personal, it's just that I know what's involved. Have you tried Camelia Belmont? She's not easily swayed by guys like Aaron," Angela said.

"I haven't heard of her. What firm is she with?" Suzanne asked as she doodled the name in her notebook.

"She's at McCaffrey, Rhodes and Rodriguez. Remember Arturo Rodriguez?" Angela said.

"Absolutely, he's darling. Maybe he'll take me on."

For a moment, the line was silent. That was her answer. Even someone like Arturo wasn't going to go up against Aaron.

"Well," Suzanne said, breaking the awkward silence, "thanks for being honest about it."

"Sorry about that. Will I see you at the Wong's holiday party tomorrow night?"

"Absolutely. See you then," Suzanne said, and hung up.

It only took one more phone call to disqualify her next-to-last option. Angela's unvoiced opinion had been correct. Arturo Rodriguez no longer did divorces. Even hers. But he did offer up his associate, Camelia Belmont. Suzanne huffed a sigh, stubbed out her second cigarette, and took a long swig of wine. Here she was, the wife of one of the most influential trial attorneys in the southwest—hell, in the whole Western U.S.—and she couldn't even get a partner level attorney to help her get divorced.

The powerlessness of her situation came skidding into the room and slapped Suzanne hard in the face. Angry, grieving sobs burst through her veneer of calm control. As the sun went down and lights winked on across the hills, Suzanne let the torrent of bitter tears burn away the final wisps of her life with Aaron.

Finally, it was time. It was over. She just hoped it wasn't too late.

TO BE CONTINUED …

Be the first to know when

Death At The Crossroads

is released, and get deals, discounts,

and more when you join my mailing list.

https://pjdonison.com/

Already a subscriber? Thanks so much!

Manufactured by Amazon.ca
Bolton, ON